PENGUIN MODERN CLASSICS

Pather Panchali

BIBHUTIBHUSHAN BANDOPADHYAY (1894–1950) was one of Bengali literature's greatest writers. His best known work is the autobiographical novel *Pather Panchali*, now published in Penguin Modern Classics in a new translation. This novel and its sequel, *Aparajito*, have been translated into several languages and also inspired Satyajit Ray's iconic and award-winning cinematic trilogy. Bandopadhyay was posthumously awarded the Rabindra Puraskar in 1951, the most prestigious literary award in West Bengal, for his novel *Ichamati*.

RIMI translates classic and speculative fiction from Bangla to English. Her works include Sunil Gangopadhyay's *The Adventures of Kakababu*, volumes I, II and III, Bibhutibhushan Bandopadhyay's *Pather Panchali*, and Acharya Kshitimohan Sen's *United in Prayer*. She also takes a keen interest in the goings-on of stray animals, and can often be spotted on the streets of Mumbai courting new canine acquaintances.

PENGUIN MODERN CLASSICS

Pather Panchali

BIBHUTIBHUSHAN BANDOPADHYAY (1894–1950) is one of Bengali literature's greatest writers. His best known work is the autobiographical novel *Pather Panchali*, now published in Penguin Modern Classics in a new translation. This novel and its sequel, *Aparajito*, have been translated into several languages and also inspired Satyajit Ray's iconic and award-winning cinematic trilogy. Bandopadhyay was posthumously awarded the Rabindra Puraskar in 1951, the most prestigious literary award in West Bengal, for his novel *Ichhamati*.

[illegible] translates classic and speculative fiction from Bangla to English. Her works include Sunil Gangopadhyay's *The Adventures of Kakababu*, volumes I, II and III, Bibhutibhushan Bandopadhyay's *Pather Panchali*, and Achintya [illegible] Sen's [illegible]. She also takes a keen interest in the goings on of stray animals and can often be spotted on the streets of Mumbai [illegible] her canine acquaintances.

BIBHUTIBHUSHAN BANDOPADHYAY

Pather Panchali

SONG OF THE ROAD

Translated from the Bengali by Rimi

PENGUIN BOOKS
An imprint of Penguin Random House

PENGUIN BOOKS

USA | Canada | UK | Ireland | Australia
New Zealand | India | South Africa | China | Singapore

Penguin Books is part of the Penguin Random House group of companies
whose addresses can be found at global.penguinrandomhouse.com

Published by Penguin Random House India Pvt. Ltd
4th Floor, Capital Tower 1, MG Road,
Gurugram 122 002, Haryana, India

First published in Penguin Books by Penguin Random House India 2019

10 9 8 7 6 5 4 3 2

This is a work of fiction. Names, characters, places and incidents are either the product of the author's imagination or are used fictitiously and any resemblance to any actual person, living or dead, events or locales is entirely coincidental.

ISBN 9780143102953

Typeset in Sabon by Manipal Digital Systems, Manipal
Printed at Repro India Limited

www.penguin.co.in

This is a legitimate digitally printed version of the book and therefore might not have certain extra finishing on the cover.

To

Sudhamay Sengupta

For the love of books and people, and the grace of finding poetry in providence

Contents

Translator's Note

I HAVE—AND I am sure I share this misfortune with many—an uncontainable practical joker for a friend. A couple of years back, he had a group of us worked up in quite a lather over the sort of book he had 'caught' his teenage daughter reading.

'She's reading about some manic-depressive murderer!' he had said, to general expressions of shock. 'Fellow has hallucinations, thinks he is talking to his dead father, goes on a serial killer rampage . . . I think there's even a part where he tries to rape someone. And here she's trying to tell me that the book is in her school syllabus!'

We were all suitably horrified, and suggested ways to nip this delinquent taste in literature in the bud. It turned out, however, that the book *was* in fact in the school's syllabus, and that it was Shakespeare's *Hamlet*.

The prank served to underline an interesting cultural phenomenon for me. Often, when we speak of 'classic' fiction, the label triggers certain unconscious assumptions in our minds about a given text. That these are 'serious' pieces of literature, for example, and cannot—indeed, should not—be treated as entertaining stories to read for one's amusement. It's puzzling how this stereotype developed, for many of the fictional classics of the Western canon are, in essence, popular fictions from an earlier era—tales of high drama featuring grand romances, swashbuckling adventures, unabashed ribaldry, and tear-jerking tragedy. This disconnect between reputation and content has affected *Pather Panchali* as well. Its sombre cinematic treatment, coupled with its 'classic' tag, has often lent the novel a funerary air in popular imagination. Which is unfortunate, because the original *Pather Panchali* is very far from being a melancholic elegy. It is a vibrant ballad that begins with joy and ends in determination. As in life, its tragedies are many, but they are handled with fortitude and grace, and never dwelt upon merely to elicit sympathy. Instead, it brims with exuberant sensuousness; the joy of exploring benevolent woodlands, the delight of savouring unknown berries, the serene happiness of watching seasons change on a vast landscape of rivers, moors, and quiet groves. *Pather Panchali* chronicles the glorious discoveries along the path of everyday life—from spots for secret picnics and the true flavour of desserts, to the pleasure of fulfilled dreams and lessons embedded in disappointed hopes.

Unfortunately, the same attitude of reverence that confers a 'serious' mantle on a book also occasionally affects the tone of its translation, and not necessarily to its benefit. As Tagore famously said to the critics of his first two translations, *Geetanjali* and *The Gardener*:

> Perhaps you miss that sense of enjoyment in the English rendering [for in my translations the verses are] bereft of their music and suggestiveness of language.[1]

[1] Andrew Robinson and Krishna Dutta, *Rabindranath Tagore: The Myriad-Minded Man* (St Martin's Press, 1996).

In translating *Pather Panchali*, I have thus focused on preserving as much of this 'music and suggestiveness' of the original text as possible, to limit the scope of misreadings that might mar the spirit of the novel. Bibhutibhushan wrote about the daily lives of people by using the words and expressions that they used amongst themselves. The cadence of the common man's everyday is central to the appeal of his works. *Pather Panchali*, too, is rich in rural turns of speech, local vocabulary, and references to the agrarian life of southern riverine Bengal. Of course, mapping local speech patterns of one language into another is an impossible task, but I have tried to remain as faithful as possible to the vibrant colloquial nature of the text, and to the author's project of not 'gentrifying' his characters' interactions for the sake of his more urbane readers.

Naturally, some of this has been challenging to translate directly into English. For one, certain idioms sat so uncomfortably in their English garb that I thought it prudent to trade in their direct translations for phrases that would be familiar to English speakers. For another, the world of *Pather Panchali* is replete with phenomena and institutions that have no equivalent in English that one can refer to for immediate clarity. *Kuleenpratha*, for example, is a caste phenomenon little known outside Bengal, and would require an explanation for both national and international audiences.

Finally, the world Bibhutibhushan lived in and wrote about has been so utterly transformed over the last century (*Pather Panchali* first came out in 1928) that translating certain aspects of it—the names of trees and plants that the characters spoke of with such easy familiarity, for instance—now require consultations with specialized lists of information. Much of the wood-ringed, moor-bordered region is now a bustling township, with few remnants of the rich and diverse botanical landscape that Bibhutibhushan chronicled so vividly. The old agrarian way of life has rapidly given way to an industrial and service-oriented economy, rendering many of the rituals and festivities mentioned in the book a set of barely remembered names. Thus, to adequately translate the landscape of that lost time and place, it was important to craft little cultural bridges into the text that addressed these losses in knowledge, so that modern readers could fully appreciate why Choitro Shonkranti held such a glowing place in Indir's memory, or why Shorbojoya went to the Koluichondi feasts despite it reducing her to bitter tears.

Speaking of changes over time, I have made the conscious decision to move away from standardized spellings for Bengali names in this translation, choosing instead to be as phonetically accurate as I could without actually using the phonetic alphabet. While unfamiliarity might make these spellings appear visually cumbersome, I think it is an important step towards rectifying the received tradition of using spellings that nearly always mislead the reader about the local pronunciation of words and names. Indeed, in keeping with the spirit of preserving cultural authenticity, I have also kept as much of the local pronunciation of pan-Indian words as possible within the direct speech of characters. Brahmin has therefore become 'brahmon', Mahabharat 'Mohabharot', Dasaswamedh 'Doshashwomedh', and so on. In addition, I have not streamlined Bibhutibhushan's habit of switching between the given names and nicknames, and of identifying characters (especially women) by their relationships with other characters instead of by actual names. 'Mejo bourani' has therefore become 'the second-eldest [mejo] mistress [bourani]', while Durga has been 'khuki' ('little girl') in her childhood and Dugga later in life, Chondro has become Chondor, and Rani has frequently been called Ranu.

Every translator has some regrets, for it is impossible to completely transpose an entire culture, place and time into a different language. My regret, happily, is a small one. As a postcolonial child who grew up on reams of popular English literature from the turn of the last century, I have been charmed and amused by the fascinating names that places seem to have in the United Kingdom. With the blindness that comes of familiarity, I had thought this phenomenon an exclusively British one, or at any rate one that was not prevalent in India. Upon rereading *Pather Panchali*, however, I realized that almost every place in the novel had just such a whimsical or meaningful name; constant use had simply inured us to their meaning. Of these, I have translated 'Nischindipur' to the Abode of Contentment, for it is a particularly thoughtful choice on Bibhutibhushan's part. Certain other names have also found their way to their English counterparts, because when one discovers a pond called the Pond of the Sisters-in-Law, one has the irrepressible urge to share it. In other instances, however, I have limited myself to the original names, for fear of burdening the text with a little too much of the local colour. 'Prawn Belly' would have been rather a whimsically charming name for Ichamoti, for instance, but knowing that 'icha' means prawn in the local parlance—or that Holudbere is Yellow Pickets and Chuadanga is Perfumer's High—was unlikely to affect one's appreciation of the story.

Ironically, despite the immense changes it has wrought, it is the nature of our altered times that has made *Pather Panchali* immensely meaningful to the twenty-first century. Like a displaced Opu, we too are facing a near-irreversible destruction of our own homeland, and with it the cultures and ways of life that had sustained our joys and sorrows for centuries. In Opu's desperate yearning for his lost homeland, we find echoes of our own anxieties for our threatened lands. In the ballad of his travel through life, we find the reflections of our hopes and dreams. And in the God of the Travelled Road's exhortation to always move forward, we can only hope that we shall find the will to find a way.

Rimi
August 2019

PATHER PANCHALI

1

HORIHOR ROY'S TINY ancestral home marked the easternmost border of the Abode of Contentment. A few acres of inherited land and annual tokens of respect sent by his disciples were his only income, and cracks were beginning to show in the family's budget.

Indir Thakrun was demolishing a bowl of puffed rice in the veranda. The previous day had been Aekadoshi, and the mandatory fasting had left the elderly widow ravenous. Horihor's little girl, Durga, sat close by, her wistful eyes watching as each fistful travelled from the old metal bowl to her paternal aunt's mouth—a hopeless chasm of no return. Once or twice it seemed like she was about to say something, but each time, she swallowed her words at the last minute.

When the bowl was finally empty, Indir Thakrun looked up and immediately saw the longing in her niece's eyes. 'Will you look at me!' she exclaimed. 'A whole bowl of puffed rice, and I didn't even save a little bit for my little girl!'

Though this had clearly been Durga's own unvoiced tragedy, she managed to put on a brave face. 'Is okay, Piti. You hungwy today. You eat.' But her bright young eyes lingered longingly on her aunt's empty bowl.

Indir Thakrun looked swiftly around. The usual watching eyes were absent, if only for the moment. Satisfied, she grinned conspiratorially at her niece and quickly broke one of her two ripe bananas in half. Then she held one half out to the child. The strained nonchalance of Durga's face dissolved instantly into an enormous grin of pure delight. Taking the treat eagerly from her aunt's hand, she jammed one end in her mouth, and began sucking it like one would a hard-boiled sweet. Her eyelids fluttered shut in contentment.

At that very moment, a sharp voice rang out from within the cottage: 'Dugga! Have you sneaked off to your aunt's again?'

The child's eyes snapped open. Unable to answer through a mouthful of the forbidden treat, she glanced beseechingly at her aunt.

'She's not doing anything, younger sister-in-law,' Indir Thakrun supplied hurriedly, trying to divert the child's mother's temper. 'She's just sitting here with me.'

'She has no business "just sitting there" when you're eating!' snapped the invisible voice. 'Greedy, disobedient child! How many times do I have to tell you not to hang about people when they are eating? Come inside at once!'

There was no counter to such a direct order. Casting a last, longing look at the sunny veranda and her helpless aunt, Durga slowly followed the direction of her mother's voice.

~

Though fed on his sparse coin, Indir Thakrun was only distantly related to Horihor—a cousin of sorts on his mother's side. But her kinship to the village was far older than his. Her family, the Chokrobortis, could trace their roots back to several generations in Contentment. On the other hand, Horihor was the son of an immigrant, only a first-generation resident. Indeed, had it not been for Horihor's father's keen desire to acquire a second wife, the Roys might not have set foot in Contentment at all.

The story of their arrival went like this: Ramchand Roy, then the eldest living son of the Joshra-Bishnupur Roys, had lost his first wife while he was still quite young. A man becomes easily accustomed to the comforts of conjugal life, and Ramchand felt the pangs of widowerhood rather keenly. His father, he noted gloomily, wasn't making any effort to secure his bereaved heir a much-needed second wife. Naturally, as a decent young man, he couldn't bring up the matter of his own second wedding; however, when waiting hopefully in silence for several months failed to fetch him a bride, he decided to begin hinting at the travails of his singlehood.

During hot afternoons, when the household had retired gratefully for naps into dark, cool rooms, Ramchand would begin to roll about in his bed, moaning and groaning loudly enough for the whole household to hear. When alarmed relatives rushed in to ask what was wrong, Ramchand would pretend to wilt in agony. 'Does it matter?' he would ask, forlornly. 'It is my lot to suffer in solitude for the rest of my life! There's no one to tend to me when I have a headache, no one to care for me when I have an upset stomach. Indeed, if I were to die tomorrow, there is no one in this house to even care! Oh, this loneliness—I can't bear it!' Then he would roll about on his bed some more, and groan pathetically.

It's hard to say, after all these years, whether Ramchand's father was finally worn down by the constant assault on his afternoon naps, or whether he had intended all along to wait a while before finding his son a second wife. But shortly into Ramchand's campaign for a companion, his second marriage was arranged to the only daughter of Brojo Chokroborti—a rich farmer from the neighbouring village of Contentment. And that was how the Joshra-Bishnupur Roys first established their connection to this village.

Ramchand's father passed away soon after the wedding, and Ramchand—still quite young—moved his family to Contentment to be under the guardianship of his father-in-law. However, he took care to pick a different neighbourhood than his in-laws, lest people talked.

People eventually did talk, for Ramchand's wife and children were obliged to spend nine months out of twelve under his father-in-law's roof. It wasn't that Ramchand was a dissolute or a wastrel; in fact, under his father-in-law's care, he attended the local Sanskrit school in Contentment and eventually became a fairly well-respected scholar. But he was plagued by an incurable lassitude. All disciplines of profitable engagement bored and exhausted him. He much preferred to spend his days in conversation and games of dice, excusing himself from the community courtyard only briefly to eat lunch and dinner in his in-laws' kitchen.

Occasionally, his friends and neighbours felt compelled to remind him that even the most accommodating of fathers-in-law could only contrive to be alive for so long. If Ramchand failed to settle into a career while Brojo Chokroborti was still around to help, how would he support his wife and child when the old man passed away?

Ramchand, however, set great store by the reputation of his wife's family's wealth. 'Brojo Chokkoti's rice fields will feed generations after he's gone,' he assured his friends airily. 'My needs are too humble to make even a dent in it. Even if he doesn't work a day in his life, my son will probably still have crumbs of his grandfather's wealth left in the coffers after he's done raising my grandsons, haha!'

Then he would turn back to the pasha board, and the intricacies of dice would wipe everything else from his mind.

Unfortunately for Ramchand (and certainly for his son and future grandsons), Brojo Chokroborti embraced the life eternal rather earlier than expected, and his son-in-law discovered—as people in these situations often do—that much of the older gentleman's affluence was empty reputation. What little cash existed was barely enough to cover his outstanding accounts, and Ramchand—as had been noted before—had neither the skill nor the discipline to extract wealth from the land.

The family would have fallen almost instantly into poverty had it not been for a cousin of Ramchand's. This cousin had also married into Brojo Chokroborti's family and moved to Contentment, but had done considerably better for himself. He and his family were willing to share their better fortune with Ramchand's household. Things began to look particularly promising for the Roys when Neelmoni—the eldest son of this other household—found employment in the Commissariat, thus bringing both money and prestige to his extended family.

However, like most instances of good fortune, this happy state of affairs lasted all too briefly. A few years after Neelmoni's employment and subsequent emigration from Contentment, Ramchand's cousin passed away quite suddenly. Neelmoni's opinion of his native village had plummeted almost as soon as he had left it, and he now insisted on taking his grieving mother back with him to his place of work. Their house in Contentment was closed up, with no hopes of being reopened in the foreseeable future.

The wave of poverty that had arched over Ramchand for years now crashed down, nearly drowning him and his family. The honorarium he received from his handful of disciples was barely enough to scrape together a living for one person, much less three. He, his wife, and Indir were compelled to frugalize the family's bare-bones budget even further, making do with the least necessities for themselves so that they could bring up Ramchand's young son, Horihor, as well as they could.

~

If Ramchand's family suffered because of his inherent lassitude, the roots of Indir's sufferings could be traced to a long-dead king.

Ballal Sen ruled the united provinces of Bengal from 1160 to 1179. One of his chief legacies was the resurrection of traditional Hinduism in the region. He is credited with the introduction of the *kuleen* system, by which certain brahmin families were deemed to be 'kuleen', or of a particularly prestigious extraction. To keep their bloodlines uncorrupted by non-kuleen blood, women of such families were only allowed to marry their male counterparts, or remain unmarried forever. Since having a spinster daughter at home was a matter of consternation and shame, this stricture raised the marital demand for kuleen men exponentially. Several of them became professional bridegrooms, marrying scores of women throughout their lives and visiting them for a night or two at their family homes on a rotatory basis. They made quite good livings off dowries, and from the tokens of respect that each bride's family was obliged to pay them on every visit.

As the daughter of a particularly prestigious brahmin family, Indir had been married young to a famous kuleen from the eastern districts. Being rich in wives scattered over many villages, the gentleman could only occasionally grace Contentment, and then only stay long enough to put a tick against Indir's name in his big book of brides. He would then leave for the next wife on his list—after, of course, having collected his groom honorarium and travel expenses from Indir's father. Despite being married to him for several years before she was widowed, Indir had only vague memories of him—she couldn't even remember his face properly.

One of their rare unions, however, had produced a little girl. Indir named her Bishweshwori, the Empress of the World. And while the child failed to live up to the literal meaning of her name, she did, in fact, become the soul and centre of her mother's world. These years, spent with her beloved daughter in the affectionate security of her parents' home, were probably the happiest years of Indir's long, hard life.

Eventually, however, her parents passed away, and since kuleen men are not obliged to take care of their wives and children, the guardianship of Indir and Bishweshwori passed on to her brother. This new household was a great deal less affectionate than the previous one. Still, it provided mother and daughter with a roof above their heads and food on their plates, and Indir was able to arrange a fairly decent match for her daughter as soon as she was of an acceptable age. But then Indir's brother, too, passed away, and his household disbanded rapidly. With no other male relative to claim shelter from, Indir realized that she was looking homelessness in the whites of its eyes.

It was at this juncture that Ramchand moved his family from Joshra-Bishnupur to Contentment, and his wife—Indir's aunt—invited her distraught niece to join the Roy household.

That was a long, long time ago.

Many springs have decorated the village trees since then, and many winters have stripped them bare. The Chokrobortis' open field has become the Mukhujjes' dense orchard, and now even that orchard is considered ancient. So many of the old families have died out or gone, leaving the woods to claim their empty homes and lands. And so much of the ancient woodland has been cut down to set up new neighbourhoods. Ronson Sahibs have replaced Jonson Sahibs and Jonson Sahibs have replaced Ronson Sahibs at the indigo plantation by the river, and generations of water lilies have bloomed and perished in the Shellcutter's Pond. Men who were once pillars of village society are now ashes and dust, the memory of their authority long lost. Even their names have been forgotten, save by the very ancient. Time, like the burbling waters of the Ichamoti, has carried away an entire generation of lives from the Abode of Contentment: unsung, uncherished and unremembered.

Only Indir lives—and remembers. Not the lithe young woman of her own fond memories, but a wrinkled widow of seventy-five. With broken cheeks, a weak hip and a bent spine. A permanent fog clouds her eyes, and the world floats uncertainly in it. When someone approaches, she raises a shrivelled palm to her forehead, as if to ward off the glare of the midday sun. 'Who goes? Nobeen? Behari? Oh, it's you, Raju . . .'

But the Contentment of 1834 shines like a beacon in her memory. Brojo Chokroborti's house used to be behind this forlorn little house, inside that now-overgrown bamboo grove. Forty years ago, there was no man richer than him in these lands. Every festival that was celebrated in the village was centred around his house. On the full-moon day of Kojagori Lokkhi Puja, not a single cooking fire was kindled in the village, for Brojo Chokroborti hosted every household for every single meal of the day. The pavilion-like veranda outside his enormous kitchen had to be wiped clean and set with fresh banana-leaf plates on a steady cycle all day, as the women of his household fed group after group of people till they were fit to burst. On the last day of the month of Poush, a full one maund of freshly harvested rice was ground in his household alone, to make puddings, crepes and sweet dumplings in honour of the year's harvest. Women from other farming families streamed through his large milling shed for days before that auspicious day, laughing and chatting as they husked and ground the yields of their own land with the Chokrobortis' tools.

If she closes her eyes, Indir can recall those festive days with perfect clarity. There, in the middle of the milling shed, is the second-eldest daughter-in-law of the other Roy household, husking her family's grain. Her strong, fair-skinned arm pushes forward and pulls back in rhythm with the husker, the gold at her wrist glinting in the autumn sun. Indir had never in her life met a more benevolent woman, nor one more beautiful. People used to say she was the very embodiment of the goddess Jagaddhatri, the Nourisher of the World. When Indir was newly widowed, and thus compelled to observe the twenty-four-hour fast of Aekadoshi, this young woman—who was only distantly related to Indir and certainly had no obligation to care for her—would personally prepare her as opulent a breakfast as widows were allowed, then wait upon her as she ate.

Long gone now, all of them. Those men, those women . . . even those old houses. Brojo Chokroborti's house and grounds are little more than unkempt woodland these days. His famous temple courtyard, once alive with light and lively chatter, is now a forbidding grove of bamboos. One can hear foxes baying from within even during the day. Time hadn't spared a single soul who could keep Indir company, someone with whom she could talk about old friends and old times—or about the sorrows and slender joys of this, much harder, life.

~

After his parents' death, young Horihor had left Contentment in search of better prospects. Occasionally, a hurried postcard or a money order for a few rupees would reach Indir, but no one set eyes on him for the next ten years. Left alone once again, Indir had clung to the old house. She had known no other home for thirty years, and quite literally had nowhere else to go. Horihor's money orders were paltry, which made her worry about his well-being even more. She had survived chiefly on the measured charity of her neighbours, liberally punctuated with starvation.

Then, about seven years ago, Horihor had abruptly returned to Contentment. He had brought with him a pretty young wife, a girl he had married during his years away. The young couple settled into the old house, and within a year had their first child—a little girl they called Durga. Indir had been beside herself with joy. She foresaw the Roy household once again filling up with children and feisty adolescents, pictured their eventual weddings, and even imagined herself surrounded by laughing great-nephews and great-nieces. Decades of loneliness and misery had left her pining for the slightest taste of happiness. And within the narrow confines of her rural life, Indir had learnt of no other happiness than having a household of one's own, filled with the laughter of one's own people.

Of course, this was before the quarrels began.

Shorbojoya had been prepared for a hard life even before she stepped over the threshold of her dilapidated new home. But she hadn't been prepared to share it with a barely related 'sister-in-law', especially one who thought that she was the family elder. She was amazed to learn that while her husband had worked himself to the bone in faraway lands just to make ends meet, this woman had been occupying his home, living off the money that he felt obliged to send.

It soon became clear to Shorbojoya that Indir had taken advantage of Horihor's mother's kindness and permanently attached herself to a family that could barely afford to support its own. Her dislike of the older woman began to manifest itself in sharp words, and before long, shouting matches became a daily staple of the Roy household. The smallest matter could trigger Shorbojoya's quick temper, and the closer poverty bit to the bone of her family, the harsher she became with Indir. Sometimes these fights would reach such a fever pitch that Indir would wrap up her belongings in an old sari, pick up her old brass drinking jar, and declare that she was leaving the house for good. But her old bones couldn't carry her far, and she would collapse as soon as she reached the shade of the bamboo grove that grew all over Brojo Chokroborti's old temple courtyard.

The child, Durga, was the only thread that held the women together. Indir's own daughter, Bishweshwori, had died only a few months after her wedding. For decades, Indir had nursed the loss within herself. Perhaps now, with the slow ebbing of her life, she had become eager to fill that void—to slake forty years of parched maternal instincts. So she lavished all her love on this 'Khuki', this little girl born of her beloved Horihor. Khuki's childish lisp, her wobbly first steps, her constant curiosity about the simplest things—everything flooded Indir's shrivelled old body with maternal ecstasy.

Ever since Horihor's return, Indir had ceded the main rooms to the young couple and moved herself into a thatched hut at the back of the house. It wasn't large, but it was big enough for all her worldly possessions: a brass jug that she kept filled with puffed rice, a few ancient saris in various states of disrepair, a couple of clay pots in which she hid stolen delicacies from Shorbojoya's pantry, and a pile of scraps that she had been meaning to make into a blanket for the last few years, but had never found the time to begin. Shorbojoya refused to come to the hut unless she absolutely had to. But Durga, since her earliest childhood, had spent nearly all her evenings in it, sitting on Indir's old patchwork quilt and listening to her aunt's fairy tales.

Indeed, Indir had told Durga every story she had ever known—some of them over and over again. An anecdote about dacoits was Durga's particular favourite. After the usual staple of myths and fairy tales, she would come closer to her aunt, look at her beseechingly and say, 'O Piti—now that dakat stowy!' The 'story' was a bare-bones, third-hand outline of an evening twenty-five years ago, when a group of dacoits had robbed one of the neighbours. But Khuki never grew tired of listening to it.

Then there were the songs and rhymes. In her long-lost youth, Indir had quite the reputation amongst the village women as a willing songbird. They would stop her on the way to the women's bathing steps, and request song after song. Her repertoire then had been large enough to fulfil all their requests, winning her village-wide praise. The grind of the intervening decades had displaced all thoughts of music from her mind. Now that she had her Khuki to entertain,

Indir worried that she might forget her cherished songs before she could successfully bestow them upon her niece. So she repeated each poem and musical piece every evening, making sure her ageing mind held on to the lyrics till Khuki knew them all by heart. Sometimes, as a test, she would stop abruptly in the middle of a verse and pretend she had forgotten the rest. For instance, she'd croon:

O Lalita, lily-like lass
Have you heard what's new?
A thief sneaked in our Radha's room . . .

Then she would stop, and look expectantly at Khuki. But her bright-eyed, brilliant niece was impossible to trick. She would immediately lean forward, and exclaim:

A bun-haired lad of blue!

No matter how long since she had last heard the song, Khuki could always recall the lines perfectly. It filled her aunt's heart with pride and joy. But then Shorbojoya would call her daughter in for dinner, and the session of music and tales between aunt and niece would wrap up for the night.

So when Indir left home in a tearful rage, it was Khuki who went looking for her. And after the first couple of times, she knew exactly where to find her missing aunt. 'I'll talk to Ma, Piti,' she promised her aunt every time, pulling her by the arm. 'I tell her not to scold you again. Now come home! Come home, Piti. Is so dark here!' After a while, Indir would allow herself to be led back home.

Every time Shorbojoya witnessed this return, she would twist her lips in open disdain. She knew it was inevitable, for where else could that old leech go? She didn't even have a clay oven to her name, much less a home. And yet she insisted on repeating this empty drama of 'leaving' over and over again! It was an obvious manipulation, and it infuriated Shorbojoya. She could have forgiven—though with bad grace—Indir's eating into her family's slender resources. But she could not forgive the dependent old woman's hollow shows of independence. And she especially could not forgive the woman's influence over her daughter. It infuriated her to see Durga fall for Indir's pathetic act every single time, and become closer to her 'aunt' than she was to her own mother!

2

HORIHOR'S ANCESTOR BISHNURAM Roy had been one of the first brahmins to settle in Joshra-Bishnupur at the invitation of the local landlords. The Choudhuris had wanted to set up a brahmin neighbourhood in the village as part of their legacy, and to that end had donated tax-exempt land to a handful of prestigious brahmin families.

This was before the British had fully consolidated their occupation of the land. Power was in a flux, and travelling far outside one's village offered a buffet of terrors. Land routes were stalked by thuggees, thyangares and other groups of highwaymen. River pirates terrorized the waterways. Thieves and dacoits hounded homes, barns, temples and inns. Most of these robbers were poor, lower-caste men trying to supplement their income. But upper-caste criminals were far from rare. Indeed, many of the richest families today owe their initial wealth to dacoit ancestors. During the day, all of these men—upper and lower caste alike—went about their lives like everyone else. At night, however, they convened in secret meeting nooks to worship the goddess Kali (whom they had fashioned into their patron deity), and went out to loot and pillage in her name. To this day, hidden shrines to this avatar of the goddess, locally called the 'dakate-Kali', can be found in remote crannies of old villages.

Of all the above enterprises, being a highwayman was the least profitable. All too often, thuggees and thyangares discovered that their freshly murdered victim had nothing of value on them, or had only a few measly pennies. Standard practice in such cases was to bury the corpse and go back to the highway, in the hopes that the next victim would make the night worth their while. Like pirates and dacoits, most thuggees and thyangares were also men from the lower castes: milkmen, fishermen, woodcutters, palanquin-bearers and the like. But just like its sister professions, they sometimes had an upper-caste employer or colleague. Biru Roy, son of Bishnuram Roy, was rumoured to be such a man. He paid monthly stipends to a group of powerfully built men, skilled with the spear and wooden club, and frequently accompanied them on their post-sunset hunts. His men staked claim to a section of the highway north of Contentment, unavoidable for people travelling east towards Chuadanga or Taki. And even though people tried their best to avoid travelling after dark, Biru Roy and his men managed to fill the ground with so many corpses that even today, ploughing those fields turned up human skulls and bones.

On the night that the Roy family was cursed, an elderly brahmin and his young son had been travelling eastwards from the market town of Kaligonj. It was late autumn, and the man had been out visiting acquaintances and disciples to raise money for his daughter's impending wedding. They had cooked and eaten their lunch at an inn in the smaller market town of Horidashpur, and had planned to spend the night at Nawbabgonj. It wasn't that the brahmin hadn't known about the dangers of the road. But he was in a hurry to get home, and had estimated that by walking fast, he would reach the inn at Nawbabgonj well before darkness fell. What he had forgotten to take into account were the short daylight hours of near-winter, and also perhaps the slowness of his own elderly pace.

The duo had reached as far as Shonadanga when the sun slowly began to dip westwards. Alarmed, father and son started to stride across the landscape, desperate to make it past the infamous grassy moors before darkness fell. But their speed was in vain. The thugs caught them just before the Pond of the Sisters-in-Law.

The father took the first blow on his head. Clutching his bleeding pate, he broke into a desperate run, shouting at his son to follow. But given that he was old and his son very young, it wasn't long before the thuggees overtook and surrounded them. Village lore said that Biru Roy was with his men that night. Recognizing a fellow brahmin, his victim begged for mercy. He offered to let Biru Roy's men kill him and take all the money he had raised, if only they would let his young son go.

'Think about my family and ancestors!' he is supposed to have begged. 'This is my only son. Without the prayers and offerings from him and his progeny, the souls of all our ancestors will be doomed!'

It hadn't occurred to the poor, simple man that a seasoned murderer would have little interest in the well-being of his victim's soul. He would be far more focused on quashing the danger of being recognized by a runaway prey. So, in the early hours of that night, two more bodies were buried at the shores of the Shellcutter's Pond, and Biru Roy and his men returned home richer by a few paltry rupees.

About a year after this, Biru Roy was returning home by boat from his father-in-law's house at Holudbere. Durga Puja was only a few days away, and he and his family had spent a happy few weeks with his indulgent in-laws. The entire party was cheerful and relaxed. In those days, big boats had to first cross the broad saltwater inlet south of Noneepur, then ride the high tide for two days till they reached south Shreepur. Only then could they enter the Ichamoti. Joshra-Bishnupur was a further four days' journey west from there, with parts of the river route running parallel to the highway that Biru Roy's men terrorized.

After two days on the Ichamoti, the crew stopped at Taki to shop for the upcoming Durga Puja at the Roy household. The next night, they dropped anchor on a quiet stretch of saltwater, next to an island in the middle of the river. The place was close to the confluence of the Ichamoti and the Dhobolchiti rivers. The meeting currents created a soothing, watery burble that filled the air. Light from the full moon washed the night in a pearly sheen, and the happiness on board was palpable. Home was only a few hours away, and Durga Puja—one of the year's biggest festivals—was imminent.

The crew cleared a cooking space for themselves amongst the tall kans grass, and another one for Biru Roy's family a little distance away. Both groups had begun preparing their dinner, when a sudden muffled noise beyond the clearing made everyone look up. A few boatmen left the circle around the crew's cooking fire to investigate. Before they could move into the surrounding thicket, however, the terrified screech of a young voice filled the air, followed rapidly by the splash of a heavy body sliding into water. The entire crew ran towards the noise, straight into the waist-high thicket of kans grass. But it was too late. All they discovered was the obvious sign of struggle on an empty bank, and the marks of something being dragged into the water. Seasoned helmsmen glanced at each other. Everything about the incident screamed the presence of a large saltwater crocodile that had just made off with its prey. And since they were the only people on the little island, it was equally clear that the prey had been a member of their party.

A headcount was immediately ordered, and that is when tragedy hit Biru Roy and his wife. The only person missing from the two large boats was their eldest son. Being young, he was supposed to wait for dinner in the family boat. But being young, he had sneaked out for the thrill of a moonlit walk along the shore. And then the shore had come alive, and claimed him as its own.

The usual acts of desperation followed, even though everyone knew that saltwater crocodiles left no trace of their prey. Small boats were lowered into the water, and boatmen scoured the river for the little boy. Dinner lay forgotten, half-cooked and cold. Men splashed their oars heavily into the water to draw out the crocodile, but in vain. It was almost as if an invisible arbiter was balancing last year's slaughter on the road with this year's loss on the water. The ignorant Biru Roy learnt, far too late, that while the Pond of the Sisters-in-Law might be deep enough to hide the evidence of his crimes from human eyes, it wasn't deep enough to hide them from the dispenser of cosmic justice.

Biru Roy died shortly after the group returned to Joshra-Bishnupur. The Roy family that survives today is descended from his younger brother. But the death of his eldest son on the Ichamoti started a strange pattern in the family. None of the family's firstborn sons survived to adulthood. Indeed, most of them died even before they reached puberty. People began to say that the family had been cursed, finally touched by the sin of slaughtering a brahmin. And that was how Horihor's mother—Ramchand's second wife—heard of the curse. However, she was not inclined to give in passively to destiny. Almost immediately upon hearing about the curse, she arranged to travel to the famous shrine at Tarokeshwor. There, she begged and pleaded with the gods and holy men to grant her son a reprieve from the family curse. As the result of her appeals, she was finally given a protective amulet. She tied it securely around her son's arm right after her return to Contentment, and instructed him never to remove it from his person.

Perhaps the amulet is more powerful than the sins of his ancestors, or perhaps the curse on the Roys had lost its power over the years, having satisfied its vengeance with the lives already taken. Either way, Horihor is now middle-aged, and is still very much alive.

3

A FEW DAYS later. It was late evening outside, and Khuki had already gone to bed. Her aunt was not at home. She had fought bitterly with her mother, and had left Contentment for the house of a distant relative. That had been two months ago. Ever since then, and particularly since her mother had entered the birthing chamber, there wasn't really anyone to look after Khuki. No one noticed what she ate, or when she slept. So, with nothing else to occupy her empty evenings, Khuki had taken herself to bed.

After a few minutes of sleepless loneliness in the dark room, Khuki began to sob softly for her aunt. She cried for her aunt every night in bed, away from censorious eyes and ears. Then, still whimpering, she drifted into sleep. A few hours later, she was roused abruptly by the babbling of adult voices. A group of women seemed to have gathered outside their kitchen, in the area where the water pots were kept. Khuki tried to stay awake and identify the voices. There was Kuruni's mother, the village midwife, Nyara's grandmother . . . and a few other neighbouring women. Everyone sounded busy and worried.

From her bed, Khuki could see that the light in the birthing chamber was on. Long shadows clustered around it, whispering urgently. On a different night, Khuki would have been scared by the air of worry and anxiety. But tonight, her sleepy eyes were drawn to the glow of the full moon. The veranda outside her room, usually infested with shadowy darkness after sundown, was awash with the golden moonlight. As the night deepened, a moist, cool river breeze began to waft into the village, rustling the tops of the bamboo grove on its way. Soothed by that rhythmic sound, Khuki slowly slipped back into sleep again.

When she next woke up, it was around the middle of the night. She had been roused by the sound of running feet and a confusion of loud voices. The women were still gathered around the birthing chamber, but speaking much louder than they had been earlier. She heard her father run across the courtyard towards them, anxiously demanding, 'How is she, younger aunt? What is it?'

Then Khuki heard her mother. It couldn't have been anyone else—she knew that voice too well. But why was her mother grunting and groaning? What was wrong with her? What exactly was going on in the birthing chamber? Heavy with sleep and alarm, Khuki sat up in a tangle of bedclothes, but couldn't decide what to do next. After a few minutes of helplessly looking around, she fell back on the bed. Her mind was such a whirl of worry and wonder that she didn't even notice when she sank back into sleep again.

The sound of a kitten crying pierced the night. Khuki had no idea how long she had been asleep this time, but she shot up at the sound. The stray female—the one that lived in the woods and came by the house sometimes—had just given birth to a litter. Khuki had secreted the pile into her aunt's unused mud stove to keep it safe from predators. Clearly, that safe haven had been breached.

'It's the tomcat!' she thought to herself, thoroughly alarmed. 'Oh no—he's going to eat the kittens!'

However, when she sprinted over to her aunt's veranda and put her hand inside the cold oven, she found that the soft pile of kittens was still there, fast asleep and perfectly safe. There was no sign of the tomcat anywhere. Could the kittens have gone back to sleep in the few seconds that it took her to reach her aunt's hut? No . . . that didn't seem likely. But if it wasn't the kittens, who could have been making that wailing noise? And why?

Khuki trudged back to bed, sleepy and puzzled. As she drifted into sleep again, she was fairly certain that she heard another kitten-wail.

It was morning when she woke up next. To her surprise, some of the women from the previous evening were still milling about their courtyard. The midwife, Kuruni's mother, approached her with a big smile.

'You had a little brother last night, Khuki—didn't you realize?'

Khuki was astonished. She had had no idea!

'Bless your sleep!' exclaimed the midwife. 'Here we were, screaming and shouting all night . . . didn't you hear *anything*? I'd better make offerings at the pirbaba's mosque at Kalpur on my way back—saved us from a catastrophe last night, he did!'

The moment Kuruni's mother walked away from her, Khuki ran to the birthing chamber and peeked in. If she had a new brother, then it stood to reason that he would be found near her mother. Even at this hour, the inside of the chamber was hazy with smoke. The midwife had built and banked a cow-dung and coal-powder fire inside. Khuki had to look around a few times before she could make out the shapes within. There was her mother, lying on a makeshift bed next to the temporary fence. She was fast asleep. Beside her lay a tiny, doll-like creature . . . barely bigger than an actual glass doll. Was *that* her brother?

At that very second, the creature opened its eyes, blinked a few times, then raised two impossibly small fists in the air and let out a wail. Durga was astonished. He sounded exactly like a newborn kitten! It suddenly occurred to her that the wails she had heard the previous night had been of this creature's making—not the kittens' at all. Amazing!

As she watched the tiny thing continue to wail, the astonishment in her heart melted into a flood of pity, which swiftly transformed into protectiveness and rapidly blossoming affection. Her poor little tiny brother! Just as helpless, poor darling, as those newborn kittens! Had it not been for the forbidding presence of the midwife and Nyara's grandmother, she would have run inside the chamber and held him tightly to her chest!

A few days later, Shorbojoya's confinement finally ended. Now that her brother was out of the birthing chamber, Khuki spent hours of her day in his company. She pushed him gently on his little swing, singing songs and reciting rhymes she had learnt from her aunt. Often, as evening descended on the village and birds began returning to their nests in a chattering swarm, she sat next to her brother and cried silently for her missing aunt.

The entire neighbourhood had been coming by to see the new baby. Their decrepit old house echoed with their admiration.

'Such a lovely smile—did you see that, fourth-eldest sister?' women asked each other as they crowded around the baby. 'Such hair, such a beautiful face! That smile can light up a whole house!'

'If only Piti could see him!' Khuki thought, wistfully. Everyone else was getting to meet her brother . . . why not his own aunt? Where had her piti gone, anyway? Did anyone know? Would Khuki ever see her again?

Though still very young, Khuki had worked out that Piti was unwanted in their home. Neither of her parents had any love for her piti, nor any interest in bringing her back. Her little cottage at the back of the house had already begun to look abandoned. The unlatched doors remained open on most days and nights. Bat-dung had accumulated in the outer veranda. No one bothered to dust or sweep the place, and saplings were already pushing their way through the cottage floor. Whenever she looked at the slowly dilapidating cottage, Khuki's eyes brimmed with helpless tears. Every song, every rhyme, every story that she had ever heard had been on that veranda. Was she just supposed to forget those magical times?

Happily, a miracle struck only a few days later. Hori Palit's eldest daughter hurried up to their house in the middle of the morning.

'Saw your old woman on my way to the bathing steps—she was coming into the neighbourhood with a small bundle and a water pot,' she informed Shorbojoya. 'Went straight to the Chokkotis' house. Still too upset to come home, I take it? Anyway, what I came to tell you was—end this ugliness now. Send Dugga over to meet her. If Dugga takes her by the hand and leads her home, she'll come back. Never could say no to your daughter, that woman.'

Indir had, in fact, moved to Hori Palit's own house by the time the news of her arrival reached the Roy household. Several of the neighbourhood women had flocked over to see her. And as she rested after her long, arduous walk back to Contentment, they filled her in on the birth of Horihor's son.

'O Piti!'

Startled, Indir looked at the door. Her Durga stood framed in the doorway, wild hair streaming behind her, panting like she had run all the way from her house to Hori Palit's as fast as she could. She was grinning from ear to ear, but her eyes were bright with unshed tears.

Indir's ancient face split into an enormous smile. She held out her hands to grasp her beloved niece, but Durga dove straight into her lap, clinging to her aunt as if both their lives depended on it. Her little body began shaking with silent sobs. Several of the assembled women wiped tears from their own eyes. Hori Palit's middle-aged wife leaned forward, touching Indir on the shoulder. 'There you go, sister-in-law,' she said, gently. 'Your own darling girl has returned to your lap as your niece.'

Later, when she reached her old house and saw the newborn boy, Indir almost went mad with joy—laughing, cooing and crying at the same time. After decades of unrelenting sorrow, the stars were shining on her family again! She was back in her familiar little cottage, her niece was in her arms, and now the family had finally been blessed with a much-awaited son.

The next day, the old woman began taking charge of her recalcitrant little cottage. She dusted and swept the room with vigour, pulled out the taro and lebbeck saplings that had taken root on the floor, and began restoring the little thatched hut to its former pristine glory. Durga was delighted. Despite the arrival of her wonderful new brother, life hadn't felt quite right to her ever since her aunt had left. Now, finally, everyone was back where they belonged—and her happiness knew no bounds!

After lunch, Indir took to splitting bamboo and chopping them into smaller sticks. Durga sat next to her and chatted incessantly, carrying each load of sticks indoors as it was done. There were no longer any houses between Indir's back veranda and the river; only bamboo groves, old woodland and mango orchards. Of course, the river wasn't exactly close. It was a quarter of a mile away at least, and that was if one went directly through the woods. But with nothing except trees in its way, the breeze was still moist and cool when it reached her hut, and unfailingly soothing. Sitting in that breeze under the pleasant afternoon sun, hand moving rhythmically over the bamboo, Indir's thoughts floated back to the days of her youth. The village used to be a completely different place then. So different, in fact, that memories of it now felt like a happy daydream.

He had come thrice that she could remember . . . her husband. Once he had brought a treat wrapped in a piece of cloth—Bishweshwori had been two years old that year. They were little rounded lumps, white and sweet. Ola, that's what everybody called them: small balls of local white sugar. She'd had a little taste, too: a single sip from a small pot of water that someone had dissolved one of those things into. Then one evening, during the lamp-lighting hour, a man had arrived under the guava tree in their courtyard. He said he had a letter from her in-laws' village. There was no one at home to read the letter (her brother Golok had passed away just the previous year). So Indir had taken the letter and walked to her uncle Brojo Chokroborti's temple courtyard, where the neighbourhood men gathered in the evenings to play games of dice. She can still recall the moment vividly: her Brojo Jyatha, Potito Roy's younger brother, Jodu Roy (both from the Roy family the next neighbourhood over), her own second-eldest and fourth-eldest uncles, and Golok's brother-in-law, Bhojohori, had all been sitting around the dice board, while her own third-eldest uncle read the letter silently.

'Who brought you this letter, child?' he had asked in surprise, when she had first handed him the letter. That surprise quickly changed to something else.

After the letter had been read, Indir had to go immediately back to her house and remove all traces of being a married woman from her body. She scrubbed the vermilion from her parting and took off her iron wedding bangle. Then, with a great deal of sorrow, she had removed her pair of silver bracelets, knowing that she would never be allowed to wear them again. Those bracelets had been dearly cherished. Her parents had given them to her when she was in the first flush of her youth, and over the years they had become her only symbol of frivolous indulgence. Finally, with all her adornments gone, she had gone down to the Ichamoti and bathed in its ink-dark waters. Afterwards she had put on, for the first time, the plain white widow's garb that she would have to wear for the rest of her life.

So many decades ago, all of this . . . yet it felt as recent as last night's dream.

Nibaron—poor Nibaron. The wilderness behind her hut keeps reminding her of Nibaron. He was her uncle Brojo Chokkoti's son. Sixteen, handsome, and the apple of absolutely everyone's eyes. 'Such a glowing complexion!' everyone used to say. 'Such a beautiful head of hair!'

There, where the undergrowth now covers the foundations of the house—that was his sickroom. His fever was fatal, but he still lingered for three days. Poor child, he was desperate for a drink of water. But Ishan Kobiraj had strictly forbidden it. He was only allowed to suck on a pinch of anise seeds wrapped in a piece of cloth. Finally, after three days and three nights of constant thirst and suffering, he passed away on the fourth night. Even seconds before passing, till literally his last breath, he had begged everyone for water . . . for just one drop, for just a second's taste. But no one had so much as wetted his lips. Physician's orders, after all. But the desperation of those pleas had cut everyone deep.

Once he passed, Nibaron's mother—Brojo Chokkoti's wife—quietly stopped eating and drinking. It went on for four full days. People coaxed and pleaded with her, but to no avail. It was obvious to everyone what she had made up her mind to do. Finally, on the fifth day, the elderly Ramchand Chokkoti, her husband's much-older brother, went to her room himself. He didn't try to reason with her. Instead, he simply folded his hands in supplication.

'Who's going to look after this old man if you leave us, Ma?' he pleaded gently. 'Will you abandon this infirm child of yours in his helpless years?'

Now, Nibaron's mother was the daughter of an old, distinguished family. The duty to nurture had been bred into her bones. It was said that she never started her day without first washing her husband's feet and drinking that water. No one had ever seen a morsel pass her lips till every soul under her roof had been satisfactorily fed. Like a true old-fashioned matriarch, she cooked elaborate meals for her large household and fed everyone till they were fit to burst, but ate only simple fare herself. And that at three in the afternoon, after even the servants had eaten. She was also incredibly generous. Few people returned from her door empty-handed. The village used to compare her to the goddess Onnopurna, the Vanquisher of Hunger. In beauty and in deeds, they said, she was the goddess incarnate—a mother to all who needed succour.

So, when her elderly brother-in-law came before her as a supplicant, it hit something deep within her—her innate instinct to protect and serve. She slowly lifted herself out of bed, and poured herself a drink of water.

The entire household breathed a sigh of relief.

But the loss of her son, and the cruelty that she had been forced to show him in his final days, had crushed her spirit. She passed away only a year and a half after this incident.

On afternoons like this, when looking out into the woods that was once her house, Indir could almost hear those final excruciating exchanges between mother and son.

'Just a little water, Ma . . . just one taste, no more, I promise!'

'No, darling—for shame. Ishan Kobiraj has said no water, not even a taste. You know this, sweetheart . . .'

'I beg you, Ma, please . . . I'll fall at your feet. Just one sip, Ma—please! Please!'

The rustling of leaves in the breeze brought her back across those five long decades. Noticing the lull in her aunt's responses, Khuki asked, 'Are you sweepy, Piti? Come, less haff a nap.'

'Aww, my sweetheart . . . I'm all right. Let's finish up these sticks today. It's too late for a nap, anyway. How about you hand me that large piece of bamboo?'

4

IT HAD BEEN almost ten months since the birth of the Roys' little boy. Khoka was now a slender, wispy child, with an impossibly small face. So far, he had managed to acquire just two teeth, but the lack in numbers was made up by the frequency of his beaming smile. The neighbours often ribbed Shorbojoya about the grin, insisting that she must have had it especially commissioned from the workshop in the sky.

And if someone added a little starter-laughter of their own, Khoka's grin would blossom into interminable bouts of delighted giggling. His mother would finally be compelled to say, 'That's enough laughter for today, my darling. Let's save the rest for tomorrow, shall we?'

So far, he had mastered two words. When happy, he chanted 'Je je je!', and showed off his teeth in an enormous grin. When upset, he screamed 'Na na na!', and bawled furiously. The rest of his time was chiefly spent in testing the strength of his two teeth. Clumps of clay, the end of his mother's sari, pieces of wood—anything that he could reach went straight into his mouth. Feeding times inevitably ended with him biting down hard on the bell-metal spoon, and Shorbojoya struggling to get it out.

'Aww, look at you, you silly boy!' she would giggle, enamoured by his antics. 'What will you grin with, darling, if you break your two lovely teeth?'

But Khoka would refuse to let go. Finally, Shorbojoya would have to put her fingers inside his mouth to pry it out.

Since Durga could not be trusted to keep an eye on the baby all the time, a raised pen of split bamboo had been constructed in the veranda outside the kitchen. This is where the baby would stay while Shorbojoya did the housework, or went down to the pond to bathe or fetch water. From a distance, it made Khoka look exactly like a tiny criminal on the dock. He appeared not to mind this wholly undeserved slight, however. Much of his time in the pen-like cot was spent crawling around enthusiastically, gurgling with laughter and talking to creatures invisible to adult eyes. But there would be moments when he would pull himself up by the rails and stare into the bamboo grove behind the house in complete silence, a look of sombre wonderment on his little face.

The swish of wet clothes in the back lane—the one that led directly to the women's bathing steps at the pond—was his signal that his mother was on her way home. Usually, this would make him gurgle with renewed delight and scramble to the edge of the cot in anticipation. Lately, however, he had learnt to be more cautious. Before leaving for the pond, Shorbojoya would clean and dress her son in fresh clothes, then draw a thick line of kajal around his eyes to ward off the evil eye. In the time that it took her to bathe and do the daily laundry, however, Khoka would smear much of the black pigment all over his freshly cleaned face. Upon her return from the pond, his exasperated mother would call him a little magpie, then advance purposefully upon him with a damp cloth. No matter how hard he screamed or how red in the face he became, she would scrub him till he was clean again, and then pin him down to reapply the repellent of evil eyes. These were the moments when Khoka was decidedly not fond of his mother, and he endeavoured to express it as loudly as he could. But his otherwise-doting mother would pay no attention to his wishes when there was dirt to be removed.

Sometimes, instead of fighting, he attempted to escape when Shorbojoya approached him with a washcloth. But his mother was wily, and knew his ways well. All she had to do was say, 'My baby says "tuuuuu!" Show us how to rock, my darling. Show us how to sing! Tuuuuu!'

Immediately, Khoka would plop down in his cot and begin to rock back and forth. He would start moving his tiny hands to an internal rhythm, and launch into the only song he knew:

Je je je ae aaeeeeee aeeeeiiii
Je je je je je aee
Je jaeeeeeiiiii . . .

At the very next moment, he would be swept up in his mother's lap, and the dreaded washcloth would be scrubbing him clean.

Sometimes, while working, Shorbojoya would suddenly realize that she hadn't heard her baby's babbling for a while. Her heart would thud harder in her chest. Did he manage to slip out of his cot? Did he crawl out of the courtyard? Did a fox sneak in and carry him off? She would scramble to the veranda, falling over her feet in her haste . . . only to find Khoka sprawled in his cot, fast asleep. His fair-skinned little body looked like a basket of spilled magnolias in the sun, rising and falling gently with each breath. Nothing could rouse him when he slept this deeply—not red ants, not flies, not the black tickling ants. In the last ten months, these moments of repose had been the only spells of silence in this remote old house by the woods and bamboo groves. The rest of the time, its dilapidated rooms overflowed with his joyous singing and his unstoppable gurgles of delight.

People often say that mothers are the greatest pillar of society, for they gift civilization its greatest asset: its men. We praise women, and justly so, for unselfishly bearing and raising our boys without expecting any recognition or compensation in return. But in that praise, do we not often forget the gifts that a child bestows upon its mother? It is true that our children enter the world empty-handed, without the coins to pay for their care. But what worldly wealth can compare to the joy of seeing that first gummy smile, to hearing those first lisping words? Can any earthly treasure be as precious as watching the wonder with which our babies slowly discover the world? No, we do not minister to our children solely out of the goodness of our hearts. Parenting is not an act of charity or duty, akin to giving alms to a beggar. Children pay us for every moment of care that we give them. They pay for it with the sheer joy and wonderment that we feel in watching them grow.

Payment of this kind was especially in evidence in the Roy household on those mornings when a harried Shorbojoya would try to get her husband to watch his son for a while.

'Here, hold your son for a bit,' she would say. 'Dugga isn't home, and your sister has already gone down to the pond. There's no one to look after him but you. Take him . . . I'll only be gone a few minutes.'

When her husband expressed alarm at the prospect of watching a baby, Shorbojoya would snap in exasperation.

'So should I just give up on housework and sit with your son in my arms all day? Good lord, I only asked for a few minutes!'

Horihor would then try to point out, sensibly, that he was busy with the family accounts or his own writings, and watching a child would disrupt this serious work. In response, his quick-tempered wife would simply put the baby down on the floor and storm out of the room.

Left with no choice, Horihor would sigh and go back to his papers, leaving the child to his own devices. When he looked up a few minutes later, his little boy would inevitably be doing something that he absolutely shouldn't, such as chewing his father's slipper. Before Horihor could find the words to tell him off, however, his son would be distracted by something else entirely . . . such as a sparrow. Things that were perfectly common to an adult were still objects of utter amazement and delight to him. Khoka would bestow his famous two-toothed grin upon the bird, and begin singing his happy 'Je je je!' song at it.

And just like that, Horihor's exasperation would melt into an overwhelming love for his little boy. Watching him wave his tiny palms at the bird, he would think of another afternoon not too long ago, when the midday train had deposited him on an empty station in the heart of rural Bengal. It was the station closest to his in-laws' house. Horihor had last visited their village several years ago, and had quite forgotten his way. Several people had had to guide him from the station—not just to the village, but all the way to the house.

The courtyard of the house, when he reached it, had been empty. After a few minutes of him repeatedly announcing his presence, a fair-skinned, willowy girl had stepped out of the main door to answer him. The moment their eyes met, however, hers had widened. Then, without speaking a word, she had quickly turned around and run back into the house.

Horihor had been just as taken aback to see her. There were no young women in his in-laws' household, as far as he knew. Then who could the woman have been? Could it have been his wife? If yes, then . . . goodness! How she had grown!

Then a more sobering thought struck him: had he really been away from home for that many years?

Confirmation came later that night. A few hours after dinner, Shorbojoya finally came into his room, wrapped in a length of cheap red-bordered white silk. It was her mother's only good sari, painstakingly preserved through decades of poverty. It was also the only sari in the entire household that was good enough for a night of such an unexpected reunion. Despite his glimpse of her earlier in the day, Horihor was amazed all over again. The child bride he remembered from his wedding day bore no resemblance to the beautiful young woman now in his room. Her face, her hands, her feet—even the way she moved—had been utterly transformed. It was as if the gods had broken her down and then remade her from scratch. True, the change had robbed her of her old, artless innocence. But even Horihor realized that the loveliness bestowed in its stead was a rare gift.

Though it was she who had come to his room, Shorbojoya appeared startled when she met Horihor's eyes. Despite her years as a married woman, she was, in actual fact, still a new bride. She had only met her husband once after their wedding, and that only briefly.

Horihor broke the silence first. Taking her right hand into both of his, he guided her to the only furniture in the room: the bed.

'Make yourself comfortable,' he invited, smiling warmly. 'How have you been? Well?'

Relieved at the gentleness, Shorbojoya smiled back at him. The awkwardness between them seemed to melt away.

'And why was I forgotten for all these years?' she demanded cheekily, with the familiarity of a real wife. 'What possessed you to disappear for so long?'

Then her smile became a mischievous grin. 'Or was I being punished for being a bad wife, hmmm?'

Horihor burst out laughing. After being away for so many years, the rural tone and style of his wife's speech was like honey to his ears. Then his eyes fell on her arms. There was no trace of gold on her wrist or forearms. All her bangles were cheap glass, except the pair of wedding bangles made of white shell. Suddenly, Horihor was overcome with sympathy for his beautiful young wife. First the daughter of an impoverished household, then the wife of an absent young man. Who could she expect presents from, really? Who could she even ask? No no . . . this was his fault. He had been most remiss in his duty towards her.

From behind what remained of her shyness, Shorbojoya, too, was watching her husband. She had sneaked quick peeks at him throughout the day, but she now felt that those passing glimpses hadn't done her husband justice. Being out and about in the west had tanned Horihor's fair skin golden, and had given him the sort of self-assurance that was seldom seen amongst the young men of her world. From her parents' conversation, she had gleaned that he had become quite the scholar in his time away. Surely all that learning would now help him make a decent living? Please, gods, may he not leave her again! These last years had been unspeakably miserable. Everyone had assumed that her husband had abandoned her to become an ascetic. Of course, she never allowed herself to believe that, but in her heart of hearts, Horihor's return had felt like an improbable dream. At every single wedding or thread ceremony in the village, people had showered her with ostentatious pity; they had been certain that *she* would never have children of her own, or even her own household. She had become used to putting up a brave face to this aggressive sympathy, but far too many of her nights had been spent in bitter tears. What if her friends and neighbours were right? What if her husband never did return? Her parents barely eked out a living for themselves. What would happen to her when they passed away? Whose door would she have left to go to, to claim kinship and beg for shelter? These thoughts had haunted her every waking moment.

Today, she could put those worries to rest. Today, the floating bark of her life had finally found its shore.

'Did you recognize me this morning?' Horihor asked, grinning.

'Not at first . . .' Shorbojoya confessed. 'But I knew pretty much immediately.'

'As if!'

'No, honestly! Didn't you see how quickly I covered my head and went back into the house? It wasn't a guess. I *knew* it was you!'

Then, after a second's pause, she asked in a softer voice, 'And you? Did you recognize me too? Did you *know*?'

And thus the conversation had flowed throughout that night, washing over matters relevant and superfluous. Shorbojoya couldn't hold back tears when she spoke of the passing of her older brother; Horihor asked which village Beena had been married into (he had forgotten the name of Shorbojoya's younger sister—happily, a dinner-time conversation with his father-in-law had refreshed his memory). But through it all, Shorbojoya's mind kept going back to one specific question: was her husband back for good? Would he finally take her to his own household? Or would he simply go away again and leave her to her fate? A few times in their conversation, she almost asked him about it. But something within her rebelled at the idea of appearing clingy, especially if it was to a disinterested husband.

'Let him do as he likes', it whispered within her soul, even as the rest of her yearned to know. 'Why invite pity if all he wants to do is go back to his Goya and Kashi?'

In the end, Horihor solved the dilemma himself. 'Let's head back home together tomorrow, what d'you say?' he said.

Shorbojoya was certain that the whole house could hear the sudden thumping of her heart. But she tried her best not to give away her excitement.

'Tomorrow?' she forced herself to ask, as normally as she could. 'But you've only just arrived. I don't think Ma and Baba will let you go before they've had the chance to coddle you for a few days. Besides, my medlar-flower has invited you to her house for lunch the day after . . .'

'Who is your medlar-flower?'

'My friend . . . we swore to undying friendship on the medlar blossom. She moved two neighbourhoods away after her wedding.' Then she grinned her mischievous grin again. 'Medlar-flower sent word that she's coming tomorrow. She means to sneak a good look at you from behind the doors and windows!'

And thus the darkness of the rural night had slowly faded into the grey-blue of a village dawn. Their new beginning had no witnesses, save for the lone brainfever bird in the drumstick tree outside the window. The road ahead was long and shrouded in the mysteries of the future, but at least, at long last, they had each other.

And now here was this child, Horihor thought, watching his son happily singing at the birds. Who had thought, on that fateful night, that they would have come this far?

5

SHORBOJOYA HAD REFUSED to speak a full sentence to Indir Thakrun since her return to the household half a year back. She fully believed that the old woman was an ill omen for her family. Not only had every single relative she'd ever lived with died before their time, Shorbojoya was also sure that the woman was now trying to siren away her own children. Durga certainly seemed to care more for her 'auntie' than she did for her own mother. Well, Shorbojoya wasn't going to stand for it! In the last six or so months, she had made it quite clear to Indir that she was no longer welcome in the Roy household. She had instructed her, in so many words, to start looking for alternative arrangements before her time under Shorbojoya's roof ran out.

Indir had no idea what these arrangements could possibly be. In her seventy years, she had been cast adrift by fate several times, and the charity of neighbours and family was the only thing she knew to turn to. If there was indeed an alternative way for women to survive, she had certainly never found it. It did occur to her, however, that she could beg sanctuary from someone else. Decades ago, her daughter had been married to a well-off farmer in Bhandarhati. Of course, the poor girl had passed away soon after, and her once-son-in-law had gone on to marry again and have several children, who now had several children of their own. But if she managed to reach him, and then throw herself upon his mercy, would he really turn a former mother-in-law away?

At six the next evening, a bullock cart stopped outside a large house in Bhandarhati. A young man came out from within to answer the carter's call. A man of about fifty followed him out, saying, 'Who is it, Radhu? Ask them where they're coming from.'

Indir peered out from under the cart's awning. Who was this heavy-set man of obvious authority, with more salt than pepper in his hair? Was this her son-in-law? No no, surely not! Where was the tall, willowy Chondor that she remembered? Suddenly, all the despair, confusion, and worry that she had been bottling up inside for months crashed upon her. She began sobbing helplessly. Forty years. Forty years! That was how long she had lived without her darling daughter—how long her little girl had been dead! These days she could barely remember her face. And here was the poor child's once-husband—older and well-settled, bearing no trace of her anywhere on him!

But surely, surely he would still grant her sanctuary? Chondor was a good man. He would be good to her. He must! She had nowhere else to go!

Meanwhile, the sight of a sobbing, gasping older woman had left Chondor Mojumdar stunned and speechless. It took him a good few minutes to work out that this woman, crying pitifully about his first wife, was in fact his first mother-in-law. Once he worked that out, he quickly came forward and bent to touch her feet. At this, relief flooded Indir. She forced her sobs down and pulled the sari a little over her head.

'A place . . . under your roof, Babaji,' she gasped. 'Haven't many days left. No one else to give shelter . . . just a little food, some old clothes . . .'

Hurriedly, Chondro Mojumdar instructed his eldest son to unload Indir's things from the cart and take her indoors. After the passing of his second wife, the household duties had fallen to his widowed daughter, Hoimoboti, and his eldest daughter-in-law. They would see to this new member's needs.

Chondro Mojumdar's house was built on two enormous raised platforms, supported by the trunks of palmyra trees. Each platform housed an *aatchalaa*—a house with an eight-sided roof. The large space within was filled to the brim with trunks, safety chests and other furniture. There was barely enough room to walk. Within this edifice of plenty, Chondro Mojumdar lived with his four children, three daughters-in-law, and four or five grandchildren. Indir soon discovered that in the absence of his second wife—who, like Bishweshwori, had preceded her husband into the afterlife—the household was run by his widowed daughter Hoimoboti and his eldest daughter-in-law.

Indir took to Hoimoboti immediately. She was a cheerful and kind woman, and had no hesitation about calling Indir grandma. 'Did you meet me when I was little, Grandma?' she asked, while chopping fruits for Indir's meal. 'No . . . I don't think you've ever visited us before. Do you still have your teeth? Should I dice a sugarcane for you?'

Outside, in the kitchen veranda, the household children were fighting and laughing over their dinner.

'Ma, look! Umi poured ALL her daal on my plate!'

'Why do you keep sitting next to her? Haven't I told you to sit somewhere else? And you, Umi! Think you can do what you like, do you?'

Umi began to defend herself, and the rest of the conversation drowned in a confusion of voices.

A few days passed. Indir couldn't settle into this new household. The crowd of furniture overwhelmed her. The children were strangers to her, and far too loud. She had food and shelter, but no one to talk to. The ways of the household, the people in the neighbourhood, even the roads around were new to her. Had Indir stopped to think about it, she may have realized that Chondro Mojumdar's family was everything she had always thought she wanted: a surfeit of resources, paucity of want, and a house full of happy children. As it was, she missed the peace of her own little hut. She missed walking down familiar paths, and a neighbourhood that she had spent an entire lifetime in. But most of all, she missed Durga and the baby.

Finally, on the twentieth day of her arrival in Bhandarhati, Indir could no longer withstand her inner turmoil. She wrapped up her scant belongings, and took her leave of the Mojumdar household. Her exit didn't have much of an effect on anyone in the family. Hoimoboti had several things to occupy her time—Indir had merely been one more charitable responsibility. Her sister-in-law, on the other hand, hadn't taken well to being burdened with the care of her father-in-law's former mother-in-law, so she was glad to see the old woman go. As to what Mojumdar Moshai himself felt . . . well, that was between him and his god. But he certainly said nothing to stop Indir. Age had taught him the value of peace, and he was not prepared to upset his eldest son and daughter-in-law for the sake of his dead wife's mother.

Much later that night, Indir collapsed gratefully on the veranda of her beloved hut. With the children beside her watching the moonlit coconut leaves shimmer gently in the familiar river breeze, she felt contentment finally descend on her.

For the first few days of her return, her darling Khuki had refused to speak to her. But Indir won her back with stories, head rubs, and the promise to never go away again. Soon, they were back to sitting side by side, Indir gently caressing the girl's hair and listening to her stream of questions and observations. She sometimes wished that she could buy the girl her first pair of adult earrings, but both aunt and child knew that that was impossible. Indir could not even afford to replace her own tattered blankets. In fact, she had been going up to old Ramnath Ganguly's house in the Ganguly neighbourhood for exactly that reason.

'O Ram, the cold is upon us again!' she would begin. 'And here I am without even a single piece of warm cloth. Nothing to wrap these old bones in once I leave the bed. So I thought, let me go ask my brother Ram. Surely, he . . .'

At this point, Ram Ganguly would cut her off. 'Yes, yes, Didi. Of course. It's just that things are a bit hard this month. Come back another time, okay?'

This had been going on for a few weeks. Indir had almost given up hope of getting something out of her wheedling, when one day Ram Ganguly actually produced a thick shawl of Kushtia-woven red cotton.

'Here you go, Didi. Got this for you from last Wednesday's market. Nine-and-a-half annas, it cost me. No one's going to find you a better shawl in all of Nawbabgonj market—I can guarantee you that! Winter's suddenly looking very cosy, eh, Didi? Haha! Go on, try it . . . do you like the print?'

Indir was beside herself with joy. She had been begging as a matter of habit, but though used to scraps of charity from neighbours, she hadn't expected something actually new, something that would belong to her alone. She unwrapped the gift with trembling fingers, and quickly wrapped it around herself. A toasty warmth engulfed her.

'So warm . . .' she breathed, awed. Tears of gratitude ran down her cheeks. 'Bless you, my brother, bless you. May your sons Kanai and Bolai live a hundred years! No one cares about poor older folk any more. We're just cast aside to suffer. Been asking Awnnoda these past three years for a sari, but does he ever give in? Oh no, not he! Bless you, Ram. May you live many, many more years!'

Later, when she tried to show off the shawl—the first new thing she had possessed in decades—to Shorbojoya, Shorbojoya's strained patience snapped.

'Look, sister-in-law, if you want to live a beggar's life, do it somewhere else. The Roy family still has some dignity left. If you want to live here, then begging at our neighbours' doors has to stop! Do I make myself clear? There's no place for a beggar in this house!'

Indir said nothing. She had long become used to people's rage and shaming, and Shorbojoya in particular lost her temper ten times a day. When Shorbojoya shouted at her, she thought in passing of the old rhyme:

Kicks and sticks matter not at all
If rice and roof keep up my gall

So Indir ignored Shorbojoya's outburst, and continued to show off her new red shawl. Durga, in particular, was in awe of it. She ran her small finger over the thick red fabric, feeling the weave. 'Cost many paisas . . . no, Piti? So pwetty. So wed!'

The next day onwards, Indir took to sun-bathing next to the lane that led to the women's bathing steps, her new shawl draped around her. As the women of the village walked by on their way to and from the pond, she would casually call out to them, to the best estimation of her failing eyesight.

'Who goes? Raji's mother? Bit late today, aren't you?'

Then, lest the conversation turn towards Raji's mother's morning chores, she'd quickly add, 'Do you see this shawl? Ram from the Ganguly neighbourhood bought it. Especially for me, you know. Brand new! Cost him nine-and-a-half annas at the big market . . .'

The women mostly moved on with token praise. A few of the more mischievous younger girls said, 'Oooh, a *red* shawl? Getting married again, are we? You'd make a lovely winter bride in that shawl, Grandma!'

6

TOWARDS THE TAIL end of that winter, Dashi Thakurani from the next neighbourhood over stopped by mid-morning with a big smile.

'Where's our daughter-in-law? Ah, there you are! Do you have my two paise on you?'

Shorbojoya had been absorbed in housework. Now she stared.

'The custard apple that Aunt Indir bought from me yesterday?' Dashi Thakrun prompted. 'The one she said you'd pay for today? Only I'm in a bit of a hurry, so . . .'

Shorbojoya seemed to find this a little hard to grasp. 'Someone *bought* a custard apple off you?' she asked doubtfully.

Dashi Thakrun was a keen businesswoman. She'd never in her life let anyone have so much as a tamarind or a hog plum for free, and she knew how to extract money from unwilling debtors. In the face of Shorbojoya's doubt, her amiability disappeared.

'You think I'm lying?' she snapped. 'For two paise? Ask your sister-in-law if you don't believe me! My custard apples are four paise each. But your sister-in-law didn't have the money, so I thought, what's a little loss? Let the poor old woman have her treat. And I gave her one for two pice. And now I am the liar?'

Humiliation and rage choked Shorbojoya's voice. Custard apples were so abundant this year that even goats and calves had begun to turn away from them. Why people would go out of their way to pay for one when they lay rotting by the wayside was beyond Shorbojoya's understanding.

But of course, Indir hadn't paid for her own treat, had she? Oh no. She had bought her custard apple on credit, knowing full well that Dashi Thakrun's sharp tongue would goad the money out of Shorbojoya. Never mind that the family could barely make ends meet. As Shorbojoya always knew, Indir didn't actually care about the family that took her in. She only cared about what she could get out of them.

It was at this critical juncture that Indir, who had been out, shuffled into sight. Shorbojoya could barely keep from launching herself at her.

'You're buying *custard apples* now?' she shouted. 'Do you think our money grows on trees? Three-fourths of your life you've spent eating into this family's income! Can't you be a decent person for once and think about us before you think about yourself?'

Indir was used to sharp comments all day, but this frontal attack in front of the thin-lipped Dashi Thakrun thoroughly alarmed her.

'I forgot . . . getting old . . . last time, I promise . . .' she stammered, desperately casting about for the best words to mollify Shorbojoya. 'Just two paise though . . . please, Bou? When I saw the ripe custard apples, I thought, who knows if I'll live to see tomorrow? Let me eat what I want today . . . Go on, Bou, don't be that way . . .'

This did not have the desired effect. Shorbojoya had heard Indir's spiel about having only a few years left to live far too often to be affected by it. '"Just two paise"?' she snarled. 'If two paise is so cheap, then why don't you pay it yourself? Why drag the debt to our doorway? I'm not giving you a single paisa. Go sell that ancient stuff you cling to! Your debts are no longer mine!'

With that, she swung up the metal water pot to her hip and stormed out of the back door.

Dashi Thakrun waited for a few minutes in the ensuing silence. But no money was forthcoming.

'Cut my own nose off if I've seen so much drama before!' she finally said, irritated. 'I tell you, Aunt Indir, you shouldn't have bought that fruit off me if you didn't have the money. Don't go buying things on credit when you know you can't pay. Anyway, your family troubles are yours, but those two paise are still mine. I'll come again in the evening. Make sure you have them by then. I'm a poor woman selling my wares, don't cheat me of my money.'

When the altercation happened, Khuki had hidden herself indoors. Now, as Dashi Thakrun walked away from their veranda, she wobbled out of hiding on her toddler legs and stumbled after her. 'Piti only wanted a custudd apple,' she tried to explain to the woman, lest Dashi Thakrun thought poorly of her aunt. 'Is not wong to like custard apples . . . wight Dashi Auntie? Ma shount haff scolded her. Piti gave me half of you custudd apple—so good! Where you get fruits, Dashi Auntie? Is there twees in your house?'

When Dashi continued to stride away without paying her any heed, Khuki shouted her chief message from the edge of their courtyard.

'I have a paisa hidden in my dolly's box, Dashi Auntie! Can't give now, Ma locked the woom. But I give you in the evening! Only don't tell Ma, Dashi Auntie, it secwet . . .'

That afternoon, Indir left home. All her things fitted into a small bundle that she carried in her left hand. Her drinking pot of sheet metal she took in her right, and her tattered carpet was rolled up under her arm. The frayed edges of the carpet trailed the ground around her feet as she shuffled across the Roys' courtyard. Khuki ran after her, alarmed and in tears. 'Don't go, Piti! Where you going? Don't leave me-e-e! Piti, I cwy if you go . . . don't go!' When pleading didn't work, she began tugging at the frayed edge of the old carpet. But this afternoon, Indir was implacable.

Shorbojoya had returned from the bathing steps a while back, and was in the process of cooking lunch. She watched the whole engineered drama with bitter vindication. Trust the woman to try and harm the Roys even with her exit!

'You're going to leave just before lunch, are you?' she shouted after the old woman. 'Just up and leave without a meal, hoping we'll be cursed for throwing you out on an empty stomach? Wicked I've seen, vindictive I've seen . . . but never someone this evil! No wonder your life is a lonely, rotten desert!'

Indir didn't respond. She made her way out of the courtyard and began plodding down the path towards the village. Khuki followed her auntie for quite a while, begging her to come back. But for once, Indir was deaf to all pleading. After a while, Khuki was forced to give up.

Indir reached Nitai Ghoshal's house in the early evening. It was two neighbourhoods down from the Roys'. Nitai Ghoshal's wife was amazed to hear about the young Roy bride's cruelty, and graciously allowed Indir a place under her roof. After two months, however, the welcome wore thin. Indir left, and sought shelter at Tinkori Ghoshal's house, and fairly quickly thereafter at Purno Chokroborti's place. She had hoped that after a few weeks, someone from the family would come to take her back. She had practically raised Horihor—surely he wouldn't abandon her? But after three months of living off grudging charity, her hopes dimmed. She was pretty sure that Durga would drag her home, if only she knew where her beloved auntie was. So she dragged herself back to the old neighbourhood, in hopes of running into her precious niece. But despite trekking there and back a couple of times, she didn't cross paths with Durga.

Finally, the villagers decided they needed to find a permanent place for the old woman, if only to keep her from turning up at their houses. Everyone promised to give her a little something each month to cover expenses. Chintey, the milkwoman from the east-side neighbourhood, had an old thatched hut just off the end of the village, inside a bamboo grove. This was where Indir was sent. The hut was small, and was fenced in with spotty old cane. Still, it was her own place . . . for as long as the villagers kept up with the rent, that is. Shorbojoya, for one, had gone around informing the village women that the Roys didn't care what happened to her. 'That woman couldn't even put my little babies before herself!' she told her neighbours acidly. 'She can go die in a cesspit for all I care. I don't want to see her face around my house ever again!'

Gradually, the help from the neighbours began to dwindle. The old woman left the hut less often, because there was nothing to be had from begging. She began blaming herself for her temper on that fateful day several months ago. What had possessed her to leave her own home? Khuki had come crying after her for such a long way. Even Bou had wanted her to stay and have lunch. What a stupid, stupid woman she had been, to leave all that in a fit of pique! Tears of despair and self-pity ran down Indir's broken cheeks. Oh, to endure such cruelty in her final days! If only her poor daughter had been alive . . .

April drew to a close. The day had been very hot, but a weak breeze had begun to blow around early evening. Indir had been going from door to door, hoping for kindness on the holy day of Choitro Shonkranti. But nearly everyone was away from home, celebrating the last day of the Bengali calendar at the annual Chorok fair. Eventually, she dragged herself back to the hut, and collapsed on her old carpet. A small earthen cup of water lay by her head. The sheet metal pot was long gone, pawned for four annas so she could buy rice. At a distance, the village was still alive with festivities. Drumbeats from the Vaishnav neighbourhood reached even her remote bamboo grove, but Indir barely noticed it. Worry about the future consumed all her thoughts. It was a fear that ate away at her all the time now.

'Pishima!'

Indir was jolted out of her fevered sleep. There was her Khuki, climbing on to the raised courtyard of her hut! She was wearing a fresh sari, one end of it knotted to hold several little treasures. Oh, how she had grown in these months! Behind her came Behari Chokroborti's youngest girl, Raji. Indir barely had time to take in the surprise before Khuki had flung herself into her arms. Indir immediately wrapped her weak arms around the girl, and clutched her tightly to her thin chest.

'It's a secret, Pishi, don't tell anyone! We went to Chorok . . . and on our way back we came secretly to see you! Look what I got from the fair!' She began to unknot the little bundles at the end of her sari. 'Sweets! These are all for you—two paise's worth of murki, and these two kodmas. And look, I bought this wooden doll for Khoka!'

Joy and relief nearly choked Indir. She sat up a little more and began inspecting her niece's little treasure trove. 'Let me see, let me see . . . god bless you, my precious darling. Such generosity for your poor old auntie! May you become a queen one day, a queen! Where's the doll? Oh, that's a nice doll. How much did they ask for it?'

After pouring out several months' worth of pent-up chatter, Khuki finally asked about Indir's high temperature.

Indir tried to dismiss it. Fever had become such an everyday thing for her lately that she had forgotten what it felt like to live without it. 'It's just a little heat from the day,' she said. 'I'd been going around all day in the sun, so . . .'

Khuki was young, but she understood all too well why her aunt had needed to walk about the village under the April sun all day. She ran her small hand down Indir's emaciated frame, showering it with all the affection and tenderness of her loving young heart. 'Come home, Pishi. Evenings are so empty now. No stories, no nothing . . . come home tomorrow, all right? First thing in the morning.'

Hope burst anew in Indir's heart. 'Did your mother ask you to say that?' she asked eagerly.

'Oh no, not *her*!' Raji piped up. 'Khurima doesn't want Dugga coming here. We get such a telling-off if we even ask about you! But still, you should come back, Pishima. Khurima might shout a bit at first, but if you say the right things she'll be all right.'

'Tomorrow, Pishi, don't forget!' said Durga, wrapping her brother's doll up again.

'We have to go now. Don't tell anyone we were here, all right? But tomorrow! Leave here as soon as you can!'

So the next morning, Indir bundled up her few remaining possessions and began the long walk towards the Roys' household. On the way, she met the Vaishnavite Gopi Boshtom's wife, who gave her a big smile. 'Our sister-in-law's fury has finally died down, has it? Took her long enough!'

Indir's face practically dissolved in a grin. 'Oh yes. Durga came to visit last evening. So many tears! "Ma asked you to come home, Pishi. We miss you, Pishi." So then I thought, why delay the inevitable? If I leave now, I'll probably get there by mid-morning . . .'

It was, in fact, well after noon when she reached her old home. The house was empty. The long walk, after days of fever and severely rationed meals, had exhausted Indir. So she lowered herself on the raised platform outside her old hut and waited for her family to return. She was just about to doze off when Shorbojoya returned from the bathing steps by way of the back door, wet clothes still in hand. Eager to ingratiate herself, Indir smiled warmly at her. 'There you are, Bou. Have you been well? It's so hard to stay away from family at this age. So I thought, let me go back home before death comes calling . . .' Then she looked hopefully at her younger sister-in-law.

Shorbojoya had been struck dumb at the sight of the old witch's toothless smile. But at the threat of moving back in, her temper flared. 'What do you mean, "home"?' she bit out.

Indir swallowed. The hostility in the younger woman's tone wiped the hopeful smile off her face.

Shorbojoya didn't even give her time to stutter a reply. 'I told you when you left that you were never to return.

This is not your "home", it's ours! How dare you show your face here again?'

Indir was not prepared for such brutal cruelty. She felt like she'd been turned to stone, unable to shuffle out of the way of Shorbojoya's wrath. She hadn't expected a warm welcome, but never had she imagined that she would be so unceremoniously turned away from her own household's door. All her usual tools of survival—the wheedling, the flattery, the ingratiating smiles—deserted her, and she let out a helpless, childlike sob.

'O Bou! Don't throw me out, Bou. I only have a little while to live. Let me live it in my own house. This is my family land, this is my home . . .'

'Oooh, "family land!",' mocked Shorbojoya. 'Like I haven't seen all the sleepless nights you've spent working at its upkeep, eh? Look, sister-in-law. I'm asking you nicely. You've already taken all you could from us. There's nothing here left to give. Leave us now and never come back. Or I swear I'll scream and make a scene!'

After a few seconds of impasse, Indir trudged back to her bundles in a daze. She had been so stunned by the course of events that it didn't even occur to her to protest her exile. As she picked her bundles up and slowly made her way out of the compound, her eyes fell on the old broom leaning against the wall. It had clearly not been used in months. That was *her* broom. This beloved little piece of land, that lemon tree that she had planted, this much-favoured old broom, her beloved Khuki, the new Khoka, her Uncle Brojo's place next door . . . these were the things that had made up her entire universe. In seventy years of existence, she had neither known another life, nor sought one. This house had been her anchor through decades of poverty, loneliness, and loss. Now she felt like a suddenly unmoored boat. In the face of this incomprehensible loss, her mind simply shut down, and her body shuffled forward in a blind haze.

A few minutes later, the matriarch of one of the other Roy households saw the old woman drift past the large drumstick tree.

'Hey, Grandma! Aren't you heading the wrong way? Home's behind you!' she called out loudly.

Indir appeared not to hear her.

'Granny's lost her hearing good and proper,' mumbled the matriarch, and went back to her chores.

Later that evening, a stranger from one of the non-brahmin neighbourhoods came hurrying up to the secluded little house to find Shorbojoya. 'O Ma Thakrun! Your old woman is dying! She was going back to her hut, but collapsed near the Palits' house. Send someone to have a look. Is Dada Thakur at home? No? Well, send him along as soon as he returns.'

Indir was indeed dying. The blazing sun had been too much for her already fragile health, and she had passed out on the road near the Palit neighbourhood. At first the Palits had carried her into their temple courtyard, and tried to revive her with the usual waving of fans and massaging of hot oil on the back and chest. But when it became clear that revival was unlikely, they had carried her back outside and put her down at the side of the road. Their neighbours had gathered around, speculating about her.

'Why would she leave the house at all?' one faction wanted to know. 'It's a killer, this heat we've been having.'

'She's just fainted, that's all,' posited a more optimistic faction. 'Give her some water and she'll be fine in no time.'

Bishu Palit had no such delusions. 'That's not a faint,' he said. 'She's on her way out. We've sent word to Uncle Hori, but well, it's pretty far from his place . . .'

Slowly, as word spread, Dinu Chokroborti's eldest son, Foni, arrived from the brahmin neighbourhood to see what was really going on. The Palits were relieved. 'Thank goodness you're here, Baba Thakur. Here, give her some of this Gonga water first. This far from the brahmon neighbourhood, we couldn't even find someone of her own caste to give her water on her deathbed . . .'

Foni handed his gooseberry-wood walking stick to Bishu Palit and sat next to Indir's head.

'Pishima?' he called quietly. 'Can you hear me? Are you feeling ill?'

Indir opened her eyes. There was no recognition in them. The spark of life had already left her.

Foni spooned a little water into her mouth. Indir held the water in her mouth, but her throat didn't move.

'Give her some more,' Bishu Palit advised from the side. Foni complied.

A little later, when Foni gently closed Indir's sunken eyes, a flood of unshed tears rolled down her thin, broken cheeks.

And thus, with Indir Thakrun's death, the old days of the Abode of Contentment truly, finally, came to an end.

7

IT HAD BEEN four or five years since Indir Thakrun had passed away. This was the last month of winter, but temperatures were still quite low. A low fog hung over roads and fields. On the evening of Saraswati Puja, a few men from Contentment had undertaken the ceremonial search for the elusive blue jay. The search took them off the main roads, and deep into the narrow mud tracks that ran through the surrounding woodlands.

One of the group suddenly said, 'Oh yes, Hori . . . I've been meaning to ask. Have you people really given your banana orchard over as surety? Against a loan from that milkman Bhushno?'

The man he addressed was impossible to reconcile with the Horihor from ten years ago. Gone was the lithe young man with the wind in his hair. This Horihor was a middle-aged family man, immersed completely in balancing income and expenses, and lustily battling shopkeepers over the going rate of gourds. His chief source of income these days was in being a travelling collector, going from village to village to cajole taxes out of people for the local landlord. He had also spent some years tracking down all the families that had once accepted his father as the family priest. He had convinced most of them to accept him as their new guru, and received tokens of respect from these families every now and then. Still, his income remained slender. The life of the maverick young wayfarer—one who had watched sunsets from the top of the wall at Chunar fort, spent nights in the bayleaf woods of Kedar, eaten sour oranges straight from the trees at the orchard next to the Shah Quasim Suleimani's dargah, cooked his own meals beside the river at Dasaswamedh Ghat, and sat next to the molten silver of the ice-cold Alakananda river—now seemed like figments of a distant dream.

This deeply domesticated Horihor was about to turn his head and voice assent, when he was distracted by the absence of someone who should have been at his heels.

'Where'd the boy go?' he asked anxiously. 'Did anyone see . . .? Khoka? KHOKA-A-A!'

Seconds later, a slender, beautiful boy of about six came running out of the fog towards his father.

'Don't keep falling behind,' Horihor admonished. 'Here, come this way . . . go on, walk ahead of us. And stay on the track!'

The child didn't seem at all perturbed by the telling-off. He was entranced by the foggy mysteriousness of the winter woods. 'What was that thing in the last bush, Baba?' he asked. 'The one with the large floppy ears?'

Horihor didn't respond. He was busy making fishing plans with Nobin Palit.

'O Baba,' the child asked again, determined to know. 'What was that thing that ran out of the bush? The thing with the large ears?'

'I don't know, son, do I?' said Horihor, annoyed. 'This is the trouble with bringing you along. It's always "What is this?" and "What is that?" from the moment we step outside. Come now, don't dawdle.'

Undeterred by the admonishment, the child happily kept pace with the adults.

'Tell you what, Horihor,' continued Nobin Palit. 'If you're serious, let's go to Bainsha's Lake one day. Eastside's Nepal Parui is renting out boats. A forty to sixty kilo haul, easily. No fish below at least a kilo, so they say. And sometimes, you know, late at night? "Shnaa shnaaa!" from the middle of the lake. Just like a calf wailing for its mother . . . know what I mean?'

Several of the men gathered close. Fishing had just taken a juicy turn.

'Bainsha is an ancient lake, you see,' continued Nobin Palit. 'Deep waters. Black like the middle of the night. Choking under a wilderness of lotuses. Now, that noise could have been an enormous catfish. Or, who knows, it could have been a yakshi. With these ancient lakes, you never know. Anyway, the people on the boat were stuck there all night, shivering in the cold, barely holding on till first light . . .'

At this fascinating juncture, Horihor's little boy suddenly yelled, 'There, Baba, there! There it goes again! Floppy ears!' Then he promptly took off after the creature.

'Come back! Come back!' screamed a panicked Horihor. 'There are thorns! You'll get lost!'

When his son showed no sign of stopping, he plunged into the undergrowth after the child and brought him forcibly back to the path. However, none of his disapproval made a dent in the boy's excitement.

'What was that, Baba? Did you see? Such big floppy ears!'

'Stay on the path!' admonished his out-of-breath father. 'Uff. This is why one shouldn't bring children along! Tell you a hundred times to stay on the path and what do you do? Run straight off it as soon as some pig moves in a bush!'

'Not a pig, Baba! It was ti-i-i-iny. Look, it was exactly this high . . .' The child proceeded to squat on the path to show how high the elusive creature was.

'No one wants to know how high,' said his irritated father. 'Keep to the middle of the path. No moving to the sides!'

'It was a rabbit, Khoka,' said one of the other men kindly. 'They like living in the hay this time of the year.'

Khoka was stunned. A rabbit! A real, ear-twitching rabbit! He had only ever seen rabbits in the pages of his schoolbook. It had never occurred to him that they could also be seen in real life. The idea that mythical schoolbook creatures could be found in perfectly normal bushes, and that too in the familiar neighbourhood woods, took his breath away.

The group had progressed from the narrow wooden path to an open field. The remains of an old indigo boiling room lay in one corner of the field, right on the banks of the river. Back in the days of the indigo plantations, this field used to be the headquarters of the Bengal Indigo Concern. John Lermore had his own bungalow here, and from this very field had cracked his whip over the fourteen other indigo bungalows under his care. His dominance was so absolute that he could make tigers and cows drink together from the same pond—so people said. Yet now, only a few decades later, his name had been all but forgotten. Only the most ancient people could even remember his time in the village, and his once-famous bungalow was now a pile of ruins.

Even in the faint light of the evening, the rest of the field gleamed. Yellow laburnums were scattered all over the field, and every tree was in full blossom. Circles of wild woodrose sprouted everywhere, creating little havens of cool darkness within them. Jewel-blue bluebells bloomed on vines wrapped around trees, peeking out from under the thick foliage to glitter in the sun. Spiky amaranth, blue-pea, and numerous other wildflowers grew in thick bushes all over the field, carpeting the field in bright colours. The river curved along one end of the field, golden in the light of the setting sun. Everything glittered and glowed. There was no sign of poverty or of middle-class miserliness anywhere. Nature had upturned her bowl of plenty upon the land like an empress bestowing largess . . . and the little boy could not tear his eyes away. His world, so far, had been rather a narrow one, limited to his home, his friend Nyara's house, their neighbour Ranu Didi's place, and those parts of the neighbourhood that were close to their remote little house. This evening—with its woods, rabbits, indigo ruins, and the misty, boundless field of bright colours—was a revelation to him. In his heart, he was certain that he had stumbled upon the gateway to a magical land. For surely, nothing as mundane as just another village could exist beyond that glittering golden river. That snaking woodland road *had* to be the path to a wonderful unknown . . . perhaps to the amazing land of Shyamlonka, or to the kingdom of exiled princes and flying horses! Perhaps the all-knowing birds, Byangoma and Byangomi, were hidden amongst the trees at this very minute, whispering secrets to each other! Oh, if only he could hear them, like the prince who had feigned sleep beneath their tree! Then all the wonderful adventures of his mother's fairy tales could be his!

Meanwhile, Nobin Palit was holding forth on the profits he had reaped by planting sweet potatoes on a northern plot of the indigo field. Someone else remarked that, speaking of profits, he had heard a rumour that Moti Daan of Nawbabgonj had been seen pricing the bricks of the bungalow's ruins. This was unexpected news, and caught everyone's attention. The group spent several invigorating minutes speculating exactly how rich Moti Daan had become, and how he had managed to get there. Gradually, the conversation flowed to other important matters, such as the actual date of Dinu Ganguly's daughter's upcoming wedding, and the fact that the Kundus of Asharu market had lost their shop to fire.

'Where's the blue-throated bird, Baba?' asked Horihor's son, impatient for a view of the promised creature.

'Any minute now,' said his distracted father. 'Keep an eye on the acacia. And don't move from my side, now . . .'

The child focused all his eagerness on the acacia tree. After a few seconds of no birds, though, his attention began to wander. There was a clump of plum trees close by. Compared to the ones in the village, these were surprisingly short. The height of the trees was what usually prevented him from having the delicious red plums as soon as they appeared. The hook-ended bamboo stick that his family used to cut down fruit was too heavy for him to use. Nonetheless, he had tried sneaking out with it one day. But someone had spotted him dragging it along, and had promptly informed his mother. And of course, she had immediately come running.

'Barely out of your fever and already after red berries! How many have you had? Open your mouth! Let me see!'

Luckily, the weight of the bamboo stick had prevented him from pulling down even one berry, so he had escaped punishment that day. After sniffing his mouth, his mother had hugged him in relief, and promised to make him a whole pot of red-plum pickles . . . but only if he promised to stay away from the fruit while it was still on the trees. And he had promised.

However, his mother wasn't here now. If he quietly stretched a bit, then maybe, just maybe, he could pull a few off the lower branches. On the other hand, his father *was* here. The chances that his father would let him eat wild plums was practically non-existent.

The child sighed. Life was hard, and decidedly difficult to navigate.

Sensing his son's distraction, Horihor tried to win his attention back. Pointing towards the ruins of the actual indigo bungalow, a little distance away from the river, he said, 'See that heap, Khoka? That was once the neel kuthi. See how big it was? Now don't fidget!'

The bungalow, while it stood, had indeed been large. Now, however, its remains sprawled across the land, like a grotesque monster lying in wait. Further away from the group, hidden from curious human eyes by the surrounding ruins, a single stone remained upright in the darkness. It marked the grave of Lermore's toddler son. With some effort, during daylight, the inscription could still be read:

Here lies Edwin Lermore
Only son of John and Mrs Lermore
May 13, 1857—April 27, 1860

One of the wild yellow laburnums grew right by the grave, shading the child's resting place with its branches and leaves. When strong winds blew in from the river's bend at Two-and-a-Half Point, it showered the grave and headstone with golden petals. History may have forgotten the life and death of the little foreign child, but the land has not forgotten one of its own. He has become part of Contentment, and his unsung memory lives on in its trees, its grass, and its wildflowers.

When Horihor finally returned home with his son, Shorbojoya flew out of the house in barely suppressed anxiety.

'What took you so long? I was worried! Out for the first time this late, and not even a thin wrap to protect him! Anyway, how was it? Was he good? Were you good for Baba, my darling?'

'Good!' Horihor snorted. 'Running after everything he saw, that is how he was. Almost grabbed a bunch of cow-itch flowers on the way back. Can you imagine the screaming if I hadn't caught him in time?'

Then he smiled at his son, who was still in a daze about the evening's adventure.

'"I want to see the neel kuthi field! I want to see the neel kuthi field!" Well, now you've seen the neel kuthi field. Was it everything you had hoped it would be? Hmm?'

8

IT WAS AROUND nine in the morning. Horihor's son was sitting in the sunny courtyard with all his toys piled around him. These were: a discoloured wooden horse bought for four paise, a dented tin whistle, a toy pistol worth two paise, a few cowrie shells, a handful of inedible dried red berries, and his collection of lucky stone chips. The berries had been a gift from his sister, who had brought them home because they were so pretty. The stone chips were lucky because they always fell in the right quarter while playing hopscotch, and were thus cherished. The cowrie shells, however, had been quietly removed from his mother's basket of Lokkhi Puja things, and thus Khoka was very careful about keeping them hidden from view.

This morning, the whistle had already had its turn. The horse, too, was lying on one side, like abandoned cattle in a rescue corral. He had just begun playing with the pistol when his sister, Durga, called from beneath the jackfruit tree.

'Opu! O Opuuuu!'

At the sound of a human voice, Opu automatically shoved the cowries inside his tin toy box. Then, in a perfectly normal voice, he called back, 'What is it, Didi?'

'Shhh! Come here. Quickly!'

Opu climbed down the veranda and ran to his sister. Durga was now ten or eleven years old. She was not as fair-skinned as her brother, but their features were very similar—especially their large, expressive eyes. This morning, she was dressed in an unwashed sari and a few cheap glass bangles. A halo of thick, unoiled, curly hair surrounded her thin face. When he came close, Opu saw that she was holding a coconut-shell bowl tightly to her chest, and glancing warily around.

'Is Ma back from the bathing steps yet?' she asked, as soon as Opu reached her.

'No, Didi.'

'Good. I need some oil and salt.' She tilted the bowl towards him to show him a heap of sliced green mangoes. 'I'm going to pickle these.'

'Mangoes! Where'd you get them?'

'Shh! From below the Shindurkota mango tree in Potli's garden. So, can you get the salt and oil?'

Opu hesitated. 'Um, I haven't bathed yet, Didi. My clothes are stale. Ma will beat me if I touch the oil pot in stale clothes.'

'Oh, come on! She'll never know. She's gone to do the laundry at the pond. That'll take her ages!'

Opu looked uncertain. On the one hand, there was his mother's wrath. But on the other . . .

'Fine,' he said. 'But give me the shell. I'll pour the oil in that.'

Durga immediately handed him the shell bowl. 'Now don't spill the oil on the floor, or Ma will know!' she whispered urgently. 'You are such a clumsy boy!'

After a few minutes, the mangoes were ready. Durga doled out her brother's share in a second coconut shell.

'Are all those for you?' her brother asked, eyeing her shell.

'"Allll those?" I've only taken a few more! All right, fine. Have two more. But that's it!'

Then she admired her handiwork.

'Looks good, doesn't it? Such a lovely colour. A chilli would make this perfect. Can you get a chilli? I'll give you one more slice if you do.'

Opu bit his lip. 'Ma keeps the chillies on the top shelf. It's too high for me.'

'All right, fine.' Durga shrugged it off. 'I'll get some more mangoes in the evening. We can use the chilli then. The tree beside that little pond has more fruit this year than it can hold—it all comes tumbling down in the afternoon heat!'

For the next few minutes, the two siblings stood in peace under the jackfruit tree, relishing their summer treat. A quiet woodland peace reigned. The Roys' family home was practically in the middle of the woods, away from the bustle of the neighbourhood. Earlier, Horihor used to at least have his cousin Neelmoni as a neighbour, but after Neelmoni's death the previous year, his wife had taken their children and moved back to her father's household. Gradually, the land and house had been taken over by the woods, and this Roy household had become even more isolated from the rest of the village. Their nearest neighbour now was Bhubon Mukhujje, and his place was a good five-minute walk away.

The house hadn't been repaired in years, either. Chunks of the front veranda had fallen off. Wild cow-itch and kalmegh had taken root in the cracks and crevices of the walls, and all the windows had to be held together with coconut-coir ropes, for the latches and hinges had long been broken.

There was a resounding 'jhonat!' of the back door shackle. Moments later, Shorbojoya's voice rang out. 'Dugga! Dugga! Where are you?'

Alarmed, the siblings looked at each other.

'Go go! See what she wants!' Durga whispered urgently to her brother. 'Wait, swallow that before you go! There's salt at the corner of your mouth, rub it off!'

Her own shell was still half full. She quickly pulled her brother behind the jackfruit tree, and began gobbling down the slices as fast as she could.

'Dugga-a-a! Are you even home?'

Opu was swallowing his own share as well, for there wasn't time to stop and chew. In between gulps, he smiled guiltily at his sister, well aware that what they were doing was a pretty big offence in their mother's eyes.

Once they were done, Durga pulled back her forearm and threw the shell over the bubble-bush border along their own land, and as far into Neelmoni Roy's wilderness as she could. The chance of anyone finding an incriminating shell amongst those thickets was close to zero.

'Rub that salt off, you monkey!' she whispered harshly to her brother. 'It's still there!'

After a few minutes, she entered the kitchen, looking perfectly innocent.

'You called, Ma?'

'Yes, I did!' Shorbojoya snapped. 'Do I have to run this household all by myself? Can't you at least do a little chopping and cleaning? I spent all morning with the laundry, and now I have to do everything else?' Then she looked behind Durga. 'Where's the other monkey?'

Opu was waiting just outside the door. At this cue, he stepped in. 'Ma, I'm hungry.'

'Wait, my darling, wait,' snapped Shorbojoya. 'Let your mother rest her bones a minute before she gets back to serving you! It's always "Ma, I'm hungry" or "Ma, do this for me" . . . Dugga, see why the calf is lowing, will you?'

But she reached for a cucumber even as she spoke, and sat down to peel it on the curved blade.

'Ma, don't we have any roasted rice left?' asked Durga, making her face as pitiable as she dared.

'No no—no chaalbhaja!' Opu protested. 'It's really going to hurt the teeth after all those sour mangoes . . . er . . . um.'

His sister's glare made him stutter and stop midway through the protest.

Shorbojoya looked up from her blade. 'Mangoes?' She turned to glare at Durga. 'You'd gone out again, hadn't you?'

Durga paled. 'Who, me? No! I was . . . I was standing right there, under the jackfruit tree. Ask *him*, he's the one that said it!'

Things would have taken rather a dire turn, but just then the milkmaid Shorno announced her presence outside.

'*Now* she comes!' muttered Shorbojoya. 'And here the calf has been bawling since dawn. Dugga, go out and hold the calf.'

Then she raised her voice to the milkmaid. 'O Shonno! Is this what you call the milking hour? The poor calf has been crying all morning to be fed. Try and come a little early from now on.'

As soon as they were out of their mother's sight, Durga turned and brought down her fist on her brother's back.

'"Oooh, my teeth hu-u-u-rt! Oooh, I ate sour mango-o-o-es!"—you idiot!' she growled. 'See if I ever give you anything again! The mangoes near the melon trees at Potli's garden are sweet like jaggery . . . think I'm going to share those with you? Not a chance! Stupid boy!'

Later that afternoon, Horihor came home from work. These days, he was employed as an accountant for Awnnoda Roy's estate.

'Where's Opu . . . isn't he around?' he asked his wife.

'Opu's sleeping,' said his wife tartly. '*He's* not the one that's never around.'

'Ah. So Dugga . . .?'

'Left right after lunch. Food is the only reason I see her at all. Always at someone's orchard or garden, that one. And in this summer blaze! I keep telling her that she's a big girl now, but does she listen? If the fever comes back, it will be her own fault, let me tell you!'

A few minutes later, as he sat down to eat, Horihor said, 'Listen, something happened today. I'd gone to Doshghora for their tax reminder. There was this man there—quite the local leader, you understand? Five or six granaries on his own property alone. So he comes up to me and touches my feet. Says, "Remember me, Dada Thakur?" Now, truth be told, I didn't. And I told him so. Then he tells me that Baba used to be his family's guru. Now that he's found me—Baba's successor, you know—he and his family want to be formally initiated. By me, that is, as the new guru. Anyway, I told them I needed a day or two to think.'

Shorbojoya had been standing with a bowl of daal, listening. Now she set it down on the floor next to Horihor's plate and sat down eagerly in front of him.

'Why think? Why didn't you agree right away? If they are well-off . . .'

Horihor lowered his voice. 'Well, that's the problem. They're not just a regular lower caste, see? They're Shodgope. And you know you like to talk. Can you imagine what people would say if they found out I had accepted Shodgopes as disciples?'

'Who am I going to discuss your disciples with? I won't say a word. Take them on, my dear! The eight rupees from the Roys barely see us through . . . and they only pay every second or third month! And then there are the loans. The third-eldest sister-in-law from the Mukhujjes cornered me today on the way to the pond. Said she regrets loaning us money without collateral, and wants the full amount back immediately. And Radha, Boshtom's wife, has been tearing into me every time we meet. My Opu doesn't even have a whole cloth to call his own. I've repaired so many holes in the one he wears that I've lost count. Thank goodness he doesn't care. But it breaks my heart to see my poor boy dance about happily in tattered rags. Honestly, I can't bear this any more. Sometimes it all gets so much that I think I'll just walk out. Leave it all behind and just go wherever my two eyes lead me!'

'They did make another offer,' Horihor said, slowly. 'These people, they want the prestige of settling a brahmon family in the village. If I agree to live in their village—you know, be at hand for pujos, ceremonies and such like—then they'll build us a house. Maybe even give us some paddy fields.' His voice took on a bitter note. 'Honestly, Lokkhi has abandoned us gentlemen for these lower castes. Look at how well-off these farmers are! It's us who are all "give us this day our daily rice", and tearing out our hair in worry . . .'

At this piece of news, Shorbojoya almost leaned over her husband's plate in excitement.

'Say yes! I beg you, say yes! What do we have amongst our own people? Just an old house that's falling apart, in the middle of the woods. There we'd be honoured residents under the protection of a rich man. Things would be so much better, for all of us!'

Horihor smiled complacently at his wife's eagerness. 'It doesn't do to agree to a first offer, my dear. These are the lower castes, after all. If I seem eager, they would think, "Ah, I see! So Thakur's rice pot was about to run dry!" Then they'd forever think of themselves as my saviours. I'd never win their respect back. Waiting's better. It'll also give me time to discuss the matter with Mojumdar Moshai. Let's see what he says. After all, it's not like we can leave this neighbourhood at will. The moment word gets out, all these buggers will come and say, "First pay us back our loans, or we won't let you move." So let's wait and see what Mojumdar Moshai says.'

While this conversation was happening in the kitchen, Durga was outside, trying to sneak in. At first, she had thought that she had picked a good time to sneak in, for it was the time for her mother's nap. She could slip in through the kitchen door and steal an hour's sleep indoors, without her mother being any wiser. But then she discovered that not only was her domestic adversarial unit not asleep, she was still in the kitchen, and backed up by the presence of the paternal figure. Changing her plans, she swiftly retreated from the shaded kitchen doorway, and tiptoed over to the main door of the house. Shorbojoya, however, had locked that door from within. Giving up on hopes of resting indoors, Durga then tested the raised veranda that ran around the house. Unfortunately, the sun had had all morning to bake it into a slab of intolerable heat. She could barely stand on it, much less rest.

Foiled at every step, Durga retreated to the shade beneath the jackfruit tree while she weighed her options. As she thought, she untied a handful of dried red fever-nut berries from the edge of her sari, and began playing toss-up with them. That she could simply walk in through the kitchen never occurred to her. To let her parents—her mother, especially—catch her coming home at this hour, with wild berries tied to her sari . . . no, no, that was simply not an option.

So she stood under the jackfruit tree for a while, chewing her lips and absently playing toss-up. Then suddenly, her face brightened. A brilliant new idea had just occurred to her. She retied the fever-nut berries to her sari and flew out of the compound, a big grin on her face and her unruly curls flying behind her.

9

THERE WAS A large peepul tree a short way away from the Roys' house. One could only see the top of it if one stood on the raised veranda outside and craned one's neck. Opu loved staring at the tree-top. The enormous height of the tree, and the mysteries hidden inside the dense canopy made him think of magical, faraway lands. Not that he knew very much about such places; his mother's stories of exiled princes gave only the briefest sketch of the actual places they took place in, focusing chiefly on the princes' adventures. But to Opu, this very lack of knowledge enhanced their appeal. He could spend hours just thinking about these mysterious lands, making the details up as he went along.

The idea of distance, in general, enchanted him. Even real places, if they were far enough, seemed to him like hidden gateways to storybook lands. The high blue arch of the skies above, the disappearing speck of a flyaway kite, the misty indigo field he had seen as a child . . . all of it made him think of the nebulous adventures that were happening at that very moment, in lands that lay just beyond the average human's reach. With a little effort, he could imagine himself as part of those adventures, far away from this mundane village, with no known way of returning home.

And the funny thing was, the fantasies of being away from home actually made him acutely homesick. Even though he knew he hadn't really gone anywhere—that, in fact, he was still standing in his own courtyard—he desperately wanted to find a path that would connect the lands in his imagination to his village. The thrill of adventure was a fantastic feeling, but it also made him want to cling to his mother. However, since adventures couldn't be stopped midway, he chose a totem instead to mark time (today, it was a white-chested river kite flying higher and higher into the sky). As long as the totem was visible, he would grit his teeth and allow his imagination to soar, proud that he had enough grit not to abandon an adventure midway. Then, the moment it was out of his sight, he would rush indoors, find his mother, and hug her fiercely.

Usually, these times would coincide with his mother's busiest housework hours, so she would be in the kitchen, knee-deep in chores.

'What's wrong this time?' she would ask with perfunctory concern, for she was used to his random, unrelenting hugs. 'Let me go, darling, I have food hands. You'll have to bathe again if you touch them. Here, see these prawns? I'm frying them for your lunch. You love prawns, don't you? Go on now, don't be naughty. Let me get on with my work.'

Sometimes, after lunch, his mother would lie down on the floor next to the window and read aloud from their tattered copy of the Kashidashi Mahabharat. The afternoon sun would blaze outside, and the white kites would hide inside the coconut tree and screech plaintively. Opu would sit close to his mother, pretending to practise his handwriting. But his real focus would always be on the unfolding narrative. After his favourite bits had been read out, he would say, 'Ma, how about that story? That one about the cow-dung picker?'

'The cow-dung picker? Which one was the cow-dung pick . . . oh, do you mean the Hori Hoar story? That's in the *Onnodomongol*, Baba. Not in this book.'

Then she would put a fresh betel-leaf wrap in her mouth, and begin reciting in tune:

The king said, 'Listen, oh monk's son,
I'll reveal tales of miracles done
Somdutta, king; of the Land by the Sea
Jealous of gods, and of brahmons, was he . . .'

Opu would quickly hold his palm under his mother's face and say, 'Ma, a little paan?'

Shorbojoya would take out a bit of chewed betel from her mouth and put it on his palm. 'This is too bitter,' she would say, in passing. 'It must be the cutch. I keep telling your father not to bring this particular type from the market, but he never remembers.'

Then the reading would continue. Opu would stare at the sun-drenched leaves of the lebbeck and wild jasmine outside the window, and slowly lose himself in the stories. Of all the books at home, the Mahabharat was his favourite. And of all the people in the Mahabharat, he had a special soft corner for that once-abandoned child, Korno. That part where Korno's chariot wheels sink deeper into the mud and Korno tries desperately to pull them out, begging Orjun to be fair and not attack while he's busy . . . that part filled him with hopelessness and dread every time. As his mother's reading approached that particular bit, his eyes would brim with tears in anticipation of the tragedy. And when she reached the part where Orjun refuses and kills Korno anyway, those tears would roll down his baby-soft cheeks in genuine sorrow. Not even hugging his mother could stem them then. And yet that was the story he wanted his mother to return to over and over again.

There is a special sort of satisfaction in crying at the misfortunes of storybook people. Even in his young, little-boy heart, Opu recognized that satisfaction. His mother's afternoon readings were dear to him, precisely because they allowed him to taste the joys and sorrows of life while still nestled in the safety of his own home. He was too young to properly understand most of the travails chronicled in his mother's books, but his heart swelled in sympathy for each misfortunate character anyway. And despite the tears their tales inevitably brought on, that sorrow was a feeling he savoured and cherished.

Once his mother left to resume her housework, he would walk slowly outdoors and stare at the top of the peepul tree again. At that time of day, the tree-top would either still be shimmering in the late afternoon blaze, or have the bright red light of early sunset slowly spreading through its leaves. Somewhere beyond that shimmering light lay the land of the Mahabharat. Of that, Opu was certain. Even now, Korno was probably in his final battlefield, unarmed and unarmoured, pleading with Orjun to play fair—even as he knew he was looking certain death in the eye. Valiant though he was, supreme warrior though he was, Korno chiefly elicited Opu's sympathy. And that is why, in Opu's eyes, he was the true victor of that final battle. Orjun was the hero, true; he killed his enemy, won the battle, was given honours and kingdoms, and was rightly covered in glory. Opu admired him . . . but he did not *feel* for him. His personal joys and sorrows were seldom revealed in the book. Korno, on the other hand, felt like a real person—like someone he might know, trapped in the miseries of everyday life. In the book, he suffers betrayal, feels rage, and succumbs to despair. Hardly any of us have ever been a hero, but all of us have known despair, all of us have known unfairness, and all of us have known sorrow. And that is why, despite losing the battle, Korno always won Opu's support and sympathy.

Which is not to say that Opu ignored the heroic in favour of the tragic. If anything, he felt that the Mahabharat didn't have enough fighting in it. To make up for this unfortunate lack, he had accumulated his own personal armoury of branches and bamboo sticks, which he employed to re-enact the battles with extra vigour. When no one else was around, he would quietly slip into a clearing in the middle of the bamboo grove behind their house, or into the overgrown garden of their late neighbour Neelmoni Roy. Then, assured that no one could see him, he would brandish his bamboo sword and his branch-and-coir bows and arrows, playing both sides of the epic battle with equal vigour. He would also keep up a running commentary on the battle from the original book, for while he felt that the book didn't have enough fighting, it was important to him that his re-enactments be exactly like the real thing. And if he occasionally embellished a little . . . well, who was going to know?

'So then Drono fired ten arrows at the same time. When Orjun saw the ten arrows, he fired back with TWO HUNDRED! Oooh, the sound! Arrows flying everywhere! The sun was blocked out—everything went dark! And then, and then . . . Orjun jumped down from his chariot with a sword in his hand! Durjodhon came running, Bheem came running! Everyone was fighting! Swish, swish, clanggg!!! And then, the darkness was lifted, and . . .'

And so it went on.

Things had similarly heated up the other day in his makeshift battlefield. The old arms master, Drono, had just been pushed into a tight corner, and Orjun's famous monkey-flagged chariot was advancing menacingly on him. Opu, as Orjun, was on the verge of releasing a hundred arrows into his old teacher. Then, just as his commentary had reached a fever pitch, peals of laughter abruptly broke out in the wilderness. Startled, Opu threw down his 'bow' and quickly turned around.

His sister was standing beneath a bough of wild jasmine, holding her sides and laughing.

'Oh Opu!' she said affectionately a few seconds later, still grinning broadly. 'What are you muttering about, you mad boy? And what are you doing with those branches?'

Then she ran up to him and kissed him fondly on the cheek. 'Is this a game? Oh, my crazy little brother!'

Opu's cheeks flamed. He desperately wanted to deny his involvement with bamboos and muttering, but his didi had caught him red-handed.

Happily, Durga had far bigger fish to fry than embarrassing her little brother.

'Come with me,' she said, gesturing him to follow. 'I just found something!'

Intrigued, Opu obediently followed her through the shrubs and trees till they came upon another, smaller, clearing.

'Look!' Durga said, pointing at the branches.

Opu was amazed at the sight. 'Didi! So many custard apples! Can we bring them down?'

'I've been thinking about that. We definitely need something to cut them down. Can you get the bamboo hook from home?'

Opu ran off to get the fruit-cutting tool. But even with it, the little girl and boy could only get a handful of the lowest-hanging fruits.

'Let's take these back for now,' Durga said, collecting the fallen fruit. 'We can come back here tomorrow and bring Ma with us. It's on her way to the bathing steps . . . she can get the ones we couldn't reach.'

After the loot had been securely knotted into the end of her sari, Durga grinned at her brother.

'Hey, want a nose ring?'

Without waiting for a response, she broke off a little white blossom from the cluster of wild spinach behind her, and stuck it on Opu's nose with the sticky glue from the broken end. Once dry, she lifted his face by the chin and examined her handiwork from side to side.

'That looks great! It really suits you, Opu.'

Opu disagreed. He didn't hold with wearing flowers, and he certainly didn't like being dolled up. But he didn't dare say any of that to his sister. Durga was his sole source of everything delicious and forbidden, things his parents would be horrified to discover that he had ever tasted. Sour berries, java plums, salted green mangoes—all the things that made life worth living came to him via his didi. If he had to occasionally wear a bud on his nose for that privilege, then he'd suffer that indignity in silence.

Durga walked straight into the kitchen with her early-evening haul. For once, she knew her mother wouldn't be furious about her bringing things home from someone else's gardens. Neelmoni was family, after all. Besides, custard apples were good for you, unlike unripe mangoes.

Shorbojoya was indeed pleased.

'Where did you get these? Such lovely ripe custard apples!'

'They're growing wild in Neelmoni Jyatha's garden, Ma! Opu and I could barely get a handful of the whole lot. You should come with us tomorrow to get more—I'll show you where they are. It's not like anyone else is around to eat them. They'll just fall to the ground and rot.'

Then she pushed Opu in front of her. 'Look who I found on the way, Ma . . . hee hee!'

Shorbojoya rounded her eyes in excessive surprise. 'Oh my! Who is this pretty child? I don't think I've ever met such a pretty child before!'

Opu blushed hard. He yanked off the white bud from his nose and mumbled, 'I didn't want to . . . Didi put this on me . . .'

Then he looked shyly at his mother and grinned.

Just then, the sound of a hand-drum floated into the kitchen. Durga grasped her brother's hand.

'Opu! That's the monkey man! Let's go!'

And with that, she flew out of the house once again.

It wasn't the monkey man, though. It was Chinibash the reluctant confectioner, out selling his wares from door to door. Though it was his ancestral business, confectionary wasn't Chinibash's first preference for a living; he had tried his hand at almost everything else: running a paddy-supply business, a jaggery business . . . and many, many other businesses. People said that trading in fish was about the only thing he hadn't tried at least once. All his businesses inevitably failed, because he didn't have the capital to see them through leaner patches. During those times, he tried to tide things over by selling vegetables from door to door, or by defaulting to his family's trade of making sweets. After a few months of stable confectionary income, he would quit again and start a business ferrying limestone, or anything else that promised a greater return than selling sweets in a small village.

Chinibash slowed a little when he saw the children at the doorway. Normally he wouldn't have, for the Roys were too poor to ever buy anything from him. But this was the month of Joishtho, and tomorrow was the tenth day of the waxing moon. It was one of the most auspicious days of the year, for it was on this day that Ganga had descended on earth to wash away ten kinds of human sin. Perhaps even the Roys, despite their poverty, were waiting to buy a few sweets for their Doshohora Puja.

'Want something?' he asked the older child brusquely.

Durga shook her head.

Chinibash sped up. He was on his way to Bhubon Mukhujje's house, where he knew he would make a big sale. Bhubon was a comfortable second in the village in terms of wealth, beaten only by Awnnoda Roy's large estate. His family celebrated all festivals and rituals in style.

With nothing better to do that evening, Durga and Opu trailed a short distance behind him.

Since the death of his own wife, Bhubon Mukhujje's household had been run by his sister-in-law—his third-eldest brother's wife. She was a woman of considerable local influence, for she ran a successful lending business amongst the village women. This made several of the women beholden to her, and try their best to appease her at every turn. At home, she ruled the roost with precision and terror. By the time Durga and Opu drifted into their large courtyard, she had already bought a large heap of sweets for the puja: shondesh, roshogolla and murki—puffed rice coated in caramelized jaggery. When Durga and Opu came in through the outer doorway, she had been in the middle of handing out a second pile of sweets that she had bought for the Mukhujje children's evening snack. Watching the Roy children slip into her courtyard and shamelessly eye her family's food made her temper flare.

'Go inside and eat your food!' she snapped at her son Shuneel, and gave his shoulder a push. 'What possessed you lot to eat here? In a moment you'll start dropping crumbs, and then all the pujo sweets will be desecrated!'

The Mukhujje children knew to follow her commands instantly. They swiftly disappeared into the house.

Chinibash, meanwhile, had been packing up his wares. Now he lifted them on his head and made his way out of the Mukhujje's main entrance.

'Let's follow him to Tunu's house,' Durga whispered to her brother. 'Let's see what they buy!'

As they turned to walk out of the main doorway, they heard the third-eldest mistress speaking about them inside the house.

'What an unbelievable pair. That girl—she's a greedy little thief if I ever saw one. If you want sweets, buy and eat them in your own house! Why chase after the confectioner to other people's houses? Disgusting, I call it! And no wonder. Like mother, like daughter, I always say. That madame had probably put them up to it in the first place!'

Durga and Opu continued to walk, swallowing the words in silence.

After a while, Durga said, 'As if Chinibash's sweets are that good! We don't even want his stuff . . . do we, Opu? Just you wait. When it's time for Rothjatra, I'll get Baba to give us four paise; two for me, two for you. Then we'll buy *real* fairground murki. Hot caramelized jaggery . . . thi-i-is much for two paise. The best sweet anyone could have! Just you wait and see!'

Opu kept quiet for several seconds. Finally he said, 'How many days till roth, Didi?'

10

A FEW MONTHS passed.

Shorbojoya was on her way home from Bhubon Mukhujje's well, a large pot of water balanced on her hips. Her son followed closely behind, fisting his small hands in the free end of her sari.

'Stop doing that!' Shorbojoya finally said. 'I have lots to do right now, Khoka. I don't have time for your mischief.'

Opu refused to let go. 'Do your work in the evening. Go to the bathing steps first! Now! Go now!'

Shorbojoya gave him a quelling look.

'No-o-o-o!' whined her son. 'Go to the pond! Then come back and give me my lunch!' Then he set his features in the most piteous expression he could manage. 'Aren't I allowed to be hungry? I haven't had a real meal in four days!'

'And whose fault is that? Did I ask you to run around in the sun and bring home a fever? It's not like I'm sitting around doing nothing. I'll go to the pond when I finish all my other chores.'

Opu held on to the sari tightly. 'You work all the time! What will it matter if you skip a day? I'm hungry-y-y-y!'

Shorbojoya softened. 'If you don't let me go, how can I start making your lunch? Come on, Baba. I promise I'll be quick. Lunch will be ready before you know it. Now, how many gourd-leaf fries will my little boy have? Hmm?'

After about an hour, Opu sat down to eat with a great show of enthusiasm. He mashed the hot rice with great delight, and bit into two gourd-leaf fritters at the same time. After only a couple of handfuls, however, his enthusiasm began to wane. He began taking long, gurgling sips out of his water glass, chased the fried leaves around with his rice, scattered some accidentally on the ground, and in between put a few reluctant morsels in his mouth. Then, before his mother could say anything, he finished his water in a sudden single gulp and ran off to wash his hands.

'No! You come back here!' his mother called after him. '"I'm hungry, I want my rice! I want my fried leaves"—is *this* how much you eat after all that? How will you live on so little, you silly boy? Opu! Come back!'

When her son showed no signs of compliance, she mashed some of the rice into a bowl of warm milk and sat down right in front of him. Opu tried his best to avoid the little milk-soaked rice balls, but his mother had considerable expertise at bypassing his reluctance.

'Let's see, my angel, just two more gulps . . . did you know there's going to be an idol immersion at Tunu's place this evening? Open up, sweetie, just one more . . . There will be lights and drums—so much fun! We'll all be going! Won't that be nice? This is the last one, I promise . . . no, no, don't purse your lips! Honestly, it's a wonder you're still alive!'

This was the scene that Durga walked into. As usual, her tangled hair stood out at all angles, and her feet were covered in dust. The moment she saw her mother, she was stopped short.

'Come in, come in,' Shorbojoya greeted her daughter with biting deference, her earlier warmth vanishing. 'Good of you to finally grace this humble house with your august presence. Now please oblige your mother by swallowing your lunch. I'm sure you'll have to run out at any moment to keep all your pressing noon-time appointments. No?'

Durga swallowed. She had indeed been planning on leaving right after lunch. The orchards and woodlands of the village were her whole life. She knew which berries were the sweetest, whose orchard had the sweetest plums, and which bush of berries ripened first each season. Even when she walked on human paths, she kept a sharp eye on the sides for pretty insects, or little treasures like the yellow nightshade, the fruit of which made perfect little toy brinjals for her doll box. Even shards of broken, throwaway clay were swiftly wrapped up in the ends of her sari to use as hopscotch markers later. Orchards, games and treasures for her doll box—these were the soul and centre of her life.

Shorbojoya, meanwhile, was slowly giving in to her rising temper.

'Look at you! No oil, no combing, loose hair flying everywhere . . . who's going to say you're a brahmon's daughter? You look just like a tribal girl! Just as well, since no doubt that's who you'll end up marrying. All the other neighbourhood girls are lighting lamps and praying to Shib Thakur for good husbands . . . but not my daughter! Oh no! Old enough to be married, and here she's running around the jungles doing god knows what! What's that knot in your sari?'

Durga looked around helplessly. She had hoped to slip indoors and unload her morning's pickings into the doll box, precisely so her mother wouldn't find out about them. She hadn't been prepared for a confrontation.

Her obvious fear sharpened Shorbojoya's suspicion.

'Open up!' she demanded. 'Let's see what secret treasures you've brought home this time.'

Reluctantly, Durga began to unknot the loose end of her sari. 'It's, um . . . I saw these under the sophera shrubs . . . only from Uncle Neelmoni's garden, nowhere else. There is this yellow bird that comes every day . . . so I thought . . .'

'To hell with your yellow bird!' thundered Shorbojoya. 'This house is not your dumping ground! If I see any more useless junk coming in, I'm going to take your stupid doll box and drown it in the old pond—you see if I . . .'

Her threat was cut off suddenly, for with an abrupt burst of noise, the third-eldest mistress of the Mukhujje household swept into their compound. She was followed by her daughter Tunu, her nephew Shotu, and four or five of the other Mukhujje children. The woman didn't acknowledge any of the three Roys. Instead, she turned to her nephew.

'Get the box. Let's see what she's been hiding.'

Shotu dashed into the northern room and hauled Durga's doll box out into the courtyard. Tunu immediately threw it open and pulled out a beaded necklace.

'Look, Ma! My necklace. Must've stolen it the day she came over to play!'

'Auntie, look!' Shotu exclaimed. 'Tiny mangoes from our Shonamukhi mango tree! She hid it under her other toys so we wouldn't know!'

The invasion had happened so rapidly that Shorbojoya had been stunned. She finally managed to recover somewhat at this point.

'What is all this, third-eldest aunt?' she asked anxiously, coming forward. 'What's going on?'

'Ask your precious daughter what's going on! Become a seasoned thief, that one. Look at this necklace! We let her come into our house, play with our children's toys . . . and this is how she repays us? We hadn't even guessed! Who would? Only when Shotu came home this morning did we know. And look at these fruits! That daughter of yours is no normal child. Always lying in wait in other people's gardens, waiting for fruit to ripen on other people's trees . . .'

The rapid turn of events had petrified Durga. She had moved to one corner of the courtyard when the Mukhujje contingent had come in. Now she stood with her back against the kitchen wall. Shorbojoya turned to her, radiating fury.

'Did you steal this necklace from Tunu?'

Before Durga could respond, the third-eldest mistress began screaming in rage.

'You're asking the thief for confirmation? Is it not enough that my girl pulled the stolen necklace right out of your daughter's box? Are you going to pretend we need more proof? That girl stakes out our mango trees before summer even properly hits! We barely get to see our own yield—that's how fast she is with her fingers. And you're asking *her*, like my word isn't good enough? Do you think I'm lying?'

'I didn't say you were lying, Auntie,' Shorbojoya said in a placatory tone. 'I was just asking my daughter a question.'

The third-eldest mistress waved her hands under Shorbojoya's nose. 'You can ask all the questions you like but it won't change facts. That daughter of yours is too far gone. If she's this big a thief at this age . . . well, just you wait and see what she turns into when she grows up! Tunu, have you taken your necklace? Good! Shotu, take those mangoes. We're leaving. Can't ever taste our own mangoes. That vile female is forever at the trees. Everything of ours ends up in this house! As if we don't know who encourages it . . .'

Shorbojoya was usually adept at giving back just as good as she got, but Durga's crimes had forced her to swallow every possible retort during this blitzkrieg. This last insinuation, however, was too much for her.

'I don't know anything about that necklace,' she called out, 'but there's really no proof that those mangoes are from your trees, Auntie. They could be from anywhere. And even if they were from your trees, they're fallen buds, anyway. So unripe that they're almost inedible. What difference does it make if a child picks them up for fun?'

The third-eldest mistress had been about to exit the Roys' compound when she heard Shorbojoya. The unexpected attack enraged her so much that she couldn't speak for a few seconds.

'You've got a fine tongue on you for the mother of a thief!' she finally ground out. 'Okay, so the buds don't have our names on them. Could you tell me which of *your* many gardens yield such high-quality fruit? And by the way, your name wasn't inscribed on my money either. But that didn't stop you from begging and begging and begging for it, did it? It's been a full year since I gave you that money. All I've ever heard in return is "I'll return it today", "I'll give it tomorrow". Well, I want the full amount back this evening. Keep it ready. And there had better not be any excuses when I come for it.'

With that killing blow, she swept out. A few seconds later, she was heard telling someone on the street in an unnecessarily loud voice, '. . . stole my daughter's necklace, would you believe? And our most expensive mangoes! And then the mother says to me [here she mimicked Shorbojoya with extreme exaggeration], "The blossoms don't have your name on it, how dare you accuse us of stealing?" Imagine! The nerve!'

Then she lowered her voice a little to imply a confidence, although it was still clearly audible.

'Like mother, like child, don't you know? Where do you think the children learnt to steal? That one's just as dangerous as her girl. The whole family is full of thieves, you mark my words!'

Throughout the ultimatum and the public broadcast, Shorbojoya had been standing in front of the kitchen, furious but mortified. This last accusation, against her entire family, finally galvanized her into action. All her pent-up fury unleashed itself towards the cause of this entire showdown. Stomping up to her daughter, she fisted her daal-soaked hand in her hair and began blindly landing punches on her shoulders and back.

'You vile thief!' she screamed. 'How many times do we have to swallow insults because of you? Why don't you go die and give us some peace? Get out! Get out of my house! If I see your face here again, you'll know what real pain feels like!'

Durga, who had been frozen in fear so far, was perhaps relieved at this direct order. She writhed and pulled till her head was free of her mother's fist, then raced out of the back door. A tuft of her tangled curls remained in Shorbojoya's food-smeared fist. Shorbojoya threw down the locks on the courtyard and glared after her daughter. Her fair complexion was flushed with rage, bitterness and humiliation.

Opu had been watching the entire event with disbelief and alarm. He had been surprised to see Tunu Didi pull out the necklace from his didi's box—he, for one, had certainly never seen it in the box before. But he knew for a fact that the mango buds were not stolen goods. Only yesterday, his sister had come running to tell him that the strong wind was likely to detach some of the newly blossomed fruit from the Shonamukhi mango tree in the Mukhujje's orchard.

'We'll just go wait for it to come down, okay, Opu?' she had said.

And that was exactly what they had done. Their plan was to oil and salt the little baby mangoes, but their mother's inconvenient presence at home all day had prevented it from happening. Brother and sister had been hoping she would take a nap today, so that they could sneak some oil and salt into the back garden for a secret afternoon snack.

So yes, the third-eldest granny could say what she liked, but picking fallen buds wasn't stealing. His sister didn't steal a thing from the Mukhujjes, and that was a fact.

He dearly wished that he had the nerve to say this to the Mukhujje contingent, or at least to his mother after they left, but the sudden violence in his mother had absolutely terrified him. He swallowed the rest of his milk-and-rice like a good little boy, cleaned himself up without being prompted, and tiptoed out of the kitchen to sit with his box of books. Though he could actually only read from the *Children's First Book*, he had begged and borrowed three other books from around the village. Two of these were thick English books that he couldn't read at all, but it felt good to simply have them in his box. The third was a tattered copy of Dashu Roy's *Book of Ballads*. Today, however, his heart wasn't in the books. He was worried about his sister. Where was Didi? She had just come home, hungry for her lunch. And then that awful third-eldest granny had come and ruined it all.

He also felt a fierce anger rising against his mother. Why did she have to beat Didi so badly? She had actually ripped out a fistful of her hair!

But he didn't dare breathe a word about his feelings to his mother—not after what she had done to his sister. Nor could he bring himself to ask her where she thought his didi might have gone.

After a few minutes of flipping through the books, he packed everything away and quietly slipped out of the house. Where could his didi really have gone? Perhaps to the bamboo grove . . . but there wasn't anything to eat there. For food, she would have to go to one of the orchards.

Gathering his courage, Opu searched the closest orchards alone for the next couple of hours. His didi wasn't in any of them. On the way to the last one, he met Rajkeshto Palit's wife returning from the bathing steps.

'Auntie! Auntie!' he called after her. 'Have you seen my didi? She hasn't eaten all day. Ma beat her so badly, Auntie . . . then she ran out of the house. Have you seen her after that, Auntie?'

Palit's wife hadn't. After failing to find his didi in the orchards, Opu decided to check the bamboo grove anyway. One never knew; maybe his sister had eaten elsewhere and was now resting in the grove. He went deeper than he usually did, calling out for his sister. Only his own echoes came back from the darkness within, sending chills down his spine. Still, he soldiered on for as far as he dared. When the silence of the grove began to close in on him, he gave up and ran back home. But even there, he stayed out of his mother's sight. He was still too bitter to speak to her.

Hours passed. Daylight began to withdraw from the ground and collect at the tops of trees. A little later, it began to die from the tree-tops as well. Opu stood in one corner of the courtyard, staring at the peepul and willing his sister to return. The long-tailed yellow bird flew into their courtyard, as it did every evening. But his sister didn't return. Waiting alone at home became impossible. Maybe Didi was hiding in the Mukhujjes' garden? He should've looked there! It was the closest. The moment the thought occurred to him, Opu shot out of the house.

When he reached the garden, several of the Mukhujje children were playing hopscotch. Runu, his favourite of the Mukhujje lot, came running and took him by the arm.

'Look everyone, Opu is here! He's going to be on our team. Come Opu, it's our turn next.'

Opu pulled his arm away. 'No Runudi, I'm not here to play. Have you seen Didi? She hasn't been home all day. I've been looking for her, but . . .'

'Dugga's missing?' Runu thought for a second. 'Have you checked beneath the medlar tree? She likes to play there alone sometimes.'

The medlar! His sister did like to play there. How had he not remembered that?

'Come for hopscotch tomorrow, Opu!' Runu's sister Raji called after him. 'We've drawn a new court behind the husking shed. Bring Dugga!'

Opu barely heard her. He had pulled out of the Mukhujje's orchard in a run, and didn't stop till he was right under the medlar tree.

His didi wasn't there.

Opu looked helplessly around. Even in the darkness, a few date-palm trees were visible in the woods beyond the medlar tree. They led to a small pond, and more importantly, to a pair of guava trees. Had his sister gone there? She had told him a few days back that the guavas had just begun to bear fruit. Maybe she thought she could eat them in peace, this far from the village roads?

He advanced a few paces. The woodland darkness was thick here, and full of unnamed terrors.

'Didi?' he called out tremulously. 'Are you there? Come out, let's go home now. You need to eat.'

Silence greeted him. Eerie, fearsome silence.

He tried calling out a few more times, but all he succeeded in doing was scaring away an animal hiding under the sandpaper tree to his right. He left, defeated and scared.

He was so worried about his sister's disappearance that he almost walked right past the velvet-apple tree. For some reason, the darkness of evenings under this particular tree terrified him. There was no reason why he should be this scared of a tree, of all things . . . and that was why his instinctive fear terrified him even more. He stood on the path, biting his lip. Should he close his eyes and just run past the tree? Or should he go back a bit and take the longer road past Potlidi's house?

Wait! Maybe Didi was at Potlidi's house! They were friends. Why hadn't he thought of that?

Backing away in relief, Opu took the path towards Potli's house. It was late evening already, and Potli's mother was cooking dinner indoors. Their fisherwoman Bidhu was standing under the open loft, waiting to be paid for the day's catch. Potli's grandmother was sitting on the raised courtyard with all the children, telling stories to keep them awake till dinner time.

'Grandma!' Opu called from the path. 'Have you seen my didi? I've just been to the large medlar, looking for her . . .'

'Dugga? She just went home. Right now, in fact. You can catch her if you run.'

Opu ran. He had just entered their own compound when he saw his sister once again fleeing towards the back door, arms trying to protect her head from her mother's blows. Their mother followed close behind, bringing down something repeatedly on her daughter's head and back.

'How dare you come back here!' she was screaming. 'God knows what filth crawled into my womb that I had you for a daughter! I wish I could take you to the milkwood pine and leave you there!'

Opu froze. The milkwood pine marked the village crematorium. Did his mother just say she wanted his didi dead?

In an attempt to avoid facing her, he waited in the darkness till his mother stomped back to the kitchen. Then he tried to tiptoe into his book-box room, giving the kitchen doorway a wide berth. Unfortunately for him, his mother had only gone into the kitchen to light the evening lamp. He was right in the middle of her path as she walked out with it.

'And where have *you* been all day?' she asked archly. 'No food, no rest . . . who'll know it's your first day of eating rice after the fever?'

Opu wanted to ask her a whole host of questions. Why did his sister get a second beating? Where had she been hiding all day? Had she eaten? But the memory of his mother's rage kept his lips sealed. Instead, he climbed on to the veranda and entered the room like a clockwork doll, quietly pulling out his box of books. For the next several minutes, he stared unseeingly at the same page of Dashu Roy's *Book of Ballads*.

After half an hour or so, Shorbojoya entered the room with a bowl of warm milk.

'Drink this, sweetheart . . . don't say no,' she cajoled, setting it down in front of her son.

Opu immediately picked the bowl up and took a small sip. Then he set the bowl down.

Shorbojoya was taken aback. Battling her son to make him drink his evening milk was a daily staple of her evening chores. What had brought on his sudden compliance?

When he didn't pick the bowl up again, she said, 'What, just one sip? No, my darling, finish the bowl. How will you survive if you don't have your milk?'

Opu wordlessly lifted the bowl to his lips again.

After a few seconds, Shorbojoya noticed that her son was holding the bowl to his lips, but his throat wasn't moving. Catching his mother looking at him, Opu put down the bowl and suddenly let out a loud sob.

'What—what is it?' asked Shorbojoya, surprised. 'Did you bite your tongue? Put the bowl down, sweetheart. Let me see.'

Opu had sworn never to speak to his mother again, but fear for his sister broke down his fear of her. 'Didi!' he gasped. 'Ma, where's Didi? I want her back!'

Shorbojoya kept quiet for a few seconds. Then she came closer to her son and began running her fingers soothingly down his back.

'Don't cry, sweetheart. Don't cry. She's probably hiding in someone's orchard—Potli's or Nyara's. Where else can she go? She's a real troublemaker, you know. Left home this afternoon after refusing to eat her lunch . . . and then she stays out all evening! Don't cry, baby. Your sister is fine, I promise. Probably hiding inside the Palit's gardens, filling her tummy with stolen mangoes and bell-fruits. I'll send someone to bring her home soon. Don't cry!'

A few moments later, when Opu's sobs subsided a little, she held the bowl of milk up to his lips again.

'We'll wait till your baba is back. As soon as he's home, I'll ask him to go get your sister, all right? My silly little boy—crying for his sister! Finish your milk, you goof!'

Later that night, Opu and Durga were lying next to each other on the bed in the northern room. Horihor had gone out to fetch his daughter just before dinner. Right now, having finished his meal, he was smoking his hookah in the next room. Shorbojoya's place was empty, because she hadn't yet finished her post-dinner chores.

Durga hadn't spoken a single word since coming back. She had eaten her dinner in silence, then gone straight to bed. Opu had wisely left her alone while their parents were still around, but now he tapped her gently on the arm.

'Didi . . . what did Ma hit you with in the evening? Did she really rip out your hair?'

Durga didn't respond.

'Are you mad at me, Didi? But I didn't do anything!'

'Oh yeah?' Durga whispered back. 'Then how did Shotu find out where the necklace was?'

Opu sat up in defensive fervour. 'Not me! I didn't even know it was there! Shotu had come over last evening while you were out. We were playing with his big red ball . . . you know? Then suddenly he started poking about your things. I told him not to. I said, "Brother, don't touch my sister's things, she gets mad at me." He must have seen it then. But I didn't say a word!'

Then he leaned over to run his palm down his sister's back.

'Is this where Ma hit you? I'm so sorry, Didi. Does it still hurt?'

'Yes . . . she hit so hard that I was bleeding. See?'

'Didi! Goodness, the cut's still raw! Should I rub some lamp oil into it?'

'Never mind, it'll heal,' said Durga, her good humour restored. 'Listen, the star apples in the Palits' garden have just ripened. We'll go tomorrow, you and me. All right? I ate a couple this afternoon when I was hungry. Sweet as jaggery!'

11

THIS IS HOW the thing happened.

Opu had finished the handwriting exercise his father had set him. He put away the palmyra leaf scripts for Horihor's inspection and went inside the house to look for his sister.

Durga was in a corner of the inner courtyard, bullied by her mother into performing the punyipukur ritual. A small square hole had been dug beneath the papaya tree and filled with water to signify the 'Pond of Virtue'. The chickpeas and green peas that she had scattered around it had begun to sprout. Durga was standing over this 'pond' and flying through the rites as quickly as she dared. When she saw Opu come in, she lowered her voice to whisper.

'Don't go anywhere. I just have the montro left . . . then I'll take you to a special place.'

'Which place, Didi?'

'You'll see when we get there. Now, one minute . . .'

She turned back to her pond of virtue, folded her palms and chanted the 'mantra', which was really just a verse.

Pond of Virtue, garland of flower,
Who worships at this noon hour?
I, Leelabotee, that is who.

Lucky sister of brothers,
A woman of virtue.

Opu was watching the rites with interest. At the end of his sister's recitation, he snickered. '"A woman of virtue", oooh!'

Durga grinned in embarrassment. 'Shush! Go wait outside. This is a girls' thing, what are you doing here anyway?'

'Hee hee! "Lucky sister of brothers, a woman of virtue." Virtuuuuuue! Hehehe!'

'Oi! You shut up, or I'll tell Ma. You'll see the beating you get! Now scoot!'

After a minute, she joined her brother outside.

'Let's go. Bhoda's mother said that the pond at the fort is full of ripe water chestnuts!'

The 'fort' was merely a large house that had belonged to the Mojumdars—the oldest residents of this whole area. They had dug a broad moat around the house to protect it from humans and animals. The family had long since died out, and their house had broken down completely. Even the moat had largely been filled in, and the area was now a messy woodland with a bamboo grove. Only one part of the moat still had water, but it was pretty deep water. This was called the Fort Pond, even though it was neither a pond, nor an actual fort.

The Mojumdar property had been at what was now the north of the village. These days it could only be accessed through an ancient orchard of mango and jackfruit trees. Brother and sister ran along the narrow old path through these orchards. When they reached the pond, however, they saw that all the chestnuts along the sides had already been picked clean. The remaining ones were right in the middle of the pond, where the water was the deepest.

'What shall we do, Didi?'

'Hmm . . . can you find a piece of bamboo? A longish one. Then we can haul those clusters in.'

While Opu looked around for a suitable bamboo, Durga began plucking and eating berries from a nearby lebbeck tree.

'Didi, don't!' Opu called in alarm. 'Those aren't for us—only birds eat those berries.'

Durga was in the process of making a small heap of depipped berries. She dismissed her brother's concern with a snort. 'As if! I've been eating these berries for years. Such lovely sweet berries. Why shouldn't we eat them? Here, try some and see.'

Opu looked conflicted. 'Don't these make you insane? That's what people say . . . okay fine, give me one. Just one.'

'Pretty sweet,' he pronounced after chewing for a few seconds. 'But there's a bitter aftertaste, Didi, whatever you say.'

'Yeah, all right, but that's the *aftertaste*. Doesn't mean the berry isn't sweet, right? It's jaggery-sweet! How could this make anyone mad?'

To demonstrate her confidence, she tossed another handful into her mouth and chewed in contentment.

These two young things were still new to this earth. Their senses looked upon their surroundings in wide-eyed wonder, eager to taste the wide array of flavours it had to offer. Sweetness, in particular, entranced them. Their family couldn't afford to buy them human-made sweets, so they went hunting in the woods for the abundant natural sweetness of fruits—from the humblest berries to the regal mangoes.

A suitable bamboo was found after a while. Durga pulled up the loose end of the sari and tucked it tightly into her waist.

'You stay here, all right? I'll go in. Oh look! Water lilies!'

She waded in with the bamboo and pulled two water lilies to herself. Shaking off the water, she threw them at the shore. 'Opu, catch!'

Opu dutifully caught the plants and put them aside.

But pulling in the chestnuts proved a lot harder than the lilies. First, they were in the middle of the pond. Second—as Durga soon found out—the pond-bed sloped sharply downwards after barely a few feet into the water. She nearly lost her footing the first time, but managed to steady herself after only a little flailing.

'Tell you what, Opu,' she said after some thought. 'I'll go in. You stand behind me and hold tightly to my aanchol. If you see me slip, just pull me back.'

Opu was only half listening. His eyes were glued to a bright yellow bird, flitting from branch to branch and whistling a surprisingly tuneful note.

'What bird is that, Didi?' he asked.

'Never mind the bird! Hold my aanchol!' said Durga, unwinding the loose end of her sari from around her waist. When it had unwound fully, she threw the untucked end at him.

Thus began the grand battle for water chestnuts.

At first attempt, Durga had almost managed to stretch the bamboo to the nearby cluster of chestnuts. However, Opu's strength gave way at a critical juncture, and the free end of the sari ripped out of his hands and flopped in the water. Opu laughed out loud at his own ineptitude. After she righted herself, Durga started laughing too.

'Useless!' she gasped. 'You're like a grain-thrasher made of velvet-apple wood—cracking at the first go!' She took a few deep breaths. 'Okay, we're going in again. Hold tighter this time!'

This attempt actually yielded a small cluster. Durga tested the fruit with her fingers. 'Still too raw,' she declared. 'No milk inside yet. Oh well. Once more.'

Opu tightened his grip on the sari once more, but this time it slipped almost immediately. Brother and sister burst out laughing. The merriment of their youthful voices echoed and tinkled throughout the quiet woodlands and bamboo grove.

A little later, Durga was still in the water, trying to wield the bamboo all by herself. Opu, however, had given up. He lay on the shore, under the shade of a sandpaper tree, looking around the wilderness. Suddenly, he caught a glint of something under an older lebbeck further ahead. He sat up.

'Didi! Did you see that?'

Durga had been completely focused on the water chestnuts. 'See what?' she called back.

'That glint there, when the sun shone through. Wait!'

Opu ran up to the other tree and began digging up the loose soil with his hands. After just a few seconds, he held up a glittering piece of . . . something.

'Didi . . . look!'

Durga, meanwhile, had scrambled to the shore. She took the thing from her brother's hand and examined it closely. It looked like a rounded piece of glass . . . sort of. It was glass-like in that one could see through. But it also had facets and veins, unlike any glass she had seen before. And it refracted whatever light fell on it in seven shades of the rainbow. Glass didn't throw off light like that.

'Opu . . .' Durga whispered, unfamiliar hope beginning to flutter in her chest. 'I think this might be a diamond.'

At this, Opu did some quick mental recalibration. He knew of diamonds by name, of course. 'Gold and silver, diamonds and jewels' was mentioned countless times in his mother's stories. But he had no real idea what they looked like. In fact, for reasons he couldn't remember any more, he had sort of decided that diamonds looked like fish eggs: yellow and cold to the touch, but hard, not soft. Apparently, he had been wrong.

Durga had already wrapped the thing in her sari. Now brother and sister made swiftly for their home, water chestnuts forgotten.

Shorbojoya wasn't home when they got there. When she came back from the neighbourhood, she found her children waiting for her just inside the back doorway.

'Ma, look at what we found!' Durga said in an excited whisper. 'From the Mojumdars' old land, buried under a tree . . .'

'I saw it first,' Opu piped up. 'I told Didi it was there.'

Shorbojoya took the thing and turned it around slowly.

'It's probably a diamond. No, Ma? Doesn't it look just like a diamond?'

'How do you know it's a diamond?' Shorbojoya asked doubtfully. She wasn't any more familiar with jewels than her children were.

'We found it in the Mojumdars' garden! They were rich people, living alone in the woods. Pishima used to say that they had buried a lot of their treasures in those woods. Someone found a gold coin in that garden once . . . Ma, this must be a diamond! Why else was it buried?'

Shorbojoya tried not to jinx the hope that was rising in her chest.

'We'll wait for your father to come home,' she told her children, keeping the thing with her. 'He'll know what to do.'

Once they were out of their mother's earshot, Durga turned to her brother, grinning. 'Good times are coming,

Opu! You'll see!' she whispered. 'A diamond will change our lives!'

Opu giggled along with his sister, without really understanding why.

Once the children had left, Shorbojoya took the glittering thing out again and slowly turned it in her hand. The roundness reminded her of ornate knobs attached to the lids of fancy vermilion holders. She realized that she could see a whole host of colours inside the thing. They came and went as she slowly turned it in the light. Suddenly, a chill of anticipation ran down her spine. This thing, whatever it was, was obviously not glass. She'd never seen such strangeness in a glass before. What if this *was* a diamond?

A lifetime of hardship had given Shorbojoya a near-mythical estimate of a diamond's value. She put it at par with the philosopher's stone, or the jewel hidden on a snake's head—things that had no specific value in the marketplace, but which, in stories, could buy entire kingdoms.

Just then, Horihor came home with his bundle. Shorbojoya immediately went up to him and held out the thing.

'Look at this, my dear. What do you think this is?'

Horihor took the thing from his wife's hand. 'Where did you get this?'

'Dugga went to pick water chestnuts in the Fort Pond. She found it there.'

Horihor looked at the thing from different angles. 'Glass, probably. But I can't be sure.'

The hope in Shorbojoya's heart rose a little higher. Had it been mere glass, would her scholarly husband not have recognized it at once?

'Might it be a diamond?' she ventured, afraid that her husband might dismiss the idea immediately. 'The Mojumdars were rich, you know. People have found treasure on their land before.'

'Hah, that's a good one! Diamonds! Come now, as if!'

Indeed, at first, Horihor was fairly certain the thing was glass. But then he thought, well . . . what if this was one of those rare times when miracles actually came to pass? The Mojumdars had indeed been rich—this much was true. Maybe this was once part of their jewellery or ornaments, but had fallen out while . . . well, had fallen out, somehow. Or maybe it was part of a buried treasure. Fables did warn against dismissing something before fully examining it. It was how a poor brahmin had lost all the treasures that fate had sent his way. He didn't want to be that brahmin!

'I doubt this is anything,' he warned his wife. 'But I'll take it along to the Gangulys' and see what they say.'

While her husband was gone, Shorbojoya sat over the cooking fire and put all her hopes into fervent prayer. 'Please god, let it be a diamond. Good things happen to so many people . . . you know how hard life has been lately . . . how much we could use that help. Please god, please! Let it be a diamond!' Her heart thudded in time with her escalating hopes.

After a while, Durga entered the kitchen, her eyes shining. 'Has Baba come back yet?'

Shorbojoya was about to answer, but Horihor stepped in right behind his daughter.

'It's nothing, just like I said. The Gangulys' son-in-law from Calcutta, Shotyo Babu, is visiting right now. Chandelier crystal—that's what he called it. Absolutely worthless. Honestly, the things you people get into your heads. As if diamonds and pearls could be found just rolling about on the streets. Hah!'

12

IT WAS EARLY one afternoon of the same summer.

Shorbojoya had just returned from the bathing steps and had started cooking lunch. After a while, she reached for the flower bowl next to her. Her fingers came back empty.

'Arre! Where did the cumin go?' she exclaimed. (The flower-bowl had long since been relegated to being a spice-holder, remaining a 'flower bowl' only in name.)

A smothered giggle floated in from the veranda outside.

'Now, who could have taken my cumin?' Shorbojoya called out, fixing narrowed eyes on the kitchen door. Sure enough, her son's beautiful, mischievous face peeked in for a second, and withdrew with a giggle the moment he caught his mother looking.

'I saw you! No point hiding any more, Opu—give the cumin back!'

Her son's head merely peeked in for another swift look.

Shorbojoya knew her child well. When he was just a little baby—barely a year old, if that—she would wash his face in the evenings, draw a thick line of kohl around his large eyes, put a large kohl bindi on his forehead, and cover his head and ears with a cheap blue woollen hat with bobbles sewed on. Then she would carry him to the veranda to take in the evening air. To keep him entertained, she'd sing him nursery songs, drawing out the words excessively.

Come, bi-i-i-irdie with a swe-e-e-e-ping tail!
Play with my ba-a-a-be, play with him wel-l-l-l.

Her son always laughed, but his chief delight was in suddenly flashing her one of his famous toothless grins, then swiftly burying his little head in the crook of her back, where her neck and shoulders met.

'Arre! Where is my baby?' Shorbojoya would trill in mock surprise, much to the baby's delight. The moment she turned and pulled back her head to reveal his face, he would glance at her, grin again, and promptly burrow into her chest. This back and forth would go on for several minutes, long after Shorbojoya's neck had started aching from all the swinging. Her baby had been a new entrant to this world then, and having freshly discovered the joy of games, was unwilling to let go of them easily. Only once *he* was exhausted would he stop the hide-and-seek, then stare into an indeterminate distance from his mother's lap. Relieved and suddenly overcome with affection for her adorable, crazy baby, Shorbojoya would lift his little face by putting her finger beneath his chin, and shower him with kisses.

'You've learnt so many tricks already . . . my clever little darling! My golden child!' she would croon. The beautiful golden child, however, took no notice of her praise. Even as his mother kissed him and crushed him to her chest, he would have found his way to dreamland. After a few moments of suspicious passiveness to her kisses, Shorbojoya would raise her head to look at her baby . . . and find him fast asleep.

'Oh no!' she would exclaim. 'Will you look at this boy! I thought I'd feed him right after dusk, but he's already a ball of sleepy clay!'

Though he had barely been eight months old then, and now he was a boy of eight, Shorbojoya knew all too well that if he thought she was participating in the game, he would keep up the hiding till sundown. It wasn't like she couldn't have found the cumin pouch herself, if only she had looked. Her innocent little boy hid things in such obvious places that even a blind man could find them. But she liked to let him have the illusion that he was a master at the hiding game—such an expert that even his own mother had to really struggle to uncover his stash.

So instead of getting up, she merely turned away from the wok and called out loudly, 'Opu, if you don't give the cumin back, I'm going to stop cooking right now. Then if you come to me asking for lunch, you'll see what I do to you!'

There was another giggle from the courtyard. Then Opu ran in, face alight with mischief. He dropped the pouch in the flower bowl, and swiftly retreated behind his mother again. Shorbojoya turned back to her wok, relieved.

A minute later, someone behind her went, 'Grow-w-w-w-w-w-w-l!'

Shorbojoya rolled her eyes. No indulgence, she reminded herself.

'Growwwwwwwl!' said the fearsome monster again, in a slightly deeper voice.

Shorbojoya sighed and turned around.

Her son had pulled down the dusty old jute sack from the bamboo shelf, and had draped it around himself.

'Opu! That thing hasn't been shaken out in a year! It's crawling with god knows what! Take it off!'

The sack monster got down on all fours and crawled forward.

'No! Don't come closer! Opu, my angel, my sweet good boy . . . here, look, I'm so scared. I'm really, really scared, all right? I'm shaking! Now take the sack off, Baba.'

The jute monster considered this plea for a moment.

'Baba, if you touch me with that dirty sack on, all this food will go to waste. Good boy, darling boy—take that filthy thing off. And go see what your sister's up to. That's something to do, right? Lord knows how many mites have already crawled in your hair, you silly child . . .'

Opu finally took the sack off. The thing was used to sun-dry batches of red lentil poppers, so it had indeed attracted a fair number of ants and mites. Many of these were now hurriedly crawling up and down his limbs. His hair, eyebrows and face were coated with old lentil powder and house dust. But he was smiling. A big, goofy grin shone through the cobwebs and filth.

Shorbojoya wanted to crush him to her chest, like she used to when he was a baby. But if he wasn't unclean earlier, he definitely was now. And the way their finances were, she couldn't afford to waste food.

'Go wash your face with some of that water,' she said instead, pointing to the pot she filled every day from the Mukhujjes' well. 'Crazy child! The things you do . . . and don't forget to give your sister a shout while you're outside. That unkempt beast was supposed to take a proper bath today . . . no wonder she left home as soon as she could . . . here, take this washcloth. Dust yourself off before you wash. My crazy little boy!'

After a while, she sat her son down to guard the kitchen while she went to refill the water pot. The moment she stepped out on the courtyard, she saw Durga speeding towards the back of the house.

'Dugga!' she called out. 'Where were you all morning? Come here!'

Thus caught, the poor girl came slowly around to the front of the house and stood in front of her mother. Her mother glared pointedly at the knots on the free end of her sari.

Seeing no way out, Durga began undoing the knots.

'I was at Raji's,' she offered nervously. 'For the gram saplings? For my punyipukur?' She licked her lips nervously. 'So Raji's aunt, she said . . . she was unpacking mangoes, and she said . . . she gave me two mangoes. Totally on her own! Honestly, Ma . . .'

'Of course,' said her mother, her voice thick with sarcasm. 'As we all know, thinking about your punyipukur drives the sleep from your eyes . . . You stupid girl—hair flying everywhere, feet covered in dust—do you even want to be normal? Or not? And what's that? Painted feet? Have you been stealing the lacquer dye from my Lokkhi's basket?'

Durga's stance suddenly became a great deal more confident. She wiped her face with the now-empty free end of her sari, and pushed her hair back. 'Of course it isn't from your basket! Ask Baba—didn't I give him a paisa to buy me a sheaf of dye from last week's market? Look in my doll box to see how many I have left. This aalta is mine!'

Just then, Horihor came indoors to re-light his bowl of tobacco.

'Again?' Shorbojoya exclaimed. 'Listen, if you need to smoke every hour, then you first need to stock the house with actual firewood. Bamboo fire only lasts as long as it is stoked. I can't keep giving you fresh fire if I'm not in the kitchen!'

But she returned to the kitchen all the same, and used an old brass stirring spoon to drop a piece of rekindled bamboo in his bowl.

A little later, when the children had wandered off, she lowered her voice and asked him, 'So . . . what happened?'

Horihor's shoulders dropped. 'Bishshesh Moshai is away. At his in-laws' village to settle some property dispute. Without him, his family won't . . . I mean, he's the boss of everything, don't you know. So the whole thing is now delayed. That's on one hand. On the other, the dates for the initiation ceremony will dry up from the onset of the monsoon months . . .'

'But what about the moving? Can't we at least move?'

'No no . . . how cheap would that look? No initiation, but already asking to move in? No, it all needs to wait till Bishshesh Moshai comes back.'

Shorbojoya gave up. She had really, really hoped that this would work out, but it was clear that her husband wouldn't push for it.

'There's still hope for respect if we move abroad,' she said with some bitterness. 'In this village it's just, "Aren't you lucky to stay on the ancestral land? Every neighbour knows all about your family! Here, have a load of old debts!" When every other household is bursting with mangoes and jackfruits, our home is empty. The girl brought home two half-rotted mangoes today—and that was because someone took pity on her.'

Then she jabbed her head towards the west, indicating the Mukhujjes' house. 'They send men to take away baskets of mangoes from your brother's orchard next door. Our children just stand at the doorway and stare. How am I supposed to see them suffer like that, and just keep carrying on?'

At the mention of the orchard, Horihor's face abruptly flooded with anger. 'Oh, that traitorous scoundrel! The orchard is worth at least twenty-five rupees in rent each year—easily! That swindler had it for *five*! You know, I went and practically begged him not to lease it. "That orchard is all my children have," I said. "And besides, it's my cousin's property—let it stay in the family. You have no dearth of money or things, Uncle. Areca nut, mango trees, black plum—you have two large orchards to meet your every need. Break your lease on that orchard, Uncle . . . go on." You know what he told me? He told me that back when he was alive, Neelmoni Dada owed him three hundred rupees. Getting the orchard for cheap was his way of paying himself back. As if someone as well off as Neelmoni Dada would go to Bhubon Mukhujje, palms outstretched! Basically, he saw that our sister-in-law was a simple soul, and tricked her into the contract.'

'A simple soul? Hardly! Do you know what she's been telling the women? "Relatives make the worst enemies." She *wanted* the Mukhujjes to have the orchard, just so we couldn't have it. "Even a cheap lease is better than relatives, that way I'll at least get to see some returns from my gardens"—that's what she said.'

'Did sister-in-law think I wouldn't pay her?' asked Horihor, hurt. 'She didn't even tell me that she was planning on leasing the orchard. I would have paid . . . Those scheming Mukhujjes plied her with luchi and mohonbhog, that's what happened. She, simple soul, was hoodwinked into signing the lease.'

13

THE YEAR'S FIRST summer storm finally broke that evening. The clouds had been gathering all day, but even then, the storm had a hurried feel to it, arriving before it was fully expected. In a moment, the world beyond the Roys' walls was transformed. The bamboos that spent the rest of the year leaning into their compound were whipped aside, making the house suddenly look far more exposed and vulnerable. In a minute, whistling dust-laden winds began to blow bits of bamboo leaves, hay and jackfruit leaves into their courtyard, making swirling little heaps all over the place. From beyond the walls came the faint but unmistakable sound of fruits dropping to the ground.

'Opu!' Durga shouted over the sound of rushing winds. 'Mangoes! Let's go!'

She raced out of the house, her brother at her heels.

'You pick under the Shindurkota trees, I'll cover the Shonamukhi,' she called back as they ran.

All around them, branches were being whipped from side to side. Swirling dust severely impaired vision, and sharp-edged bamboo leaves whistling by made staying the course difficult. When the children reached their late uncle's orchard, the place had become a battleground. Ripe fruits, unripe fruits, twigs, branches . . . everything was being ripped off and hurled around like missiles. Leaves eddied in the winds and flew into their faces. To make things worse, hundreds of soft, spiky dandelions blew into the orchard and began snowing around the mango trees, getting in the way.

And yet Opu ran around in wild excitement, shouting every time he heard a mango fall.

'Didi! There's one! There, that's another—on that side! Let's get them all!'

Durga was grinning widely. But unlike her brother, she worked silently and efficiently. For all his excitement and dancing about, Opu had only been able to locate two mangoes. Durga, on the other hand, had already picked five or six.

Suddenly, a bubble of human noise broke through the winds. The Mukhujje children were almost upon the Shonamukhi mango tree. The roaring storm had swallowed the sound of their approach, so they saw the trespassers before the trespassers saw them. Shotu's yell of outrage was the Roy children's first intimation that they were not alone.

'Look, everyone! Opu and Dugga Didi are stealing our fruit!'

The siblings looked up, alarmed. Backed up by his band, Shotu advanced swiftly upon Durga.

'Why are you in our garden, Duggadi? Didn't Ma warn you never to steal from us again? Get out, or I'll tell Ma. How many have you stolen already?'

After a forced glimpse into the mango knot in Durga's sari, he called out to this sister, appalled. 'Tunu, come see! She's already taken six of our mangoes!'

'What does it matter, Shotuda?' Ranu interjected. 'There are still so many trees to pick from. Let them pick their mangoes. We'll pick our own.'

'These are not *their* mangoes—these are ours! Plus if she stays here, she'll take all the best mangoes. Don't you know what she's like? No Duggadi, you get out of our garden right now. I'm not going to let you steal from our mango trees.'

Under normal circumstances, Durga would not have let things go this easily. The orchard was prime picking ground, and she had known the place as her uncle's garden all her life. But the memory of the brutal beating Shotu's mother had engineered a few days back gave her pause. Perhaps giving in was the smarter option. In an attempt to salvage her dignity, she threw down the mangoes and suddenly acted like a wonderful new idea had just occurred to her.

'Opu! Come on, we'll go to a fantastic secret garden! Huge mangoes, all of them thi-i-is big! You and I will run around and pick all of them. Thank goodness we can't stay here, eh? The other place is so much better!'

Then she walked out of the orchard, her head held high. Opu followed closely behind.

Once the Roy children were gone, Ranu turned on her cousin. 'You're really selfish, Shotuda! Why did you have to throw them out?'

Ranu had always been soft-hearted, and the helplessness in Durga's eyes had genuinely hurt her.

Opu was rather naive for his age. Once out of the orchards, he said, 'Where's this secret garden, Didi? Did you mean the Sholtekhagee mango trees in Putu's family garden?'

Durga didn't want to confess that she had had no actual garden in mind. Instead, she thought for a second.

'Uh, actually, I meant the trees around the Fort Pond. Let's go there.'

The way to the Fort Pond was a good fifteen minutes on foot, by way of narrow overgrown lanes that connected ancient, abandoned orchards. The ground there was thick with spindly shrubs and spiky undergrowth. Almost no one went to those orchards any more. One, because they were too far; and two, because they were too overgrown to be worth the effort.

The wind reached a fever pitch as brother and sister approached the Fort Pond, nearly drowning out their voices. Dark clouds had rolled in during their trek, and the sky was as dark as in the after-dusk hours. The lebbeck and elephant-apple trees cast long shadows, making the base of the mango trees as dark as night. Mangoes were falling rapidly, but with the howling winds, it was almost impossible to guess exactly where the sound of their fall was coming from. Most of them fell into the thick porcupine-flower bushes anyway, retrieval from which meant certain injury. Still, a determined Durga chased the falls and collected about eight to ten mangoes.

Just then, the skies opened up. The force of the howling winds lessened slightly, but the new pitter-patter of the first large drops made speaking to each other just as hard. Durga ran over to her brother through the spiky ground-shrubs, and pulled him under the dense foliage of an ancient tree.

Soon, the pitter-patter turned into a torrential downpour. The force of the water wrenched leaves from their nodes and washed them down to the orchard floor. A mist rose from the summer-warmed earth, infusing the air around them with the sweet smell of freshly drenched soil. The storm had dropped a little, but now it picked up again, adding its howl to the steady 'jhup, jhup!' of the rain. Had this been a normal downpour, the canopy under which the siblings stood might have been thick enough to protect them. But an easterly began to tear through the orchard just when the rain was at its heaviest, whipping aside branches and pouring through the leaves. Within minutes, brother and sister were drenched from head to foot.

In the darkness and brutal rain, it suddenly occurred to Opu that he was very far from home.

'O Didi,' he whispered, his voice shaking. 'It's raining really hard . . .'

'It's all right. Just come to me.' Durga pulled her brother close and covered him with the loose end of her sari. 'It can't rain this hard for long—you'll see. This will stop in no time. Heavy rain is a good thing, see? The Shonamukhi tree will be deserted now. We'll stop by on our way home. All right?'

Then the two of them began shouting an old couplet over the cacophony to ward off the rain.

Currants on citrus leaves, I say,
O Rainfall, go away!

A roll of thunder ripped through the howling wind and rain. For a second, blinding white light illuminated a slice of the dark orchard. A cluster of sponge gourd at the top of a tree flashed into existence, then plunged back into darkness. Opu threw his arms around his sister and clung tightly.

'There's nothing to fear,' Durga said soothingly, though her own voice was far from steady. 'Say "Ram Ram". Ram Ram Ram Ram . . . say it, it'll be fine . . . Currants on citrus leaves I say, O rainfall go away. Currants on citrus leaves, I say, O rainfall go away. Currants on citrus leaves, I say . . .'

A hard gust blew the rain at them. The loose end of Durga's sari was blown off Opu's shoulder. Shrapnel of water needled their faces and eyes, and rivulets dripped from their drenched hair. Lightning flashed across the dark sky above. Then an unearthly sound filled the air. Gurrr . . . grrr . . . grrrummm! It sounded like an enormous iron rod was being dragged across the skies.

'Didi!!!' Opu croaked.

'Nothing to fear, sweetie, come closer . . . eesh, your hair is like a drenched crow's nest!'

The sound of the downpour rose from the steady 'jhup jhup' to a roaring whoosh. The rumbling of the clouds rose to a deafening pitch. The wind shrieked around them, bending trees to its will and whipping twigs and leaves into hissing swirls. Thick, ancient branches broke with long-drawn-out murmurs and cracks. Durga had been nervous before, but now she began to worry about the orchard actually collapsing on top of them, and burying them alive. From under her arm, Opu whispered, 'O Didi . . . what if the rain never stops?'

Almost on cue, a tongue of blue flame slithered across the sky again, and another ear-splitting metallic growl filled the orchard. To the siblings' terrified ears, it sounded exactly like a mythical giant's mocking laughter.

Opu squeezed his eyes shut in terror.

Durga swallowed in fear, but she made herself look up. Was the lightning going to fall on them? No . . . all she saw in the brief blue light was a flash of sponge gourds in the tree in front of them.

Before she could be relieved, someone began dragging the iron rod across the skies for the third time . . .

Next to her, Opu was shivering from the cold and terror. Durga could hear his teeth chattering. In a final attempt at survival, she pulled him closer into her arms and began chanting in earnest.

Currants on citrus leaves, I say,
O Rainfall, go away!
Currants on citrus leaves, I say,
O Rainfall, go away . . .

Her voice was shaking with fear.

It was almost lamp-lighting hour in the Roy household. Both the rain and unexpected storm had subsided a short while ago. Shorbojoya was standing at the main doorway leading out of the Roys' compound, worry etched on her face. A few minutes later, Rajkrishno Palit's daughter came along the newly flooded lane, splashing her feet delightedly in the water.

'Have you seen Opu and Durga, Ma?' Shorbojoya asked her anxiously.

'No, Auntie, not today. Some rain though, eh? The frogs probably had to sing themselves hoarse for a shower like this, hehe.'

'They left before the storm,' Shorbojoya said, not really listening to the girl. 'Said they were going to pick mangoes. It's hours later now . . . everything's almost pitch-dark. Where can they be? And on top of all that, this awful weather . . .'

After Rajkrishno Palit's daughter had walked on, Shorbojoya slowly walked back indoors. She was just wondering how she could put together a search for her missing children, when the back doorway of the compound's boundary wall was suddenly pushed open. Durga came in first, drenched to the bone and carrying a large coconut. Her face was alight with joyous victory. Opu followed behind with the coconut's node and leaves, just as wet and just as happy. At the sight of them, Shorbojoya almost collapsed in relief.

'Oh my goodness, look at you! You two look like a bowl of soaked rice!'

She pulled Opu close. 'Your hair looks like a drenched nest—my poor baby.' Then she turned to Durga and smiled a big, happy smile. 'Where did you get that coconut? It's so large!'

Both her children shushed her urgently. 'Hush, Ma, hush! The third-eldest aunt is on her way to the garden . . . there, I think she just went past. This was lying at the foot of the tree right next to their garden fence!'

'She's definitely seen Opu. Probably saw me too,' Durga said, still exhilarated.

'We'd gone there to see if any of their Shonamukhi mangoes had fallen in the storm. Then, on our way out . . . we didn't even realize it was a coconut! Just saw a pile of leaves lying under the tree. Exactly at the foot, you know? So I told Opu, pick those up. Ma doesn't have a good broom, she can make a good one from those leaves. Then, when we picked the leaves up . . .' She looked happily down at the fruit she was cradling. 'Quite a large one, no, Ma?'

'And I picked up the leaves like *this*, and then I ran so hard!' Opu added proudly, illustrating his brave rescue with gestures.

Shorbojoya examined the coconut. 'Yes, it's quite big. Not fully ripe yet, though. Keep it near the water pots. I'll wash it before taking it to the kitchen.'

'You always say, "We don't have any coconuts", "We don't have any coconuts",' complained Opu. 'Well, we got you a coconut! Now you have to make me fried coconut puffs, Ma, I'm not letting you off this time . . .'

Shorbojoya smiled at her son. In the semi-darkness of the evening, her children's beautiful, rain-washed faces looked like the buds of newly blossomed jasmine. Wet hair framed their faces. Their lips had turned blue in the cold.

'Come here. Let me change you out of those clothes first,' she said. 'Pour clean water on your feet and climb up the veranda.'

A little later, Shorbojoya picked up her bucket and water pot, and went down the path towards the Mukhujjes' well. Before she entered their large compound, however, she heard the ringing notes of the third-eldest mistress's voice. The woman was screaming the house down in rage.

'. . . then why even bother shelling out a fistful of money to lease the garden? Those thieving beggars take home even the scraps! That girl lurks in that garden all day and all night, just so she can take even our straw and hay home. Because that's what her thief mother taught her to do! Did you think that older woman is any less vile than her children? Oh no! When the rains stopped, I thought to myself, "Well, *that* was some storm! Let me go see how the garden is doing." And what do I see? That girl! Scarpering with a whole coconut!!! Lord, I beg you, lord! Don't stand for this evil enmity! They're trying to ruin us! Ruin us! Haul them to hell, lord! If there is power in this lamp-lighting hour, then let my words come true: let those vermin never taste their stolen fruit. Let them end up under the milkwood pine before that coconut is cooked . . .'

With a jolt, Shorbojoya realized that she had turned to stone in the middle of the path. She thought she might faint. The third-eldest mistress was wishing death upon her children! What could she do? Oh, what could she *do*? The innocent joy on her children's faces filled her mind.

'Oh god!' she prayed fervently. 'Please don't let this vile woman's poison touch them!'

Her body revolted against going into the Mukhujje compound. Fear for her children's lives had nearly pinned her feet to the ground, but she made herself turn around and slowly walk back home. The narrow path from the Mukhujjes to the Roys was lined with toothbrush trees and bamboo groves. A full moon shone upon the way, and fireflies glowed within the darkness of the grove. But Shorbojoya saw nothing of the night's glory. All she could think of was a way to ward off the third-eldest mistress's curse. Could it be stopped if the coconut was returned? It should, shouldn't it? After all, the loss of the coconut had brought it on, so surely returning it would keep her children safe? Shorbojoya quickened her pace. As soon as she was home, she called out to her daughter.

'Dugga! Take that coconut back to Shotu's family. Right now.'

Her children stared at her, astonished.

'Right now?' Durga finally asked.

'Yes. Right now! Their back door is still open. Go in, hand it over, and say, "Here, this is your coconut. We found it beside your garden, but now we're returning it to you." Then come back.'

Something in her voice warned Durga not to argue.

'It's very dark outside,' she said instead, after a moment's hesitation. 'Can I take Opu along? Opu, come on. You can stand guard on the path.'

Once her children were out of the house, Shorbojoya lit the evening lamp and took it out to the holy basil plant in the courtyard. She draped the loose end of her sari around her neck in supplication, and folded her hands in front of the plant.

'God, you know they didn't pick that coconut out of spite. Don't let that woman's curse touch them! Please god, keep my children safe. They're innocent—they mean no harm. Keep them in your sight, god. Look after their welfare. Please, god. Please!'

14

PROSHONNO FROM THE village had had 'Gurumoshai' appended to his name for as long as people could remember, for he had been the only teacher in Contentment for years. His school was run from behind the tills of his little grocery shop at one end of the village. In the absence of any real ability to teach, Proshonno Gurumoshai relied chiefly on his bamboo switch. He had great faith in the power of pain, and so did the parents who deposited their children in his care.

'Just make sure that they're not blinded or lamed, and we're fine,' they assured him. With this licence, Proshonno Gurumoshai used his switch with such abandon that all too often, his students escaped blindness and lameness purely by chance—and that by a hair's breadth.

It was a cold morning in the month of Poush when Shorbojoya woke her son up with a bright cheerfulness.

'Wake up, darling! You're going to start school today. Isn't it exciting? You'll have so many new books. And a new slate! Baba will drop you off himself!'

Opu thought at first that his mother was playing a trick on him. Why would *he* have to go to school? Only really bad children—the ones who broke things, didn't listen to their parents, and fought with their siblings—were sent to school.

It was a way of locking them up for the day. So he turned over in the bed and went back to sleep.

After a few minutes, Shorbojoya popped her head back into the room. 'Get up and wash your face, Opu. Baba's waiting. I'll tie you a big bag of puffed rice, all right? You can eat it at school. Wake up, my sweet golden boy. It's getting late.'

Opu peeped from under the blanket and stuck his tongue out at his mother. She was being extra persistent in tricking him today, but he wasn't going to fall for it.

It was only when Horihor came indoors and asked what was keeping his son that Opu realized it wasn't a prank. He was actually being sent to school! Disbelief and betrayal battled for room inside his head. What had he done to deserve this?

When his mother came to give him his packet of food, he could barely hold back his tears. He was never going to trust his mother again! She was letting him go to *school*!

'I'm never coming back to you,' he choked.

Shorbojoya was busy making sure that her little boy had everything he needed. 'Aww, don't say such things, sweetheart. You'll be home before you know it,' she said. Then she raised his chin with her thumb and forefinger, and kissed him on the forehead. 'May you learn a lot. May you grow up to get a great job, and make lots of money. There's nothing to be afraid of . . . My dear, it's his first day—please tell Gurumoshai to go easy on him.'

And with that, father and son were off. After a short walk, they reached Proshonno Gurumoshai's school and shop. His father deposited him near the open end of the room and leaned in to impart his words of wisdom.

'I'll come here to pick you up when school is over, all right? In the meantime, you sit quietly and work hard. Listen to Gurumoshai. Don't be naughty.'

His fatherly duties thus fulfilled, Horihor then straightened up and walked away, as if he hadn't just abandoned his only son—his only son!—in the vast and terrifying unknown of a school. When Opu finally gathered enough courage to look up a little from his lap, his father had already disappeared around the bend in the lane.

For the first few minutes, Opu was so scared that he couldn't even make himself move. He sat on his mat, staring fixedly at the little school bundle in his lap. After a while, he took a deep breath and unpacked his slate. After a few seconds, he lifted his head a little further and stole a wary glance at his new teacher.

Said teacher was at the front of the shop, weighing out sea salt for a customer. None of his attention was on his students.

Opu relaxed a little. The boys closest to his new gurumoshai were sitting cross-legged on their carpets. They were reciting the numerical tables completely off-key, moving violently back and forth in time to their broken rhythm. Another group, sitting further away, was trying to drown them out by chanting the rules of grammar. An older boy, with a large mole on one cheek, was intently watching the dark space below Gurumoshai's raised platform seat. In one corner of the room, a boy leaned against one of the bamboo poles that was holding up the roof of the school, and stared at the empty lane leading back to the village. He was also chewing a palmyra leaf—the one, in fact, that he had been given to write on. Two of the few remaining boys were sitting quite close to Opu. They were holding a single slate between themselves, watching Gurumoshai warily and whispering to each other. Curious, Opu tried to peek at their slate.

Goodness! They were playing tic-tac-toe! Alarmed, Opu quickly looked down to his own slate and began practising his spellings.

A few moments passed in silence. The sea-salt customer took his order and left. Suddenly, just when Opu was becoming absorbed in his list of words, Gurumoshai called out, 'Fonay! What are you doing on that slate?'

The two boys playing tic-tac-toe swiftly hid the slate under their bundles. But Gurumoshai's eagle eyes were impossible to deceive. 'Shotey! Get those slates here!' he barked.

The boy with the mole swept down from the front of the shop and snatched up the incriminating slate. He practically flew down to the teacher's platform and placed it in front of Gurumoshai. Gurumoshai examined the chalk crosses and circles with obvious satisfaction.

'So this is what your slate is for, eh lads? Shotey! Haul those two up here by their ears.'

Opu suddenly giggled. The greedy eagerness on Gurumoshai's face, the alacrity with which the mole-boy swept down once again and hauled up the offenders by their ears, the terrified look on the boys' faces—it all looked like a comically exaggerated parody to him.

Gurumoshai whipped his head around. 'Who's laughing? You, new boy! What's so funny? Is this a music hall to you?'

Opu's throat instantly dried up in fear.

'Shotey, get me a brick from under the tamarind tree. Get a big strong one.'

Terror seized Opu's body. Even if he had the courage to flee, he could not have forced his legs to move. When the brick arrived, however, he saw that it was for the tic-tac-toe boys, not him. For some reason, Gurumoshai had decided to spare him. He didn't know whether it was because he was new, or because he was young. Honestly, once he realized he wouldn't be beaten that day, his relief was so overwhelming that the reasons didn't seem important.

The school mostly convened in the early evenings. The school-house was some distance away from the other houses in the village, surrounded by woods and connected to the main village road by a narrow, wooded path. The grocery shop things were up front with Gurumoshai, around or under his broad bamboo platform. The students sat in rows that began a little behind the platform. The walls of the schoolroom didn't extend much beyond the platform, so the actual sitting area for the students was an open space; there wasn't even a basic fence connecting the bamboo poles that held up the roof. The students, therefore, had a clear view of the deep woods on both sides of the school, and of the orchard at the back that Proshonno Gurumoshai had inherited from his father. The proximity to large trees kept the place mostly in shade, but if strong winds blew through the foliage, then the late afternoon sun sometimes shone through the thick branches of the pomello, velvet-apple or Peyaraphuli mango trees.

Most of the eight or ten boys who attended the school had picked up the habit of swaying back and forth on their woven mats as they rhythmically chanted their lessons. Gurumoshai sat on his perch up ahead, watching his pupils with his head tilted back to rest on the bamboo pole right behind his perch. Oil from his hair had turned that bit of bamboo yellow. Every now and then, his voice would ring out in reprimand.

'Kyabla! Why are you staring at that boy's slate?'

'Nutu, how many times do you have to go to the loo? If I see you leave your seat one more time . . .'

After dusk, Raju Roy or Dinu Palit from the village would often come over to the shop for their evening chat. They sat on the platform with Gurumoshai, and talked about a hundred different things. Opu liked this part of the school day the best. Stories were far better than lessons. When Rajib

Roy recounted tales from his time as a tobacconist, he leaned forward to catch every word. In his ever-fertile imagination, he saw himself in Rajib Roy's place: a young man deciding to start his own shop, because a business was where the goddess Lokkhi preferred to dwell. He imagined sitting behind the closed shopfront, intently chopping tobacco leaves with a small axe. He saw himself going down to the pond to fetch his own water, and cooking his own pot of fish broth and rice. He imagined being all alone in a secluded little shop on monsoon evenings, reading the Mahabharat by the golden light of a lamp, as frogs croaked by the back pond and it rained relentlessly outside. A shiver of delight ran down his spine at the very thought. When he grew up, he was definitely going to open a tobacco shop next to an isolated pond.

The best evenings at school were when Rajkrishno Shanyal Moshai visited. Shanyal Moshai lived in the adjacent neighbourhood, and Opu adored the man. He could serve even the slightest of tales in the most delectable of ways. Most of Shanyal Moshai's stories were about travelling, for he loved to travel. Indeed, he was addicted to it. Dwaraka, the Shabitri mountains, Chondrokona . . . he had found out about all sorts of famous distant places, then gone and visited them all. And unlike normal men, he never travelled alone. He took his wife and children along on his trips, spent months seeing everything there was to see, and only returned when his money ran out. For months, his neighbours would see nothing of the family, and wilderness would slowly begin to take over his land. Then suddenly, one day, two bullock carts would trundle up to the house. Shanyal Moshai would descend enthusiastically, and start directing hired hands to cut through the stinging nettles and assorted saplings that had sprung up in his absence.

And the amazing thing was that once he was back, it was impossible to tell Shanyal Moshai apart from all the other village men—even the ones who had never so much as left the neighbourhoods of their birth. He would slip into the daily village routine with such ease that new acquaintances would probably think him the epitome of the old-fashioned rural gent, comfortably growing roots where he sat. Then one morning they would come over for a chat, and see a big lock hanging from the closed front door. Shanyal Moshai would have taken off again!

When he came to visit at the school, the man would stride in with a thick walking stick in hand, his deep voice booming.

'How's business, Proshonno? I see you've spread the net quite wide. How many flies today?'

Opu would immediately stop chanting the tables and pack away his slate. As far as he was concerned, Shanyal Moshai's presence meant the end of lessons for the day. In his eagerness, he would slide forward a couple of hands' length in the direction of Shanyal Moshai's palmyra mat, his eyes shining with anticipation. And he would never be disappointed. Thanks to Shanyal Moshai's repertoire of tales, he heard amazing stories about his own village that no one else ever talked about. For example: a long time ago, Moti Hajra's brother Chondor Hajra had gone to chop down a tree at a place called Naltakuri's Stream. It was the monsoons, and the downpour had already washed away the mud from here and there. In one such washed-away place, Chondor saw the gleam of something brassy. It turned out to be the rim of a brass pot, so he dug it out and brought it home. Then he saw that the pot was filled with ancient coins! And that was how Chondor Hajra came into his life of showy luxury for a few years . . . till he blew it all away, of course. This was a true story, for Shanyal Moshai had seen the whole thing unfold with his own two eyes.

Talk sometimes turned to the distant places one had to travel to by rail. There was a hill somewhere called the Shabitri Mountains—obviously a very faraway place, since no one else had ever spoken about it. Shanyal Moshai's wife had had a very hard time climbing it. Then there was Nabhigaya, where Shanyal Moshai had performed the ritual of offering food to his ancestors' souls, then almost come to blows with the money-grabbing priest who officiated the ceremony. He'd eaten a wonderful thing called a 'pNyara' in that place . . . the sound of the name was so comical that Opu almost giggled out loud. He was definitely going to find and eat a pNyara when he grew up.

Sometimes Shanyal Moshai spoke of places and things that Opu didn't quite understand. Like a 'chikamasjid', which Shanyal Moshai had had to walk through a tamarind forest to see. Now, what sort of a thing could a chikamasjid be? Shanyal Moshai said that a lot of people used to live in it once. So Opu assumed that it must be some sort of a house, now abandoned. By the time Shanyal Moshai and his family had walked through the forest and emerged on the other side, evening had already descended. A colony of bats had suddenly burst out of the house, and had flown right over their heads. Opu could easily imagine himself in the scene: a wild tamarind jungle, no one else around, approaching a broken old house (he imagined this house to look like the western corner of Ranudi's house, which had a hidden room). Then suddenly a whooshing sound above . . . and hundreds of bats would escape into the night!

In yet another distant land, Shanyal Moshai had seen an ascetic who survived solely on alms. This fokir lived beneath the shadow of an old sacred-fig tree. If people brought him a pipe of cannabis, he would ask them what their favourite fruit was. When they told him, he would point to a random tree in the vicinity and say, 'Go, get me what you see on it.' People would walk up to the tree and be astonished. Pomegranates would be hanging from mango branches. Bananas would grow where guavas should have. Many people had seen this miracle, not just Shanyal Moshai—or so Shanyal Moshai said.

At this juncture, Raju Roy would say, 'That's just playing around with magic. You know, there was the time when my mother's brother . . .'

But Dinu Palit would talk over him. 'Since you did bring up magic, let me tell you a story. Not a story, actually; something that I saw with my own eyes. Do you know Budho, the carter from Beledanga? Rajib may not have seen him, but my brother Rajkrishno certainly knows who I'm talking about. He would wear those wood-and-rope slippers and come to Nitey blacksmith's smithy to have his plough straightened. He died in his hundredth year—and *that* was some twenty, twenty-five years back—eh, brother Rajkrishno? What I mean is, he was already an old man in our youth . . . and even then we couldn't best him in arm-wrestling. So this one evening—this was almost an age ago, I was only about nineteen or twenty then—we were returning from Chakda after bathing in the holy Gonga there. The only thing on the road was Budho carter's cart, and inside the cart there was me, my aunt, and Ononto Mukhujje's son Ram—the one that's recently moved to Khulna, don't know if you've heard. It started to get dark once we reached Kaanshona's moor. You remember the terrors of that region, my brother? Open moor on all sides, womenfolk on board . . . and it wasn't like we didn't have a fair amount of cash with us, either. I was very worried.

When the cart had reached that place—you know, where the new village has now come up—four dark-skinned, muscular fellows slid out of the darkness. They slipped behind us and caught the bamboo at the end of the cart. Two on this side, two on the other. My good sirs, I froze! But the strange thing was that none of the four men said anything. They just held on to the bamboo and kept trotting along, trotting along, trotting along. Budho, I saw, was glancing back from time to time and rapidly blinking his eyes. He caught me looking and signalled that we shouldn't speak. Finally, when we were almost at the Nawbabgonj police station—the market had just come into view up ahead—one of the men calls out, "Ostadji, forgive us! We didn't realize it was your cart." And our Budho says, "No! I'm going to take you to the station and hand you over. Let the police take you away in ropes." At that, all four men started begging and pleading. After some time, Budho said, "All right, fine. I'm letting you go . . . but just this once. Don't do this sort of thing again." The men touched Budho's feet, then disappeared back into the night. Saw the whole thing myself. That's the power of spells. They'd tried to slow down the cart by pulling on the poles, so Budho nailed their hands on to the poles! Mantras and the tantras, my friends. Powerful stuff . . .'

By the time the stories wrapped up, the ember-like sunlight of the late tropical evening would glow from beneath the curve of the horizon, and suffuse the surrounding woods. Tailorbirds would come to rest on the gently swinging moonseed vines hanging from jackfruit and cluster-fig trees. The smell of earth from the untiled schoolroom floor would mix with the smell of palmyra mats and old books, and seep into the smell of the woods that surrounded the schoolroom all day.

The image of a doe-eyed, enchanted rural boy will forever be painted on the memory of those golden-hued evenings. A little boy, with his school bundle under his arm, clothed in much-repaired pieces washed with fuller's earth, following his older sister down the unpaved lane from school to home. In that eternal bubble of time, the fading light of the sun will forever shine upon brother and sister through the canopy lining the path, and draw shifting patterns of darkness and light on the narrow avenue. The boy's hair will always remain silky-soft, combed lovingly into place by his mother. His large eyes will forever look around in awe, bespelled by the richness and beauty of the evening. This little woodland-ringed village will forever be his whole world, and in that world, his mother will always feed him with her own hands, and his sister will always dress him for school. The world outside that little circle of beloved familiarity will forever remain an ocean of the unknown. His child's mind will never grasp the idea of its vastness, nor believe that places beyond his village could one day become just as familiar as his own childhood home. How could he, when, within that charmed bubble, he will always know for certain that the land of the mundane ends just beyond his village, giving way to the lands of fairy tales and adventure? That road over there—the perfectly ordinary one that passes through the bamboo grove behind that garden—that can take one to the *other* edge of the Shellcutter's Pond, where men can find hidden treasure on fortuitous days. Days on which it rains for hours, the soil begins to fall away in clumps . . . and the mouths of buried brass pots peek out, packed with gold. The child in the bubble will spend a lifetime of delicious hours wondering how many more such pots might be hidden around his village, and where. Perhaps under a wild cluster of taro plants, the gold glinting from beneath the thick, dark green colocasia leaves?

Within this miraculous timeless circle, where innocence and wonder will forever be preserved, who really knew what truly was, and what could be?

One evening, something wonderful happened at school. None of the neighbourhood men had come by, so there were no stories. Opu was sitting in his row reading his copy of *Information for Children*, when Gurumoshai called out, 'Dictation! Slates out, everyone.'

Though he dictated without looking at a book, Opu understood immediately that the words were not gurumoshai's own. He was reciting from memory, much like Opu could recite verses from Dashu Roy's *Book of Ballads*. Nonetheless, he was struck by the majesty of the words. He didn't think he would ever hear so many beautiful, majestic words spoken at the same time. Many of them were formal and unfamiliar, so he didn't fully understand the meaning of the piece. But the interweaving of the familiar and unfamiliar, the rise and fall of the rhythmic recitation, the sudden clarity of a few easier words—all of it, together, painted an enchanting picture of unequal beauty for him, draped in mists of incomprehension and mystery.

Years later, when he was older, he found the recited passage in one of his textbooks:

> This, then, is that mountain of cascading waterfalls, centred within the realms of human habitation. Its peaks are adorned with the permanent indigo of their immutable union with multitudes of mistral-surfing, mist-accruing clouds that traverse the paths of the sky. The elevation of the plateau-land, beneath a densely knitted verdant marquee of the forest and woodlands, is temperate, restoring, and exquisite. At the foothills,

the joyous waters of the Godabori expand its ripples and crests . . .

And so on. This passage confirmed something that he always knew, but couldn't quite put into words; he knew that the unknown existed, just beyond the reach of the everyday world. That evening, two years ago, when he had gone out with his father for a blue jay sighting—that was the day he had truly discovered the glory of the unknown. He remembered the thrill in being surrounded by unknown plants and unknown birds, and also the thrill of seeing a schoolbook creature hop out of a perfectly ordinary bush. He remembered staring at the narrow path that weaved through those brightly coloured, unknown flowers. Where else could that road have led to, if not further into the land of mysteries?

His father, of course, had tried to convince him that the road was perfectly ordinary. 'That road leads to the Shonadanga moors, Khoka,' he had said. 'You can take it to go to the Shonadanga moors, then to Madhobpur, then to Doshghora . . . then right up to the ferry wharf of the Dhobolchiti river.'

He knew the truth, though. He knew that the road went far beyond the Dhobolchiti wharf. Grown-ups couldn't be expected to understand, but roads like that went right up to the land of the Ramayan and the Mahabharat—a land of adventures and fairy tales that he thought of when he stared at the top of the peepul tree near his home.

Why else would he think of that road today, while Gurumoshai was reciting a description of this hidden, wonderful place? It was because that road—the one that led to the cloud-topped mountain with the cascading waterfalls—was another such road that secretly led from the mundane lands to the magical. In these quiet rural evenings, perfumed by the soothing aroma of wildflowers, the enchantment of that magical unknown often descended upon him. How far could those blue peaks be, he wondered, as he walked down the woodland path latticed in darkness and light.

Well, it didn't matter how far. He was going to find them, and visit them when he was older.

Had he confided his plans to a grown-up, they might have pointed out that he was conflating several separate universes in his mind. For instance, none of the things that his gurumoshai dictated today—the cane-lined shores, the dancing waters of the Godabori, the verdant valley or the indigo-peaked mountain range of unrivalled beauty—were part of any land actually described by either Balmiki or Bhobobhuti, and so they couldn't exist with either the Ramayan or the Mahabharat. But in the innocent imagination of that young village boy, the connection was unquestionably real, undeniably familiar. Lands whose existence was a geographical impossibility in the real world had been given the seat of eternal truth in the heart and mind of a trusting child.

15

DURGA HAD BEEN roaming the village looking for her brother. She had gone to every place he could think of, but Opu was nowhere to be found. Her search had brought her to Awnnoda Roy's house, so she thought, 'Let me stop by and meet Auntie.'

As she stepped through the main gateway, however, she realized that she was about to walk into a domestic dispute. So instead of announcing her presence, she stood just inside the door and listened. In the absence of his wife, Awnnoda Roy's household was run by his widowed sister, Shokhi Thakrun. Shokhi Thakrun was standing in the outer veranda, screaming her wrath down upon her niece-in-law, Awnnoda Roy's son's wife.

'I'll touch that one's feet, I tell you! I'm that impressed! Seen hundreds of women, never one as desperate as her. When you know your husband can pulp your bones, shouldn't you at least *try* to keep him happy? Oh no, not that one! She'll throw it in his face! And then there's my nephew. That poor man . . . honestly. For three days now, he's been begging. "Put the seeds out in the sun, darling. Darling, put the seeds out in the sun." But does she listen? Oh no! In one ear and out the other! Doesn't even fear a husband like that! Wives in our time husked paddy and did the housework. Not this one! She's too busy making herself up and sitting pretty, like she's too good for housework. Painted princess! That's what we've got in our household, a painted princess!'

Here, Shokhi Thakrun began to pull faces, and demonstrated how she thought 'painted princesses' might primp in front of the mirror.

So far, her niece-in-law had been weeping quietly in the inner courtyard. She had several blooming bruises on her arms and back, and was obviously still in pain. At the last jab, however, she finally spoke up, though in a sniffling, nasal whine.

'When do I sit like a painted princess? I roasted five kilos of moog daal just yesterday. Sat down after lunch, no sleep, no rest, and when the five o'clock train went past I was still baking in the heat! Roasted it, pounded it—it was late night when I finally finished. The pins and needles from it haven't died yet, all night I felt feverish—and now this beating first thing in the morning. Why? Do I sit and eat off someone else's labour?'

Awnnoda Roy's son Gokul had just come home with a young bamboo in one hand and a hoe in the other. Hearing the last of his wife's words, he lost his temper again.

'Still carrying on, are you?' he roared. 'Oh, you're really asking for it now! How many times did I tell you to put the paddy seeds in the sun? Good sowable seeds, this wet weather—if those seeds sprout right now, then which one of your precious fathers will feed us for the rest of the year? Huh?'

At this, his damp wife suddenly reared back in fury. 'Don't you bring my father into this! What has my father done to you that you're always taking his name?'

Before the words were properly out of her mouth, Gokul threw down the bamboo and jumped up on the inner veranda with the hoe raised. 'It's you or me today, woman!' he screamed. 'I'll beat that family loyalty out of you if it's the last thing I do . . .'

His wife screamed. Durga screamed. A host of people surreptitiously watching from within the house screamed. Shokhi Thakrun began shouting her opinion at everyone. In the blink of an eye, everyone who had been inside the house had run out to the inner courtyard.

The family's field hand had quietly been watching things from the outer courtyard so far. Fearing murder, he now jumped up on to the outer veranda, ran indoors to the inner courtyard, and wrenched the hoe out of Gokul's fist. At that point, Gokul had almost reached his wife, who had backed herself into the wall, arms raised against a strike. Her eyes were pools of terror.

The field hand held the hoe away in one hand, and with the other pulled on Gokul's arm. 'Da Thakur, what are you doing? Come away. Come outside now.'

Gokul was almost thirty-six, but chronic malaria had left him rather weak. He knew that struggling against the muscular field hand would only emphasize his frailty to the audience. So he allowed himself to be led out of the house, raging.

'A whole basket of paddy seeds, and she just won't listen!' he ranted to the field hand. 'Now if it sprouts in this wet weather, what are we going to sow in the field this season?'

The field hand made noises of acquiescence as he guided Gokul away from the house. Durga, too, left quietly. She was relieved that Uncle Gokul had been stopped, but she also realized that this wasn't the time to stop by for a visit.

On her way home, she saw a strange new man. He had set up an open-air brazier under the Indian plum tree near Panchu Barujje's house. Several of the neighbours' broken utensils were piled in small heaps around him. The man was shortish, with a weather-beaten, dried-out look. He could have been thirty-three, or he could have been fifty-three. It was hard to tell. A three-tiered necklace of dried basil seeds was looped around his neck. There was an old slicing scar on his right cheek. Veins stood out on his arms like ropes, and a halfway-clean dhuti was all he wore. Several of the neighbourhood children had gathered around to watch him work. Durga went and joined them. The man looked up at her.

'What do you want, Khuki?' he asked.

'Nothing,' said Durga. 'I'm only watching.'

Later, when she went home, she told her mother about the beating at Awnnoda Roy's house. Shorbojoya was immediately sympathetic.

'Gokul is no better than a brutish, obstinate farmhand. That wife of his will spend the rest of her life being knocked about, poor girl.'

'Auntie really loves me,' Durga said. 'Whenever something nice is made at their place, she keeps a little aside for me. It hurt to watch her cry, Ma. And then Grandmother Shokhi began shouting at her, like it was her fault . . .'

For the next three or four days, Durga went regularly to see the brazier-man at work. The man asked her her name, her father's name, the details of their household. Then he said, 'Don't you have things to repair, Khuki? Why don't you get them?'

So Durga came home and repeated the offer to Shorbojoya. 'Ma, there's a really nice man doing repairs under the plum tree in the next neighbourhood. Can I take our broken pots and pans to him?'

The man said his name was Peetom. He called himself a coppersmith, and was very clearly a devotee of both Krishna and Radha. When putting lit charcoal in front of the bellows, he would call out, 'Victory to Radha . . . Radhe Gobindo!'

Several of the neighbourhood men would gather around his brazier in the morning, chatting and watching him work. The man would voluntarily light their bowls of tobacco and put them in front of their hookahs, face crinkled with a deferential grin. 'Oblige me, Baba Thakurs,' he would say. 'May we all find a place at the feet of Radharani . . . but yes, the coconuts were a total loss this year. This past Joishtho, I thought, good warm weather, let's put the plants in and see what happens. Six times four—that's how many I bought. But the frogs, Baba Thakur. Ruined all my saplings. Dug them out by the main root. No saving any of them. Turned my coins to mud . . .'

Mukhujje Moshai had been sitting under the tree all morning, chatting constantly with the man in the hopes of getting a pot repaired for free. 'How's the malaria in those parts?' he asked.

'Oh, brimming, Baba Thakur, brimming. Everyone is down with it. Roasting our bones and feasting on it, this malaria . . . here's your pot, Baba Thakur. Good as new now. That'll be six paise.'

'Hah, "six paise"!' said Mukhujje Moshai, as if it was a joke. 'You just repaired a little thing for a brahmon. In the month of Kartik, no less. Your blessings will be far beyond a mere six paise. Well, I'll be seeing you around.'

As he began to rise, Peetom's hand flashed out and grasped the pot by its rim. 'No, Baba Thakur, forgive me,' he said with his melting-in-subservience smile. 'I can't do it for free. Haven't had the first sale of the morning yet. I'll just keep the pot here with me. You go home and send the six paise whenever convenient.'

Shorbojoya thought about her daughter's proposal. 'These people sometimes take broken old utensils and give new ones in exchange,' she said, after some time. 'Ask this man if he'll do that, will you?'

Oh, Peetom absolutely would. So Durga made several trips from the plum tree to her home and back, carrying all their old pots, bowls, spout-pots and utensils to him. She began spending more than half of each day underneath the tree, watching the lighting of the charcoal by the bellows, and the soldering of tin. Peetom had promised to beat a piece of brass into a ring for her. He had also assured her that her family wouldn't have to pay for any repairs—for them, he'd do it for free. When Durga relayed this to Shorbojoya, Shorbojoya was flooded with goodwill for the coppersmith.

'Oh, such a nice man! This coming Wednesday is Opu's birthday—ask him over for lunch, Dugga. We'll only have the usual rice and daal, but it'll still be a brahmon's leftovers. He'll be honoured.'

On Wednesday morning, Durga went to the plum tree to convey the invitation, but the place beneath the plum tree was empty. She asked the people sitting about, and was told that the coppersmith had packed up his brazier and bellows the previous evening, and had left the village around lamp-lighting hour, just when oil lamps were being lit in the surrounding homes. Confused, Durga went around the village in a wider circle, asking everyone if they had seen him that morning, or if they could tell her where he had gone. No one seemed to know anything.

Fear made Durga's mouth run dry. What was she going to tell her mother? More than half their utensils had been left under the plum-tree smithy! She spent the day looking high and low for any trace of the man. Peetom had once mentioned that his main shop and smithy was in Jhikorhati. The reason they didn't immediately get new things for old was because the new things were kept at this shop, and Peetom had to send word to his brother when he needed them. In fact, just a couple of days ago Peetom had assured Durga that his brother was on his way to Contentment, bringing the Roys' new utensils with him. So much for all that! During her search, Durga discovered that they were the only family that had trusted Peetom enough to leave their things with him. Not a single other family had lost so much as a piece of the family brass.

When she came home at the end of the day, she was on the brink of tears. Shorbojoya was amazed to hear about the man's perfidy.

'What, just left? Goodness! I've never heard of such a thing! Go tell your older uncle next door, see if he can do anything.'

But nothing could be done. Horihor was away from home when this happened, trying to drum up income on foreign shores. By the time he returned, it was already too late. Still, Jhikorhati was visited, and Peetom searched for. But the locals hadn't seen a man of his description, and he most certainly did not have a shop in that market.

Time passed. Kartik turned to Bhadro. Summer was on its way out, and autumn was in the air. One evening, just as Opu was getting ready to leave the house, his mother called out to him. 'Where are you going, Opu? I'm roasting rice and chickpeas. Don't you go now . . . have your food first.'

Opu pretended he hadn't heard. He knew that his mother had sat down this early in the evening to roast rice and chickpeas because he loved them . . . but what could he do? The boys must be running wild in Neelu's house by now! He needed to be there! So he took a deep breath to collect his courage, and ran straight out of the house. Behind him, he heard his mother calling, 'Why's the boy like this? Opuuu! I rushed back from the pond to make this for you . . . don't you like it fresh and hot? O Opuuu!'

Opu stopped running only after he had reached Neelu's house. But alas, despite running out on his snack, he was too late. The evening's games had just been concluded, and boys were breaking off into small groups and leaving. Seeing his disappointment, Neelu said, 'Want to go see the baby birds in the southern fields, Opu?'

Opu did, so the two of them set out together. The southern fields were about a mile from the village. The paved east-west road from Nawbabgonj cut straight across the local paddy fields, splitting the land into two halves. Opu had never come this far from home before. Once the last familiar sight disappeared behind them, he began to worry. What was this vast, unknown land that Neelu had brought him to?

'Let's go home, Neeluda,' he said, after only a short walk through the middle of the fields. 'It'll be lamp-lighting hour soon—Ma will scold me. And I can't walk past the velvet-apple tree on my own after dark . . .'

But Neelu had lost his way. After several attempts at finding the road, the two finally found a narrow path that went past someone's large mango orchard. Tired and a little scared, they took the path. While darkness was still some time away, storm clouds were gathering overhead. Suddenly, Neelu stopped walking and grasped Opu's shoulder. 'Brother Opu, look!'

Opu looked around, a bit startled. But he didn't see anything to be scared of. 'What is it, Neeluda?' he asked.

Then he followed Neelu's eyes, and saw that their path led straight to someone's courtyard. It had a small thatched hut in a corner, and a hog-plum tree.

'It's Aturi Daini's house!' Neelu whispered, his voice shaking.

Aturi Daini—the Birthing-room Witch? Oh no! What made them come down this path in this near-darkness hour? Aturi Daini stole the life out of boys who came to steal her hog-plums! Everyone knew about that fisherman's boy, whose life she had wrapped in a taro leaf and thrown into the pond! When a fish swam up and swallowed the leaf, the poor boy's taste for hog-plums had been rather permanently cured. And that wasn't all. His sister had also told him that the witch could suck the lifeblood out of little boys simply by looking at them! The poor boy wouldn't even know that anything had happened; he'd go home, have his dinner, and go to sleep. And then he'd never wake up. Even under the comfort of their own blankets, inside the safety of their own home, these stories had terrified Opu. 'Don't let's tell these stories at night, Didi!' he had begged his sister. 'Tell me the one about the princess with the cloud-coloured hair!'

And now here he was, standing just a few feet away from the witch's actual home. And, and . . . there was someone over there, standing just behind the split bamboo fence, watching them! No, not them. She was watching *him*. Opu's entire body froze in terror.

The person came out of the bamboo gate. It was the daini herself. Her eyebrows were drawn together, and her hollow-cheeked face leaned forward, as if to see him better. Opu tried lifting a foot, and realized he couldn't. For some reason, Aturi Daini was furious with him. She had spelled him, and was now advancing upon him with deliberate steps. In a minute his life would be wrapped up in a taro leaf and fed to the fishes.

This was all his fault. He had left behind food that had been made in his name. His mother had returned early to make him his favourite snack, and he had pretended not to hear her calls. This was his karma. He looked helplessly around for help, knowing there was none. In desperation, he began pleading with the advancing witch. 'I don't know anything, Old Auntie! I promise I'll never do it again. Let me go this time, I beg you. I'll never come this way again, promise! Let me go, Old Auntie . . . just this once . . .'

Behind him, Neelu had started sobbing. But Opu's throat was so constricted in terror that he couldn't even cry.

The witch merely bared her teeth at them in a terrifying grin. 'My poor babies . . . why are you crying?' she crooned. 'What has scared you, Baba?'

When the boys remained frozen, the baffled old woman tried to reassure them with humour. 'It's not like I'm going to steal you two away, Baba. Do you want to come in and rest for a while? I have salted mangoes—let me give you some.'

Opu's terror doubled. The witch was offering bait! How could he get out of this?

A little worried by the frozen silence, the old woman advanced towards them a further few steps. 'There's nothing to fear here, Baba,' she tried again. 'I won't do a thing to you. Why are you so scared of me?'

This is it, thought Opu. It's all over now. This is what I get for not listening to my mother. The witch will snatch away my life and put it in a taro leaf. With every passing second, he expected the smiling human face in front of him to morph into a grotesque monster, and laugh a booming, blood-curdling laugh. Just like the fake queen in *The Monster-Queen's Tale*! And yet he couldn't move. This is how pythons hypnotize their prey, he remembered. They caught their eyes and mesmerized them. The little fawns could see them slithering forward, but they couldn't run away. They stood, like he was standing, waiting for an inevitable, horrible fate.

'My mother will cry,' he whispered, his lips moving with difficulty. 'I've never stolen your hog-plums . . . my mother will cry, Old Auntie, let me go . . .'

Terror had almost turned him blue. He could no longer see clearly. The trees, the field, the house behind the witch, Neelu . . . everything had begun to dissolve together into a shimmering, blurry mist. The only real thing was himself, a pair of cruelty-laden witch eyes . . . and the distant voice of his mother, calling him to come eat his roasted rice.

Suddenly, a burst of desperate survivalism coursed through him. Breaking the enchantment with a half-voiced scream, he threw himself off the path and into the field. Then he ran blindly through a thicket of leadwort and glory bower, followed closely by an equally terrified Neelu.

The old woman stared after the pair in amazement. For the life of her, she couldn't work out why two young boys would act so strangely. 'Didn't try to grab them, didn't try to hit them . . . what on earth were they spooked by? Whose child was that?' she wondered.

When Opu reached home, the lamp-lighting hour was already past. Shorbojoya was sitting in the kitchen, lighting the oven to heat oil for palmyra puffs. Durga was sitting in front of her, scraping pulp and squeezing juice from a palmyra fruit.

Seeing her son, Shorbojoya said, 'And where were you all day? Left when it was barely evening, and now you come back . . . don't you ever feel hungry or thirsty?'

His mother's words of concern created a riot of emotions inside Opu. This was the woman whose food he had scorned! Oh, how could he? Several different things scrambled to pour out of him in such a rush, that he ended up saying nothing at all. The only words he could squeeze out were the most mundane: 'Do I have to change my clothes before I eat, Ma? This dhuti is from the morning . . .'

After he was changed and washed, he noticed, with some amazement, that his mother wasn't making any move towards giving him his roasted rice. Instead, she sat happily in front of the oven, testing the thickness of the palmyra batter.

'Let me fry a few at this thickness,' she said to her daughter. 'If it comes out too thin, you can get a bit of rice flour from under the plank bed.' Then, turning to her son, she said, 'Wait, Opu. I'll give you a big bowl of puffs straight off the wok. Won't that be nice?'

Opu finally managed to find his voice. 'Why the puffs, Ma? What happened to the roasted rice?'

'Well, you didn't want the roasted rice, did you? It went cold, so I gave it to Durga. Now, just give me a second. I'll fry a batch up—hot and fresh, just for you.'

The house of cards that Opu had been building in his mind all evening came tumbling down. Throughout his terrifying ordeal, he had been thinking how upset he'd made his mother by leaving home without eating the special meal she had made for him. He had imagined her anxiety and restlessness, waiting for him to come home so she could affectionately feed him his roasted rice and chickpeas. He imagined her thinking things like, 'Oh, my poor son! I came back from the pond as quick as I could, but he still left without eating. I'm going to give him his food the moment he comes back!'

But clearly, his mother had wasted no time thinking about him at all! She had fed *his* special meal to Didi at the first opportunity. Then they had moved on together to the next thing they wanted to do—never mind how Opu felt about his lost meal! Silly him, wasting an evening thinking that his mother actually cared about him!

Meanwhile, Durga was saying, 'Fry them up quickly, Ma. It looks like rain. You know the roof won't hold if it starts pouring. It'll end up like the other day.'

The rain clouds were indeed gathering. The last light of dusk was wiped from the top of the bamboo grove. A cool, moist breeze began to filter through the village, like a forerunner to a storm. Durga felt excitement begin to course through her. Every time black clouds blanketed the sky, she felt like an epic storm was coming—a downpour to uproot civilizations and bring forth chaos. It never happened, but thinking about it still gave her a delicious shiver of fear. She kept getting up to go peek at the sky from under their thatched roof, tasting her anticipation at the sight of the clouds.

Shorbojoya finished frying the first few puffs. 'Give this to him in that bowl, Dugga,' she instructed her daughter. 'He must be hungry. Nothing has passed the poor boy's lips all evening.'

This was what finally undid Opu. He had held on in the face of his mother's callousness, but this show of affection broke his determination to suffer her cruelty in silence. Taking the bowl from his sister, he flung it across the kitchen.

'I'll never eat your puffs . . . never!' he cried. 'Go away!'

Astonished, Shorbojoya could only stare. Only she knew how she kept the household together, how many insults she swallowed regularly to keep putting meals in front of her children when there was practically nothing left to eat. And here was her wretched son, ruining not one, but two such meals in a single day! She turned to him, her anger and grief boiling over. 'What is wrong with you today? Have you completely lost your mind? Throwing away good food, made especially for you? Ashes, that's what's written in your fate this evening! Eat that, hot off the oven!'

Opu was appalled. He had never heard anything so cruel from his mother. He was hoping his mother would apologize, say a few words of sympathy and coax him into eating. Instead, this heartlessness! He shot to his feet.

'Am I not allowed to feel even slightly bad that I couldn't eat my roasted rice, Ma? Do you think I have not been thinking about it all evening? I'm never coming back to your house, you see if I do! Why should I eat ashes? I won't eat ashes. You want me to eat ashes so Didi gets all the good food, don't you? I'm never coming back to your house again! Never!'

Then, with the same blind desperation that had carried him out of Aturi Daini's house, he took off for the back door, his mind a raging bubble of insult and injury. In a second, he had disappeared into the darkness.

The unexpected dramatics of the evening had completely blindsided Durga. She found her brother's trembling lips and absurd outburst hilarious. Once Opu shot out of the house, she almost rolled on the kitchen floor, laughing. 'Hehehe, that Opu . . . he's our little mad boy, Ma! Did you hear what he said?' Then she mimicked her brother's emotionally charged speech: '"I couldn't eat my roasted rice"—hehe, hehehe—"doesn't that hurt my feelings?" A complete silly goose, Ma! O Opuuuu . . . don't go! It's going to rain! OPU-U-U-U!'

Opu had run out of the back door and followed the path along it straight into the bamboo grove. It was now properly night, and the cloud cover had made the darkness within the grove impenetrable. He could feel the shrubs around his feet and hear the scurrying noise of unseen night creatures. Under normal circumstances, he wouldn't even have thought about coming here this late in the day. But now he stood in the darkness, muttering, 'Never going back. Nevv-vuh going back!' After the first rush of excitement was over, however, fear began to creep in. He raised his eyes towards the Sholtekhagee mango tree a little ahead, and shivered. What if a ghost came down and took him straight to the top?

Well, it would serve his mother right, for one. How she would cry! She would wail and say, 'Why did I have to tell my baby to eat ashes? That's why he went out of the house in the dark, with the clouds on his head. And then, and then . . . he never came back!'

Imagining his mother's remorseful grief gave Opu a few minutes of glowing, vengeful satisfaction. But when that glow faded, he felt the need to slowly feel his way back towards the familiar path along their boundary wall. The forest was stirring, and he was suddenly very aware of every single flutter. The prospect of dying at the hands of a ghost was no longer quite as appealing. A sudden sound from around the mango tree made him shudder. He wished he could just walk back into the house, but that would mean admitting defeat. He had more self-respect than that! After the way he left, there was no way he could go back home without someone finding him first, and cajoling him to return.

Just then, his sister's and mother's voices rang out from Ranu Didi's back garden. They were calling for him. Now his sister was coming out of their back door. Oh thank goodness—she was going to take the bamboo grove path home! Opu ran and stood right next to their back door, where he couldn't be missed.

Durga saw her brother when she was almost at the door, about to go in.

'Ma! He's hiding here!' she shouted in relief. 'You naughty boy! Hiding here all quiet-like, while the two of us go all over the neighbourhood looking for you!'

Then mother and daughter cradled him between them, and took him home.

16

WHEN IT WAS time for him to travel again, Horihor said, 'Let me take the boy along. He barely gets to eat anything at home. If he travels with me, then perhaps a little milk here, a little ghee there . . . his body may heal a little.'

Opu had never left the village. Not once, since the day he was born. The canopy of the old medlar, the Goswamis' garden, the large elephant-apple tree, the banks of the river that curved along the village . . . maybe, on an adventurous day, the sight of the cobblestoned road that led to Nawbabgonj—these were the borders of his world. The idea of distance enchanted him, but he had never had a taste of it. The closest he had come to leaving the village was when his mother took him down to the river, during the summer months of Boishakh and Joishtho. The two of them would stand on the bathing steps to enjoy the late afternoon breeze. Fields of summer hay would lie on the other side of the river like a bright, unending carpet. The acacia trees dotting the fields would be heavy with blossoms, yellow against the bright blue sky. Grazing cows would move slowly across the landscape, raising their heads every now and then to low in the quiet afternoon air. A wilderness of moonseed vine would hang from the young night jasmine tree, making it look positively ancient from a distance.

As dusk approached, the cowherds would begin to herd their charges towards the river for a wash and a drink. Okrur Majhi's small fishing boat would appear around the bend, on its way to lay his two-pole fishing trap for the night. Beyond the bustle, the flowering shrubs that dotted the hay fields would gently undulate in the cool evening breeze. Opu would look past it all and focus on the far point where the fields met the blue sky. From his bank of the river, the emerald of the distant woods would look like a smear of colour above the lighter green of the field, blending into the sky's darkening blue. He would stare at the majesty of the distant vastness and think . . . well, he couldn't quite express what he thought, for he didn't have a name for the sense of thrill and wonder that the view of the horizon filled him with. But on the days that his sister came along with them, he would grasp her arm and eagerly point the majestic view out to her.

'Didi, Didi—look! Do you see? Behind that tree?'

'Yes?'

'Isn't it so far away?'

Durga would grin affectionately at her little brother. 'You want me to see that it's far away? That's what you're excited about? Opu, you're one nutty boy.'

That had been his life so far. Today, he was finally about to take his first step towards that magical faraway. Anticipation had kept him up for several nights in a row. Every single morning, he counted the days to see how many were left till they began their journey. That day of discovery was finally here.

Just beyond the boundary of Contentment, the main village road took a turn to the right, leaving the cobblestoned road to Nawbabgonj behind. A little ahead, it merged with the mud road leading to Asharu-Durgapur.

The moment father and son stepped on to the mud road, Opu said, 'Baba? Where's the road that goes to the railroad?'

'It's going to be on our way,' said Horihor. 'We'll cross it soon. Now keep pace.'

What? The railroad was going to be *on their way*?

Once, a little while back, their red cow had lost its calf. They had searched the whole village for two or three days, but the calf hadn't been found. So he and his sister had been sent to the southern fields to look for it. It was autumn, in the month of Poush. Stalks of ripe black gram had covered those fields. As they looked for the calf, he and his sister kept dipping down to pick the fruit from the stalks and pop it in their mouths. On the raised cobblestoned road further ahead, bullock carts had been trundling along, ferrying loads of date-palm jaggery to the market at Asharu.

He hadn't noticed it at first, but his sister had stood for a while, staring at the misty horizon on the other side of the cobblestoned road. Suddenly, she had said, 'Opu . . . want to do something? Want to go see the railroad?'

The proposal had taken Opu by surprise. 'Railroad? But that's really far, Didi. Can we go that far?'

'It's not that far! We can easily go. It's supposed to be just on the other side of the cobblestoned road . . . right?'

'Umm . . . if it's that close, shouldn't we be able to see it? Maybe if we climb on the cobblestoned road . . . Didi, let's do that first. We can easily climb on that road. Then we'll see.'

The two of them had spent several minutes standing on the cobblestoned road, looking around for signs of the railroad. Finally, his sister had said, 'Yes . . . I think maybe it *is* too far . . . no? I suppose we won't be seeing the railroad today.'

Opu had agreed. 'If we can't see it, it is too far. If we go, we mayn't even make it back tonight. We should just go home.'

But their eyes had lingered on the horizon. A longing for far-off lands, coupled with a desire to witness the near-mythical railroads, was strong in both hearts. Finally, in a tone of desperation, his sister had said, 'Opu . . . let's just go. How far can it be? If we go right now, we'll be back before afternoon. That way we can also see the afternoon train! We can tell Ma that we were looking for the calf and forgot the time.'

The decision thus made, brother and sister had looked around carefully for inconvenient witnesses. Once certain that no one was watching them, they had clambered down the other side of the cobblestoned street, then flown like the wind across the fields on the other side. Past the green hay, past the marshlands—straight south! The wind had whooshed past their ears. As they had raced ahead, the red cobblestoned road to Nawbabgonj grew smaller and smaller against the horizon behind them . . . and then fell away from view completely. Alone in a sea of green, brother and sister had run, run, run! Past the sapling field, past the travellers' free watering-house, past the Pond of the Sisters-in-Law: run, run, run! Everything familiar was left behind. Only when a small, unknown lake broke into the surrounding greenness ahead of them had his sister finally stopped to catch her breath.

'If Ma ever comes to know, she's going to skin us alive,' she had said, grinning in delight.

Opu had grinned back, but it was tinged with a touch of fear.

A big, deep breath, and then they were off again. Run, run, *run*!

That had been the first time in either of their lives that they had been beyond familiar boundaries, beyond watchful eyes and enforced limits. Exhilaration had coursed through their bodies. The joy of pure freedom, never before tasted, had made their young blood sing. They had been in no state to stop and ask for directions, in no state to stop and consider the consequences of running wildly into the unknown. So when those consequences finally arrived, they had been both unexpected and deeply unpleasant.

A little ahead of the small lake had been a much larger lake. It had loomed right in front of them, filled with water grass and shola-pith. And then . . . then his sister had realized that she had lost her way. In their glorious run of freedom through the fields, they had seen no villages to mark the way: only paddy fields, marshland and thickets of cane. Walking through the latter two proved impossible; the canes were too thickly clustered to break into, and the marsh kept trying to swallow their feet. Which left the fields. Meanwhile, the afternoon sun had grown so fierce that even in the autumn chill, he and his sister had been drenched in sweat. As they had walked about, trying to work out which way to go, his sister's sari kept catching bushes of low-lying thorns and ripping open in different places. He himself had had to pull thorns out of his feet twice or thrice. In the end, finding their way to the railroad had become the least of their worries. Tired and scared, they had begun to believe that they were too lost to even find their way home. When they had finally found the cobblestoned road again—after much treading of marshy water and trudging through deserted paddy fields—the golden afternoon had already sunk into the deep reds of early evening. When they reached home, his sister had

had to spin baskets upon baskets of lies to save both their hides from the wrath of their mother.

Today, that very railroad was simply going to pop up along the way? He wouldn't have to run, wouldn't have to lose his way, wouldn't have to lie to avoid a beating? He could barely trust such unbelievable luck!

After walking together for a little while, a raised road came into view. It cut across the paddy fields, just like the road to Nawbabgonj did. A small pile of bright red cobbles were heaped on the side of this raised road. Whitish iron poles lined it, linked to each other with ropes. The poles bracketed the raised road on both sides for as far as he could see. His father said, 'Look, Khoka, that's the railroad.'

That was the railroad???

Opu raced past his father, past the open gateway, and scrambled straight on to the road. He turned to look up and down the road several times, awed. A hundred questions popped into his head at the same time. Why were there two iron bars on the ground? Did railways carriages slide along on those bars? Why? Why wouldn't they go on the road, like carts? Wouldn't their wheels slip off the bars? Why not? They looked slippery! And those shiny ropes . . . are those 'wires'? Why could he hear a 'Whoooosh!', 'Whoooosh!' from inside the wires? Was this what's called 'news from the wires'? Goodness! What a noise! Who's sending the news? How does news travel through wires? Wait . . . where's the 'station'? Is it on that side? Or on that side?

He turned to his father and said, 'Baba, when's the train? I'll see the train and then go.'

'See the train and then go? What? No no, we need to hurry. The train is going to come in the afternoon—that's a good two hours from now.'

'I don't mind, Baba. I'm going to see the train!'

'And sit under this sun for two hours? No, no, no! Come on, come on—we have a long way to go.'

'But I've never seen a train, Baba! I'm not going till I see this one, yes. Two hours is not long . . .'

'Now, Khoka. Don't be that way. This is why I never want to bring you out with me. I'll show you the train on our way back, all right? Now let's go.'

Defeated, Opu followed his father down the other side of the railway road, barely holding back bitter tears.

~

Imagine you are walking away from everything you know.

The way ahead is unknown, and you know nothing of the things your eyes might see. You are young and eager, and your eyes are alight with a world-swallowing hunger. They devour the newness around you with amazement and delight.

At such times, you should feel no less than the famous explorers who charted new lands. For it isn't necessary to visit actual undiscovered terrains to savour the joy of discovering the unknown. If I take my first steps on a road I've never been on before, if I bathe in a river I've never before dipped my toes in, if my sun-warmed body is cooled by the soothing breeze of a village I have never before visited—then it does not matter to me if other people have visited these places before me. In the world within my head, every place I have not yet visited is an undiscovered land. When I visit one, I 'discover' it—with my mind, my heart, and with all of my senses. I taste of its newness, and I am elated.

~

Aamdob. Such a lovely name! It was a little village of small farmers. As they passed, they saw the women sitting in their outer courtyards, chopping up hay, tying goats to the trees, and feeding rice to the hens. Men were drying jute and chopping bamboo to size. Before they knew it, they had crossed Aamdob's last little home, and were walking through the field beyond. On the other side of the road was a large lake, glistening in the sun. Wild paddy grew around it. Every few minutes, a shock of white arced gracefully out of the green and into the blue—the cluster of paddy was dense enough to hide the storks pecking within. Wild swathes of water lilies grew all over the lake, making it difficult to see the water underneath.

Father and son reached Kholsheberia. Vast fields of autumnal paddy bordered the lake outside the village, only a few days away from golden ripeness. The sky, freshly cleansed by the rains, was the striking azure of late autumn. Sunlight fractured on the edges of bright white clouds, creating a maze of shimmering colours over their heads. Opu stared at the sky as he walked, transfixed. Through the colours he could see a castle of clouds, an ocean of clouds . . . an entire dreamland made of light and clouds. He had never seen a sky this vast, not from within the confines of his village. The distant lands that he had always dreamt of—the ones that always lay just beyond the horizon—were finally unveiling their mysteries to the eager eight-year-old.

It took them quite a while to finish their journey.

'Why do you stare at everything?' his father admonished. 'What is so enchanting about every single thing you see? Walk quickly!'

It was past the lamp-lighting hour when they reached the home of Horihor's disciple, Lokkhon Mohajon. Lokkhon

Mohajon was quite a rich farmer, and generally well-off in terms of domestic plenty. He welcomed them, with considerable pomp and respect, into a small house on the outer edge of his large domestic compound.

The next morning, Lokkhon Mohajon's younger brother's wife noticed a strange young boy on their compound. She had come down to the family pond to take a bath. Just as she was stepping into the water, she noticed the boy in the banana grove beside the pond. He was striding up and down amongst the plants, brandishing a short length of bamboo and speaking passionately . . . apparently to himself. So she walked up to him.

'Whose house are you visiting, Khoka?'

All of Opu's bravado was limited to his mother. Once he left home, he turned into a painfully shy boy. So when a strange woman suddenly spoke to him, his first instinct was to throw down the bamboo and run like mad in the opposite direction. But after a few painful seconds, he managed to whisper, with considerable shyness, 'Umm . . . that house.'

The woman looked slightly surprised. 'My elder brother-in-law's house? Oh! Then you must be the guru's son!'

A little later, the woman proudly escorted Opu back to her own house. The two brothers' households were separate, though they were on the same compound. This new one Opu came to was only a few steps from Lokkhon Mohajon's house, but it was on the other side of the pond. Though hesitant at first, the woman's affectionate behaviour quickly dissolved Opu's shyness. He began walking around the rooms, curiously examining their things. These people had so much stuff! He hadn't even laid eyes on half the things they had, much less imagined having them in his own home. There was a clothes rack decorated with cowries, iron ceiling hangers painted in bright colours, birds made of wool, glass dolls, ceramic dolls, little trees made out of shola-pith, and so many other wonderful things. He nervously picked up a few things to examine closely, then quickly put them back.

The woman hadn't had a good look at him outside. Now that she watched him, she thought that the boy was still a child at heart. The look of bewildered awe in his eyes was something that she would expect from a five-year-old, not a boy of eight. Never before had she seen such innocence in a boy his age. Neither had she seen such a lovely complexion, such beautiful bone structure, or such a pretty face. His eyes looked like they had been painted with an artist's brush! Maternal affection for this beautiful boy flooded her heart.

Opu, in the meantime, had come further out of his shell. After exploring the rooms, he sat down in front of her and began chatting. The previous day's journey had given him a lot to talk about, especially the wonder that was the railroad. After a little while of hearing him talk, the woman got up to make him a bowl of hot mohonbhog. The bowl was large, holding more mohonbhog than Opu had ever been served at once. The semolina had been roasted in so much ghee that his fingers were soon glistening with it.

The taste of the first morsel astonished him. He had never before, in his entire life, tasted anything so wonderful. There were raisins in this mohonbhog! Why? His mother never put raisins in the mohonbhog at home! It was not like Opu was a stranger to this treat. Back home, he would sometimes harangue his mother till she made him the dish.

'You *have* to make me mohonbhog today!' he would demand. 'I'm not going to take no for an answer, Ma, I'm telling you that right now!'

His mother would grin. 'All right, all right. I'll make you your precious mohonbhog this evening,' she would say. But that mohonbhog was nothing like the concoction he was eating right now!

The truth was that Shorbojoya couldn't afford even the basic ingredients of mohonbhog. Neither semolina, nor ghee, and certainly not nuts and sultanas. Instead, she would boil a little rice flour in water, blend in some jaggery, and cook till the thing was reduced to a sticky, stretchy mass—more like a poultice than food. This was what she had always served as mohonbhog, in a little bowl of cracked brass. So far, Opu had eaten that poultice with great delight. It had never occurred to him that actual mohonbhog—a dish considered fit for the tables of heaven—could be anything other than the sweet paste that his mother cooked. But if this porridge, swimming in raisins, nuts and ghee, was the real food of the gods, then he had to admit that the mohonbhog his mother made him, with all her love, was at best a pale earthly imitation. As soon as he realized this, sadness and sympathy for his mother flooded his heart. Poor Ma! he thought. Did she even know what real mohonbhog tasted like? In a vague way, he began to understand for the first time that his mother was poor . . . that *they* were poor. And that was why there was never going to be food like this in his own home.

His next invitation was to the house of a brahmin neighbour of Lokkhon Mohajon. He had been asked to lunch, and a girl from that house came by at noon to escort him to their place. Once there, he was invited to sit in the veranda outside their kitchen. The place had been freshly mopped and purified with a sprinkling of holy water. Low wooden seats had been placed on the floor, and plates and bowls placed in front of it. The girl who had come to call Opu was called

Awmola. She was quite fair-skinned herself, with large eyes and a pretty enough face, and probably around his sister's age. Awmola's mother sat close to Opu and supervised his eating with great hospitality. For dessert, she served him chondropuli: half-moon-shaped coconut and condensed milk dumplings that she had made herself. After lunch was over, Awmola walked him back to Lokkhon Mohajon's house.

That evening, while playing with the local children, Opu's toe was caught in a split bamboo from the garden fence. The bamboo was young and raw, and it bit into his toes, refusing to let go. There was blood everywhere. All the other children froze in fear, but Awmola ran up and forced his toe out. Had she not rushed to help, he may have lost the toe entirely. When he couldn't walk, Awmola made a paste of miracle-leaf leaves to put on the wound, then carried him home in her arms. Fearing a scolding from his father, Opu didn't tell anyone at Lokkhon Mohajon's house about the accident. But all through that night, he dreamt of Awmola. He dreamt of himself going around the village in Awmola's lap, of sitting next to Awmola, playing with Awmola, of Awmola tying a bandage around his bleeding toe, of Awmola and himself running up and down the railroad. Awmola's large, smiling eyes kept him company all through his sleeping hours. When he woke up in the morning, the first thing he did was to run outside to look for Awmola. But it was too early for games, and the Mohajons' garden was empty.

After a little while, however, the other children began to arrive. Eventually, the games began, but Awmola didn't come. The dawn hours began to roll towards mid-morning. The women of the household sent word from within that breakfast was ready. But Awmola still didn't show up.

'Has Awmola Didi come here today?' he asked the woman who had made him his mohonbhog. The woman didn't know—she hadn't seen her.

As morning turned to noon, games were concluded for the first half of the day. The children left for their own homes, and his father called out to him to go take his bath. And yet no word from Awmola!

Betrayal and rejection drowned all the affection Opu had so warmly nurtured for Awmola all night and morning. 'Fine!' he thought to himself. 'Awmola Didi doesn't have to come. I'm never going to talk to her again anyway. In fact, if she comes, everyone will see how much I'm not talking to her!'

That evening, the children gathered in the gardens again, and the games began at their usual time. But once again, Awmola was missing. For all that he was determined never to speak to her again, Opu lost all interest in the games when she didn't turn up. Five or six of the local children called out to him, but he didn't want to join them. Awmola wasn't there—what was the point of games?

Awmola finally returned the next morning. Opu did not speak to her. When she sat, he pointedly didn't go anywhere near her, but kept shooting surreptitious looks her way to see if she had noticed that he was shunning her on purpose. Much to his chagrin, Awmola seemed not to notice his boycott for several minutes. In fact, she was immersed in games, and not particularly aware of anything else. Later, when she realized Opu was avoiding her, she went directly up to him.

'What's wrong, little boy? Why aren't you talking to me? What've I done?'

Opu pouted. He couldn't quite explain why he was upset, but the babble of words building inside him burst out anyway.

'As if! Why should anything be wrong? No one's done anything! Nothing's wrong—I'm *fi-i-ine* . . . why didn't you come yesterday?'

Awmola was rather taken aback. 'Is that why you're angry? Because I didn't come yesterday?'

Opu nodded vigorously.

Awmola burst out laughing. Taking Opu by the hand, she led him straight to the kitchens. Once they found the woman who had made Opu mohonbhog, Awmola repeated the whole conversation to her. The woman burst out laughing as well. Finally, tamping down a little so she could speak, she said, 'So then, Awmola, it looks like you won't be going back to your own home after all. Since our Khoka can't live without you, we should probably move you to our house permanently, eh?'

Awmola was old enough to understand that there was a double meaning to those words. In a tone of embarrassment, she said, 'Go on, sister-in-law! If you're going to be that way then I'm never going to come to your house again!'

After a while, when Awmola left to go back home, Opu tagged along. Once at their place, Awmola opened a cupboard and started showing him all her things: big glass dolls that looked like memshahebs, colourful birds made of wax, wax trees with fruit, and many, many other things. All of these treasures had apparently been bought from a fair, one that took place in Kaligunj during the period of holy bathing in the Ganga.

And then there were the toys. Opu hadn't even known such toys existed. There was an amazing monkey, made of rubber; no matter where you went, the monkey would look at you and blink its eye. Then there was a doll with a tambourine, made out of something Opu didn't recognize. If you pressed its tummy hard enough, it would throw its arms around like a person suffering an epileptic fit, and bang the tambourine loudly. But the thing that amazed Opu the most was a tin horse. All you had to do was wind up the horse, just like Ranudi's youngest uncle wound up the big clock in their inner veranda. Then, if you put the wound-up horse on the ground, it would move completely on its own! For quite a distance, too—almost as if it was a real horse! The further the horse walked, the more Opu's amazement grew. Once it stopped moving, he picked it up to examine its belly and its back.

'This is amazing!' he said to Awmola. 'Where'd you get it? How much did it cost?'

After a while, Awmola brought out an ornate container for women's vermilion. Instead of vermilion, however, the container held a piece of crinkly golden paper.

'What is this?' Opu asked. 'Tinsel-paper?'

Awmola smiled. 'Why should tinsel paper be in a box, Opu? Haven't you seen gold leaf before?'

Well, no . . . he hadn't seen gold leaf before. Was gold really this golden? He picked the little sheet up with his finger and turned it around slowly, watching it gleam.

Later, on his way back from Awmola's house, he thought of his sister. 'My poor Didi,' he thought. 'She has never even *seen* toys like this. Stupid girl just runs around collecting dried berries and seeds, and gets beaten up for stealing other people's dolls.'

The sympathy that he'd felt earlier for his mother now filled his heart for his sister. He had realized, vaguely, that they were poor, but never before had he been able to compare his sister's poverty to the affluence of other girls her age. Now that he saw Awmola's wealth, he understood how truly poor his sister was. If only he could get some money, he thought. He would definitely buy his sister at least that mechanical horse. And maybe a rubber monkey. The kind that looked at you and blinked, no matter which way you went.

The woman who had fed him mohonbhog had a pack of cards. Well, not a pack, exactly, but a collection of lost or leftover cards from lots of other decks. When he visited, Opu sometimes looked through the mismatched deck. Back home, the village women would sometimes gather at Ranudi's place in the afternoons to play cards. He had sometimes watched them from the side. He found cards rather strange. Imagine grown-ups fighting over pieces of paper because they had pictures on them! But he loved the names they had. King! Ace! Jack! All in all, he conceded that cards were good fun, though he didn't know anything about the actual games. Neither did his sister. Nor, for that matter, did his mother. Shorbojoya tried to join the village women's card circle every now and then, but her ignorance in this regard was well known. 'Don't take her,' the women warned each other when she tried to get in. 'She knows nothing about cards!'

On the rare occasion that his mother managed to find a partner, she tried her best to pretend that she was a seasoned player. She would glance at her cards, then look around the room, a knowing smirk on her lips. But within moments, her partner would exclaim, 'Younger sister-in-law! Why did you play the ace? Didn't you get a knave of trumps in the last hand? There, it's right in front of your eyes!'

Caught out, his mother would try her best to pretend it was an accident. 'Oh no, I completely forgot it was there, sister-in-law! I had *no* recollection of that!'

As the game proceeded, she began looking around again, smiling slightly. Like she knew exactly what everyone else had been dealt and was just biding her time. But it would only take a little while before her partner would suddenly say, 'Wait a second, show me your hand . . . younger sister-in-law, you had a perfect running flush! Why didn't you show it?'

His mother would try, once again, to bluff her way out. She would smile a superior and secretive smile and say, 'There's a special something in that flush, sister-in-law. It'll come into play later. It wouldn't do to disclose it now.'

The truth, of course, was that she had no idea what a running flush was, or what to do with one.

'"A special thing"?' her partner would snap. 'It was a running flush! You ruined a perfectly good hand! No no, younger sister-in-law, you give your cards to our third-eldest sister right now. We've seen enough of your "special" skills for one day.'

As everyone in the room laughed at her, his mother would struggle to put a smile on her lips, too. She liked to pretend that it was all merely a joke, and that they teased her because she was their friend.

'If I could get my hands on a pack of cards,' Opu thought, 'then Ma, Didi and I could play at home.' He imagined themselves sitting down in the afternoon, after lunch was done, in front of the window that had a clear view of the back woods; the one whose shutters smelt of old wood, and whose frame had been so completely hollowed out by termites that mustard-like yellow dust fell out of it when shaken. The bitter odour of bedstraw shrubs would waft in from the woods, and the green glass beetle of his didi's acquaintance would keep landing on and flying off the kalmegh plant in the inner veranda. The three of them would sit on the old woven mat in the window's square of sunlight and play for as long as they liked.

So what if none of them knew what makes a running flush? In their game, there would be no need to show a flush—*that* would be their rule! No one would be thrown out for not knowing things. No one would be insulted, and no one would mock or laugh at anyone else. Everyone would play in whatever way they liked best. Card games meant sitting together and making cards move from one person to another . . . right? So who cared if there was no running flush?

The next evening, Opu was invited to the mohonbhog woman's house for dinner. The array of utensils and dishes amazed him. Why was there a floral porcelain bowl for salt and lemon slices? Ma never had a separate bowl for them—she put them both right on the plate! This woman had served each curry in a separate bowl. And she had made so many different curries! Also, also . . . was that enormous lobster for him alone? Would he really not have to share?

And there, in the middle of his plate . . . luchi! Luchi-i-i! Oh, this must be the land of dreams come true! The glittering land of plenty that he and his sister dreamt of, as they ate their rice with stir-fried colocasia stems or boiled bottle-gourd 'curry'. It was a land of fairy-tale feasts, built on their desperate desire for every delicacy that they had seen or heard about but never tasted. As they sat through mornings and evenings without food, this was the land their hungry, covetous minds went to! A land of deliciousness. Of perfectly puffed hot, white luchis straight out of the bubbling wok of ghee—as many as they each could eat! And now, for him at least, that land was real!

At the next day's games, Opu stuck with Awmola while picking teams. Their chief opponent, Bishu, was older, athletic, brash and unafraid of taking risks. Opu's slender feminine form was no match for his prowess. When Bishu ran, it was immediately clear that Opu would not be able to catch him. Awmola pursed her lips in open irritation. Opu kept trying for the rest of the game to win so that Awmola would be pleased with him. But despite his best efforts, he lost again.

When teams were being picked again, Awmola chose Bishu. Tears threatened to roll down Opu's cheeks. The games turned bitter in his mouth—Awmola was speaking only to Bishu, her body turned towards him. All her jokes and laughter were for him. When Bishu had to go home for a bit, she kept asking him to come back as soon as he could.

'She's only doing it because the number of players is going down,' Opu tried to tell himself. 'If I go, Awmola Didi will ask me to come back, too. In fact, she'll ask me way more than she asked Bishu!'

A minute later, he pretended he had just noticed the time.

'Oh look, it's almost noon—I have to go, everyone. Bath time!'

Awmola didn't even notice. Only the blacksmith's son, Narugopal, said, 'All right, brother. See you this evening, then.'

Halfway to the house, Opu turned around to see how things were faring without him. The boys and girls were chasing each other and laughing, just as they always did. Awmola had been made the new Old Woman, and she was grinning widely as she stood protecting the den. There was no sign at all that he had ever been part of the group.

By the time he reached their rooms in Lokkhon Mohajon's house, deep hurt had replaced Opu's tears. He didn't speak to anyone for the rest of the day. So Awmola Didi didn't want to be friends with him. Fine. Who cared? It wasn't like she was that special, anyway.

Two days after this, Horihor finally returned to Contentment with his son.

It had only been a few days, but Shorbojoya had been going out of her mind, missing her son and worrying about him. Durga hadn't been having much fun, either. Just before leaving, she and Opu had had a big fight over the possession of dried pumpkin shells, valuable in the world of entertainment as toy boats. The battle had been so intense that they had refused to acknowledge each other's existence for a few days. Since his departure, several shells had accumulated in the kitchen, but Durga had not taken them to the river or ponds to play boat.

'Why did I have to fight with him and twist his ear?' she scolded herself. 'Let him come back. All the shells will be his alone—I shall never fight him over pumpkins again.'

For nearly fifteen days after his return, Opu went around telling everyone about the strange and wonderful things he had seen during his amazing adventure. When it came to the wonders, he was spoilt for choices. There was, of course, the railroad. It was easily the most astonishing thing he had seen. Whoever knew carriages slid on iron bars? But then there were the clay vegetables. It was amazing how lifelike they were! Then there was that doll—the one that threw its arms and legs about and banged the tambourine when its belly was poked. How on earth did someone get that to happen? Oh! He must also tell everyone about Awmola Didi! And then there was the road: the long, never-ending stretch of sunlit road, empty except for his father and himself, weaving endlessly through green fields and woods. He saw so many distant lakes from that road, with such astonishingly large swathes of water lilies and lotus! Or perhaps he should tell everyone about the lovely blacksmith family, who, when his father asked for water, instead invited them into their home for a hearty meal of milk, sugar lumps and toasted rice.

His sister was enchanted by his description of the railroad.

'How many poles, Opu—did you count?' she asked him over and over again. 'Were they very tall? How tall? Did the wire connect all of them? And the train—did you see the train?'

Oh, bitter regret! The train had been the one thing he hadn't seen—all thanks to his father's absurd stubbornness. All they had to do was sit quietly by the road for five or six hours. But no, his father refused to listen to reason, so here he was, back from his adventure across the railroad, without actually having seen a train!

A few days later, Shorbojoya was hurrying back from the pond. As she stepped on to the outer veranda, she felt something break against her chest. At the same time, she heard the low twang of taut string giving way and saw two sticks at two ends of the veranda simultaneously fall away. Everything happened in the blink of an eye. Since it didn't interfere with her work, Shorbojoya gave it no further thought.

A little later, Opu came home. He walked through the doorway and began walking towards the outer veranda . . . then stopped short. The breadth of the veranda was missing its new adornment. The enormity of the loss was so immense that for a few seconds he simply stood rooted to the spot, unable to move.

The first thing he recovered was his voice. 'Who tore my teligirap line?' he called out, high and shrill.

There was no response.

Shaking off the last of his numbing horror, Opu advanced carefully upon the house, looking around for clues. There was still the mark of wet feet on the veranda, drying innocently in the early noon sun. He had no proof, but a voice inside him whispered, 'This is Ma. It's never anyone but her. Those are her feet. Go ask her, you'll see.'

Inside the house, his mother was washing jackfruit seeds. Nothing about her suggested that she'd just committed a terrible act of wanton destruction. Opu positioned himself like the Abhimanyu of travelling jatra groups, leaning slightly forward for maximum effect. Then, in a sweet, piercing voice reminiscent of a flute playing the seventh note, he cried: 'Didn't I have to work hard for those stalks, Ma? Didn't I have to trample gardens and woods for them?'

Startled, Shorbojoya turned to stare at her son. 'What have you got from the woods? What are you talking about?'

'Like I didn't suffer for it, Ma? Like my legs weren't bruised by thorns?'

'What on earth are you on about? What's happened?'

'What's happened! I worked so hard to hang up my teligirap wires . . . and you tore them down, didn't you?!'

'That was one of your crazy things, was it? I was rushing back to finish everything by your lunchtime, how was I supposed to know what you've been doing in the veranda . . . teligirap or what girap? Anyway, it's torn now. There's nothing I can do.'

And with that, she calmly turned back to the seeds.

Oh, the cruelty! To think that he once believed his mother actually loved him! Of course, that childhood delusion of his had long been shattered, but he had never before thought her capable of *such* cold cruelty. It was like her heart was made of stone! He had spent hours—hours!—scouring Uncle Neelmoni's lands, the large mango orchard of the Palits, his Proshonno Gurumoshai's bamboo groves . . . and several other perilously dangerous jungles in the neighbourhood!

He had had to bring down moonseed vines from the highest branches, and get just the right kinds of stalk to weave them all together into a long telegraph line. Everything had been ready for playing railways at home . . . and now this heartless destruction!

He wanted to say something just as cruel to his mother, something that would hurt her just as much as she had hurt him. After a few seconds of fruitless rummaging about inside his head, he said, probably for lack of any better threat: 'I won't eat my rice today. I won't, I won't! I will not have lunch in this house!'

'Like feeding you lunch fetches me a king's ransom?' said his heartless mother. 'You don't want your rice—fine, don't eat it. It's not like you'll come running into the kitchen even before I've taken the pot off the flames, will you? "I won't have my rice" indeed! We'll see what's what at mealtime.'

In the blink of an eye . . . here's you, here's me, here's Opu's mother contentedly washing her jackfruit seeds . . . but where's Opu? He's dissolved into air—like a lump of camphor left out in the open! Only Durga, coming home through the back door, caught a glimpse of him: a boy-shaped whirlwind whooshing by.

'Opu! What's the matter? Where are you going?' she called after him. 'Opuuuu! Listen to me!'

From within the house, her mother said, 'Well, don't ask *me* what happened. That boy always has his fingers in one crazy thing or another! Hung ropes of god-knows-what across the veranda, no warning, no nothing . . . I was coming in, it tore. Not like I did it on purpose! But now he's cross. "I won't have my lunch", "I won't have my rice" . . . fine, don't! It's not like I get the bells in heaven tolling for me for cooking your lunch!'

In the event of these little frictions between mother and son, Durga had to play both mediator and scout. When she finally managed to find her brother—after much shouting of his name in the orchards and woods—and bring him home, it was past two. He had been sitting morosely on the trunk of a fallen mango tree in an orchard that belonged to the Roys from the next neighbourhood.

The hours between afternoon and evening, however, had transformed him completely. Gone was the boy who had nearly left the motherland in bitter disillusionment, vowing never to return. Instead, Opu was running from one end of the outer veranda to the other, tightening the rope of vines and plant sheathes that spanned its length. When he was satisfied, he stepped back and watched his own handiwork in awe. It was just like the real teligirap wires! Once again, he had his own railroad to play with!

A few minutes later, he entered the Mukhujjes' household in search of Shotu. He was dying to show off the wondrous new game to the older boy.

'Shotuda . . . we have a teligirap wire on our outer veranda to play railroads with—want to come join?'

'Who strung up the wires?'

'I did. Didi got the plant sheathes, but I strung up the wires . . . come no, Shotuda? It'll be fun . . .'

'Nah, you go play with your "wires". I'm busy.'

With dimming hopes, Opu realized that he simply wasn't the sort to band the older boys together and lead them into a new game. After all, who would listen to young Opu? Still, he couldn't give up without trying one last time.

Clinging, without any real hope, to the edge of the courtyard, he said in a defeated voice, 'Come no, Shotuda? You, Didi and I can play. It's going to be a lot of fun.' Then, in a tone used to tempt children, he said, 'I've made a big pile of pomelo leaves for tickets. You can have some if you play . . .'

Shotu wasn't interested. Opu was too shy to push further, so he walked quietly out of the Mukhujjes' house. Tears were threatening to spill out of his eyes. Why wouldn't Shotuda come play with him? He had asked him so many times! What was the point of having a railroad at home if no one came to see it?

By the next morning, however, he was excited again. He and his sister had crafted a shop in the corner of their courtyard with throwaway bricks and were on their way to collect goods for sale. In these expeditions, Opu followed his sister's lead; Durga was much more familiar with the woods and gardens, and knew of more plants than he did. Together, they brought back a very respectable variety of stock for the shop: custard apple leaves to be sold as betel leaves, inedible brown fruit to be sold as potatoes, petals of the honeysuckle to be sold as fish, little ivy gourds as regular gourd, unripe snake gourd as ripe cowpea, clumps of soil as raw sea salt.

'What shall we do for sugar, Didi?'

'There's that pile on the way to the bamboo grove . . . it has some very fine sand. Ma got some to toast rice in. White and clean—it glistens in the sun. Perfect sugar!'

The two of them took off again for the bamboo grove. Wandering through the grove for secondary stock, a strange treasure caught both siblings' eyes at the same time. High up, behind the protruding branch of a tall lebbeck tree, hidden by the dark green of its own vine and leaves, was a profusion of perfectly rounded, beautiful red fruit. Despite much effort, the two of them could only dislodge a small part of the vine. Only three of the fruits on it were ripe and ready for the shop, but that was enough for Opu and Durga. They dusted off their unexpected treasure and raced back home. At the shop, these fruits were given pride of place: right in the middle of the counter, so that even passing customers couldn't fail to notice them.

Now that the stock was complete, buying and selling began in full force. Durga bought betel leaves so often that she almost single-handedly put the shop out of stock. She was in the process of ordering some of the other wares when Shotu stepped in through the main doorway. Opu immediately jumped off the shopkeeper's seat and ran to greet him.

'Shotuda! Come look at the shop we've put together. Here, see these red fruits? Didi and I got them from the woods. What are these—do you know?'

'Yeah, bitter apples,' said Shotu dismissively. 'We used to get hundreds of them in our garden. What else have you got?'

And so the game carried on. Opu was ecstatic to have Shotu, the leader of the older boys, actually come to his house to join him and his sister's games. By his very presence, he elevated their playshop from childish puttering-about to serious game-playing.

After several regular transactions, Durga came in with the shop's first big order.

'Give me two maunds of your finest rice,' she demanded. 'Tomorrow the groom's folks are coming to finalize my doll's wedding, so I'll have a lot of guests for lunch.'

'Are we invited?' asked Shotu, leaning over the display.

'Invited! You lot are going to be part of the bridal procession. I'll come in the morning with a gift to formally invite you. Shotuda, could you tell Ranu to make some sandalwood paste tonight? I'll come in the morning and . . .'

Before she could finish, Shotu's arm shot out over the display. The very next minute, he was racing out of the Roys' compound. Opu jumped off the shopkeeper's perch and ran after him.

'Didi! He took them! He took them all!' he managed to shriek in his piercingly high, flute-sweet voice.

Durga simply stood for a few seconds, stunned. Then her eyes fell on the shop display. Its chief attraction, the three precious fruits, were gone. She turned and followed the boys as swiftly as she could.

Outside, Shotu had taken the road that went by the much-feared velvet-apple tree. Under normal circumstances, Opu wouldn't have had a hope of catching up with him; not only was Shotu older, he was also taller and stronger—not slender and feminine like Opu. But while Shotu was merely running away for the sake of it—he had no real fear of reprisals—Opu was almost running for his life. He had fallen in love with the red fruits. They were like his own secret treasure, and he couldn't bear the idea of losing them. So by the time Durga caught sight of them, Opu was almost at Shotu's heels.

As Durga began catching up with the two, Shotu suddenly swooped down, turned around, and hurled something at her brother. Then he turned back and disappeared down the road that led to the velvet-apple trees. Opu stumbled to a halt in the middle of the road and covered his face with his hands. Durga hurried up to him.

'What is it? Let me look . . . what did he do?'

'Threw dust, Didi. In my eyes. It hurts so much!'

Durga quickly caught his hands and lowered them. 'Stop rubbing your eyes, it only makes it worse. Let me blow in them, it'll get the dust out . . .'

But Opu put his hands up again, rubbing his eyes harder. 'It feels terrible! Why can't I open my eyes? Didi, I think I'm going blind!'

'Let me see. Let me *see*—move your hand.'

After some coaxing, Durga finally managed to get him to lower his hands. Then she soothed his eyes by breathing on the loose end of her sari, and pressing the breath-warmed cloth on his eyes. After a while, Opu was able to open his eyes a little.

'Is that better? Can you see again?'

Opu nodded. But he was in no mood to talk.

'You go back home, all right? I'll go straight to Shotuda's mother and grandmother and tell them exactly what he did. What an awful boy! I'll tell Ranu, too. Everyone will know about him. You just go home carefully, okay?'

Opu nodded again.

Upon reaching the Mukhujjes' back door, however, Durga hesitated. The third-eldest mistress was a force to reckon with, and Durga was quite certain whose side she would take. After a few more minutes of dithering, she finally decided to just go home. Entering their compound via the front doorway, she found Opu holding on to the left-door beam, silently crying. Her brother wasn't a crybaby. He had bouts of dramatic exits and pouting silences, but he seldom shed tears. Durga realized that the day's events had hurt him deeply. Not only had he lost his fruits—which he had clearly developed an attachment to—but he had also been insulted and hurt by Shotu, a boy he had so badly wanted to befriend.

Durga couldn't bear to see her little brother cry. It made her chest tighten with misery.

'Don't cry, Opu,' she whispered, taking him gently by the hand. 'Come on, we'll play with my cowrie shells. I'll give them to you, okay? Are the eyes still hurting? Look, I think you've ripped your dhuti . . . come on, let's go inside.'

~

Opu seldom left home after lunch. He preferred to stay in and explore the ancient family home. The room of leftovers, in particular, enthralled him. It was full of old things that were no longer used: an old-fashioned wooden lockbox, a large cane basket, an old wooden clotheshorse, a few low bathing seats. There were boxes here that he had never seen opened; jars and pots he didn't know the contents of. But then his chief curiosity was not about the things, but about the times gone by, when these things were new and would have been in use. He liked to think about a time when his grandfather's lockbox was regularly opened, when clothes were carefully draped on that ancient clotheshorse. Had the abandoned temple courtyard in the bamboo grove been whole then? Did children laugh and play where the golden laburnum now grew wild? What could their names have been? Some of them must have lived in this very house, sat where he was sitting right now. He wished he could know more about them. But their time was a long-ago time; they had all disappeared, leaving no trace of themselves behind.

Sometimes, when his mother went to the pond and he was alone in the house, he was sorely tempted to open the old boxes and jars and see what treasures were hidden inside. There was a bundle of old notebooks and palm-leaf manuscripts on the highest shelf in the room. He knew from his father that they once belonged to his grandfather, Ramchand Torkalonkar. He would never dare to do it, but he dearly wanted to get his hands on the bundle—to smell the old-paper smell and rifle through them, reading for himself what his grandfather had written (for he could read now, and that too quite well). On other afternoons, he simply sat beside his favourite window—the one that opened to the woods behind the house—and read his mother's torn copy of the Kashidashi Mahabharat.

His father was very proud of his academic prowess. Sometimes, he would take Opu to the Gangulys' temple courtyard, where the older men of the village congregated for their evening assembly, to show off his reading skills.

'Read this bit, Baba. Show everyone how well you can read,' he would say, pointing to a section of the Ramayan, or the lyrics of a ballad. Opu would oblige, and have the gathered men heap praise on him. Old Dinu Bhotchaj would complain, as he always did, about the lack of literary proficiency in his progeny.

'My grandson, Horihor . . . what can I say. He's about the same age as your khokha. Shredded two *Introduction to Alphabets* beyond repair, and still doesn't know all the letters! Taken after his father, that one. After I close my eyes . . . that's it. Father and son will have to join the labourers in the fields.'

Horihor offered words of token sympathy, but his heart swelled with pride. He accepted these testaments to his son's superiority as his family's due.

'Education is not your line,' he wanted to say to Dinu Bhotchaj. 'You can't spend your life inflating interest rates, and then expect erudition in your sons. We may be poor, but my father didn't write those heaps of manuscripts for nothing. He established a culture of learning in the family. That culture is not for the likes of you.'

~

The woods that Opu liked to stare at began only a few feet from the Roys' boundary wall. From the back window, the top of the woods seemed like frozen waves of green: the hill-glory-bower speckled with white flowers, thick green vines spreading across branches, spiky leaves of the ancient bamboo leaning through the golden-yellow laburnum and dillenia. At the foot of the trees, shrubs of turmeric, wild colocasia and bitter arum fought for sunlight and breathing room. Those that lost the battle were buried under the victor, dying slowly in the darkness; only a few steps away, late autumn sunshine streamed through a gap in the foliage and glistened on a luckier bush of wildflowers.

Opu and his sister had known these woods and groves since the day they'd been born. Their fresh, evergreen vibrancy coloured every moment of their lives. They knew every bit of this land; its beauty and mysteries filled their young hearts with wonderment and joy. The sweet smell of yellow-nicker blossoms, glimpses of the dancing wagtail, the family of squirrels in the porcupine-flower tree, the many nameless berries and leaves that the two regularly used in their games, the elusive bird that hid within the shrubs and warbled high, solitary notes—all of it made the woods feel like a magical wonderland. Opu couldn't quite explain why, but the smallest things about the woods filled him with a strange, deep happiness.

Somewhere deep within these woods—so the saying went—there was an ancient, dilapidated temple to the goddess Bishalakkhi. She was once the resident deity of the village, just as Ponchanon Thakur is now. Her temple had been set up by the Mojumdar family, who—back then—ruled supreme in these areas. Once, after something particularly good happened to the family, they attempted to thank the goddess by sacrificing a human in her honour. Outraged, the goddess visited the family in their dreams that very night, and informed them that she was leaving the temple, never to return. That was several generations ago. Since then, the

Mojumdars have died out, the temple has broken down, the temple pond is in ruins, and the entire area has been taken over by the wilderness.

Only once—and even this was many, many years ago—had the goddess been seen again. Shawrup Chokroborti had been returning from a short visit to a distant village. Alighting at the pier after dark, he noticed a young woman standing just off the road. Now, the pier was quite a walk from the nearest human settlement, and the girl—who looked about sixteen—was very beautiful. To say Shawrup Chokroborti was surprised would have been an understatement. Before he could say anything to her, however, the girl spoke.

In a voice that was sweet, but also inflected with slight pride, she said, 'I am Bishalakkhi, the resident deity of this village. In a few days, cholera is going to sweep through this village. To avoid the worst of it, tell people to worship the goddess Kali on the fourteenth day of this lunar cycle, then sacrifice a hundred and eight pumpkins in her honour at the Ponchanon temple.'

After that, she vanished into the surrounding mist . . . right before the stunned Shawrup Chokroborti's eyes. Cholera did indeed visit a few days later, and took a lot of lives.

Over the years, Opu had heard this story several times. When he stood at the back window in the quiet afternoons, staring into the woods, he often thought about the goddess. Was it so improbable that he'd meet her one day? Perhaps some morning, when he was busy unwinding some moonshine vine from a branch . . . a sixteen-year-old would appear in front of him. She would be wearing a red-bordered white sari, and necklaces and bangles just like Ma Durga.

'Who are you?'

'I am Opu.'

'You're a very good boy, Opu. What boon do you want?'

After staring at the woods for a little longer, Opu would go have a lie-down. The moist, cool breeze from the river would shimmer through the rooms of the house, filling it with the bittersweet smell of the autumn wilderness. Far above the village, seagulls would scream into the silence. During these moments, Opu would feel a strange sense of self-contained detachment. As if this little village was beyond the reaches of temporal joys and sorrows; as if he existed outside the reach of either the past or the future, responding only to the echoing call of a wandering traveller-god. He could never tell the exact moment when sleep would finally take him. When he would wake up, the afternoon would be long gone. Dusk would have descended upon Contentment. But instead of disappointing him, dusk on those days would fill him with exhilaration and hope. The sweet smell of the woods would make him think that he had lived a day just like this one before, and that it had been a day of great joy. And he would be convinced that he would soon live another such day in the future, with just as much joy waiting for him.

Opu had often traipsed after his sister on her treasure hunts through the woods, hoping to go deep enough that they would come out on the other side. Indeed, they had sometimes gone so deep within that the woods had seemed like forests, and the midday sun had barely made inroads through the thick foliage. When they looked up to see the sky, all they saw instead were clusters of unknown fruits, orchids on high branches, and an unbroken canopy of dark green leaves. Despite this, they had never found an end to the woods. After a few such expeditions, Opu became secretly convinced that there was no end to the woods behind their house: it went on and on and on. Beyond their mundane village, past the indigo-bungalow fields, along the bend in the river . . . straight into the magical land of the epics. Perhaps it was under that very bamboo grove—the one in the distance—that an older woman had come to a man on the eve of a great war, asking him for the gift of his god-given armour and earrings. Perhaps, in that abandoned courtyard now overrun with wilderness, a thin, underfed little boy had been tricked into drinking rice water instead of milk. In that clearing under the golden-apple tree that he had come upon once—that was probably where Orjun's arrow had pierced the earth, bringing forth the sweet water of the underground river to quench the thirst of a dying Bheeshho, laid out on a bed of arrows. And that patch of wildflowers next to the small pond in Ranudi's orchard? That was really the garden by the Saraju river, where Doshoroth had accidentally killed the only child of blind brahmin parents. It had happened right there, next to the big jambolan tree.

There was a book at home—yellow with age, without a cover, with the first few pages destroyed by silverfish. It was called *Beerangona Kabyo*, or *The Ballad of the Brave Woman*. The author's name was missing. Opu loved reading that book. Sometimes, when no one was home, he would read the verses out loud to himself:

Near at hand I saw a lake, and on its shore
A royal warrior, rolling in dust.
Broken thigh! I cried out aloud
My lord, why send me such an awful dream?

On the days of the Koluichondi feast, he and his mother would visit the choked pond in the fields to the north of the village for their ritual picnic. No one but Opu had ever realized that the pond was secretly the Dwoipayon Lake. On the shore of that lake, the defeated warrior of *Beerangona Kabyo* lies for all eternity—dishonoured, forgotten, waiting for death. There is no one to look after him, no one to come visit. When dusk erases the distant plots of banana and brinjal from view, and the farmhands begin to make their way home from the fields . . . then, staring at the unending unknown beyond the Shonadanga moors, Opu often thinks about the poor, the betrayed, the forgotten people of the epics. The little boy who had never tasted milk, the famous warrior who was left alone to die . . . he had shed many a quiet tear thinking about them all.

His father was not at home that afternoon. Had he been, Opu would have had to sit down with his books as soon as lunch was over. Afternoon would melt into evening, but his father wouldn't let him go. Opu would bury his chin in his chest, trying to hide tears of frustration. How many more times did he need to go over the rubrics of Shubhonkori arithmetic? Wasn't he going to have any time to play today? Why was Baba being so mean?

Then suddenly, his father would declare the end of lessons for the day. Opu would rush through the wrapping up of books and palm leaves, then race out to the back courtyard and literally dance for joy. Evenings at the back of their house were magical. The shadows would begin to darken within the woods, even as the last light of dusk glittered on the high branches of his uncle's golden-apple tree. The sight of the brick playroom he and his sister had set up, the 'telegraph' vines that had never been taken down, the glistening brown of the lapwing as it landed on the white morning glory bush, the woven palm-leaf screen, the smell of the freshly turned earth—all of it would fill him with a sense of tranquil happiness that he couldn't describe in words.

One evening, Shorbojoya had put the rice pot on later than usual. Opu was sitting near her on a woven mat. It was completely dark outside. Cricket-song filled the kitchen.

'Ma, how many days till pujo?'

Durga was sitting on the side, slicing vegetables on the curved blade. 'Twenty-two days—isn't that right, Ma?'

She had been making plans for weeks. Baba would be coming home for Durga Puja. He would be bringing presents for Opu, Ma, herself: dolls, new clothes, lacquer dye for the feet! These days, her mother doesn't let her go to other people's houses for meals on festive days. She has almost forgotten what luchi tasted like. When she was younger, she would have gone around the neighbourhood homes on the night of Kojagori Lokkhi Puja, collecting the puffed rice and murki that had been offered to the goddess during the day. The wooded paths, as she made her way around, would be a chequer of darkness and golden moonlight. The sound of conch-shells would sound from every home, and the smell of luchis being fried in ghee would waft out of the more affluent kitchens. Sometimes people would generously send them a plate of cold offerings, including a piece or two of stale luchi. Her mother would save it, along with the heaps of puffed rice and murki she collected, doling out small portions to her children and herself for days.

But then last year, the third-eldest mistress had said, 'What is this, younger sister-in-law? Letting the daughter of a respectable family go out to collect proshad like a lower-class girl? Don't send her around like that again—it shames us all.'

Since then, her expeditions on Lokkhi Puja nights have been curtailed.

'Do you want to play cards?' she asked, chopping the last of the vegetables.

'Oh yes,' said her mother. 'Go get the pack from that room, let's have a game before dinner.'

Durga stood up, but then she bit her lip and looked at her brother.

'It's all right, I'll come with you.' Opu laughed, getting up.

From behind them, their mother called out, 'Oh, the drama! Where's all this fear when you roam the woods all day long? But ask her to go to the next room at night, and madam shivers in fear!'

Their pack was the mismatched one that Opu had brought back from Horihor's disciple's sister-in-law. All three players were equally inept, but that seldom interfered with their enjoyment of the game. Opu hadn't yet learnt to tell the different cards apart, so he would often show his hand to his opponent in the middle of a game and ask, 'Is this a diamond, Ma? Can I play a diamond here?'

Durga was very happy tonight. It wasn't often that they could afford to have a hot dinner. Most nights they would simply eat the cold leftovers from lunch. Today, however, they were having freshly made rice, *and* their mother was going to make a curry especially for dinner. It was almost like a festival night! She was ecstatic.

Opu said, 'Tell us that story while we play, Ma. That Shyamlonka story?'

Before his mother could respond, he suddenly lay down in front of her, putting his head in her lap. Running his hand entreatingly down her arm, he begged like a little boy. 'Recite those lines no, Ma! "Shyamlonka grinds spices/Her tresses sweep the floor . . ."'

Durga said, 'How's she going to play if she recites poems for you? Sit up . . .'

Shorbojoya said, 'Where did you get these mushrooms, re Durga?'

'You know the woods behind the Goswamis' orchards? Where you and I once went to look for the calf, Opu? There. There's a lot of them right there, Ma, in the middle of the woods. No one else knows, or they'd have cleaned it out.'

'You went into those woods?' Opu asked, impressed. 'It's seriously like a jungle there, Ma. I've only been there once.'

Shorbojoya was watching her son with an almost overwhelming love. This was her Opu! Only a few years back, he was her little toddler, constantly in her arms. When she stretched her index finger and sang, 'Come down to us, moon/And put a bindi on my son!' he would happily lean his moon-like face forward and push his forehead on to the finger. That Opu was now playing cards! Could anything be more amazing? If he made mistakes, lost a round or was dealt a poor hand, Shorbojoya, despite being in the opposition, felt his disappointment tug at her heart!

When they were in the middle of the rounds, Durga said, 'Ma, do you know what happened today . . .'

'Didi!' exclaimed Opu. 'If you tell Ma I'm never talking to you again!'

'Fine, don't talk to me. So what happened was, Raji's family had laid out their poppy seeds in the sun. Now, this one here doesn't know what poppy seeds are. So he asks Raji, "Rajidi, what are these?" And Raji says, "It's licorice. Want to try some?" Ma, he actually stood there and chewed the poppy seeds! Didn't realize what it was! Such a silly boy—isn't he, Ma?'

Opu grinned at her. Though he had said he wouldn't speak to his sister, he knew that such a thing could never happen. That day, when Shotuda stole his three bitter-apples, his didi had spent the rest of the day hunting the woods for replacements. Finally, well after the lamp-lighting hour, she had returned with a whole cluster of them tied in the loose end of her sari. 'How about these, eh?' she had grinned. 'Don't you feel silly for crying, now?'

That had been a few days ago, and he still hadn't been able to decide what made him happier: having so many of the pretty red fruits, or the deep affection for him that he had seen in his sister's grin.

Meanwhile, his sister had begun collecting the cards for the next round. 'It's a game of sixes, Opu. Play carefully!'

'What's that smell, Didi? Is it a flower?'

'It's the flowers of the milkwood pine,' their mother explained. 'There's a milkwood pine in your uncle's garden, just behind their house. Haven't you seen it?'

Brother and sister moved closer to Shorbojoya in excitement. 'Is it true that a tiger once got as close to this house as that milkwood pine? Was it during your time? Ma?'

But their mother suddenly scrambled up, throwing down her cards. 'Oh no! The rice! Let me pour out the starch, then I'll tell you the story . . .'

Later, at dinner, Durga was effusive about her mother's cooking. 'The mushrooms are perfect, Ma!' she said, happily pushing another mouthful of rice and curry into her mouth.

'Yes, that's right, perfect!' chimed her brother. 'I could get you mushrooms too, Ma. I see them growing all over the place. I used to think that they're umbrellas left behind by frogs, that's why I never picked them . . .'

Shorbojoya's heart soared with the praise. Her darling children! Still, what did she have to help her along? Nothing! Not even proper ingredients. People called the third-eldest mistress to cook for feasts in their homes. If they called her instead, gave her the things she needed . . . well, she'd show the third-eldest what cooking really was! Yes, she would!

When her children went out to wash their hands, she called, 'Make him go off the road, Durga—don't pour water on his hands till he does. Opu, why do you have to stand in the middle of the path to wash your hands?'

Opu, however, refused to move. Going off the path meant going towards the pitch darkness of the woods, away from the light of the kitchen. Who knew what lurked in those shadows? He could never understand why his mother made such a fuss about this every night. When your life was at stake, what difference did it make if you washed your hands and mouth in the middle of the path?

A little later, all three of them were in bed, fast asleep. The moist breeze of late autumn infused their broken old house with the thick scent of milkwood pine. The slender crescent of the waning moon rose above the woods and gardens, making the pre-dawn dewdrops glitter. Sudden bursts of wind rushed through the village, shaking the lavender trees and scarlet gourd shrubs in its way. Sometimes, Opu would wake up at this very moment. Staring into the fragrant darkness, his mind would fly back to the tale of the goddess Bishalakkhi.

Few people remembered her any more. The time of her worship had long since passed. Those that had built a temple in her honour were now history. People said that the ancient ditabark tree beside the river hadn't even sprouted from seed when they had been around. As their footprints disappeared from the cool, mossy banks of the fish-laden Ichamoti, so did the worship of the goddess.

But the goddess has not forgotten her village.

When the night deepens and the humans sleep, she goes from plant to plant, bringing flowers into blossom and caressing baby birds in their nests. In the final hours of full-moon nights, she fills the honeycombs with the sweetness of yellow-nicker and jackfruit flowers. She knows the bush under which the malabar nut hides, she knows the patch in the woods where the baby milkwood pines blossom. She knows the exact curve along the river where the blue-petalled morning glory has been building its colony amidst the dark green moss, and within which thorny bush the tailorbird hides her warbling babies.

All through the night, the misty glow of her soothing beauty pervades the woods. Unnamed fragrances mix with moonlight and silence, creating a pool of mystical repose. Then, as night turns to dawn, she melts into the disappearing darkness. No one has laid eyes on her since Shawrup Chokroborti.

17

THE RICHEST MAN in Contentment, Awnnoda Roy, had recently found himself in a bit of a fix. Officers of the Land Survey had set up camp on the fields just north of his neighbourhood, determined to re-evaluate the legal ownerships of Contentment's lands. Had it just been the surveyors, Awnnoda Roy might have managed to keep his holdings secure. But this time, senior officials had accompanied the field team and set up a base office on the banks of the river. They had also brought along a number of junior enforcement officials. It was a big production, and it showed that they meant business.

Almost all the gentlemen of the village owned some parcels of lands—fruit of their ancestors' machinations and labour. But for the last couple of generations, the gentlemen of the brahmin neighbourhood had lived in placid, slothful unproductivity. The boats of their lives had been dragged out of the ebb and flow of life's currents, and buried securely into the silt of their inheritance. The stagnant water of the shores was all they were capable of navigating. The sudden arrival of surveyors had naturally alarmed this change-averse, comfortably corrupt coterie. After all, who knew? Maybe Ram had appropriated some of Shyam's land as his own at some point, and Jodu may have been paying taxes on ten acres of land when he actually owned twelve. Not that it was anyone's business. This survey nonsense would dig up these wholly unnecessary details, and disrupt the cosy, comfortable lives that these families had made for themselves.

Awnnoda Roy was worried about these problems as well, but his true troubles were of a slightly different nature, and somewhat more severe. One of his cousins had left Contentment several years ago and settled permanently in the west. As a consequence, Awnnoda Roy had been enjoying the undisputed ownership of his mango and jackfruit orchards all these years, as well as the income from his cousin's share of the land. He had planned to quietly transfer all that property—or at least some of it—to his own name during the next survey. His cousin lived too far away to keep track of local surveys, and by the time word reached him, if it ever did, it would have been too late. But people could never mind their own business, and some busybody had written to his cousin, warning him that he was about to be cheated out of his inheritance. As a result, his cousin's eldest son, Neeren, had arrived ten days ago to supervise the survey on their share of the property.

Not only did this crush Awnnoda Roy's dreams of legally owning the land he already considered his own, it had thrown up a host of other problems as well. First, the rooms that belonged to his cousin were the best rooms in their common ancestral home. Awnnoda Roy had occupied them as soon as his cousin had left Contentment, and had been using them with impunity for the last twenty years. Now that his cousin's boy was here, he'd had to relinquish that cherished control. On top of that, the boy Neeren was a fashionable young college student with wastefully modern ways. He used one room for sleeping and another as his study—forcing Awnnoda to move heavy trunks, tall stacks of paperwork and myriad other things down the stairs from the first floor to the ground floor. It didn't end there; one of his cousin's rooms on the ground floor was being used as a storeroom to house cheap wooden beams from the Palit neighbourhood. Now he had been informed that he would have to vacate that room as well.

Late afternoon was just turning into evening that day. Awnnoda Roy was not yet done for the day, for he still had several assembled debtors to deal with. However, men of the village had already begun to assemble in his temple courtyard for their usual rounds of evening dice and chitchat, and he wanted to be done as quickly as possible.

A young woman had been sitting on the ground beside the courtyard with her little boy, her head covered with the loose end of her sari. She was clearly poor, likely a farmhand's wife. Watching the other debtors leave one by one, she finally stood up, thinking her turn had finally come.

Awnnoda Roy peered at her through his glasses. 'Who're you? What do you want?'

The woman began untying a knot at the end of the sari.

'I've managed some money . . . it was very hard,' she said in a low voice. 'Take it and release the barn key, master. Such hardships we're going through, I can't describe . . .'

Awnnoda Roy's expression brightened.

'Hori!' he called out to his junior accountant. 'Take the money from her and count it. Then check the date in the notebook and calculate the interest once more to see how much is left.'

The young woman took the money out of the knot and put it down in front of Horihor. He counted the amount. 'Five rupees?' he asked the woman.

'That's fine,' said Awnnoda Roy. 'Take it and make a note.' Then he turned to the woman. 'What about the rest of the money?'

'Take that for now, master. I'll pay the rest later. I'll work hard to raise the money. Release my barn key against these five rupees for now . . . let me feed my little Mato. Of course, our home is leaking, but I thought, let me save my starving child first. I can leave the repairs for later . . .'

The woman was speaking as if the barn key were already in her hands. Alas, she didn't know what stuff Awnnoda Roy was made of. Even before she could finish, Awnnoda Roy exploded.

'Listen to this hag's demands! Forty rupees—that's how much you owe me, with interest. "Take five rupees and unlock my barn!" The nerve of you lower-caste people, honestly. Go on now, out! Don't ruin my afternoon with your racket.'

The woman was not unknown to the gentleman who'd gathered to play dice. Only old Dinu Bhotchaj, who could no longer see too well, called out from the back of the courtyard: 'Who's that you're talking to, Awnnoda?'

'It's Tomrej's wife from the other neighbourhood. Tomrej has been dead for three or four days now, don't you know—took almost forty rupees of my money with him, counting interest. I put a lock on his barn the moment I heard. Now his wife won't leave me alone. "Open the barn, master", "Do me a favour, master", "Save my baby, master". Ridiculous!'

Tomrej's wife couldn't have been more alarmed had the actual ground beneath her feet opened up to swallow her whole. She had been confident that five rupees, within mere days of her husband's death, would have been enough surety for the moneylender to let her have access to her own grains. Now she realized that she was looking at utter devastation.

'Don't be like that, master,' she begged in dismay. 'Please . . . I sold my son's silver waist-locket at BhoNda jeweller's for that money! It was his father's last present—I didn't want to sell it. But then I thought, let my boy eat first. If he lives, and god provides, I'll buy him another one later. Please master, my baby needs to eat . . . the keys . . .'

'What did I just say?' growled Awnnoda Roy. 'Out! Get out! Tears aren't going to pay my debt. Why am I even talking to you—if your husband were here he would know what I mean. The five rupees have been credited to your name. Bring me the rest of the money, then we'll see about the key.'

To signal the end of the conversation, Awnnoda Roy took off his glasses, put them in their case, and made to stand up. When Tomrej's wife saw that he was genuinely preparing to go indoors, she let out a distraught, high-pitched cry.

'Master, please! What will happen to my child? What will I feed him? I don't have even a single paisa left—not even to buy him some puffed rice! Please, if you won't unlock the barn, give me my five rupees back!'

Her appeal so incensed Awnnoda that he bared his teeth and snarled at the woman. 'Shut your whining, you stupid hag! Like I don't have problems of my own? Here I am, losing a fistful of my money, and you're chasing after me with your "unlock the barn" and "give back my money"! How much grain do you think you have, anyway? Let me tell you—four bales, at the most. That's not even enough to pay me back! Did you think of that? Those five rupees is probably all the cash I'll ever see from you, the rest is down the drains. "Oh, sob, sob! What will my son eat?"—what do I know what he'll eat? Get off my land right now! You think I'm starving your child? Go complain to the courts and punish me if you can!'

Then he turned sharply around and went inside the house.

Once Awnnoda Roy was gone, old Dinu Bhotchaj said, 'So when did Tomrej die, eh girl? I hadn't heard anything . . .'

'Last Wednesday, master. He was perfectly fine. Brought some labeo fish from the market, I cooked it with onions and served it with rice. He ate a good lunch, like a perfectly normal person. Then he said, I'm feeling cold, put the quilt on me. So I did. After some time, I realized he wasn't making any sound. None. Before the afternoon was over, he was gone. And my Mato and I were brought down to the streets!' Her voice choked with tears. 'Please, Thakur, say something to the master. I need the keys to the barn—we have nothing else. I'll pay back the money, I really will. Somehow or another, master will get his loan back. Just ask him to . . .'

Just then, Awnnoda's cousin's son arrived at the temple courtyard. The assembled gentlemen immediately lost all interest in Tomrej's wife and her starving child.

'Come, come, Neeren Babaji!' Dinu Bhotchaj greeted the young man warmly. 'Did you go towards the fields for a walk today? This is the land of your ancestors, you know. How do you like it so far?'

Neeren smiled a little. He was a strong, well-built, handsome young man, not more than twenty-one years old. Though perfectly pleasant, he preferred to speak as little as possible. He had been raised in the west, but he currently lived in Calcutta, studying to be a lawyer. Although his father had charged him with supervising the surveying of their lands, he didn't in fact understand the matter too well, nor was he particularly keen to. Most of his days were spent reading novels and shooting fowl in the woods. He had even brought his own gun.

After some pleasantries, Neeren went upstairs. As he turned towards his room, he saw that his cousin Gokul's wife was sitting on the floor, rapidly picking up broken shards of glass. Curious, he approached the doorway silently. As hc came closer, he noticed that his expensive imported lamp was sitting on the floor, minus its glass dome. Ah, so that was what it was! Having worked out the mystery, Neeren walked confidently towards his room.

Gokul's wife hadn't heard him come up the stairs. At the sound of sudden footsteps, she whipped to face the door, startled. Neeren saw that she had spread the free end of her sari on the floor to collect all the shards and fragments. It seemed to him that she had come in to do her usual dusting, then decided to light the lamp for him, but broken the dome because it wasn't a local, familiar model. When he came in, she had clearly been trying to erase all evidence of the mishap and escape before the owner of the lamp returned. The embarrassment at being caught was written all over her face.

In an effort to make her feel less guilty, Neeren decided to make light of the situation.

'Breaking lamps around the house this evening, eh, elder sister-in-law?' he said jovially. 'All that efficient clean-up wouldn't have hidden your crime, you know. I'm a student of law! Now leave the shards alone and bring me a cup of tea—let's see how efficient you really are. Wait . . . before you go, let me light the lamp. I have a spare dome in my bag, thank goodness.'

His bustling about finally made Gokul's wife smile a little. 'Should I go down and get you some matches, younger brother-in-law?'

'You didn't bring matches? What were you doing with the lamp if you didn't have matches?'

Gokul's wife flashed him a slightly bigger grin. 'Not light, clean,' she explained shyly. 'Saw cobwebs in it when I was cleaning the room, so I thought, let me clean that as well. But when I tried to bring it down . . . I don't understand these mechanical English lamps . . . but wait, let me first get you the matches.'

Then she ran down the flight of stairs, but not before smiling shyly at him one more time.

Although Neeren had already been in the house for ten or twelve days, he hadn't really spoken to Gokul's wife before. This, despite the fact that technically she was his sister-in-law and therefore, socially, quite a close relation. But after The Incident of the Broken Dome, the awkwardness between the two dissolved. Neeren had grown up with every luxury and means of entertainment, and on top of that this was his first visit to rural Bengal. With no friends or any of his own things around to pass the time, he had been finding village life rather hard going. But now, with easy conversations with a sister-in-law his own age, he found that teatimes, at least, were easier to endure.

Durga stopped by Awnnoda Roy's house that afternoon. She peeked in the kitchen, where Gokul's wife was the only one working.

'What are you cooking, Auntie?' she asked, and not casually. She was very fond of Gokul's wife, and genuinely interested in her day.

'My favourite niece!' said Gokul's wife happily. 'Come in, my dear, come in. Mind helping me a little? I can't handle all of this alone.'

Durga was a frequent visitor to the kitchen, and whenever she came she tried to help Gokul's wife with her mountain of chores. She immediately began cutting the fish to size. 'Where'd you get these crabs, Auntie?' she asked, pointing to the little pile. 'These crabs aren't for eating.'

'Aren't for eating? But why? That fisherwoman Bidhu told me this is what everyone ate.'

'You paid for these? With actual money?'

'Of course I paid for them! But Bidhu gave me a good deal—only five paise for that whole lot.'

Durga wisely chose not to pursue the matter. To herself, she thought, 'Auntie's a darling in every other way, but she is a bit simple. Whoever heard of people eating these crabs, let alone spending money on them? That Bidhu tricked her—and all because she's a sweet, trusting person.'

With that last thought, she felt a surge of affection and protectiveness for this gullible aunt of hers, 'related' though they were only by virtue of being neighbours. Shorno, their milkwoman, had informed them the other day that Uncle Gokul had been seen beating Auntie on the head with his hard slippers. So the next morning, when Auntie didn't wet her head at the bathing steps, Durga immediately knew why. Her chest had tightened with pity and affection for her poor, sweet Auntie. But she hadn't said a word, because she didn't want to embarrass Auntie in front of the other women.

The other women, of course, had no such compunction. The eldest mistress of another Roy household had asked Auntie, 'What's wrong, daughter-in-law? No full dips today?'

Her aunt had simply smiled and said, 'Not today, Grandma. Haven't been feeling too well lately.'

Poor, simple Auntie. She thought no one knew that she had been beaten up at home, but every single woman on those steps had known. As soon as she left the pond, the eldest Roy mistress said, 'Did you see how badly that worthless Goklo had beaten her up? Her hair is still matted with dried blood!'

Wasn't that awful of the eldest Roy mistress? If she knew, she knew. Why did she have to ask Auntie that question, and why did she have to tell all the others?

Once the fish was done, Durga knew she would have to leave. But the question she had come to ask hadn't yet been broached. She glanced swiftly around the kitchen, making sure that no one else was within hearing distance. Then, nervously, she whispered, 'Auntie . . . would you have some extra paddy for making flattened rice? Only Opu was asking for flattened rice the other day, but we haven't bought any paddy for that this year . . .'

Gokul's wife also glanced around the kitchen. 'Come later in the afternoon,' she whispered back. Then she tilted her head towards the courtyard to indicate the rest of the family. 'Come after they've all gone inside for their naps, all right?'

Just before leaving, Durga asked, 'Oh, and who's your guest, Auntie? I heard that someone's come to stay in your house, but I haven't seen anyone yet.'

'Oh you haven't seen our younger brother-in-law? He's not at home right now, but you'll see him when you come in the afternoon.' Then she grinned mischievously. 'Younger brother-in-law and you, now there's a perfect match. What do you say, girl?'

Durga turned bright red. 'Auntie-e-e!'

Gokul's wife laughed out loud in delight. 'Why "Auntie-e-e"?' she said, grinning broadly. 'Is our girl lacking in any way? Let me see . . .'

Then she put her forefinger beneath Durga's chin and lifted her face to the light. 'There! Such a lovely face. As beautiful as the goddess herself! So what if her father doesn't have money for a dowry? Anyone would be lucky to have such a girl!'

Durga was both very flattered and acutely embarrassed. 'Auntie, you're . . . you're . . . *crazy*!' she exclaimed. Then she almost ran out of the kitchen to escape further conversation. Once she was safely out of the house and on her way home, she thought, 'Auntie is great, but she really is a little silly. Who else would think of such a . . . I mean, as if!'

Shorno the milkwoman arrived at Awnnoda Roy's home mere seconds after Durga had raced out. Gokul's wife was already busy with yet another of her many chores. When she heard Shorno, she came out of the kitchen and said, 'Both my hands are tied, Shonno. You know where the calf is tied—under the patchouli tree in the front courtyard. You'll have to bring it back here. The milking bowl is in the veranda over there. Take it once you've brought the calf back.'

With that, she went back to work.

A few minutes later, her aunt-in-law—Awnnoda Roy's sister Shokhi Thakrun—finished her lengthy morning puja and came outside to offer her final prayers. Turning north towards the local Kali temple, she folded her hands and bowed her head, then began chanting her prayers in the manner of a stage actor reciting a dramatic monologue.

'I bese-e-e-ech you, mother Shiddheshhhwori-i-i-i! Forgive our si-i-i-ns, mother-r-r! Make this day-y-y go well, as we continue to travel across the o-o-o-cean . . . of life! Mother Rokkhekali-i-i-i-i! Bring us sa-a-a-a-fely to the end of this day, mother-r-r-r! Save us and protec-c-c-t us, as we na-a-a-vigate these waters!'

Hearing the final prayers, Gokul's wife called out from within the kitchen, 'Auntie! I have saved a few jaggery-coconut naru for you. Have a couple of them with your water.'

Shokhi Thakrun didn't respond. But after a few seconds, her loud voice rang out across the inner courtyard. 'Daughter-in-law! Come here at once!'

Terror immediately gripped Gokul's wife. She was mortally afraid of Shokhi Thakrun and her hair-trigger temper. While distributing kindness and sympathy amongst his children, the almighty had shown a particular reticence towards her aunt-in-law. Her heart beating faster, Gokul's wife made her way over to the older woman.

Shokhi Thakrun was bent over the row of freshly washed utensils set out to dry in the veranda. When her niece-in-law reached her, she jabbed her finger towards one of the vessels.

'Look! Use your own eyes for once. Do you see? The clear mark of water—do you see that? Shonno must have picked up the bowl from here, and the water dripped from her hand on to these vessels. And you, you fool, picked them up and took them into the kitchen veranda! Gods protect us—our entire kitchen has been contaminated by that shudro woman's touch! Thank goodness I didn't touch that water jar, or I'd have to go down to the pond at this late hour for another bath!'

She proceeded to collapse on the veranda a little further away. Such was her dismay that a person just stepping into the house could have been forgiven for thinking that she'd just been informed of the death of a favourite son.

Gokul's wife stood in front of the utensils, dejected. She knew exactly where this was headed and she bitterly regretted letting it happen. 'Why did I have to ask that stupid Shonno to take the bowl?' she berated herself silently. 'Never mind indoor chores—I should have come out and handed it to her myself.'

Her lack of immediate action enraged Shokhi Thakrun further.

'Standing around like a shameless hag! What's that going to achieve, eh?' she screamed. 'Thought I'd finally get something to eat at this late hour, but no! The whole kitchen is rotten now. Go inside and throw away everything you've cooked so far! Wash each and every one of these vessels again! Then wipe every inch of the kitchen with cow-dung water! Then go down to the river and take a proper, cleansing bath!'

She stopped to replenish her breath, then pretended to talk to herself, though people walking along the lane outside the compound could easily have heard every word.

'This is what happens when worthless girls from bone-skint families worm their way into a gentleman's household. It's not their fault. How would they know about the ways of decent people? No, the fault is *ours* for bringing these starving wretches into our households. These ignorant hags ruin our caste, and destroy our household purity!'

With that final pronouncement, Shokhi Thakrun, still shaking with righteous rage, retreated to the unpolluted sanctuary of her own room. The glare of the afternoon sun was too hot for her to carry on outside.

It was almost evening by the time Gokul's wife finished complying with all her aunt-in-law's orders. By the time she went down to the river for her bath, exhaustion, the heat, and sharp pangs of hunger had almost driven her to the point of collapse.

At that hour, the bathing steps at the river were deserted. Sunshine glittered on the water and on the tops of the silk-cotton tree, but the bank was cool and dark with the shade of the thick canopy. A sailboat drifted past the bend in the river. A man was standing at the stern, holding up a cloth to the sun. It fluttered like a damp flag in the breeze. A big turtle emerged in the middle of the river, took a deep breath and promptly dove in again. The glug-glug-glug of the dive echoed for a short while in the empty, sunny landscape. A cool smell wafted across the surface of the water. A little distance away on the opposite shore, a cormorant perched at the edge of a bamboo fishing platform, waiting for that tell-tale little bubble to rise to the surface . . .

Every day, at around this lonely, quiet time, Gokul's wife remembered bits of her childhood. She and her friends had a rhyme about the cormorant, of which she now recalled only the first two lines.

Cormorant, O cormorant
Swim up to the bank . . .

Gokul's wife stood in the shallows and stared at the cormorant for a while. Whenever she thought of her childhood, she thought of her dear mother's face. Without her mother, there was no one in her family who would spare her a thought, who would wonder from time to time how she was doing. Had her mother really been old enough to pass away? Her only remaining family was a brother—an addict whom no one kept track of. Who knew where he was right now? He had come last year during the pujas, and stayed with her for a while. She had quietly slipped him what little she could from time to time—a quarter of a rupee here, a few annas there. Then one day, he abruptly disappeared. It was later discovered that he had bought a woollen shawl from a Kabuli trader on credit, and written Gokul's name in the trader's book.

Gokul's wife shuddered when she remembered the punishment that had followed. Her in-laws had heaped the vilest abuse on her family, on her parents, on her. That was the last she had heard of her brother.

In rare moments of respite from her chores, she often wept for her feckless, addled little brother. Perhaps, at this very moment, her vagabond brother was straggling along the narrow muddy lanes of some distant village, no hope for shelter and no real destination in mind. There was not a single person in their lives who could look after him. Both his life and hers were interminable waves of helplessness and misery. There was no hope of escape. Within seconds of having that thought, everything around her—the floating clouds, the shady riverbank, the silk-cotton tree on the shore, the cormorant, the sailboat anchored at the bend—dissolved into hopeless pools of bitter tears.

18

THAT DAY AFTER lunch, Opu had gone to the fisherman's neighbourhood to play with cowrie shells. It was after two in the afternoon, and the sun was at its harshest. His first stop was at Tinkori fisherman's house. Tinkori's son Bonka was under their guava tree, sharpening a piece of split bamboo.

'Oi, want to come play cowries?' Opu asked.

Bonka very much wanted to, but he was scheduled to go on the boat. His father would be furious if he disappeared to play cowries. Reluctantly, he refused.

Next, Opu went by Ramchoron fisherman's house. Ramchoron was sitting on his outer veranda, smoking tobacco.

'Is Hridoy at home?' Opu asked him.

'What'd you want with Hridoy, Thakur?' Ramchoron replied gruffly. 'Cowries, is it? No, Hride isn't at home. Be about your way!'

Walking about under the midday sun had begun to tan Opu's fair face red. He went to a few more houses in the neighbourhood, but found no one free to play with him. He was on the brink of giving up, when he struck gold under the tamarind tree near Baburam Parui's house. A large group of boys had gathered under the tree, and they were playing cowries. Opu's face lit up at the sight. Most of the boys were from fishermen families, but there was also Potu, a young boy from the brahmin colony. Opu didn't know Potu that well for they lived quite far from each other and were from different age groups. Indeed, he had only met Potu when he had started going to Proshonno Gurumoshai's school. Potu had been the boy sitting in the back row, silently chewing the edge of a palmyra leaf. Still, as the only other outsider in this neighbourhood, Opu walked up to Potu.

'How many cowries?' he asked.

Potu untucked his cowrie pouch from his waistband. 'Seventeen cowries. Seven of them gold-veined. And if I lose these, I can get more.'

Then he pointed proudly to his pouch. It was a small bag woven with bright yarn, and one of Potu's most treasured possessions. 'Do you like this, Opuda? It can hold eighty cowries—a full pon!'

The games began. Potu was losing at first, but soon he started winning. As he had discovered a few days back, his aim in the game of cowries was becoming nearly perfect. It was confidence in his new skill along with the dream of winning a whole pon of cowries that had brought him this far out of his own neighbourhood. Following the rules of the game, he would aim at a big cowrie and strike. His face lit up every time he made a shell twirl out of its square. He carefully stashed every cowrie he won into his pouch. Every so often, he would open up the pouch and peer into it, eagerly counting how many more he would have to win to fill it up.

After this went on for a while, a few of the local boys suddenly called a halt and went into a huddle. After some whispered conferring, one of them broke away and approached Potu.

'Your aim's too good, Thakur,' he said. 'You will have to aim from a foot further than the rest of us.'

Potu instantly straightened. 'It's not a crime to have a good aim!' he protested. 'You can aim as well as you like—I'm not stopping anyone from winning!'

The fishermen's boys refused to yield. Looking at the cowries he'd already won, Potu began to think that an early retirement might be the better part of greed. He'd never before won as many cowries as he had that afternoon. If the others forced him to aim from an extra foot away, there was a good chance that he would lose all the shells he had won, and then a few. No reason to take such risks.

'I think I'm done for the day,' he declared. 'I'll be going home now.' Then, seeing the violence written clearly in the eyes of the other boys, he involuntarily wrapped his fist tighter around his precious pouch.

A second boy broke away from the huddle and came forward. 'Not so fast, Thakur. Planning on making off with our cowries, were you?' His arm shot out and clamped on Potu's wrist.

Potu tried to free his wrist, but soon realized he was nowhere near strong enough. 'Why are you acting like this? Let me go,' he pleaded. By now, all the local boys had surrounded him. One of them shoved him from behind. Potu fell, but didn't let go of his pouch. He knew that was what the boys were after. So he lay prone on the ground, pressing the pouch to his stomach, determined not to give in. But he was only a boy, and a weak one at that. His strength was no match for the much older and stronger boys of the fishermen's neighbourhood. Before long, the pouch was snatched from his grasp, and his shells scattered all over the ground.

At first, Opu hadn't exactly been unhappy at Potu's troubles. After all, he too had lost several cowries to Potu's excellent aim. But when the boys shoved Potu to the ground and began beating him up, his heart constricted in sudden alarm. He began pushing through the crowd that was raining blows on Potu, shouting, 'He's just a small child! Why're you beating him up like this? Let him go—let him go, I say!'

Once he reached Potu, he tried to help him get back on his feet. But then someone's fist connected with the back of his head, and he collapsed next to Potu, right in the middle of the shoving and pushing. The punch had been so hard that for the next few seconds he saw nothing but darkness.

Opu was destined for a severe beating that day. Though older than Potu, there wasn't much strength in his delicate, effeminate frame. It was Neeren's sudden appearance on the road that saved both boys. The moment the other boys spotted Neeren, they fled. Dazed, Opu managed to stand up, but Potu had been hurt quite severely. Neeren had to help him get up and shake the dirt off his clothes. After recovering his bearings, Potu began to immediately search for his precious shells. But all of them save a scattered couple had disappeared, and with them his beautiful cowrie pouch. Potu simply stood under the tamarind tree, absorbing the enormity of his loss. Then, slowly, he walked up to Opu.

'I hope you weren't hurt too badly, Opuda,' he said, concern mixing with heartbreak in his voice.

Neeren gave both boys quite a talking-to for coming this far from home to play cowries with fishermen's sons, and in such scorching heat at that. Time passed slowly for him in the sleepy village, so to make it pass, he had started an informal school in one corner of Awnnoda Roy's temple courtyard. He exhorted both Opu and Potu to begin attending that school from the very next day, instead of wasting their time wandering about the village. Then he walked them both back to their own neighbourhoods, and saw them home.

Opu was listening to Neeren talk about the school during the walk. Potu, however, barely heard a word. All he could think of as he trudged through the lanes that took him back home was the tragedy of his lost cowries and pouch.

'My beautiful pouch,' he mourned silently. 'I got it only the other day from Chibas—and after so much pleading, too. Gone! What is it to those boys if I want to stop playing after I have won? I can do as I like, can't I? Can't I?'

Opu, on the other hand, forgot all about cowries the moment he reached home and spotted his sister. He had his own tragedy to avenge.

'Didi! I had kept a bent branch near the trunk of the night-jasmine tree. Were you the one who broke it into two?'

Durga had indeed broken the branch, but she was not about to be held accountable for it by her younger brother. 'As if it was anything special,' she derided. 'As if one wouldn't find *loads* of sticks just like that if they just looked inside the bamboo grove! Oh no, we must mourn broken twigs now—silly boy!'

Opu felt a little embarrassed, but he wasn't about to give in. 'Of course it was special!' he countered. 'Why don't *you* go get me another one just like that if it's so easy? I found that stick after hours of searching—why would you just break it?'

His eyes filled with tears at the injustice of it all.

For once, Durga didn't melt immediately to his tears. 'I'll get you as many sticks as you want,' she said dismissively. 'There's no need to bring on the waterworks.'

But his sister didn't understand the charm of bent sticks. They might just be simple dried-up twigs to others, slightly broadened at the base and tapered at the tip, but to Opu they were near-magical. With the stick in his hand, he could roam all morning and all afternoon, along the river-path or through the bamboo groves, lost in the magical worlds inside his own head. Some days he would be a prince, some days a tobacconist in a faraway shop. On other days he would be an adventurer, a general leading the charge, or even Orjun from the Mahabharat. As he walked up and down, he flourished a stick and told himself stories of these people's lives; *his* life, really, for as long as he had the stick to flourish. The lighter the stick, and the more perfectly bent, the further his imagination would go. But finding the perfect stick wasn't easy. Only he knew how hard he had had to look before he found one that gave free rein to his dreams!

Of course, Opu had to be very careful that no one found out about these stick-and-story episodes. If people saw him roaming around, muttering to himself and waving about a twig or split piece of bamboo, they would think that he had lost his mind. So not only did he avoid places that were frequented by people, he eschewed even those where there was only a slight chance of meeting someone else. His favourite places to play pretend were by the lonely stretches of the riverbank, the deserted parts of the bamboo grove, or in the dark shade of the large tamarind tree behind their house. Even then, he kept a sharp eye out for accidental passers-by. If he thought anyone was coming his way, he would immediately throw away the stick and blush furiously. Though young, he realized that flights of fancy such as his were not common amongst his peers, and as much as he loved it, he was also quite embarrassed about his secret game.

The only other person who knew was his sister. She had caught him a couple of times in the act, so he saw no point in hiding it from her any further. In fact, it was the only reason that he had asked her directly about the stick. Had it been anyone else, Opu could never have brought himself to admit that he even knew there was a broken stick in the house. Although no one knew of his secret relationship with sticks, he always felt that everyone was actually in on the secret. If he said as much as a word, they would pile on each other to mock him for being crazy. No one understood the magic of sticks—this much he had noticed. Well, they were missing out, they really were. Why, give him a properly curved stick, and he could spend all day without company or sustenance, happily striding along the empty riverbank or bamboo grove, lost in the exquisite delight of make-believe!

When his sister found out about his little game, he had begged and pleaded with her to not tell their mother. Durga hadn't. She knew her little brother was a little silly, a bit young and innocent for his age. But that only made her feel more protective towards him. Their mother didn't need to know his every secret.

The day before the Modhushonkranti ritual, Shorbojoya instructed her son to invite Neeren to their house for a meal. 'Invite your new Master Moshai home tomorrow—tell him he'll have his lunch here.'

She had planned an elaborate feast for the occasion: rice, papaya cubes in thin gravy, sour-fig curry, paste of cooked banana stem, small prawns in gravy, banana fritters and rice pudding.

She had also roped in Durga to serve the food. Durga had no experience in this sort of thing, and was consequently terribly anxious about slipping up in front of a guest. When the day finally came, she took ages to just lower the bowl of daal, as if at any moment a watching jury would shout at her for being slow or sloppy.

Neeren, unfortunately, was not accustomed to such poor fare: the rice grains were entirely too thick for his taste. The curries barely tasted of anything—neither tempering or spices, nor oil or ghee. The pudding was thin and gruel-like, its milk clearly diluted with a great deal of water. A small taste killed half his enthusiasm for dessert.

Opu, on the other hand, was relishing every bit of the rare feast. He'd seldom had such an elaborate spread at home—barely twice in his entire life, in fact. He enthusiastically asked his sister for seconds and thirds of everything.

'Have some more pudding, Master Moshai,' he invited Neeren generously.

It was a day of great happiness for him. If his life had been a book, the details of the day's marvellous meal would have been inscribed in it in letters of gold. With such glorious abundance on his plate, he was going to remember this day for a long, long time.

When Neeren finally reached Awnnoda Roy's home that afternoon, Gokul's wife could no longer keep the real reason behind the lunch to herself.

'Did you like our Dugga, younger brother-in-law?' she asked directly. 'Such a pretty girl, isn't she? A penniless family, alas. Who knows whose hands she'll end up in—her father will never have the money for a suitable match. Poor girl. Suffering is probably all she has written in her lot. Why don't you do something, younger brother-in-law? Why don't *you* marry her? Her family is the right caste, and the girl is good-looking. What more could one want? Both brother and sister have that doll-like prettiness about them, don't they?'

The next day, on his way back from the survey tent, Neeren had taken the path through the mango orchards behind the village. As he emerged from a narrow wooded lane, he saw a girl come out of the orchard and step on to the path. He recognized her—it was Opu's sister, Durga, the girl his sister-in-law had wanted him to marry.

'Khuki!' he called out. 'Are these your gardens?'

Durga turned around. When she saw who it was, a world of shyness descended on her. She couldn't think of a single thing to say. When Neeren caught up to her, she tried to step aside to let him pass. Neeren, however, indicated that she should lead the way.

'You walk ahead of me, Khuki. I need your help to find my way back home. I've no idea how I ended up by that pond back there. You people have terribly dense jungles growing all over your land!'

Durga silently led the way. Only once did she turn her head back to sneak a look at Neeren. The movement dislodged some fruits from the folds of her sari, and they rolled on the dusty woodland path.

Neeren hurried forward. 'What was that, Khuki? What fruits are these?'

Durga, dying with embarrassment while scrambling after the fruits, mumbled, 'Nothing . . . wild potatoes.'

'Wild potato fruits? Are they good to eat? How does one eat them?'

Durga was surprised. How could such a learned, bespectacled man not know about wild potatoes? Even a child of five knew about them! But shyness stole her usual fluency. 'Can't eat . . . too bitter,' was all she managed.

'Then why are you . . .?'

Discomfited by the questions, Durga mumbled, '. . . to play with.'

It was hard for her to speak normally to this bespectacled young man from the city. She knew he was the person her village aunt was trying to arrange her wedding to. Ever since she had found that out, she had been tempted to sneak a good look at him, yet felt a world of shyness descend on her whenever he was even mentioned. She hadn't even been able to raise her eyes to his face when she was serving him lunch in her own home. She certainly couldn't bring herself to look at him now.

'Tell Opu to come take his book tomorrow morning, will you?' Neeren said, after a few seconds of silence.

Durga tilted her head in assent. After a while, where the path forked into two, she pointed to the lane veering off to one side. 'This is your way,' she said, eyes firmly away from Neeren.

'Never mind me, I can find my own way now,' Neeren said. 'Let me walk with you a little longer. Can you find your way home alone?'

Durga nodded. 'Our house is just up ahead,' she said, pointing. 'There's no need for you to come.'

Before that very moment, Neeren hadn't had a good look at Durga's face. Now that he did, he thought he had never seen such beautiful, expressive eyes before (except in her brother, Opu, of course). The tranquillity in their depths reminded him of a secluded copse of medlars—fragrant and peaceful. The dark ring that surrounded the deep central pool seemed to him to be the liquid darkness of the night hour just before dawn. It held the promise of first light, of the sounds of village women heading down to the pond, of the fragrance of incense sticks, and a new awakening in every house.

For a while, Durga simply stood on the path. It seemed to Neeren that she wanted to say something else, but was too shy.

'Come, let me walk you a little further,' he said, in the hopes of encouraging her. 'I can return by the main path that passes in front of your house.'

Durga hesitated a bit, then bit back a smile. Neeren felt certain that she would say something then, but Durga only shook her head to indicate that he didn't need to accompany her. Then she turned around and walked rapidly down the path towards her secluded home.

~

Afternoon, a few days later.

After picking up dried clothes from the clothesline on the roof, Gokul's wife peeked into Neeren's room on her way down. Neeren was sitting on the floor writing letters, having given up on trying to sleep in the heat.

'Not sleeping this afternoon, younger brother-in-law? I thought I'd find you asleep. You barely had any lunch—most of your banana-flower curry was left on the plate!'

'Sister-in-law! Come in, come in. And how could a reasonable person eat that banana-flower curry? The amount of chillies you people put in your cooking—I could barely tell where the curry ended and the chillies began!'

Gokul's wife leaned against the doorframe and hid her grin behind the loose end of the sari. 'You're such a city gent, younger brother-in-law,' she teased. 'No one from your sophisticated land can tolerate even a little chilli, can they?'

'"A little chilli"? Forgive me, sister-in-law—if that is what you call a *little* chilli, then I'm not leaving this place till I've tried what you people consider a lot! I hereby abandon my well-being to fate! But then again, how much worse can it be, really? After the amount of chillies I ate today, anything hotter can only be like taking a whip to a corpse. Forget caution for a day, sister-in-law, and add as many chillies as you like!'

'As if I've locked my mortar and pestle away for fear of scarring your palate! The things you say, younger brother-in-law! Taking a whip to a corpse . . . honestly!' The absurd idiom broke the last of her reserve and she began shaking with laughter.

After a while, when she recovered from her fit of giggles, she asked curiously, 'The place where you are from, younger brother-in-law . . . how hot does it get there?'

'The place where I am from? Do you mean Calcutta or the west? You cannot even ever fathom our western heat, sitting in Bengal. In summer we can't even sleep in our rooms. We have to start flooding the roof with water from late afternoon so that it cools down enough for us to sleep indoors at night.'

'How far is this place? The west, I mean?'

'Almost two days' journey by the railroad. If you take a train from your Majherpara station in the morning, then it'll be almost midnight the next day when you reach.'

Gokul's wife came a step inside the room in her eagerness. 'Tell me, younger brother-in-law, they say they've cut a way through the mountains to make the railroad to Goya and Kashi. Is it true?'

'Oh yes, completely true. Huge mountains, too—covered in dense forests. When the train goes through the mountains—tunnels, it's called—everything goes pitch black. You can't see a thing. People have to turn on the light inside each coach.'

'But . . . but . . . wouldn't it cave in?'

'Why would it cave in, sister-in-law? Famous engineers have come together to design the tunnel, huge sums of money have been spent building it—how can it cave in just like that? It's not like the bathing steps at the village pond that it'll crumble a little every day.'

Gokul's wife did not understand what sort of a creature an engineer was. So instead she asked, 'These mountains—are they made of soil? Or stones?'

'Both soil and stones. Honestly, sister-in-law, you are such a naive village girl! Tell me, how far have you actually gone by train?'

Gokul's wife began laughing again. Her eyes nearly closed with mirth, and she lifted her chin like a child telling an obvious fib. 'Who, me? I've gone so-o-o-o far. Kashi, Goya, Mokka, Medina—I've been to every place a person wants to go to!'

Then she leashed her merriment a little and said more soberly, 'I've been on a train only once, younger brother-in-law. The other year, when I accompanied my aunt-in-law and Shotu's mother from the Mukhujje household to visit the temple of the god Jugolkishor at Aranghata. There—that's the extent of my adventures on the railroad!'

Neeren really liked how this girl wove an atmosphere of light-hearted laughter from the smallest of things. Some people have an endless fountain of joy within them, which spills over and infects everyone around them. This girl was one of them. Neeren had come to eagerly await their little chats in his room. On days when she didn't stop by, he was disappointed, and, truth be told, a little hurt.

'All of you should come to the west once, sister-in-law,' he said. 'Come and let me show you around personally.'

A note of derision entered Gokul's wife's laughter. 'That will be the day, younger brother-in-law! People of this household going on holiday to the west? Who will tend to their precious brinjal crop in the northern fields, then?'

A small silence followed.

Then Gokul's wife said in a completely sober voice, 'Younger brother-in-law . . . will you keep a request of mine?'

'What is it?'

'I'll tell you, but only if you promise to keep it.'

'You know I'm a student of law, sister-in-law. I cannot sign on a blank paper like that. First let me hear what it is that you have to say then I'll let you know if I can keep it.'

Gokul's wife left the doorway completely and came inside the room. She took something wrapped in paper from within the folds of her sari.

'Will you keep these two earrings as collateral and give me five rupees?'

Neeren was astonished. 'But why, sister-in-law?'

'I cannot tell you that, younger brother-in-law. But will you give me the money?'

'Tell me why you need the money. If I don't know why, then . . .'

Gokul's wife relented. 'I have to send it to someone,' she confessed in hushed tones. 'Here, read the address on this envelope and tell me where to send it—it's in English.'

Neeren read the address. 'This is your brother, isn't it, sister-in-law?'

'Hush, hush! Don't let anyone in this house hear you. He has asked for five rupees. Now where am I to get five rupees from? You know the life I lead in this house. A prisoner, that is what I am! So I thought—these are my own earrings, brother-in-law, not from this family. Won't you give me five rupees for them? That wretched brother of mine has no one else to turn to . . .'

Her voice grew heavy with tears.

Neeren said, 'I'll give you the money, sister-in-law. Five rupees, ten rupees—whatever you need. But I cannot take your earrings from you.'

Gokul's wife's sombre mood lifted immediately. She grinned through her unshed tears. 'That's not how lending works, my dear younger brother-in-law. What kind of a businessman are you? What'll happen to my soul if I die while still in your debt? No no, you must take the earrings. All right, I have to go now. I've left a lot of work downstairs, but didn't dare talk to you at any other time . . .'

She left the room hurriedly but turned back just as she was about to go down the stairs.

'Don't tell anyone about the money, younger brother-in-law,' she begged. 'You understand, don't you? Not a soul.'

~

Later that night, a few minutes after brother and sister had turned in, Durga whispered happily from under the blankets. 'Opu! Are you awake? Listen to this!'

Opu had been awake. He'd just been silent so far. Now he said, 'Didi, would you shut that window first? It's letting the cold air in.'

Durga got up, closed the shutters, and climbed back in.

'Do you remember when Ranu's didi's wedding is?' she asked, once back under the blankets. 'Not too long, now! I heard there's going to be loads of stuff happening around the wedding. There'll be English music—that's what I heard today. Have you ever heard English music?'

'Oh yes. They wear these hats and have huge pipes. Big drums, too. There's this pipe they play—blackish, not too big. It's called the fulut pipe. Have you ever heard the fulut pipe, Didi? It's beautiful!'

But Durga's mind had already moved on from the music. She was now thinking of something a lot more intriguing. Last evening, she had gone to visit her favourite village aunt at Awnnoda Roy's house. After some general catching up, her aunt had asked, 'Accha, Durga, where exactly did you meet my younger brother-in-law? He said he'd been lost in the woods . . .'

Enthusiastically, Durga had told her aunt the circumstances under which she had met Neeren in the wooded back lanes.

'He had completely lost his way, Auntie!' she had laughed. 'Gone all the way to that pond near the old fort—would you believe that? Lost and alone in that godforsaken jungle, hee hee . . .'

Her aunt had grinned right back at her. 'I was telling him about you yesterday. I said, "Poor girl, their family is not well off and her father won't be able to give you anything for the wedding. But our Dugga is such a good girl! You won't find girls like her in this age—she's like a transplant from the golden times. Take her home, younger brother-in-law; make her your own." So then he began asking about you, said you helped him find his way after he went astray and so on . . . anyway, I've been trying to get my father-in-law to speak to your father—it's been three days already, but I'm not giving up. Younger brother-in-law is definitely amenable—he seems to have taken quite a shine to you. And why not, when our girl is so lovely, eh?'

The next morning, Durga took the calf out from the dark cowshed and tied her in the sun. Usually, she at least tried to help her mother with some of the housework, but this morning she felt like doing nothing at all. A sense of carefree wanderlust had come over her. She felt like no fence, no rules could hold her back today. This feeling sneaked up on her every now and then, so she did what she normally did under those circumstances. She slipped out of the house, chores forgotten, and spent the morning flitting from one village backlane to another, weaving in and out of the surrounding neighbourhoods. The breeze was perfect this morning: neither too hot, nor too cold. It carried with it the sweet fragrance of lime flowers, reminding her of something . . . but she couldn't quite put her finger on what it was. The thing lurked just beyond the reach of her mind, a phantom half-memory.

She decided to stop by Ranu's house. Bhubon Mukhujje was quite a wealthy landowner, and Ranu's didi was his eldest daughter. That there would be pomp at her wedding was practically a given. The fireworks man was at the house this morning, finalizing the details of his show. Durga had heard that Sheetanath, their area's most celebrated musician, had been commissioned to play at the wedding. Several of the Mukhujjes' relatives had already begun arriving and settling into guest quarters. The sounds of their children playing with the household children filled the Mukhujjes' courtyard.

The sights and sounds of the oncoming festivities exhilarated Durga. In just a few days, she'd be able to see a fireworks show. Her first fireworks show ever! Well, all right, she'd seen some at the Ganguly household one summer during the celebration of Jhulan, Radha–Krishna's floral swing ceremony. But that little thing had only whetted her appetite. She could spend hours watching the fireworks whoosh into the sky, then burst into a handful of stars before coming down. Opu said that the boys called it 'howibaaji'. It was amazing stuff.

She went back home for lunch, but once her mother lay down on the veranda for her afternoon nap she slipped out of the house again. It was the middle of the month of Falgun. Spring had begun to melt into summer. The afternoon sun rained fire from the sky. The outer leaves of the neem tree next to Ranu's house were turning yellow and dying from the constant heat. There was no one around on the little village back path. The only human noise was the sound of someone beating a tin drum from the direction of Nyara's house.

Suddenly, the stillness was broken by a buzzing noise. A green jewel bug! Without noticing that she was doing it, Durga clutched the end of her sari in her fist in anticipation. Where was the bug?

There it was, on the path! Not a jewel bug, but a red ladybug. Oh wow! Durga's fist unclenched automatically. Carefully, she tiptoed towards the insect. It was sitting on the side of the road, the spot on its wings like tiny sandalwood markings.

A ladybug was not really an insect. Everyone said it was the god Shudorshon in insect form. It was extraordinary luck to have spotted one. So she'd heard from her mother, and indeed many others. Seeing one today, of all days, must be a sign of good things to come.

Durga lowered herself next to the insect, careful not to frighten it. Then, first pointing her reverently folded palms towards the insect and then bringing them up to her forehead, she chanted, 'God Shudorshon, keep us safe. God Shudorshon, keep us safe. God Shudorshon, keep us safe.'

This was the standard chant that she had learnt from other women. After that basic ritual was done, she looked around and quickly added a few hushed words of her own.

'God, keep Opu well, keep Ma well, keep Baba well, keep Auntie from the other neighbourhood well.'

Then she hesitated for a second before rapidly adding, 'Keep Neeren Babu well. And please, god, let my wedding be arranged with him! And let there be as much pomp and splendour at that wedding as there's going to be in Ranu's didi's wedding.'

This extreme show of faith in his powers appeared to fluster the god Shudorshon, for his insect form began inscribing helpless circles on the ground. Durga didn't notice. She continued to pray till she was content. Then she respectfully passed him and went on her way.

If anyone in the village had cared to look up, they might have noticed that at this time of the year, Contentment offered a clear view of the bright, sun-washed blue of the early Falgun sky, stretching above the treetops in an uninterrupted arch. Sometimes, the sun-washed blue briefly turned a rare peacock-blue. The narrow back lane that began from the cluster of sandpaper trees continued through the mango orchards. The air around it was warm and suffused with the sweet smell of ripening mangoes. One could hear the low buzzing of bees and jewel bugs, and the high notes of the cuckoo's call. The mango and sandpaper canopies cast a cool, dark shadow on the path, even as the Falgun afternoon blazed beyond.

The field where the Chorok festivities took place was at the end of this path. The orchards cast a small shadow on the thick grass of the field. At this time of the year, the field was covered in undergrowth. Once she reached the field, Durga went into the bushes, looking for wild plums and berries. Good, edible berries were hard to find this time of the year, having mostly ripened at the end of winter. Just the other day she had found a cluster in the bushes beyond that mound over there, but that had been pure luck. There were none to be found now. Instead she found dried remains of the berries from last winter, strewn about the bushes like a sprinkling of ground black pepper. A flock of birds had been carrying on within the bushes when she started looking for berries. When they saw her approach, they suddenly took flight in a hasty rustle of wings.

The joy that had been building in her heart from the previous night suddenly burst forth and flooded her whole being. Good times were on their way! The oncoming festivities, Ranu's didi's approaching wedding, staying up all night to watch the Chorok jatra . . . she felt like running around in joy. Seeing that she was alone, she actually spread her arms like a bird spreads its wings and ran around the field for a while. She wished she could fly; then she would go up, like those birds. Way, way up, into that clear blue sky. The body was such a light thing. If she had feathers on her arms, she was certain she could easily have glided through the air. Then, for the sheer joy of hearing the crunch, she walked up and down on the piles of dry leaves in a corner of the field. The leaves crumbled beneath her feet and filled the air with dusty leaf powder, and the slightly bitter smell of old damp soil.

The narrow path continued on the other side of the field as an unpaved road that led straight to the Shonadanga moors. A bullock cart was making its way down that road, its wheels crunching the soil underneath. Its awning was made of young bamboo. Red quilts and embroidered blankets had been draped over the awning to make it into a little private room. From within, a girl could be heard crying in a monotonous, childish voice. Perhaps some farmer's daughter was being sent from her father's house to her in-laws' place.

Durga stood on the leaves, watching the disappearing cart with sudden fascination. Would she also have to leave everything behind after marriage? Her father, her mother, Opu? Where would she go? How far would that new place be? Would those people *ever* let her come home, never mind coming whenever she wished? These were aspects of marriage that she hadn't really considered. Would being married mean saying goodbye to everything familiar and beloved—all the things that made up her whole life? This field, the flowers of the malabar-nut plants, their red cow, the jackfruit tree in their courtyard, this smell of dried leaves, the lane to the women's bathing steps . . . *everything*?

If yes, then she understood why the little girl in the cart was crying.

The river was across the unpaved road, past a small field that had recently been burnt clean. A handful of fishermen had anchored their boats near the other bank, and were casting their nets. What fish were they catching? Khoyra? If they came to this bank, she would buy two paisa's worth to take home. Opu loved khoyra fish.

After she got home, she spent a long time in the evening arranging her doll box. Her mother had spilled a lot of kerosene oil on the floor while filling the lamp, and the room was filled with its distinctive smell. Even the air seemed a little warmer. She was almost done arranging her dolls' worldly goods when Opu suddenly stormed up to her.

'Didi, did you take the small mirror out my toy box?'

All of Durga's happy detachment left her. 'Your mirror?' she sneered. 'As if! That mirror is mine. I saw it first—it was lying under the bed. Now it's my mirror, so it'll stay in *my* box. What does a boy need a mirror for, anyway?'

'How is it yours? When Ma brought the mirror from Auntie's house, I asked her for it straightaway. No, Didi, you give my mirror back!'

Then, without waiting for his sister, he leaned forward and began digging haphazardly through Durga's doll box. Durga was incensed at the invasion. She slapped her brother's cheek.

'You brat! How dare you mess with my things? I spent all this time arranging my box—now look at it! I won't give you the mirror—keep your hands off my box. Go away!'

Even before she had finished speaking, Opu leapt on her and began mercilessly pulling fistfuls of her unoiled, curly hair.

'Why did you hit me? Why did you hit me?' he kept demanding over and over, his voice high-pitched with tears. 'Give me the mirror or I'll tell Ma. I know you stole the lacquer dye from her Lokkhi's basket! I'll tell her that too!'

At the charge of theft, Durga lost whatever was left of her cool. She caught her brother's ear in one hand and delivered a few swift slaps with the other. 'I took the aalta? *I* took it? You horrible awful boy! Like I don't know you stole the cowrie shells from that same basket? I can tell tales just as easily as you!'

Their collective screaming and shouting brought Shorbojoya running to the room. By then, Durga had almost forced Opu on the floor by pulling his ears. But Opu had her hair in his fists and was pulling with all his might, which meant that she was almost at the same level herself, and couldn't move her head even an inch. Of the two, Opu was probably hurt a little bit more. The minute he saw his mother, he began crying: 'Ma-a-a, look! She took the mirror out of my box and kept it in hers. She's not giving it back! And she slapped me so hard on my cheeks!'

'No, Ma!' Durga protested. 'I was just sitting here by myself, arranging my doll box, when he came in, and . . .'

Before she could finish, Shorbojoya walked swiftly up to the pair and rained several resounding blows on her daughter's back.

'Worthless girl! How dare you hit him? Don't you remember the difference in age between him and you? And all this over a mirror! Which of your funeral offerings will require a mirror, eh? Any excuse to beat the poor boy up! Die, why don't you? Box of dolls indeed! Just you wait . . .'

Without finishing her threat, Shorbojoya bent over, picked up the doll box, and threw it out of the house with as much force as she could muster. With mounting horror, Durga heard it crash somewhere in the dark courtyard. Her mother was still snarling at her. 'Useless lump! Doesn't do a smidgen of work—only stuffing her face and roaming about the neighbourhood all day! You see what I do to your box of dolls! I'll haul it all to the bamboo grove and chuck it in. Good luck ever finding your precious playthings then!'

Even after her mother stomped back to her work, Durga remained rooted to her spot, speechless with shock. Her doll box was her life. Her mother knew that. At least ten times a day she took everything out and rearranged the box—the dolls, various bits of coloured paper, scraps of printed fabric, the sheaves of red lacquer dye, dried nuts and berries that she had scoured the woods to get, an abandoned bird's nest. Each of those things were now scattered across the dark courtyard, likely lost or broken beyond repair. She could never have imagined such cruelty in her mother. To just throw her box out into the dark! She had spent hours searching for and collecting those treasures!

Her mother's abrupt cruelty had so stunned her that she hadn't been able to say a single word in her defence; instead she had stood in the room, bearing the blows numbly.

Even Opu felt that the punishment had been too harsh. Despite the victory, he quietly slipped away to bed, covering himself with the sheets and closing his eyes.

The night grew late and dark. The oil lamp that Shorbojoya had lit spread the smell of kerosene through the room. Mosquitoes began their nightly chorus from dark corners of the room. After several minutes of sitting still, staring at nothing, Durga finally went to bed. Moonlight streamed in through the broken window shutter, and with it the fragrance of lemon blossoms.

Despite being under the covers, Durga couldn't sleep. She wanted to go out and look for her precious possessions. If she waited till morning, she was certain most of them would be gone. But she didn't dare. What if her mother beat her again, this time for trying to undo the damage of her punishment?

Several minutes passed. Suddenly, she felt a hand on top of hers.

'Didi?' Opu whispered tremulously.

Before she could respond, Opu had pressed his face into the pillow and began to sob. 'I won't do it again, Didi! Please don't be angry with me!' her brother begged, his voice choked with tears.

Durga was surprised by the crying at first, then alarmed. Throwing aside her sheets, she sat up and tried to stem the oncoming tide.

'Shhhh, shhhh! Don't cry! If Ma hears you, she'll punish me again! Don't, please . . . okay, okay, I won't be angry, all right? Now stop crying, please!'

She had no doubt that if her mother heard her brother crying, she would storm in and deliver another set of blows to her, without letting her explain the situation.

It took a great deal of effort to calm Opu down. After several reassurances of forgiveness, she finally managed to stop his tears. She then put him back to bed and climbed in beside him. Then, to prevent a relapse, she distracted him with every bit of local news and speculation she had recently discovered. First she related every story she'd heard about Ranu's didi's wedding. After several minutes of this, Opu finally began chatting of things himself. Once Durga ran out of things to tell him, there was a brief silence.

Then Opu whispered, 'Shall I tell you a secret, Didi? You and Master Moshai are going to get married!'

Durga immediately felt shy, but also desperately curious. However, she was too embarrassed to discuss the matter with her younger brother, so she forced herself to remain silent.

Opu spoke up again, 'Auntie from the other neighbourhood was telling Ranu didi's mother this evening—I heard them myself. Apparently Master Moshai is not at all averse to the idea, so Auntie said.'

Durga could not hold back her curiosity any longer. But instead of asking a direct question, she said dismissively, '"They were saying"—as if they would! You and your stories, Opu . . . shoo!'

Opu almost sat up on the bed in excitement. 'No, Didi, it's true! Here, I touch and swear by you that it's true! I was right there—in fact, Auntie brought the subject up after she saw me. They'll get Baba to write a letter to Master Moshai's father, that's what they said.'

'Does Ma know?'

'When I heard the news I thought I'll go home right away and tell Ma—but then I forgot. Should I ask her if she knows? Maybe she doesn't, you know. Auntie did say that she would have to find Ma tomorrow to tell her . . .'

After a while, he said, 'Master Moshai lives really far away. You'll ride so many trains to get there—you'll see!'

Durga received this exciting news in silence. She had seen pictures of trains in Opu's books. They were impressive things. Very long, with many, many wheels, and a big engine in front. There was a fire in the engine—that's where all the smoke came from. All of the train was made of iron, even the wheels. No wooden wheels, like those on a bullock cart. She had also heard that there were no thatched houses near the railway line. There couldn't be. Train pipes shot out flames as it went past—a thatched house or wooden wheels would catch fire and burn down.

'Don't worry,' she reassured her brother, running an affectionate palm down his shoulder. 'I'll take you with me. We'll ride the train together.'

Afterwards, as sleep began to settle on both siblings' eyes, it occurred to Durga that Shudorshon really had answered her prayers. She had asked for her boon just that morning, and here it was, already granted by nightfall! Shudorshon really was kind, her mother had always said so.

Before drifting off, Opu opened his eyes one last time and said, 'Oh, and they brought home Leela Didi's wedding sari today. Such a lovely sari. Leela Didi's uncle bought it in Ranaghat's markets. The third-eldest aunt said it was a real Baluchori.'

Durga suddenly smiled in the darkness. 'Do you know this old rhyme? Pishima used to sing it:

On the sandy beaches of Baluchor, friend,
Such miracles grow!
Heard there's a baby peacock,
In the belly of a buffalo!'

19

OPU HAD BEEN nursing a secret for the past few days. He hadn't taken anyone into his confidence, not even his sister, for the secret had been too momentous to share. He had discovered it one afternoon a few days ago while surreptitiously exploring his father's wooden lockbox of books.

It had been an afternoon just like this one—golden and hot. The shadows of the trees were dense, short, and piled around the trunk; they hadn't yet begun to elongate and thin out along the east or the west. Taking advantage of his father's absence, Opu had slipped into the room that held Horihor's locked book box. Shutting the door behind him, he had pulled out the box and had been flipping through the books eagerly, looking for stories and pages with pictures. One of the books was called *Shorbo Dorshon Shongroho*: *A Collection of All Philosophies*. The book was clearly ancient: the thick, once-white marble-paper pages were turning brown, and there were large spots of discolouration on the cover. When he had opened it, silverfish had scurried out in all directions.

Opu had always had a soft spot for mysterious old books. He had lifted this one to his nose and inhaled deeply. He didn't understand what 'collection of philosophies' meant, but the smell of the old book enchanted him. It made him think of his father, who was so often gone from home.

He had stuffed the other books back into the box and hidden this one under his pillow.

It was in this book that he had discovered the secret. It was astonishing and frankly difficult to credit—yet there it was, printed on a proper sheet of book paper, in a real book. While describing the many qualities of quicksilver, the author said that if one filled vulture eggs with quicksilver and left them in the sun for a few days, then the eggs acquired the ability of letting humans fly. All a human had to do to fly was to hold the egg inside his mouth.

At first, Opu couldn't believe his eyes. So he read that bit again . . . and again. Then he hid the book inside his own broken-lidded book box and wondered at this amazing secret.

'Do you know where the vultures' nest is, Didi?' he asked his sister.

His sister had no idea. So he asked the neighbourhood boys. Shotu, Neelu, Kinu, Potol, Nyara—he asked everyone. Some of them said that the closest tree that housed vultures was the tallest one at the other end of the northern fields. Opu was all for hunting that tree down, but his mother told him off for roaming about all afternoon under the blazing sun. To placate her, he had to stay home after lunch and pretend to take a nap. But the moment he was alone, he took the book out of his box and read those lines over and over again. How could people not know of this simple way to fly? Was there only one copy of this book, and was his father the only person to have it? Could he possibly be the first person to have discovered the flying-egg recipe?

Thrilled but conflicted, he lowered the book on his face and breathed in. The aroma of old books engulfed him. His faith in the book's accuracy was restored.

He wasn't worried about the quicksilver. Quicksilver meant mercury, and he knew that the black stuff on the back of the mirror had mercury in it. It was the vultures' eggs that he had been racking his brains about. Where on earth could he get those?

Some afternoons, his sister's silliness would interfere with his reveries of flying.

'Come see this, Opu!' she would call from the kitchen, then sprint to the clearing between the back of the house and the bamboo grove. There, she would put down a handful of rice that she had saved from lunch.

'Wait for it,' she would whisper to her brother, then raise her voice. 'Come, Bhulo . . . t-u-u-u-u-u!'

Then she would look at her brother, face alight with anticipation and joy. Anyone might think that she was waiting for the land of mysteries to suddenly pop up in front of them.

After a few moments of complete silence, a disturbance would begin deep within the grove. It would advance rapidly towards them, rustling leaves and breaking twigs on its way. Then suddenly, it would materialize in the form of a thin dog, its tail wagging frantically.

'There he is!' Durga would exclaim. 'It's like magic, the way he appears! Isn't it?' Then she would laugh in delight.

Feeding the stray had become a source of daily amusement to Durga. Despite her mother's scoldings, she always saved a little rice for him, sacrificing some from her own meal if she had to. It never failed to amaze her how she seldom saw the dog at other times, but how quickly he appeared when she called, apparently out of nowhere. Every afternoon she put the rice down, called the dog, and quickly shut her eyes. Her heart would oscillate wildly between hope and the anxiety of disappointment. 'Maybe he won't come today,' she would think to herself. 'Surely he can't be here every day—who knows where he really lives?'

But Bhulo never disappointed her. Within moments of her calling him, he would appear out of the woods, panting hard and wagging his tail. And every time this happened, a thrill of delight would shoot through Durga.

'What if I call out softly?' she would wonder sometimes. 'He lives deep inside the grove—would he still be able to hear me?'

One day she did lower her voice significantly when calling out. But within moments, Bhulo came scampering out of the woods and began devouring the rice.

Opu, however, wasn't impressed with this stray nonsense. He was too focused on flying to be distracted by this silly feeding thing that his sister had set up. He didn't even bother to look at the emaciated dog eagerly inhaling the small fistful of rice; all his thoughts were focused on finding vultures' eggs.

Finally, he found a way. The local cowherds often came into the neighbourhood homes to ask for oil and tobacco, tying their charges under Hiru barber's jackfruit tree when they did so. Opu caught up with their neighbourhood's cowherd when he was on his way back from these domestic rounds, and made a deal.

'Hey, you! You people spend all day in the fields—have you ever come across a vulture's nest? If you can get me their eggs, I'll give you two paise.'

Four days later, the cowherd came to his house with the treasure cradled in his little cloth bag.

'Look, Thakur—got what you asked for,' he said with a flourish, unhooking the bag from his waist and showing two small black eggs.

'Is this definitely a vulture's eggs? Are you sure?' asked Opu.

The cowherd immediately launched into a spirited monologue supporting his claim. Much of it was a detailed description of the hardships he had had to endure in the process of climbing to the top of a very high tree and bringing the eggs safely down. In fact, given how much he endangered himself, he wasn't going to sell the eggs for less than two annas.

Opu was alarmed. There was no way he could get his hands on that much money. 'Take the two paise,' he begged, 'and I'll also give you all my cowries. I have a whole tin—each this big and veined with gold. D'you want to see? I can show you one right now.'

The cowherd turned out to be far more worldly-wise than Opu. He refused everything except cash. After prolonged bargaining, he finally agreed to make the sale for four paise. Opu had to beg his sister to give him two extra paise to add to his own. In addition, the cowherd also took some cowrie shells. Under normal circumstances, Opu would never have parted with these shells. They were his heart and soul—he would not have bartered them for half a kingdom and a princess's hand in marriage. But what were a few gold-veined shells compared to the joys of flying?

When he finally held the eggs in his palms, he felt almost weightless; like an air-filled rubber balloon. But at the same time, a tiny bit of doubt settled in a corner of his mind. As long as he was focused on getting the eggs, he hadn't had time to think if his plan of flying was actually feasible. But now . . . He hid the eggs and went off to Nyara's family orchard. There, sitting on the stump of the black plum, he thought about the matter in solitude. Would those eggs really make him fly? If yes, then where would he fly to? His mother's old village? Wherever his father was now? On the other side of the river? Or simply high up, like the hill mynahs—closer to the twinkling stars?

That evening, Durga was looking for tattered rags to make wicks with. Forcing her hand through the shelf of tightly packed pile of old utensils and rags, her fingers touched something round. The contact made the things roll along the shelf and then off it, straight on to the floor. The room was dark, making the mystery objects hard to see. So Durga picked them up and brought them outside.

'Ma, come see!' she called. 'Some bird has been nesting inside our house! It's left two large eggs. Poor thing, the shells have been crushed to powder in the fall.'

It's probably best not to describe what happened after this. Opu screamed, shouted, dissolved into tears, and refused to have dinner that night.

For the next few days, his mother lived off the story at the women's bathing steps. 'My boy, sister-in-law . . . really, what can I say. Never in my life have I heard anything so bizarre. Have you, third-eldest sister-in-law? Vultures' eggs can apparently make people fly now! It's that cowherd's fault, I tell you—the one from that house over there. A full bundle of wicked, that one. Brought my son two eggs—a crow's or who-knows-what bird's—and said, "Here, take these, completely real vultures' eggs." And my son bought them for four paise! Such a silly boy—so naive and innocent still! Sisters-in-law . . . I honestly don't know what to do with him!'

We cannot blame poor Shorbojoya. She hasn't, after all, read *Shorbo Dorshon Shongroho*, and so knows nothing about the secret powers of quicksilver. After all, if these things were widely known, wouldn't everybody be flying around in the sky?

20

FOR SEVERAL YEARS NOW, Opu has shared a warm friendship with old Norottowm Daash Babaji. Babaji was a fair-skinned, handsome old man, always cheerful. He lived in a simple little hay-roofed hut in the Ganguly neighbourhood. He disliked loud gatherings and enjoyed his solitude, so he wasn't often seen at the Gangulys' temple courtyard in the evenings. He was a gracious host, however, and over the years, Horihor often visited him at his home. He had been taking his son along ever since Opu was a little boy, and that is how the friendship between the boy and the old man had begun. These days, Opu was old enough to visit Norottowm Daash on his own. Upon reaching the hut, he would call out: 'Grandpa, are you home?' The old man would come out eagerly and lay down a woven palmyra-leaf mat for Opu in his veranda. 'Welcome, my grandson,' he would always say. 'Come in, come in. Have a seat.'

Opu was painfully shy almost everywhere except in his own home; it was almost impossible to get a word out of him in company. But with this placid, simple-souled man, he forgot all reticence. Their relationship was sunny, unconstrained and full of delight—much like a child's relationship with his friends and playmates. Norottowm

Daash had no family; he lived alone in his hut. A fellow Vaishnav girl from his own caste came in during the day to do his domestic work for him. So Opu could sit with him and chat uninterrupted till late evening, telling him about his own life and listening to Norottowm Daash's stories. He knew, of course, that Norottowm Daash was older than his father—older, perhaps, than even the village elder Awnnoda Roy. But the difference in ages had never affected the ease he felt in the old man's presence. Indeed, it was his extreme seniority that had made Opu think of him as a kindred soul—as the sort of person one could open up to. His sense of embarrassment and wariness always fell away in the flow of their talks. He laughed heartily in that hut, and talked freely about those things that he dare not bring up around other grown-ups for fear of being labelled a rotten, overripe child. Besides, he cherished the regard in which Norottowm Daash held him. The old man often told him, 'My child, you're my Gour. I'm sure Gour had looked exactly like you at your age—as auspiciously handsome, as pure, and with just such kindly eyes . . .'

Anywhere else, talk like this would have deeply embarrassed Opu. But to Norottowm Daash, he would merely grin and say, 'Then it's time you showed me the pictures in that book!'

So the old man would bring out 'that book'—his cherished copy of *Prembhokti Chondrika: The Light of Love and Faith*. It was a dearly loved book; he read it often in the solitude of his hut, enchanted and absorbed. It was, however, a bit short on pictures. There are only two in the whole book, right at the end. After showing him the pictures, the old man always told Opu, 'I'll leave you this book before I die, my grandson. You won't disrespect it, I know.'

Sometimes, while Opu was there, one of Babaji's disciples would come around in the hopes of reciting some of their own devotional verses to their guru. But an annoyed Norottowm Daash would wave them away every time. 'It's good that you've written poems, but I don't want to hear them. After such verse-masters as Bidyapoti and Chondidaash, this stuff frankly grates on my ears. Go find someone who cares about modern poetry and recite it to them.'

An undercurrent of freedom flowed through his simple, unadorned life. Despite his youth, Opu could feel the exhilaration of it. Time spent in this hut gave him the same kind of happiness he felt from watching trees and birds, from inhaling the smell of freshly turned earth. On his way back, he would pick a palmful of karnikara flowers from Norottowm Daash's courtyard. When he reached home, he would make a pile of them on the bed. After the lamp-lighting hour, his father would make him sit down with his books. Study-time seldom exceeded an hour, but to a restless Opu, the hour felt like an interminable journey into midnight. The moment his father let him off, he would run to the bed and dive in, inhaling the aroma of the hut's karnikara. His tired mind and body would be flooded with every happy memory of the day, easing his resentment at being chained to the books and missing out vital hours of playtime. He would turn himself on his belly so he could smother his face into the flowers.

One day, in the middle of all this, Durga suddenly said, 'Opu, d'you want to have a picnic?'

With the onset of winter, women and children from the village had been going into the woods, right past their house, for the multi-day feast of Koluichondi. Their mother went too, but didn't take them with her. The feast required everyone to bring and cook their own food in the woods, and his mother never had enough in the larder for a public meal for the whole family. Other families unwrapped expensive rice, daal, ghee and milk. His mother took out thick-grained rice, pasted Bengal gram and maybe a brinjal or two. When the third-eldest mistress from Bhubon Mukhujje's household served her children rice, bananas, fresh milk and sugarcane jaggery for dessert, Shorbojoya averted her eyes. Her heart broke to see the plenty on other people's plates. Her Opu loved that dish—soft, boiled rice mashed with bananas, jaggery and milk. And here she was, unable to give him even the same quality of rice, never mind any of the other things! By the time she finished her joyless feast, sunset reds had descended on the quiet woods. Throughout the walk home, all she could think of was the excesses she had witnessed, and the bitter pain of her poor son's deprivations.

Durga had hacked away at a spot in Neelmoni Roy's overgrown courtyard till she had a reasonable clearing for their own picnic. Now she had to gather the resources.

'Stand under this tamarind tree and be a watchout for Ma,' she instructed her brother. 'I'll quickly slip in and get the rice.'

Moments later, she ran out of the kitchen holding a coconut shell full of oil.

'Here, take this,' she said, handing the shell to her brother. 'Go keep it at that place—you know where I mean. Be careful . . . don't let the cows get to it.'

Just as Opu was leaving, Mato's mother came in through the back door, carrying her youngest son.

'What brings you this way, Tomrej's wife?' Durga asked, forced by civility to delay their adventure.

Mato's mother was still fairly young, and not bad-looking. But constant battles with poverty had worn her down. The months since her husband's death had left her rather thin. Her face had lost its previous animation. 'I'd gone by the indigo bungalow to gather twigs . . .' she said. 'Do you want a plum necklace, Didi Thakron?'

Durga regularly scouted the woods and orchards for flacourtia plums herself. She shook her head.

'Go on, take one, Didi Thakron,' Mato's mother pleaded. 'I picked them fresh from the bank of the Modhukhali lake—more sweet than sour, I promise you.' She took a necklace out of the folds of her sari. 'See how big they are? The twigs won't fetch me anything till evening—I'll have to go to the market, find customers, haggle. A paisa's worth of puffed rice would tide over my Mato till then. Here, I'll give you two for a paisa, take one . . .'

Durga refused. But she couldn't bring herself to turn away a hungry child. 'Opu,' she said, 'there's a handful of toasted rice left in the metal pot—pour it into Mato's palm, will you?'

After Mato's mother left their compound through the back door with her wares, brother and sister finally left for their secret picnic spot.

The clearing was surrounded by trees and undergrowth. This was important, for it hid their little feast from even the nearest path. Durga started the cooking fire and put the rice on. It was a small earthenware pot, only slightly larger than the pot they had in their playroom. Then she dug around the folds of her sari and brought out a handful of white yams. 'Look, Opu—mete alu! Found them amongst the palmyra undergrowth at Puti's garden. We'll add them to the rice as an extra, it'll be great!'

Opu set about gathering dry leaves and vines. He was ecstatic. Even with toy-sized utensils, their picnic was really happening! A part of him still couldn't believe his luck. Were they really going to cook actual food on that fire? Or was this going to end up being just another one of their playroom picnics, with dirt for rice, pottery shards for potato, and jackfruit leaves for luchi?

The morning was beautiful. Their spot was shaded by the canopy overhead and marked by a wilderness of wildflowers. Vines of scarlet gourd moved gently in the breeze. A nearby lebbeck tree was covered in white blossoms. The tall wood-apple trees were almost in bloom. Flocks of wagtails danced and chased each other through the knee-high meadow grass that grew around the clearing. Spring had adorned the broken walls of Neelmoni Roy's abandoned house with the flowers of young glory bowers. The sudden mist of the past week had killed some of the pomelo blossoms, but the large tree beside the clearing still bore several clumps of white aromatic flowers. This far into the woods, peace and solitude reigned supreme.

Durga has lately been feeling more attached to the village than usual. A sense of impending loss made her want to cling harder to these trees and to the familiar village lanes. She could sense the sorrow of an imminent goodbye in everything she loved: the wooded path by the elephant-apple tree, the women's bathing steps, the bamboo grove behind the house. Her Opu, her darling little brother whom she cannot go a few hours without seeing, he would be taken from her as well. She was going to have to go far, far away from this village, from everything that was known and beloved.

What if she never returned? What if she became like Auntie Nitom?

Auntie Nitom used to live on this very land, in that now-ruined house. She was married off and sent away to her in-laws years ago. People said that her husband's home was in Murshidabad district—where is that place? How far is it from here? Anyway, no one bothered to keep up with Auntie Nitom. She didn't get to see her parents once after the wedding, nor her brothers and sisters. They all passed away here, far away from her, one after another. Did Auntie Nitom know? Did anyone bother to tell her? Goddess! How could people be so cruel? Why didn't anyone keep up with her? Durga had often wept in secret thinking about Auntie Nitom's miserable, castaway life in Murshidabad—wherever that was. What if Auntie Nitom came back one day? What would she do when she saw that her entire family was long gone, her old home abandoned, and the land of her birth taken over by the woods?

And what if that happened to *her* some day? What if she was sent away from Baba, Ma and Opu . . . sentenced never, ever to see them again? What if she could never return to the shade of that elephant-apple tree, to the canopied lane that led down to the pond?

Durga shivered, even in the sun. Please, gods, no! She didn't want any of that! But it felt like something unstoppably terrible had laid claim upon her. It lay in wait, only a little way off, biding its time. The feeling caught her unawares several times throughout the day: while doing her chores, while playing, while traipsing through the woods in search of fruit and berries. Something's about to happen that has never happened before. She couldn't quite put her finger on why she felt this way, or why the change seemed so imminent—just that it was. Very soon, she was sure, it would find her.

The picnic was in full flow when a young voice floated down from the Roys' courtyard, calling for the siblings.

'Sounds like Bini,' said Durga. 'Opu, could you go get her?'

A little later, a dark-skinned girl about Durga's age tiptoed into the clearing behind Opu. 'What is happening here, Durgadi?' she asked, her voice laced with awe.

'Sit, Bini,' said Durga, grinning broadly. 'We're having a picnic.'

Bini was wearing a semi-clean sari and glass bangles. She was on the taller side for a girl, and quite plain in the face. Her father, Kalinath Chokkoti, was a brahmin, but from the lowly Jugi community. His family was thus excluded from all social events. He lived in one corner of the brahmin neighbourhood and struggled to make a living. The family was acutely aware of their lower status and tried to shrink into themselves whenever they spoke to one of their higher-born neighbours.

Having been allowed into the secret picnic, Bini began to eagerly fulfil Durga's every wish. She had stepped into the middle of a wonderful thing by accident, and while she was clearly excited, it was evident that she was worried the Roy children might not include her in the festivities once the chores were done. So she tried extra hard to please.

'Bini, see if you can find some wood,' Durga said, poking the fire. 'This fire isn't strong enough.'

Bini immediately ran into the woods and returned panting, with an armful of dry wood-apple twigs and branches. 'Will this do, Durgadi? Or should I get more?'

So when Durga finally said, 'Since Bini's here, she's going to eat with us. Opu, go get a little more rice from the house', the girl's face visibly shone with happiness. She immediately volunteered to go get water for the feast.

'What are we eating with the rice, Durgadi?' she asked eagerly upon her return.

After a while, Durga poured off the rice and put the pot back on. Then she emptied the coconut shell of oil into the pot and released sliced brinjals into it.

'Look, Opu,' she called, amazed. 'They're changing colour! Just like the fried brinjals Ma makes, no?'

Opu was equally amazed. Despite the heap of cooked rice, a small part of him had been holding on to his earlier doubts about the picnic's success. Cooking rice and brinjal in the middle of the woods had seemed rather fantastical. Even now, he couldn't quite believe that they had managed it.

A little later, all three of them sat down enthusiastically to eat. The food was less than simple: white rice and brown brinjal fry on green banana-leaf plates—and nothing else. Before taking her own first mouthful, Durga looked anxiously at her brother, who was already eating. 'How's the brinjal fry, re Opu?'

'Pretty good, Didi, but we forgot the salt.'

Salt! They hadn't even thought of bringing salt to the picnic, much less putting it in the food. Nonetheless, the three of them began to happily chew mouthfuls of the unripe yam and inadequately fried brinjals. This was Durga's first attempt at cooking. She looked happily around the clearing, delighted and a bit surprised at her own prowess. Here they were, eating real food in the woods, sitting on piles of shrivelled custard-apple and palmyra leaves. Who would have thought?

Opu caught his sister's eyes and giggled in delight. He was so happy that the balls of rice didn't want to go past the smile on his face and down his throat.

'Duggadi, is there any oil left?' Bini asked timidly. 'I'd mix some with the yam and rice, just a little . . .'

'Opu, run home and get some oil,' Durga ordered magnanimously.

Life is hard, but it stores little thrills and joys along its many curves and bends. They wait for us in the middle of mundane days, anointed with the light of unexpected happiness. These three are but young travellers on that road. The sudden flavour of these surprises are still a welcome delight to them. Indeed, little joy, adventure, happiness—these are the things that make the great uncharted road of life so sweet. Even when the path makes us scale high mountains of permanent snow, we rejoice in our hopes for the unseen other side. The joy of waking up to a new day, of the small pleasures of everyday things—that is what keeps us all going in the midst of despair.

After they were done eating, Opu said, 'What will we tell Ma, Didi? Will you be able to eat dinner after this?'

'We're not telling Ma anything! We'll start feeling hungry again once it gets dark. Don't worry.'

Bini, meanwhile, was hesitating. Jugi brahmins were not allowed to touch the utensils of their higher-born brahmin neighbours. If they asked for a drink of water, people gave it to them in cheap metal pots, and they had to wash those pots after. Which is why, after some consideration, Bini finally indicated Opu's glass.

'Can you pour some water into my mouth, Opu?' she said timidly. 'Only I'm very thirsty . . .'

'You can have a drink yourself, Binidi. Here, take it.'

Bini was taken aback. She didn't dare reach for the glass.

'Take the gelas and drink, Bini,' Durga urged her. 'We don't mind.'

Later, when everything was cleared up, Durga said, 'We're not throwing this pot. It'll be saved for our next picnic, all right? We'll hang it on that plum tree till then.'

'No way!' Opu protested. 'Mato's ma comes to collect kindling in these woods. If she sees a pot, she'll take it straight away. Big thief, that one!'

Finally, Durga decided to stash the pot in a small alcove in the abandoned house's wall. When he heard this plan, Opu's heart began thudding in his chest. The wall his sister had chosen had another alcove on the other side . . . and that was where Opu had hidden his secret box of cheroots. He had first fancied cheroots when he saw Nyara's brother-in-law smoke them with his friend. The two young men had come to visit Contentment from their own village, which was supposedly very close to Calcutta. The men acted like they were quite the city gents—lighting one cheroot after another all day. Watching them, Opu had decided that he, too, wanted to taste a cheroot. After a lot of whispered discussion with Nyara, they had pooled their resources and bought a foil-wrapped packet of ten cheroots from Horish Jugi's shop. Terrified of being caught, Opu had taken his share deep into the woods and lit one. He hadn't enjoyed the taste. It was bitter and acrid, and altogether unpleasant. After barely two pulls, he had thrown the thing away. But even knowing that they would go unsmoked, he couldn't bring himself to throw away the four remaining cheroots. Instead, he had packed them inside an empty cheroot box—sourced secretly by Nyara from his brother-in-law's throwaways—and hidden them in the alcove.

Despite only two puffs, he had been terrified that his mother would smell the smoke on his breath. So he had hidden himself in the woods, eating fistfuls of ripe red plums and testing his breath into his palm, till he had been satisfied that the smell of smoke had been drowned out by the aroma of the fruit. Only then had he dared to re-enter human society.

He couldn't imagine being caught now, on such a happy day, after putting in all that effort to hide his crime!

But his sister was happy with the alcove on this side, thank goodness. She didn't even bother to check the other side of the wall. Opu breathed a sigh of secret relief.

21

SHORBOJOYA HEARD THE news at the bathing steps.

Trouble had been brewing between Neeren and Awnnoda Roy for the last few days, and more particularly between Neeren and Awnnoda Roy's eldest son, Gokul. Things had finally come to a head yesterday afternoon. There had apparently been a great deal of screaming and shouting. As a result, Neeren had packed his things and left the village late last evening.

Horimoti, the wife of Awnnoda Roy's neighbour Joggeshwor Deeghri, was holding court by virtue of being the closest observer. 'I don't believe the story they're putting out—their daughter-in-law is not the type. Then again they do say that Neeren gave her money in secret, and she sent it to who-knows-whom. The receipt came back and Gokul found it—that's what led to all this trouble. Who can really tell what's going on in people's minds? Best not to speculate—that's what I always say. I did hear Neeren, though. He was saying, "But it's all right for all of you to gang up on and torture someone? I don't care what anybody else thinks—if my sister-in-law commands, I will bear her away from this place with all the honour and respect I would have accorded to my late mother. You can raise whatever hell you please after that!" Then there was some more shouting. Finally, Neeren called for a bullock cart from the milkman's neighbourhood. He was gone before the lamp-lighting hour was over.'

Shorbojoya felt cut off at the knees. She had been asking her husband to write to Neeren's father, proposing a match between Durga and his son. In the meantime, she had invited Neeren for lunch again twice—and Neeren had come. Her husband had tried, several times, to discourage her. 'They're too rich for the likes of us,' he had said. 'Neeren's father wouldn't waste his son on a family like ours.' But Shorbojoya had persisted. She had really liked Neeren. Surely there was no harm in trying? Finally, Horihor had given in and spoken to Awnnoda Roy, asking him to write to Neeren's father on his behalf. And now this! How was she going to get Neeren's father to agree to the match after this?

A few days later, Durga met Gokul's wife in one of the back lanes of the village. In the privacy of the empty road, Gokul's wife broke down completely. She sobbed her heart out while telling Durga the whole story.

'This is my life, Dugga—kicks and beatings till the day I die. I have no one, *no one*. Only one brother, and him worthless. No place I can escape to for a few days' peace!'

Durga's heart swelled in sympathy. Gokul's wife was her favourite village aunt, and she was torn by her despair. She wanted to viciously condemn the people slandering her aunt's virtue, but she also wanted to simply soothe the sobbing woman. Outrage, protectiveness and affection mixed together in such a lump in her throat that she ended up not expressing any of them properly. 'That Shokhi grandmother, she's always been like that!' she finally settled for saying. 'Let her say what she likes—what can she do? Don't cry, Auntie. I'll visit you every day, I promise.'

When she later told her mother about the conversation, her mother perked up immediately. 'So what else did our sister-in-law talk about, Durga?' she asked eagerly. 'Did she mention Neeren at all?'

'I don't know about any of that,' Durga mumbled, suddenly shy. 'You go ask Auntie about that yourself.'

When Opu heard that she had spoken to Gokul's wife, he, too, asked about Neeren. 'What did Auntie say, Didi? Is Master Moshai coming back or not?'

'I don't know anything about your Master Moshai . . . go ask Auntie yourself, shoo!' Durga snapped.

But these reminders of Neeren brought back her sense of impending loss. She wished she could forever hold on to this house, these woods, these familiar roads. But most of all she wished she could hold on to her beautiful, silly little brother. She and Opu sniped at each other all day, but if she didn't see him for a few hours, her mind would fervently begin to list all the terrible things that might be happening to him at that very moment. It almost made her burst into tears. Right now, her brother was playing hopscotch in their courtyard. Brinjal-and-seeds, they called it in their village. His fair, vermilion-in-milk complexion had turned golden in the sun. Poor boy! A solitary game of brinjal-and-seed was all the entertainment they could afford for him. Every now and then he would come to her, asking hopefully for a few paise to buy trinkets with. Durga never had any money to give him, and it broke her heart.

A few days later.

The wedding at Bhubon Mukhujje's house was over, but not all of the visiting relatives had left. The house was still full of their many children. Durga had made friends with a little girl called Tuni. Both of her parents had come for the wedding, but her father had left just this afternoon after lunch to attend to his place of work for a few days.

The third-eldest mistress was doing something in her room when she heard Tuni's mother's exclamation from the next room. She hurried into the next room, saying, 'What is it, Hashi? What's wrong?'

Tuni's mother was frantically turning up the bedding and pillows, bending to look under the bed and between the sheets.

'I can't find my gold vermilion box!'

'What? Are you sure you didn't take it with you when you went inside?'

'No,' said Tuni's mother distractedly. 'It was right here, on the bed. My husband came home, Khoka cried out in his baby swing . . . I went inside to look after him, completely forgot about the box. Where could it have gone, Grandma? It's nowhere in this room . . .'

Everyone gathered around to search the room, but the box could not be found. The third-eldest mistress discovered, after some interrogation, that there was only one outsider in the inner veranda that afternoon. Durga. When the women of the house sent word that lunch was ready, all the Mukhujje children had gone indoors, leaving Durga alone in the veranda.

The third-eldest mistress's youngest, Tepi, sidled up to her mother. 'Ma, I saw Duggadi slipping out of the back door, right after we went in for lunch,' she whispered. 'Look, she has only just come back.'

The third-eldest mistress went into a huddle with some of the other women of the household. Then she advanced upon Durga.

'Give the box back this instant, Durga,' she growled. 'We know you took it.'

Watching the third-eldest mistress confer with the others had already frightened Durga. Now she backed up towards the wall, mumbling something incomprehensible. Her facc had gone blank with fear.

Tuni's mother was rather taken aback by this turn of events. Never before had she seen a gentleman's daughter being accused of theft. Over the last few days, she had seen Durga constantly in the Mukhujje house, and had developed quite a liking for her pretty face and friendly ways. So she tried to come between the girl and the third-eldest mistress, saying, 'No, no, third-eldest grandma, I don't think she'd take it. Why would she . . .'

But the third-eldest mistress cut her off roughly. 'You be quiet! What do you know of this girl? I know quite well what she's capable of!'

Another woman from the crowd, in tones of making peace, said, 'Look, if you've taken the thing, just give it back. Or tell us where it is. You made a mistake, but it doesn't have to get worse. Give the thing back and we'll forget about it. Why make trouble when you don't have to?'

By now, Durga had backed into the veranda wall. Her legs were visibly shaking under the crowd's accusatory glare. 'I . . . I don't know anything, Auntie,' she managed to mumble. 'I . . . I just . . .'

'Look at that guilty face!' the third-eldest mistress invited the circle of watching women. 'That face is enough to tell me that she's done it! Fine, you don't have to admit to anything. Just tell us where the box is. I'm asking nicely, Dugga—give me the box and you can go.'

The female relative who had exhorted Durga to return the box now said, 'Honestly, never heard of a gentleman's daughter stealing before . . . where's this girl from? This neighbourhood?'

The third-eldest mistress was fast losing whatever little patience she had previously had. 'You're not fit for mercy!' she snarled. 'Going to swallow my property just because we're asking nicely—are you? I'll show you niceness! You little . . .'

Then she pulled Durga by her wrist into the centre of the inner courtyard. 'One last chance: give me my box and you can go home. No? Oh, you don't know where it is? Aww, you innocent little darling . . . I swear I'll punch you till every single tooth in your mouth is powder! Last chance, while I'm still using my words—where is the box?'

Once more, Tuni's mother tried to insert herself between Durga and the third-eldest mistress, but the relative who'd spoken earlier held her back with some amount of glee.

'You just wait and watch,' she advised. 'I'm sure that girl has stolen your box. The only cure for thievery is a good beating. If she doesn't want a beating, she should return the box—the choice is hers, not yours.'

By now, terror was making Durga's head swim. She could barely stand up straight, much less defend herself. With great difficulty, she opened her parched mouth and stuttered, 'I don't know, Auntie. When the children went in to eat, I left, too . . . I've only just come back . . .'

Then she once again tried to back up against the wall, too scared to take her eyes off the third-eldest mistress.

Several of the women tried their best to convince her that she had indeed stolen the box, and there was no point in denying it. But despite near-absolute terror, Durga remained firm: she had no idea where the box was.

After a few minutes, one of the watching women turned away in disgust. 'Clearly well-seasoned, this one,' she pronounced. 'A born thief.'

'Oh yes, Auntie!' said Tepi eagerly. 'She steals our mangoes right out of our trees!'

This last sentence triggered an avalanche of old rage in the third-eldest mistress. 'You evil, disgusting scum!' she roared. 'Steal our property, will you? I'll teach you to steal, you vile thief. We'll see how long you can stand this!'

Then she pounced on Durga, grasped her by her flyaway hair, and began banging her head against the very wall she'd sought refuge on.

'Tell us where it is! Tell us where the box is!' she screamed, in rhythm to the banging.

Tuni's mother finally broke out of the arms restraining her, and ran to insert herself forcibly between Durga and her enraged relative. 'Stop, third-eldest grandma! Stop! Never mind my box, I don't want it back—how can you beat another person like this? Is this any way to act? No, leave her—let her be! How could you . . . for shame!'

Tuni, who had never seen such a brutal beating before, burst into terrified sobs. The woman who had so far been inserting her commentary into the proceedings now helpfully said, 'Oh dear, the girl is bleeding.'

Everyone turned to look at Durga. Blood was indeed flowing from her nose, dyeing the sari below her chin a bright red.

'Tepi, run to the outer veranda,' Tuni's mother instructed. 'There's a bucket of clean water there. Bring some, quick.'

The entire episode had been so loud that girls and women from the neighbouring blacksmith's house had come running into the Mukhujjes' inner courtyard via the back gate. Ranu's mother was part of that group. She had gone over to the blacksmith's family for some post-lunch catching-up, and had thus missed the developments so far.

The repeated banging had left Durga dazed and wobbly. She stood where the third-eldest mistress had left her, too addled to even sit down. When Tepi came back with the water, Ranu's mother gently lowered her to the ground and washed her face and nose with it. It was clear she was still fairly cotton-headed—not fully aware of her surroundings.

'Honestly, third-eldest sister . . . is that how one beats another person?' she chided her sister-in-law gently. 'Poor thin girl . . . for shame.'

'Shame my foot! None of you know her like I do. There's no treatment for thievery except a good tanning, let me tell you. You think this is bad? Wait and see what I do to her if I don't get my box back. Hori Roy can come home and impale me on a pike if he likes, but I'm going to get that box out of that thief!'

'All right, that's enough, third-eldest sister. Let the girl catch her breath first. The way you've hit her, poor thing . . .'

'I wouldn't have made a peep about my box if I knew this was going to happen,' Tuni's still-horrified mother chimed in. 'I don't want that box back, third-eldest grandma. Just let the girl go.'

Under normal circumstances, the third-eldest mistress would have been very unlikely to let Durga off with merely a concussion. However, she was astute enough to realize when the tide of popular opinion had turned against her. In the face of growing disapproval from her extended family, she was forced to let her suspect go.

Ranu's mother guided Durga to the back door.

'You must have left home under a seriously inauspicious star this morning, Dugga,' she said sympathetically. 'Tepi, open the door wide and hold it in place—make sure Durga has enough room to pass.'

Durga walked unsteadily through the back door and on to the path. An entire courtyard full of women and children watched her go.

'Still didn't admit to stealing—did you notice that?' said one of the visiting relatives. 'Old hand, if you ask me. Not a drop of water in those eyes, either.'

'That's because terror froze her tears,' Ranu's mother responded sharply. 'She had no water left to spare once our third-eldest sister started on her. Her fear drank it all.'

22

CHOROK PUJA WAS almost upon the village. Boidyonath Mojumdar from the village started making the rounds, account book in hand, soliciting contributions from every household for the community celebrations. When he came to Horihor, the latter was shocked at Boidyonath's expectation.

'No, Uncle,' he insisted, 'it's very unfair of you to put me down for a whole rupee. Look at me—am I in any state to contribute a rupee?'

'But you don't understand!' Boidyonath exclaimed. 'We've bagged Neelmoni Hajra's troupe of performers. No one in these parts has ever seen a troupe like that. The Paalpara Market people have booked Mohesh Jeweller's choir of devotional singers—we have to beat them at the game!'

From his fervour, one might have thought that the very survival of Contentment was dependent on winning a non-existent competition with Paalpara Market.

The argument would have carried on, but Opu interrupted it by dragging a long piece of split bamboo into the courtyard.

'Look at this, Baba,' he called out to Horihor. 'It'll make for good pens. I saw it lying under the bamboo tree near the pond, so I picked it up for you.'

Then he brought the branch up to Horihor and held it up for a closer inspection, grinning with pride and satisfaction. 'Good bamboo, isn't it, Baba?' he asked again. 'Nice and ripe . . . no, Baba?'

Days passed. Choitro arrived. The festival of Chorok was now only a few days away. The dancing ascetics had already begun doing rounds of the neighbourhoods, seeking alms. Durga and Opu had given up on meals and sleep just so they could follow them around the village through every single neighbourhood, near and far. Most of the families gave generously of their old clothes, uncooked rice and spare paise. Some even donated a few of their old utensils. At their own house, though, there was never anything to spare except a small handful of rice. After years of receiving practically nothing, the ascetics had learnt not to come by their house at all.

The dancing ascetics took almost ten to twelve days to complete their rounds. Then, the day before the Chorok festival was to begin, came Neel Puja—the worship of the blue-skinned god, Shiva.

Every year on Neel Puja afternoon, the ascetics would perform the ritual of breaking the thorns on a date-palm tree. This time, Durga brought the news that they wouldn't be performing the ritual on the usual tree. A different tree had been chosen on the banks of the river. Brother and sister joined the boisterous group of neighbourhood children as it set off towards the river. Once the ritual was over, nearly all of them walked over to the field where the festivities would be held. Thick clusters of undergrowth—chiefly toothbrush-bush, and a few other shrubs—had already been cleared from the field. A Neel Puja platform had been set up in a corner, fenced in with branches of the date-palm. The older girls of

Bhubon Mukhujje's household were already at the platform: Rani, Puti and Tunu. These girls were under far more strictures than Durga had ever been. Unlike her, they couldn't afford to run around at will. They had been permitted to visit the field only after much begging and pleading, and didn't dare go beyond the actual fairground.

'Tonight's the night the ascetics will go to the cremation grounds to raise the dead,' Tunu informed the new group importantly.

'Like we don't know!' said her cousin Rani, stung. 'One of them will play dead. They'll bundle him up and take him to the cremation grounds, under the milkwood pine. Then they'll do a ritual to reanimate him, pick up a skull from the cremation grounds, and make their way back. They sing a special song while coming back, so I've heard. Besides there are other secret rituals that no one knows about. . .'

'I know the coming-back song!' Durga piped up. 'Do you want to hear it? Should I sing? It goes like this.'

From heaven came the chariot
Landed straight on grass
Wherever Shib went,
Twenty-four crore hay-arrows
Showered en masse
From the golden era a corpse, from the ascetics the soil
Say 'Shib Shib!' everyone, and on those drums toil!

Then she grinned at the group. 'Did you see this year's Goshthobihar statue, Neeluda? Isn't it beautiful? I went by Dashu the potter's house to see. Have you seen it yet, Ranu?'

Before Rani could answer, Puti suddenly said, 'Will the skull be real, Ranudi?'

'Of course it'll be real! You can see it, too, if you come here really late in the night. But we have to go now, girls. Come on, everybody . . . tonight's not a good night for any of you to stay out. Opu, come with us. Come Duggadi.'

'Why isn't this a good night, Ranudi?' asked Opu. 'What's going to happen tonight?'

'These are not things one speaks of, Opu!' Rani admonished. 'You just come home with us!'

But Opu wasn't prepared to go home this early. He stayed back, watching his sister walk back to their neighbourhood with the Mukhujje household's girls.

Soon afterwards, the sky turned cloudy. Dense clouds obscured the last of the light, and made the fast-descending night darker. Left without friends in the Chorok field, Opu began to feel little shivers of fear go down his spine. All evening he had been told about dead people and cremation-ground skulls. It occurred to him that this might not be the evening he wanted to stay out alone. He began making his way back home as quickly as he could. But even the roads offered little comfort. They were dark with the dense clouds above, and completely deserted. When he reached the crossroads at the bamboo grove, he was certain he could smell something awful from within the grove. Scared, he began walking a little faster. A little further down the road, he finally saw another human being. At first the darkness had cloaked its identity, but then Opu recognized his neighbour Nyara's grandmother, on her way to the Chorok fields with a large plate of Neel Puja offerings.

'What's that smell, Grandma?' he asked, enormously relieved to have found someone to talk to.

'It's them,' said the old woman cryptically. 'They're all abroad tonight, don't you know?'

'Who's "they"?' asked Opu.

'You know, Shib's own people . . . we don't speak their names after sundown. Ram Ram, Ram Ram . . .'

A chill ran down Opu's spine. The darkness of night, the black clouds in the sky, the swaying bamboo grove, the cremation-ground smell, the supernatural followers of Shiva . . . it all took on a suddenly ominous meaning. His young heart filled with fear, yet also with the thrill of stepping into the dangerous unknown.

'How will I get back home, Grandma?' he asked, his voice shaking.

The old woman was annoyed. 'Who asked you to stay out this late, huh? On today of all days?' she scolded. 'Come with me now. I'll make the Neel Pujo offering and then walk you towards your place. Honestly, you boys!'

A few days later, workmen finished erecting a temporary arena for the jatra troupe in the community celebration area with enormous bamboos and colourful cloth. The entire village waited with bated breath for the troupe to finally arrive. People crowded around the arena every afternoon, certain that the troupe would be arriving that day. Afternoon turned to late evening, but the troupe did not arrive. People reassured each other that they were travelling by the night train and would definitely be at the village by next morning. When they didn't arrive in the morning, they waited eagerly for the afternoon. When afternoon passed, they pinned all hopes on the evening. And so it went on.

Opu began to practically live at the celebration area, meals and sleep forgotten. He could barely contain the excitement that gurgled within him, like a young river at the prospect of seeing a play. Even at night, when he was forced to go to bed, he'd twist and turn from side to side in excitement. His whole life was suffused with one joyful chant: the jatra was coming! The jatra was coming! The jatra was coming!

Shorbojoya had recently forbidden Durga from leaving their own neighbourhood. She had insisted that Durga was now too old for such liberties. This had forced Durga to keep her visit to the arena a secret, but she had been unable to keep herself from discussing what she had seen with her friend Rajlokkhi. Opu had overheard that conversation. Listening to his sister describe the bamboo structure and the unique red-and-blue paper decor in great detail, Opu found himself shuttling between excitement and disbelief. How could the community celebration area—that familiar, unimportant, perfectly mundane piece of land next to the temple of the five-faced god Ponchanon, where he went twice a day to play cowrie-shell matches with the neighbourhood boys—become the vessel for something as magical, as unheard-of, as utterly wonderful as Neelmoni Hajra's jatra troupe? Even though his sister had seen it with her own eyes, Opu had trouble believing that such a transformation could have actually happened.

Then one day, the news arrived that the jatra troupe were finally on their way . . . they were going to reach the village by evening. Opu could feel the blood in his heart jump up at the news. That afternoon, the local boys ran along the main road till they reached the end of the potters' neighbourhood, desperate to catch as early a sight of the troupe as possible.

Afternoon had begun to slowly melt into evening when the first bullock-cart appeared at the horizon. Slowly, one box-laden cart turned into two, then three, then four . . . then five! Potu counted the number on his fingers with delight.

'We'll follow the carts to the house they've been assigned, Opuda!' he said, vibrating with excitement. 'Will you come?'

Once the carts passed them by, the boys saw the group of people who were following behind on foot. These must be the performers! Opu noticed that unlike the men of his village, every last man had a parting in his hair, and several of them were carrying proper shoes (though in their hands and not on their feet, to protect them from the village roads). Pointing at a man with an impressive beard, Potu whispered, 'That one probably plays the king, no Opuda?'

Much later, when he came home after seeing the troupe to their host-homes, Opu saw his father sitting in the outer veranda, writing something and humming to himself. Clearly, his father had found out about the arrival of the troupe! Why else would he be singing? So he ran up to his father and delivered the good news.

'Five carts of costumes and scenery, Baba!' he exclaimed, gesticulating wildly. 'That's how big a troupe they are!'

Horihor had been writing out protective amulets for his disciples. 'What costumes, Khoka?' he asked, taken completely by surprise.

Opu was astonished at his father's ignorance. A famous jatra troupe had come into their village . . . and his father didn't even know? Opu decided right then that fathers were rather pitiable creatures.

Usually, when his father was at home, Opu had to spend the morning with his books. That was the norm. But Opu wasn't prepared to waste today on books. A few minutes after sitting down, he made a pitiful face and petitioned his father for a day off.

'Everybody's gone to the celebration grounds already! Why do I have to sit here and study? Please . . . what if the jatra begins right now?'

'The jatra won't begin right now,' his father said. 'And if it does, they'll first sound the large drums to announce it. You can go if they start sounding the drums. For now, you just sit here and read.'

The truth was that Horihor wanted to spend as much time as possible with his son. Indeed, when he was home, he could barely bring himself to let Opu out of his sight. Opu was the sole, unexpected male child of Horihor's middle age, and all the more precious because of it. For much of the year, Horihor had no choice but to live apart from his son, for his livelihood kept him out of the village. But when he was at home, he used his son's education as an excuse to keep him as close to himself as possible.

Meanwhile, tears of outrage were pouring down Opu's cheeks. Furious at his father's cruelty, he forced himself to read out loud from his book of sums, *Shubhonkori*, in a tear-choked voice:

> If such-and-such is his full month's pay
> How much does he make per day?

Later in the day, he found out that jatra troupes performed only in the evenings, never in the morning. But that didn't stop him from running to his mother as soon as she walked into the house from the bathing steps, and complaining in detail about his father's unusual cruelty. Happily, his mother was entirely on his side.

'Oh, let the boy go, why don't you?' she said to his father. 'You're not even home nine months out of twelve. Do you think he'll blossom into a scholar with just one morning's lessons?'

Unable to counter that, Horihor was forced to let his son go. Ecstatic, Opu ran straight to the celebration ground and refused to go back home for the rest of the morning and noon. When he came home for his early evening meal, he found his father sitting on the veranda yet again, writing something. Usually, this was when he had to sit with his father and practise his own handwriting. Horihor had devised several amusing tricks around the lessons to keep him interested, lest his son lose his temper with the tedium of education. For instance, instead of the usual writing assignments, he'd say, 'Let's see, Khoka, can you write, "Oh my goodness! What a terrifying ghost!"?'

Opu would burst out laughing and quickly write the sentence down. 'But that was the last one, Baba,' he would say, still grinning. 'I'm going to go play now.'

'Of course you will, of course you will,' Horihor would say soothingly. 'But can you write . . .' and then he'd say something outrageous again.

Opu would fall for the trick several times in a row.

But unlike that morning, seeing his father in their usual study spot didn't faze Opu at all. With the jatra about to start, he felt a strange, almost magical presence thrumming in the very air of the village. His father might choose to sit here, in this isolated little bamboo-grove-bound house, and do all the writing in the world. But if he so much as said, 'Bring your books here, Khoka', then an absolute riot of protests would erupt across the grove and rescue him from paternal tyranny. 'No no no!' a thousand voices would cry out together. 'No studying, no studying, no studying . . . the jatra is about to start!!!'

Suddenly, Opu felt sorry for his father. Poor Baba! How could he and his books hope to win when pitted against the magic of the jatra?

While he was still indoors, his sister whispered, 'Opu . . . ask Ma if I can come with you, too. She might let me go if you ask for it.'

Opu promptly went up to his mother and said, 'Ma, why doesn't Didi come with me? They've made a special area for the women—nicely surrounded with a split-bamboo screen. She could sit there, no?'

His mother simply said, 'Not now. I'm going to go later with the girls from the other households. She can come with me then.'

When he was about to leave, his sister suddenly called out to him from behind. Then she caught up to him, grinning broadly.

'Show me your palm,' she demanded.

As soon as Opu held out his palm, Durga dropped two coins in it and quickly folded his fingers into a fist over them.

'Buy yourself two paise's worth of murki,' she said. 'Or if they're selling litchis, buy yourself some litchis. All right?'

There was a background to this generosity. A few days back, Opu had come to her and said, 'Is there a paisa in your doll box, Didi? Can you give it to me?'

'Why? What do you want with a paisa?'

Opu had looked at her, grinned shyly, then looked down. 'I want to eat litchis,' he had whispered. Then, in the tone of one making excuses, he explained himself further.

'The Boshtoms have tied a scaffold on their trees, Didi. Picked two large baskets. Six litchis to a paise . . . each of them this big, and red like vermilion! Shotu bought some,

Shadhon bought some . . .' Then he stopped for a second and asked again. 'So . . . do you have a paisa, Didi?'

Durga hadn't had any money that day. The look of disappointment on Opu's face had cut her deep. Opu was her brother, her precious golden treasure. It broke her heart if she could not fulfil even his smallest requests. Which is why she had begged these two paise from her father last evening, saying that she wanted it for herself, to spend at the Chorok fair. Watching the joy on her brother's face filled her being with lightness.

Shorbojoya went and returned from the bathing steps shortly after Opu left.

'Do something for me, Dugga,' she called as she stepped into the house. 'Go to the Mukhujjes' garden and get me a couple of white fever-vines. Opu's health hasn't been too good these past few days . . . I'll make him a thin fever-vine broth tonight.'

Durga shot out of the house. She reached her friend Ranu's family gardens in one quick run. While looking for white fever-vine in the shoulder-high shrubs of weed, she began nodding her head in happiness and singing a verse she had learnt from her late aunt.

In the yellow wood
My nose ring I've lost, my friend,
And with it, my mood.

23

THE JATRA BEGAN. Everything else in the world dissolved into nothingness; there was only Opu and the performers in front of him.

The troupe's violinist had begun playing an opening piece in the yaman raga just before darkness had truly descended upon the arena. He was a fairly skilled musician and the forlorn notes floated far across the neighbourhood. Opu had been mesmerized. He was a simple rural boy—music like this was well beyond his staples. The forlorn tune touched spots of melancholy in his soul. He thought of his father, sitting in the isolated old house, writing in the dim light of a lamp. He thought of his sister, who had dearly wanted to come with him, but had not been allowed.

When the first players descended on to the stage, their magnificent, gold-trimmed costumes glittering under the cowrie-shell chandelier, Opu felt a second rush of sympathy for his father. Poor Baba! He didn't even know what a spectacle he was missing! Why wasn't he here, anyway? Almost everyone else from his village was there . . . he could see several men from his own neighbourhood right over there. Why couldn't his father come? He'd heard that boys' devotional choir once before . . . it was *nothing* compared to this. Such actors, such costumes, such beautiful people!

He had been completely immersed in the fast-paced plot when a familiar voice behind him said, 'Can you see everything, Khoka? This is not too far for you?'

It was his father! Goodness, he hadn't even noticed when his father had come to sit right behind him!

'Is Didi here?' he asked immediately. 'Is she with the women, behind that screen?'

Meanwhile, the plot on the makeshift stage was thickening. The throne had been usurped by the evil, scheming minister, and the king had been exiled from his own kingdom. He was forced to wander the woods with his wife and children. The violins played a heart-wrenching score to mark their exit from the kingdom. The king, his arm linked to his queen, took a step, then stopped dramatically to look forlorn. Of course, no man would have ever walked like that in real life, unless he was quite mad, but the players seemed determined to wring the last drops of tragedy from every scene. The scheming minister, for instance, gnashed his teeth and shivered so hard in villainesque rage that he looked remarkably like a person in the throes of an epileptic fit. But Opu was enchanted by it all. He had never seen anything so utterly amazing in all his life.

And then, and then . . . where did the king go? Where did the queen go? The only people left on stage were their two young children, Prince Awjoy and Princess Indulekha. The two children roamed the forests helplessly. There was no one to care for them, no one to show them the way. One day, Indulekha went to pick fruits for her little brother, and never came back. Anxious and terrified, Awjoy went to look for his sister. He found her at the end of the day, sprawled out next to the river, dead. Starvation had driven her to eat poison-berries. Awjoy threw himself down next to her and broke into a beautiful, heart-breaking song:

Where did you go, leaving me alone in this forest,
Oh dearest of my heart, the partner of my soul?

Ah, such music! Opu's previous rapt enchantment dissolved into tears. His body shook with barely restrained sobs.

And then came the big fight. Sword in hand, General Bichitroketu charged the king of Kolingo. Such flourish, such deafening clangs! There was no way at least one of them wouldn't lose an eye! The audience shouted, 'Watch out! Watch out! Watch out for the chandeliers!' But despite the fierceness of the fight, both the chandeliers and the eyes remained miraculously untouched. Now *that* was truly magical swordplay. All hail Bichitroketu . . . he truly was a hero!

In between there was a break, when the musicians and singers played their longer pieces. In the middle of it, Horihor leaned forward to ask his son if he'd had enough.

'Are you sleepy, Khoka? Do you want to go home?'

Home? *Sleep*? No no! He wasn't going anywhere—definitely not home. In the end, his father settled for calling him outside and giving him two paise.

'Here, keep this. Buy something to eat, all right? I'm going home now.'

After his father left, Opu looked around the shops that had sprung up around the arena. Looking at the crowd around the paan shop, he suddenly really wanted to buy one readymade paan, worth one paisa. He began pushing his way through the crowd. When he reached the front, he was amazed to see Bichitroketu, in full costume, buying and lighting up a Bird's

Eye cigarette. And then poor Prince Awjoy came around the bend and touched Bichitroketu on the arm!

'Buy me a paisa's worth of paan no, Kishorida?' the prince begged.

Instead of immediately obliging his prince, the loyal general shook the arm off. 'Scoot! Haven't got money for that . . . did you tell me when you two used up all of the soap this morning? Eh?'

'Don't be that way, Kishorida,' Awjoy pleaded. 'Have I never given you anything? Come on, just one paisa's pan . . .'

But Bichitroketu wasn't swayed. He shrugged off his prince's petulance and walked off with the lit cigarette.

Up close, Awjoy looked about Opu's age. Fair-skinned, good-looking, a beautiful singing voice. Opu stared at him, fascinated. He wanted to say something, anything . . . but what could he say? Suddenly, he heard himself saying with considerable shyness, 'Um . . . would you like some paan?'

Awjoy looked at him, surprised. 'Are you offering? That'd be great. Let's get some paan, my brother.'

And that was how the two became friends. Or rather, that was how Opu acquired the chance to bask in his sense of fascinated stupefaction around the prince. And Awjoy was a prince, even off the stage. His eyes, his face, his voice—everything about him was exactly what Opu had always wanted in a prince, exactly what he had dreamt of when he thought about his mother's fairy tales. And now that prince was right in front of him!

'Which way's your house, brother?' Awjoy asked. 'I've been assigned a host household, but they serve meals way too late. Who's been assigned to eat at your place?'

Pure joy coursed through Opu. 'You can come to our house, brother,' he said immediately. 'I'll come myself and show you the way. The man who eats at our place plays the large drums—he could easily go to the house you've been assigned to.'

After a few more minutes of conversation, Awjoy took his leave.

'I have one more song in the last scene,' he explained. 'How'd you like my part so far? Was I good?'

The jatra concluded in the early hours of the morning, but its magic lingered heavily in the air. As he walked back home with the rest of his neighbours, Opu felt like everybody in real life was merely an echo of the magnificent play. When one man in their group spoke to another, it sounded exactly like a bit of the dialogue he had just heard.

When he reached home, his sister came out to greet him. 'How'd you like the play, Opu?' she asked eagerly.

To his ears, she sounded exactly like Princess Indulekha, lost in the woods. The jatra fever had engulfed him completely.

'I've invited Awjoy to eat with us from tomorrow!' he announced happily.

His mother was alarmed. 'Two people?' she exclaimed. 'Where will I get enough for . . .'

'No no, not two. The one that eats now will go away. Only Awjoy will eat with us.'

'Wasn't it magical?' his sister asked, a little later. 'That song when the princess dies . . . so beautiful! I've never seen anything like this before.'

Beautiful? Opu's entire being was suffused with the jatra! When he walked, it was to the beat of the violin. When he slept, his dreams played out to the music of its orchestra.

When he woke up later in the morning, the lack of sleep from the previous night was palpable. He was still tired, and the brightness of sunbeams pierced his dry eyes like needles. Splashing cold water on them only made them burn more. But the violin, drums and cymbals continued to play in perfect harmony in his ears, rendering the discomforts immaterial. Later in the morning, when the women of the neighbourhood began going past their compound's boundary wall to the bathing pond beyond, it seemed to Opu that a parade of female characters from the play was drifting past the house. Within the very first minute, he could swear he heard Dheeraboti, the empress of Kolingo, chatting animatedly with Awjoy's mother, Boshumoti, as they made their way to the bathing steps. And of course, he saw Princess Indulekha in every gesture his sister made, every word she spoke. The actress who had played Indulekha last night was a good enough match, but throughout the years, whenever he had thought of a princess, he had always imagined a girl exactly like his sister: the same large eyes, the same beautiful face, the same lovely hair. It was like the princess of the play had died during the night, and been reincarnated as his sister.

No, that was not quite right. If anything, it was the opposite. Opu wasn't seeing shadows of Indulekha in his sister. What he had seen was his sister's shadow in all of the princess's actions on stage. The affectionate way in which she wrapped a cloth around her younger brother, the way she had gone alone to seek sustenance and lost herself in the forests . . . everything was exactly like things his own sister had done for him. In particular, Indulekha's love for Awjoy reminded him of the bitter-apple episode—how his sister had soothed and protected him then!

That afternoon, Opu went out and brought Awjoy back for lunch. Shorbojoya prepared two seats for them beside each other, and while serving the courses, sat down in front of them to interrogate Awjoy about his family. Awjoy turned out to be the orphaned son of a brahmin. He had been raised by a maternal aunt who had passed away right after his childhood years. Now, for the last year or so, he had been travelling with this troupe of performers.

Shorbojoya felt a great deal of affection for the poor orphaned child. She kept pushing second and third helpings on to him. There wasn't very much on offer, but Awjoy seemed very content with his meal.

'Ma, ask him to sing that song no?' whispered Durga, once he had finished his meal. 'You know, "Where did you go, leaving me in this forest, dearest of my heart, partner of my soul" . . . that one?'

Awjoy sang without pretence or artifice. By the end of the song, tears were running down Shorbojoya's cheeks. Such a wonderful boy, she thought. Oh, for such a lovely child to be without a mother!

Awjoy sang a few more songs after that. Finally, when it was time for him to leave, Shorbojoya invited him to come by for an early evening's meal.

'I'll be frying puffed rice at home,' she told him. 'Don't forget to come by! This is now like your own home, do you understand? There's no need to be shy. Come by whenever you feel like.'

There was still time for that night's performance, so Opu took Awjoy for a stroll along the riverbank.

'You have such a sweet voice, brother . . . why don't *you* sing a song?' Awjoy invited, once they were away from the road.

Opu wanted to agree immediately. At that moment, he wanted nothing more than to astonish Awjoy with his amazing musical prowess, then humbly collect his praise from the boy who played prince. But Awjoy wasn't just any actor—he was a professional performer with Neelmoni Hajra's troupe. What if all Opu did was show himself up?

The two of them left the walking lanes behind and sat behind the screen of a clump of bamboo trees. After much pleading, Opu finally managed to push aside his shyness and sing one of Dashu Roy's ballads: 'Awaken to your burden, oh eternal god.' He'd written the words down after hearing his father sing it.

When he finished, he found Awjoy staring at him in frank surprise.

'And you try to hide your voice, brother?' he exclaimed. 'You're wonderful! Sing another one.'

Encouraged, Opu launched into a second song: 'I spent my days by the river, in vain hopes of a boat.' His sister had picked this up from somewhere, and had been singing it in the house. He liked the tune so much that he had picked it up from her. When no one else was at home, the two of them sometimes sang it together.

Awjoy's praises were fulsome. 'You have an amazing voice, my brother,' he said over and over again. 'If on top of this you only trained a little . . .'

Being a singer had always been one of Opu's dreams. When no one else was around, he'd try to get a frank opinion of his prowess from his sister: 'Tell me the truth, Didi . . . do I have a singing voice? Will I be able to sing professionally someday?'

His sister had always assured him that he could. But that was just a sister's assurance. This was praise from an actual professional, a medal-winning singer of an actual jatra troupe! Opu was so overcome with delight that he didn't know what to do with himself. In the end, he settled for saying, 'Will you teach me that song you sing on stage?'

For the next few minutes, the two of them sat above the flowing waters of the river and sang the song together.

Afternoon began to turn to dusk. The early-evening boats went past them, splashing water from their oars. A man appeared below them on the lower banks, looking for something along the water line.

'What's he looking for?' Awjoy asked.

'Tadpoles—he wants them as bait for his fishing rod,' Opu explained. Then he said, 'Why don't you stay back here with us, brother? No more travelling. How about that?'

Awjoy's eventual departure had been a sore point for Opu ever since he'd first made friends with the boy. The entire situation reminded him of the plot of a fairy tale. He was the person who had gone into the forests, only to run into a handsome prince in exile, and made friends with him forever. Indeed, as far as Opu was concerned, Awjoy was as good as a real prince. With those eyes, with that magical voice . . . he simply couldn't be anything else. But how was he going to cope when the prince inevitably left the little village for his capital? How was he going to let go of such a precious friend?

Awjoy, too, had been gratified to find Opu. He had never found such a dedicated companion before. He told Opu that he had managed to save almost forty rupees. After he had grown up a bit, he would quit Neelmoni Hajra's troupe—the proprietor was far too free with his fists, he said. Instead, he would go to Ashutosh Pal's troupe. That was a place of real luxury—luchi for dinner every night, and a three-anna allowance if you chose not to eat! Between the two of them, it was decided that in between leaving his current troupe and joining Ashutosh Pal's, Awjoy would come to Contentment to spend a few days at Opu's house.

'But now I have to go, brother,' he finally said, getting up. 'We might start early tonight—best reach as quickly as I can. I don't know what we're putting up tonight, but if it's *Breaking Poroshuram's Pride*, then I'll play Destiny. There's a good song in that part, watch out for it . . .'

The jatra troupe performed for three more evenings. Their plays and music became the only two topics of conversation in the village. Bits of their songs could be heard everywhere: on the streets, in the fields, from cowherds taking the cattle out to graze, from boatmen going down the river. The women of the village invited the players to their homes so that they could listen to their favourite numbers again and again. Opu took this opportunity to pick up three or four more songs from the troupe's various plays. Then, one day, while Opu was visiting Awjoy in the house assigned to the jatra troupe, other players began coaxing him to sing a song. They had heard from Awjoy that he had a wonderful singing voice, and wanted to hear it for themselves. After much cajoling and encouragement, Opu finally gave in to the temptation of more praise from the professionals, and sung a song. When he was done, the troupe members hustled him into the proprietor's room and demanded he sing another one. Opu recognized the proprietor; he was the dark-skinned, pot-bellied man who sang in the choir during shows. When he finished his second song, the man said, 'Why don't you join our company, Khoka? Would you like that?'

A real offer from an actual company! Opu felt his chest expand with uncontained pride and joy. It grew further when the other players joined in, asking him to come with them when the troupe left Contentment.

Opu was ready to leave that very night, if he could. He was frankly amazed that he had lived all these years without realizing that joining a travelling troupe was the pinnacle of achievement in any person's life. But first, he took Awjoy aside to ask him an important question.

'If I join now, my brother, what parts will they give me?'

'Well, to begin with, the role of the heroine's friend and so on . . . small parts. Then, once you're properly trained . . .'

Opu didn't want to play the heroine's friend. He wanted to play the general, rushing into battle with a gold-trimmed crown and sword. Well, perhaps he'd give joining right now a miss. He'd join later—when he was all grown-up—and straightaway get the roles he wanted. Joining a jatra troupe would be, from this day forward, the one true goal of his life!

While he was thinking of that happy day, Awjoy suddenly nudged him with an elbow.

'Do you see that boy?' he whispered, nodding at a young man with skin the colour of a jeweller's touchstone. 'That's Bishtu Teli. We don't get along at all. I buy a box of matches with my own money . . . he steals it from under my pillow to light his cheroot. I tell him, "Give me back my matches, I'm scared of the darkness at night", but he never . . . the other day he hit me so hard, right here, just because I asked again. I can't even complain—the proprietor encourages him because he's a good dancer . . . I really don't want to stay with this troupe for long.'

Five days later, the troupe came to the end of their contract and began packing up. In the handful of days that they'd been here, Awjoy had become a second son to the Roy household. When she found out that he was an orphan without any surviving family, Shorbojoya had looked after him the way she looked after Opu. Durga, too, had treated him like a second little brother. She had chatted with him, learnt songs from him, told him stories about her late aunt Indir. The three of them had played hopscotch in the courtyard together. At meals, she had forced him to eat more than what he felt was his fair share. This warmth had been a rare experience for Awjoy as well. In the troupe, everyone had to look out for themselves; no one cared how their peers lived, what they ate, or where they slept. So the taste of domestic stability that he received from the Roys made it difficult for him to leave Contentment. He'd received more love from them in these few days than he had ever received in his life before. His affection-starved soul blossomed in their care, and like a child greedy for more of a rare treat, his heart broke at the prospect of leaving it all behind.

On the day that he left, Awjoy untied his little bundle of personal effects and took out five rupees from his hard-earned savings. This he tried to give to Shorbojoya, with much embarrassment.

'This is for . . . to buy Didi a good sari for her wedding . . .' he mumbled.

'No, my son, no,' said Shorbojoya gently. 'It's enough for us that you offered. Keep your money . . . you need it more than anyone else. You'll have to grow up, establish yourself, get married, settle down. Keep the money.'

Awjoy tried his best to insist upon his gift, but Shorbojoya was equally determined to make him keep the money. In the end, she managed to dissuade the boy with much pleading and gentle words, and admonishments to look after himself first. Then all three of them—mother, son and daughter—walked a little distance along the main road with him to see him safely off from Contentment. While making his final goodbyes, Awjoy reminded them several times to write to him when Durga's wedding was fixed.

A few minutes later, as his lithe frame walked down the shade of the velvet-apple trees and finally disappeared around the bend with the glory-bower bushes, Shorbojoya heaved a heavy sigh. 'Poor child,' she thought. 'Already out and about in the world at this age to make his own living. What if my Opu had to do the same? Oh, goddess, protect him!'

24

WHEN HORIHOR FIRST returned from Kashi, everyone said that he had a bright future ahead of him. No one in the entire area had learnt such a lot from such a distant place. People praised his scholarship and told each other that he was on the brink of doing something truly great. Shorbojoya had believed it all. She was sure the people in charge would be inviting her husband along soon, and awarding him a plum position in something important, somewhere. Of course, she had very little idea who these people could be or what exactly they were in charge of, but that had not deterred her hopes in the slightest. Then months upon months passed, and eventually year upon year. No horseman in royal livery arrived at their door in the middle of the night to hand-deliver an invitation to be the court scholar. Neither did the djinn from the *Arabian Nights* fly in a jewel-encrusted mansion to replace her husband's crumbling ancestral home. Instead, the worn old house came closer to giving up the ghost with every passing year; the sagging support beams sagged further, and the insect-eaten doors became even more hollow. Still, Shorbojoya did not fully give up on hope. Horihor, too, spun her dreams of an imminent recovery every time he returned from his trips. None of his plans had ever borne fruit, but that did not stop them from making them.

Life is honey-sweet chiefly because it is made up of hopes and dreams. Most of those fail to make the transition to reality, but simply having them makes reality a great deal more bearable. To have a life rich in dreams and hopes—empty though they may be—is far superior to having one without them. Reality is a trifling thing. Material success, even more so.

Horihor has been gone for three months. It had been weeks since he had last sent any money. Shorbojoya was beginning to worry, because Durga had been falling ill a bit too often lately. Things would be fine for a while—she would be walking around, eating regular meals . . . and then suddenly she would come down with high fever and take to her bed for days. Before he left, Shorbojoya had been worrying her husband about her wedding. She had already made him write two or three letters to Neerendro's father, Rajjeshwor Babu.

Her husband had said, 'Have you lost your mind? They're big people. Rajjeshwor Uncle would never respond to a proposal from people like us.'

But Shorbojoya had refused to give up hope. 'Where's the harm in trying?' she had said over and over again. 'Write again. Keep writing. Neeren saw and liked her before he left. That's practically a bride selection. It's just a matter of formalizing things now.' When a month or two passed after the most recent letter went unanswered, she had urged her husband to write again.

When Horihor went abroad this time, he had promised Shorbojoya that he would absolutely finalize a deal to have them move out of Contentment and into a better situation. While her larder depleted and her daughter carried the threat of sickness within her, Shorbojoya sat in her empty house and dreamt of the promised future.

They would have just enough, not much. An assembly of two or three thatched huts forming a new home on one side of the neighbourhood. A well-fed, lactating cow tethered in the cowshed a few feet away, bundles of hay around it in high scaffold-shelves. A small granary in their compound, full of ripe paddy. The strong, sweet smell of ripe peas would drift across the open courtyard, from the little vegetable patch next to the field outside. Bird calls would fill the house—tailor birds, blue-throated barbets, white-rumped shama thrushes. Opu would break his morning fast with warm puffed rice, soaked in a large earthen bowl of fresh, frothing milk from their own black cow. Durga would no longer suffer from malaria. Everyone would know and honour their family as brahmins, come by just to touch their feet and collect their blessings. No one would dismiss them for being poor.

These are the dreams that Shorbojoya dreams. Through the day, through the night, these are the dreams she dreams that keep her going. A voice in her mind constantly whispers, 'Maybe *this* time, after all those other failed times . . . maybe this time something will come through.'

Why has it not come through so far? From her childhood days of running around under the black plum and drumstick trees, to the years of drawing elaborate patterns on the floor for the Shenjuti ritual, she had but one wish: to be able to settle happily into her in-laws' home, to be able to draw the footsteps of the goddess of wealth at her doorway, and live a contented, fulfilled life. Why, after so many years, was she still waiting? Why did she, despite her rituals and faith, end up in this broken old house, surrounded by wilderness and bamboo groves? These are questions she tries to silence when they threaten the fragility of her dreams.

Durga had fetched a large corm of taro from who-knows-where. She had practically organized a sit-in in the kitchen, begging her mother to cook some for her. Her mother had been saying all morning, 'What's happened to you, Durga? How can you have rice and curry today? Didn't you have fever just last evening?'

Durga had tried her best to wave this fact away. 'That's not . . . it was hardly *fever*, Ma! I was just a little cold, is all. Go on, make me a little rice with this, just a little boiled kochu with rice, please Ma . . .'

'Malaria has made your greed go wild,' her mother had chided. 'All right, if the fever doesn't visit today and tomorrow, you can have some kochu and rice day after. But not before that.'

When no amount of pleading had made her mother relent, Durga had to put the taro away, disappointed. Then, almost as if trying to convince herself, she had muttered defiantly, 'I'm very well. There's going to be no fever today. I'm going to have sautéed potato and two rutis for dinner. I'll be just fine.'

After a little while, however, a yawn had forced its way up her throat. She knew this was a sign of oncoming fever, but despite mounting apprehension, she tried to convince herself that a yawn in the morning meant nothing at all. Yawns were perfectly normal, after all—they happened by the dozens to people who had never had malaria. There was no reason to get carried away.

After a little while, she began to feel the familiar chills. Her entire being begged to be taken into the warm autumn sunshine in the courtyard, but Durga refused to yield. 'Feeling cold is natural at this time of the year,' she told herself firmly. 'It has nothing whatsoever to do with fevers.'

The dreaded fever finally attacked, as it usually did, in the last hours of the afternoon. The autumn sunshine was still lingering in the courtyard. Durga slipped outside for that last bit of warmth, hoping and praying her mother didn't catch her in the act. 'This is not really fever,' she told herself over and over again. 'It feels like fever because we constantly talk about fever, that's all.' But in her heart, she knew that all her hopes for rice and curry had just been dashed. Hopeless dejection flooded her heart.

In desperation, she wondered if she could chase the fever away. 'It might go away if I don't pay attention to it,' she decided, and called her brother over for a chat. Brother and sister sat together in the dwindling sunlight, reminiscing about old adventures as they watched the red light of dusk recede from the courtyard to the top of their mossy boundary wall.

Last monsoon, the two of them had made airtight plans for stealing into the Mukhujjes' garden on a stormy summer night, and making off with some of their fallen palmyra fruits. They had managed to get into the garden just fine, but after taking only a few steps towards the palmyra tree, something sharp had suddenly pierced the underside of Durga's right foot. She took an instinctive step backwards, only to have her left foot land on another sharp object. Next morning, they had realized that their tormentor Shotu had lined the way from the fence to the tree with palmyra needles, to prevent neighbours from doing exactly what the two of them had been trying to do.

Then there had been the amazing box.

An old Musholman man had come around sometime ago, speaking the dialect of the east and carrying a large, brightly painted tin box. He had set up his show in Jeebon Choudhuri's outer courtyard; in exchange for a paisa, anyone could look through the seeing-tube into the secrets within. The old man sold his show with a catchy tune, singing, 'See Taj Bibi's roja! See the elephant fight the tiger!'

Durga had had no money. So she simply sat nearby and watched as a steady stream of children arrived, paid and exclaimed at whatever wonder lay within. Once they were done, she had eagerly asked each and every one, 'What did you see? What's inside? Is it all real?'

None of the children had been able to give her a satisfactory answer. They had been so overwhelmed by the box that they could not say what they had seen, merely that it had been incredible. No words, they told her, could possibly describe the experience of the box.

When the last of the children finished their viewing, Durga had stood up to leave as well. The old Musholman must have noticed her sitting nearby all this while, for he said, 'Leaving, Khuki? Don't you want to take a look?'

Durga had shaken her head. 'I don't have any money,' she had said.

'Never mind the money. Have a look anyway. Come on.'

At this unexpected generosity, Durga had felt a sudden shyness creep into her. 'Nah . . .' she had replied, but without conviction. Inside her chest, her heart had been thudding wildly in anticipation.

'Nothing wrong with looking in a box for free, is there?' the man had said, smiling. 'Come on. Don't worry about the money.'

Durga had brightened. She had gone up to the box, but hadn't been able to actually look inside without another explicit invitation.

'Here,' the man had said, indicating the viewing tube. 'Put your eye here and look through this.'

Thus invited, Durga had pushed bunches of flyaway hair behind her ears, and finally looked in.

Later, she could never adequately describe to anyone the wonder of the next ten minutes. Even though she saw it with her own two eyes, the magical moving things inside that box defied belief. They went beyond things that she had heard of even in the most fantastical of stories. How could living people be inside a tin box? But she had seen them! Shahebs and mems, their houses, soldiers fighting in a war . . . it had been amazing! The other children had been right. How could anyone have words adequate enough to describe this miracle?

She had really wanted to show Opu the wonders of the box. But her brother had not been with her that day, and despite searching high and low, she had never found the man with the box again.

At this juncture, Durga's fever became so forceful that she could no longer support herself sitting. The siblings' reminiscences had to be shelved as she hobbled indoors and collapsed on the bed, wrapping herself in a thin old quilt. Soon after, she was lost to the world.

Now that his father was away from home again, Opu could seldom be found within the confines of the Roy compound. He left home early in the morning with a big stack of cowrie shells, returning only when he knew lunch would be ready and waiting. The books that he had once so loved to rifle through had been left in a corner for silverfish to scuttle through. Appalled by his behaviour, his mother had scolded him several times about it. 'You're going to be ruined!' she had predicted bitterly. 'Books and studies pushed aside for months, all for a game of cowries! You wait till your father comes back. I'll tell him exactly how much you have studied while he was away!'

Sometimes the scolding would have its desired effect. Opu would sit down with his box of books and rifle through them. He would lay them out in a spread, and shuffle their arrangement in the box. After some time he would suddenly have an idea, and call out to his mother.

'Give me a bit of catechu, Ma. I need it for my inkwell . . .'

When the catechu would dissolve in the ink, he would dip his pen in it and carefully do a page of handwriting exercise. Then he would put the page out to dry in the sun. Once dry, he would examine closely how much the catechu made his writing glitter in the sunshine.

'Ooh, that's beautiful!' he would think to himself, as the dry ink glistened in the light. 'I'll add a bit more catechu tomorrow. It's going to be so much shinier then!'

The next day, he would steal a bit of catechu from his mother's betel-leaf bowl, and wait eagerly for his writing to dry. The letters, he was certain, were glittering more than they had the previous day. And so, the next day, he would steal a bit more catechu. It went on like this for several days, till one day Shorbojoya caught him at it.

'No reading, no studying, but he needs lumps upon lumps of khoyer every day!' she shouted, furious at being hoodwinked. 'Put it back in the bowl right this instant!'

'I'm not taking it just like that!' Opu tried to defend himself, slightly embarrassed at being caught. 'This stuff is needed to make ink. How can I study without ink?'

'How are all the other boys of creation studying?' Shorbojoya snapped. 'The shops would fail if they used the stuff like you do. Leave my khoyer bowl alone. Shoo!'

So Opu simply gave up on getting an education and instead decided to write plays in his notebook. He wrote so much within the first few days that the poor notebook had only a few pages left. A trusting king had been betrayed by his adviser, and had to abdicate his throne to save his life. Last seen, he had escaped into the forests. Meanwhile, Prince Neelambor and Princess Awmba had been caught by a band of dacoits, and after much fighting the princess's corpse was found on the bank of a river. The play also had a complicated character called Shotu, who had been sentenced to death shortly after his first appearance, despite no serious transgression. Some might wish to allege that the play's plot—from a boon from the sage Narod to resurrect Princess Awmba, to her eventual wedding to the king's general, Jeebonketu—was inspired by, or indeed copied directly from, the jatra that had played in Contentment at the beginning of the previous summer. And well, technically, those people would be right. But so what? Let us not forget that stealing ideas is an ancient art. After all, it was an ancient poet's description of a peacock-peppered wilderness in the rains that had inspired Kalidash to imagine his messenger-cloud. For centuries, we have marvelled at the beauty of his epic poem, but had we realized that we were simultaneously also paying our respects to that fortuitous moonlit light, when the great poet read another's work by the golden light of his bedside lamp, and made it part of his own? To light a fire, after all, we need to already have some fire. A heap of ashes couldn't do the job. Neither could a flaming torch light a pile of ash on fire, even if it tried. So if Opu needed to copy plots from jatras he had seen to write his own plays, well . . . where was the harm?

There was a book in his box called *A Collection of Biographies*. The cover proclaimed that it had been 'Composed by Bidyashagor Mohashoy'. It was an old book, somewhat the worse for wear. His father had a habit of collecting books for his son from various places—who knows where he's got this one from. Opu had read bits and pieces from this book sometimes. He wanted to be like the people in the book. When sent to the market with his father's potatoes, the farmer's son Roscoe would instead sit next to a fence in the field and practise algebra. When he ran out of ink and paper, he did his sums by scratching an old piece of leather with a blunt awl. Then there was the shepherd boy Duvall, who let the wandering sheep go wherever they wished while he sat under a tree and studied maps. That was the sort of thing he wanted to do, too! What sort of a thing was this 'algebra'? He was sure he would love to study it, like Roscoe did. He didn't want to do these . . . these handwriting exercises, these books of tables, these silly rules of mathematics. He wanted to be left alone in a large field, next to a fence, where he would study maps—whatever they were—in peace. He wanted to read thick books and become a big scholar, like those people are. But where in this village would he get the things actually worth studying? The 'algebra', the 'maps', and books of Latin grammar? Here it was the same old upon the same old: rules for counting cowries and the three-times table.

His mother could shout at him as much as she liked; the things he actually wanted to study simply couldn't be found in this village. So why should he bother sitting down with his books at all?

25

IT HAD BEEN raining quite heavily for the last few days. That evening at Awnnoda Roy's temple courtyard, the session centred on tales of the unbelievable. The assembled men told tales so tall that they rivalled the *Arabian Nights*. If someone spun a fake thriller about the indigo plantation's past, then another informed the assembly about the five-maund magnet that was mounted on top of the Jogonnath temple at Puri. It was so powerful, apparently, that it regularly pulled ships from the middle of the sea to the shore, crashing them against the submerged rocks.

Tales of the unknown were attractive at any time, but on this dark and rainy evening, they were particularly delicious. Evening began to turn to night, but no one wanted to leave their cosy conference and trudge home in the rain.

After the geographic believe-it-or-not, the subject turned to the miracles of astrology. Dinu Choudhuri was saying, 'There's no book to rival the *Bhrigu Shonhita*. The name of the star you were born under—that's all one needs. The book will give you your father's name, your family's name, details about your past and future. Match it—it'll all be true. Everything's written in the stars, brothers. It's all a matter of correct calculations. Some say that even the details of your past life . . .'

At this fascinating juncture, Rammoy suddenly interrupted the flow. 'Nah, everyone, time to go. Do you see the state of the sky? If we don't leave now, we'll never make it home tonight. Let's just hope there isn't going to be a storm with all that rain. Move, all of you. Let's go.'

The downpour had been ceaseless since that evening. Sometimes, the clouds pretended that they were done for the day. But just as the sky lightened and the rain slowed down to a pitter-patter, darker clouds swept in over the village, and the downpour began anew. The village had been enveloped in a permanent mist for days.

Horihor had sent five rupees, and that had been several weeks ago. Since then, there had been neither word nor money from him. Every morning Shorbojoya woke up with the hope that that day would be the day the money finally arrived. Several times, she had scolded her son for not being more vigilant of the post.

'Only playing about all day—why can't you go sit by the post box? The moment you see the peon, go up to him and ask him about your father's letter.'

'Playing around!' her son would retort indignantly. 'I sit by the post box all day. Yesterday the peon brought a letter for Puti's family—go ask her if I'm lying. How did I get our newspaper if I didn't sit by the box for the post? It came with Puti's letter. I've been there the whole time!'

The early rains continued to drench Contentment by day and by night. Opu took himself to the post box in Awnnoda Roy's outer courtyard in the morning, and then waited all day for the peon—just like his mother had asked him to. As the downpour began to seep through

Shadhu Kormokar's thatched roof, the pigeons holed up within it scrambled out and flew to the balustrade above Awnnoda Roy's windows. With nothing else to do, Opu watched their struggle to stay dry. He could live with the rain, within reason, but he feared the thunder. Every time lightning flashed across the sky, he shuddered and told himself, 'Look at the sky god go. Here it comes now, his big roar!' Then he quickly jammed his fingers into his ears and tightly shut his eyes.

Upon returning home one afternoon, he found his mother and sister thoroughly drenched in the kitchen veranda, sorting through a huge pile of arum greens that they'd spent the afternoon picking.

'Oooh—that's a lot of greens!' he exclaimed. 'Where'd you get them, Ma?'

Durga grinned at him. '"Oooh, where'd you get them!"—you have it easy, sitting by that post box all day. We had to go all the way to the little pond in the garden over there, the one next to the black plum tree. The water came up to our knees, on top of all this rain! Fancy giving *that* a go?'

The next day, Shorbojoya hid a bowl in the folds of her sari when she went to the bathing steps in the morning. While she was sure no one else was watching, she cornered the local barber's wife.

'Look, this is something I had at home. Pure kansha—no filler, no nothing, and an original floral design. It was a wedding present from my family. You wouldn't get something like this today if you paid for it. I heard you saying the other day that you wanted a white-brass bowl, so I thought, let me show her what I have at home . . .'

After much bargaining, the barber's wife shelled out fifty paise from the coin-knot at the end of her sari, and swiftly hid the bowl in its folds. Shorbojoya reminded her several times not to mention the deal to anyone.

A couple of days later, monsoon truly arrived in Contentment. Water fell from the sky in sheets. Ditches and pools were flooded. The bathing steps disappeared under the rising water of the ponds. Water stood knee-high on the low village lanes. Easterlies rampaged through the neighbourhood, filling days and nights with an ominous whoosh and whistling. Bamboo groves went to war amongst themselves, whipping into each other and bending down almost to the ground. The sky became permanently overcast—not even a little sunlight made its way through to the village. Occasionally, the already-grey sky would become even darker. Coal-black clouds would sweep over Contentment from east to west, like battalions rushing to war under the command of invisible generals. The gods and monsters must be at war above the sky—nothing else explained this dark pall over creation. The gods' lightning bolt might rip through it in a blaze of roaring brilliance, but darkness returned like Hydra's undying heads, swallowing all traces of it from the sky.

And then came the storm to beat all storms.

The river began to swell. People began losing roofs to the unending gale. Doorways and windows collapsed. Cows and calves began to simply stand under trees or inside the bamboo grove, too beaten by the ceaseless rain to even seek proper shelter. All the birds disappeared. Mornings and evenings in the village became utterly silent. This state of affairs continued for four, then five days. Unending rain, and an unceasing, unforgiving gale.

One morning, Opu jumped back on to the veranda after a quick reconnaissance tour of the neighbourhood.

'Didi!' he called out, drying his hair vigorously with a damp towel. 'The water has reached our bamboo grove! Want to go see?'

Durga was in bed, wrapped up in a pile of blankets. She didn't move, merely peeked from under the folds.

'How much water?'

'Ooh, quite a bit. Go see tomorrow, when your fever goes away. The tamarind tree is standing in knee-deep water!' Then, aware of the rumbling in his belly, he looked around. 'Where's Ma, re, Didi?'

There was nothing in the larder for Shorbojoya to give her boy—nothing but a bit of toasted rice, stale. Opu cried and threw a loud tantrum. 'No, not the old toasted rice! Please, Ma, don't you understand that I'm hungry? Why won't you make me some proper rice?'

Shorbojoya tried to calm him down. 'My darling boy, my jewel of a child—listen to reason. How can I cook in this weather? The oven is full of water!'

Then she brought something out from the folds of her sari, her face alight with secret joy. 'Look at what I found . . . a climbing perch! Saw it twisting about near the bamboo grove. The inlets are flooded, that's why these fishes are now coming inland. The fish pond at Borojpota has overflown into the river—can't tell which is which. That's where this perch came from.'

Durga sat up in surprise. 'Can I see the fish again, Ma? Wow! So perch really do wander about on land! Was there more?'

Opu wanted to run out of the house right away to see if there were more climbing perches in the grove. His mother had to use her considerable coaxing skills to keep him at home.

From her bed, Durga said, 'Opu, let's you and me go tomorrow, when the fever is gone. We'll get more fish and bring it home!'

Later, she thought to herself, 'Fish in the bamboo grove . . . wow! I wonder how it got there. Did Ma search the area for more? Probably not. Still, Opu and I are going tomorrow—I'm sure we'll find more. Ooh, I wish I could've seen that koi walking about. Never mind, I'll see it tomorrow. The fever will definitely go away by morning. We'll go then.'

Lamp-lighting hour descended on the village. It was the thirteenth night of the waning moon. The nearly moonless evening sky was darkened further by the dark rainclouds hanging low on the evening sky. Durga was huddled up on the bed. Opu and his mother sat beside her on the leftover space. The rain drummed ceaselessly on the ground beyond the windows. Staring at the darkness, Shorbojoya suddenly thought, 'What if a letter comes from Neeren Babaji? Like, right now? That's not too far-fetched! After all, he said himself that he liked Durga. Hinted it, anyway. Is a proposal really that improbable?'

The very next second, bitter pessimism flooded her. A son-in-law like Neeren was not in her fate. One needed to be born with a far better destiny than hers to land such a wonderful match for one's daughter. If she had such good luck, she would not have been stuck in this hopeless life.

Brother and sister, meanwhile, had set up an epic squabble over nothing in particular. Opu chose this minute of disillusionment to squish up against his mother, grinning. 'Ma . . . how about that poem? "Shyamlonka grinds spices, her tresses over the floor flow . . ."?'

'"My mother has left the country by then—poor me, oh oh!"' his sister promptly said.

Opu looked uncertain. 'That's never . . . Ma, is that right? "By then my mother had left the country, oh oh"?'

When his mother didn't immediately confirm, he laughed happily at his sister's ignorance.

Her son's innocent laughter sent a spike through Shorbojoya's heart. Not one of seven, not one of five—Opu was her only son. And her destiny was so utterly rotten that she could not even fulfil his simplest wishes. Not ghee, not luchi, not even shondesh . . . her poor child had asked for rice! And she could not even give him *that*!

But surely these miserable times were temporary? This broken house, this constant poverty—surely they will all go away if her Opu grows up the right way? She closed her eyes and quickly said a silent prayer to whichever deity might be listening. 'Please, god, raise my son to be successful. Give him a bright future! Make a proper person of my son!'

Then, slightly relieved at turning over her worries to a higher power, she began telling her children stories of the old days of the village. There had been a storm like this back when she was still a new bride in Contentment. The river and ponds had flooded the village many streets past the bamboo grove. A large boat had lost its moorings and floated right up the big lane behind the Mukhujjes' house, quite unaware that it had left the river for a village.

'How big was the boat, Ma?' Opu asked eagerly.

'You know the boats those Bihari people use? The ones that ferry lime and fuller's earth? It was that big.'

Durga, who had been quiet so far, suddenly said, 'Ma, do you know how to make a four-strand braid?'

Later, much deeper into the night, Shorbojoya was shaken suddenly out of sleep by her son's cries. 'Ma, wake up! Wake up! The roof is leaking water on me.'

She forced herself out of bed and hurriedly lit a lamp. Rain was pounding the earth outside. Their old roof was leaking in several places. Cold water was everywhere. She picked the driest place in the room and moved the bedding there. Durga was deep in her fevered sleep, lost to everything going on around her. Her mother touched the quilt she was wrapped in. It was sopping wet.

'Dugga? O Dugga!' she called. 'Can you hear me? Sit up a moment, let me move the bedding. Quickly, Dugga—everything's getting soaked!'

A little later, when her children had fallen asleep again, Shorbojoya sat up alone. The sound of rain was magnified by the dark emptiness around the house. These nights were terrifying. All alone amidst the flooded woods, the roof leaking everywhere, her husband gone to god-knows-where—Shorbojoya felt as if everything about the night was a portent of a terrible ill. Where *was* her husband? Never mind the money, where were his letters? He had never gone this long without sending word . . . was he unwell?

'Ma Shiddheshwori, I swear five and a quarter annas' food to your worship, Ma!' she prayed fervently, suddenly terrified. 'Bring me good news of my husband, Mother, I *beg* you . . .'

After dawn the next morning, the force of the rain abated a little. Shorbojoya stepped out of the house to take stock of their surroundings. The small pond in the bamboo grove had disappeared under the much higher level of standing water. After a while, she saw Nibaron's mother splashing along the path to the bathing steps, making her way somewhere through the morning rain.

'O Nibaron's ma!' she called out. 'Come here a minute—listen!'

When the woman made her way over, Shorbojoya said, with some embarrassment: 'Remember you once said . . . that you were looking for a Bindabuni shawl for your boy? Do you still want one?'

'You have one? Good, I'll bring my son over as soon as the rain holds off for a bit. Is your shawl new, Ma Thakron, or used?'

Shorbojoya, eager to make a deal, said, 'Why don't you come in right now? Let me show it to you. It's a little old, but no one has actually worn it, really. Properly washed and put away, right from the beginning.'

There was a brief pause. Then Shorbojoya said, 'So . . . are you people still husking paddy, Nibaron's ma?'

Nibaron's mother shook her head. 'Monsoons aren't a good time for that, Ma Thakron. The paddy can't be dried enough to husk. We've just husked some for our own use—that's all.'

'Will you do something for me?' Shorbojoya asked eagerly. 'Will you bring me half a bushel of what you have?' Then she moved closer to Nibaron's mother and said in a pleading tone, 'No one will go to the markets for me in this rain, Nibaron's ma. I've been going door to door with money in my hand, hoping someone might be willing . . . I have no hope left but you, my dear . . .'

Nibaron's mother agreed to help. 'I'll bring the rice by, Ma Thakron,' she assured Shorbojoya. 'But will you people be able to eat our bhetel variety? It's probably way too thick for your gentlemanly tastes.'

Days passed. Despite her fever, Durga could no longer bear to swallow the bitter concoction of boiled neem-tree bark. Her illness was still the same. There was no doctor, no ayurvedic practitioner, no medicine of any kind. Every now and then she says things like, 'Ma, will you get me one paisa's worth of biscuits from the shop? They're nice and salty—it'd be nice to eat some of that for a change.'

'Hah!' Shorbojoya thought bitterly. Here she was, unable to buy even a bit of cheap sago . . . and her daughter wanted biscuits!

The true downpour returned again that evening: roaring sheets of rain, ice-cold easterlies, sun-swallowing black clouds and incessant whooshing. The sky-water poured into the room through cracks in its doors and windows, soaking everything within reach. At first the three of them tried to stuff the old cracks with jute bags and bits of torn old clothes, but after a while even those soaked through and began to drip. Human effort was no barrier to this beastly monster of a Bhadro rainstorm.

The rain really started coming down in buckets later that night. The whole village was asleep, but Shorbojoya was wide awake, keeping vigil. In the quiet of the night, the storm sounded like an angry giant on a rampage. Every gust of howling wind shook the ancient home to its foundations. Terrified, Shorbojoya huddled closer to her sleeping children. All alone with her little ones in this wilderness of bamboos—what was she to do if this doddering old house finally fell?

'It doesn't matter if I die, god,' she prayed frantically. 'But how do I save my children? Where can I go for help at this time of night?'

As the water continued to crash to the ground outside, she tried to map out an escape plan in her head.

'The main veranda wall will probably be the first. The moment I hear the first murmur, I'll pull them out through the corner doorway at the back.'

She couldn't afford to sleep for the sake of survival, but every passing minute made sitting upright harder. For days, she had been living on boiled arum and taro greens—starving herself so she could give her children whatever little was left in the larder. Her body was weak with hunger and anxiety, and her head was frequently aswirl with dizziness and fear.

As night deepened, the storm intensified. After a particularly vicious lashing on the house, Shorbojoya tiptoed to the front doorway, terrified of looking out yet desperate to know the direction of the wind. The moment she parted the doors, a gush of cold wind whipped inside, drenching her hair and clothes in the ice-sharp rain. Everything beyond the doorway was a uniform pitch black: sky, trees, water and houses had all blended into an unnerving, indistinguishable nothingness. The howling gale had drowned out every sound, even that of the tempestuous rain. Coldness, darkness and wetness reigned supreme.

Shorbojoya slammed the door shut. What if something came along this awful night and forced its way into the house? A human or some other animal? Goddess protect her! There wasn't a single familiar man or woman within shouting distance, only shrubs and trees. She reached for her son in the darkness, but her hand fell on his blanket. It was wet. For goodness sake! She wanted to scream in frustration. Despite her best efforts, the rain had been quietly coming in through the cracks in the roof and windows! Shorbojoya blindly cast about for the box of matches. A little later, she finally managed to light the kerosene lamp. She held up the light and tried to wake her son. 'Opu, Opu—get up! You're wet through. Opu!'

Her son mumbled something in his sleep—Shorbojoya couldn't tell what. She turned to her daughter. 'Durga, roll over . . . the bedding's getting wet. Durga!'

Opu suddenly sat up, stared at nothing for a few seconds with sleep-dead eyes, then fell back to sleep again. Moments later, a loud crash shook the room. Shorbojoya rushed to the door and peeked out, braving the lashes of cold rain. It was still completely dark, but now the darkness on the side of the house facing the bamboo groves looked . . . less solid. It took her a second to understand why.

An entire side of the kitchen had just collapsed.

Terrified, Shorbojoya stood rooted to the spot. If the walls had started to fall, then surely it was only a matter of time before the entire house fell? What would she do when that happened? There was no one to turn to . . . and a tempest was roaring outside! 'Please, god,' she prayed silently, desperately, 'please don't let the house collapse on my children. Look at their young faces—have mercy, god. Let this night pass without harm . . .'

A few hours later, dawn finally began to show through the darkness. The night's gale had passed, but there was still a heavy drizzle on the village. Neelmoni Mukhujje's wife was on her way to check on their cows. Suddenly, she heard a frantic pounding on their back door. Opening the door, she was astonished to see a dishevelled Shorbojoya on the other side. She was panting.

'Fourth-eldest sister, please wake up my brother-in-law. Ask him to come to our house. Dugga is . . . she's acting really strange!'

Neelmoni Mukhujje's wife was even more surprised. 'Dugga's acting strangely? Why? What's wrong with Dugga?'

'She's had the fever for the past few days. She was fine in between, but then . . . malaria, you know? It never goes away. And now after last night's chill and rain . . . sister, if you could just tell my brother-in-law . . .'

Seeing her sleep-deprived red eyes and obvious fear, Neelmoni Mukhujje's wife said in a soothing tone, 'There's nothing to be scared of, sister-in-law. Wait here, I'll call your brother-in-law right away. I'll come along, too. Never seen a night like last night, you're right about that . . . he had to get up before dawn to move the cows when the wind blew the roof off our shed . . . wait, I'll go wake him up right now.'

A little later, Neelmoni Mukhujje, his eldest son, Foni, his wife and two daughters set out for Opu's family home. In the pale light of dawn, the village looked like it had been trampled on by the roaring monster of the night before. Nothing was in its place. The path was covered with stray bundles of hay from roofs, young leaves from the tops of trees, and twigs and branches from all over the village. Neelmoni Mukhujje's younger son picked up a twig to uncover the corpse of a dead sparrow from under a pile of young bamboo leaves.

Pointing at the leaves at the door of the Roys' compound, Foni said, 'Do you see that, Baba? The storm has flown in those lebbeck leaves all the way from that tree near the Nawbabgonj road!'

Inside, Opu was sitting next to Durga on the bed.

'How are things, Baba Opu?' Neelmoni Mukhujje asked gently.

Opu's face was etched with fear. 'Didi is delirious, Uncle. She's been mumbling all sorts of strange things in her sleep.'

Neelmoni sat on the bed and reached for the pulse on Durga's wrist. After a few seconds, he said. 'Hm . . . the fever is a bit too high. But don't worry—there's nothing to be afraid of. Foni, you go to Nawbabgonj right away. Tell the doctor, Shorot, what's going on, and bring him back here as soon as possible.'

Then he leaned closer to Durga and called her name a few times. But Durga was deep in the throes of her fever; she didn't respond. Neelmoni then looked about the leaking room.

'Tsk! The house and windows are barely holding up. The rains must've leaked in from every side. Honestly, my younger sister-in-law, you could have just come to our place. You have nothing to be ashamed of. This is all on Hori. Never did have any common sense, that one. When other people are repairing their homes and stocking up for the floods, he's gadding about who-knows-where!'

'How's he supposed to repair the house when there isn't even enough at home to feed the family?' his wife cut in.

'No man would leave his family in this catastrophic season unless things were truly dire. Poor girl . . . she's completely soaked through. Let's put on a pot of water for her first. Foni, open that window, will you?'

Later that morning, the doctor from Nawbabgonj arrived. He examined the patient and prescribed medicines. Before leaving, he assured the family that there wasn't anything especially wrong with Durga; she just needed moist rags to the forehead to bring her fever down. It was decided that a letter would be sent to Horihor, though no one was quite sure where he was at the moment. In the end, a letter summarizing his family's travails was posted to his last known address.

Later in the day, Opu tried talking to his sister. He had been sitting by her head, mopping her forehead with a moist cloth.

'Didi—can you hear me?' he ventured.

There was no response.

'O Didi,' he tried again. 'Can you hear me? How're you feeling, Didi?'

Durga half-mumbled something, but he couldn't make out what she was trying to say. He tried a few more times to get her to talk, even placing his ear next to her lips once or twice to catch what she was saying. But in her delirium, Durga either mumbled incoherently or only moved her lips without making an actual sound.

After a while, Opu gave up.

It was early evening when the fever finally went down. After a whole night and day of being barely conscious, Durga finally opened her eyes. But the fever had left her extremely weak. When she spoke, her voice was so thin and low that one had to bend towards her to catch what she was saying.

After the first flurry of relief, their mother left the bedside to return to her household work, but Opu continued to sit next to his sister. After a while, Durga lifted her eyes to her brother.

'How late is it, Opu?' she asked weakly.

'Not late at all,' Opu said eagerly. 'We still have plenty of daylight left! We finally had some sun today, Didi, could you tell? Look—there's still sunlight at the top of our coconut tree.'

For a while, neither sibling said anything else. Seeing the sun after days had filled Opu with joy. In the silence, he looked happily at the top of the trees, where the last light still lingered.

After a bit, Durga said, 'Listen, Opu . . . I need to ask you something.'

Opu leaned closer to his sister. 'What, Didi?'

'Will you show me a real railway train one day?'

'Of course! Once you're better, we'll tell Baba to take us for a holy dip in the Gonga. Then we won't just see a train, we'll actually ride it!'

The rest of the day and night passed in peace. There was no indication in either the sky or in the gentle river breeze that a terrifying gale had just swept through the village. It was a perfectly pleasant autumn day in the month of Shorot, sun-kissed and bright.

The next morning, at around ten, Neelmoni Mukhujje was sitting on his sunny veranda massaging oil on to his arms and legs, in anticipation of a bath in the river after quite a few days. Suddenly, he heard his wife calling out for him. Her tone was urgent, so Neelmoni set aside the oil and hurried indoors.

His wife looked worried. 'I can hear crying from Opu's house,' she said as soon as she saw him. 'We should go over to check right now . . . shall we?'

Husband and wife almost ran all the way to the Roy house.

Durga was still lying where they had left her in the leaking room. But now Shorbojoya was leaning over her daughter, screaming frantically to wake her up.

'Look at me, Dugga—open your eyes! Open your eyes just once . . . Dugga, look at me. Look at me!'

Neelmoni advanced swiftly into the room.

'What . . . what's wrong? Move, sister-in-law, let the girl get some air. Here, let me take a look . . .'

Shorbojoya looked up with blind, uncomprehending eyes. The presence of an older neighbour—who, by the norms of the village, was considered the equivalent of her elder brother-in-law—didn't seem to even register with her.

'Why is my daughter acting this way?' she wailed helplessly, still trying to get a reaction out of the prone girl.

Durga didn't open her eyes again.

Sometimes, eternity beckons us through familiar blue skies. Children with too much spirit and curiosity for this rule-bound world answer that call eagerly, diving into the deep blue of an unending beyond. The paths of that place are beyond mortal understanding, for they eschew the conventions and rules we hold so dear. Durga's restless, unruly, inquisitive soul had heard that call, and seen it as her biggest, most wonderful adventure. She had probably yielded her mortal life with gladness.

The physician, Shorot Daktar was brought in again for a final verdict. 'It's the final stage of malaria,' he said sombrely. 'The moment the medicines brought the fever down, her heart failed from the shock. Saw a case just like this in Doshghora the other day.'

Within half an hour, the veranda of the isolated little house was flooded with people.

26

HORIHOR HADN'T RECEIVED the letter from home.

When he left Contentment this time, Horihor had gone first to Gowari Krishnonogor. Though he knew no one in that area, he had deluded himself with the hope that work would be easier to find in a large urban marketplace. After spending a few days in Gowari, he found out that the local households of lawyers and zamindars paid a daily honorarium for reciting the *Devimahatyam* on their premises. He spent fifteen days in the hopes of getting such a job, till he finally ran out whatever little savings he had managed to bring with him from home.

Horihor was in a severely dire situation. He was stranded alone in an unfamiliar area, without a single friendly face for help or reassurance. Once his scant money ran out, he was obliged to move out of the thatched-hut hotel he had been staying in. After much asking around, he discovered that the local Hori temple provided meals and shelter to newly arrived destitute brahmins in the city. Once he went and described his situation, they did give him a bed in one corner of a small room, but Horihor was acutely uncomfortable in the place. First, he was kept up at nights by a group of ganja-smoking men, who laughed and talked loudly to each other till the small hours of the morning. Second, he occasionally woke up at night to see women coming in and going out of the temple area . . . and none of them looked like pious women from decent households, who had come to offer their prayers to the deity.

He spent a few nights there in considerable discomfort, using the daylight hours to visit every well-to-do lawyer and zamindar he could find. Sometimes, when he returned late at night to the temple, someone else would be stretched out in his corner, on his bed, comfortably snoring. Horihor would have to spend those nights lying in the veranda. When this became more frequent, Horihor had a slightly heated exchange with the people who did this—the aforementioned smokers. The lord alone knows what the group then went and said to the secretary of the temple, but the secretary babu then called Horihor in and informed him that it was against the temple's rules to let anyone stay for more than three nights, so Horihor should seek alternate accommodation from that night onwards.

So, late that evening, Horihor found himself and his bundles back on the streets, bereft of even the lowly shelter he had found at the Horishobha. He made his way down to the Khore river and washed himself in its waters. He had earned a full rupee at a timbre storehouse that day by singing songs in praise of the goddess Shyama. He now took that rupee to the market, exchanged it for smaller denominations, and with some of it bought some yogurt and puffed rice for his dinner. Eating it proved almost impossible. He had only left enough at home to cover ten days' expenses; now it was almost two months . . . and he still had not been able to send back a single paisa. How were they managing? What were they eating? His son had reminded him over and over again to bring back a copy of the *Poddopuran* for him. The boy really did love to read.

Horihor knew that his son borrowed books from his personal book box while he was away. He would do his best to cover his tracks, but having no idea about the order in which his father kept his books, he would leave the box in a telltale mess. Horihor would take one look at the haphazard pile, and know immediately about his son's pilfering.

This time before leaving, Horihor had bought a locally printed verse version of the *Poddopuran* from the Jugi neighbourhood in the village. Opu had immediately claimed it as his own and refused to give it up. He read and reread it every day, particularly relishing the bit where Shiva goes to the Kuchuni neighbourhood to catch fish. Finally, Horihor had to practically beg it back from his son.

'Give it here, son,' he had implored. 'The book's owners want it back!'

In the end Opu returned the book, but only after extracting the promise that his father would get him his own copy. Before he left, Opu had reminded him several times of that promise.

'That book of mine, Baba! Remember to get me a copy!'

His daughter, on the other hand, didn't have such elevated tastes. A simple green sari and a single sheet of good-quality red dye for her feet—that was all she had asked for.

But never mind these extra presents, he hadn't even been able to send enough to keep the household running. Later that night, he sought out a timbre storehouse to shelter his head for the night. But he couldn't sleep. Instead, he spent much of the night tossing and turning, wondering how he could send home some money.

The next morning, he was out in the streets, wandering aimlessly in the hopes of something—anything—happening. Suddenly, his eyes fell upon a red-brick house, guarded by an iron-barred gate. Staring at the house, Horihor felt a conviction take root within him: the answer to all his troubles lay within that house. He made himself cross the unlocked gate and walk towards the main entrance. It was very obviously a rich household—the stairs leading up to the drawing room were encased in marble and decorated with potted flowering plants, palm trees and tall stone statues.

Inside, a man in his late middle age was reading a newspaper. Seeing a stranger enter, he kept the paper aside and sat up.

'Who are you?' he demanded. 'What do you want?'

'I'm a brahmon,' Horihor supplied humbly. 'Trained in Sanskrit, capable of doing Chondipath and similar. Also the Bhagobot and Geeta, if you want . . .'

The man interrupted, waving his hand to indicate that his time was too valuable for this drivel. 'Nothing here, nothing here. See yourself out.'

But Horihor clung desperately on. 'I'm new in town,' he said. 'Absolutely nothing in hand. Please . . . I'm in a lot of hardship, nothing in the last few days has really . . .'

The man sat up and fished something out from behind the cushion he was resting on. In the manner of one getting rid of a pest with the bare minimum effort, he held it out to Horihor. 'Here, take this and leave . . . you'll get nothing else here. Take it.'

Had the money been offered in a different tone of voice, Horihor would have had no trouble accepting it. He'd accepted similar charity elsewhere. But despite his hardships, he couldn't bring himself to accept the disrespectful coin.

'You can keep that,' he informed the man politely. 'I don't accept charity. If I'd done a reading for you then maybe . . . but no, you can keep that.'

His luck finally changed after a few days. The owner of the timbre warehouse, Rokkhit Moshai, heard word that an acquaintance of his—a well-off moneylender in one of the rich villages outside Krishnonogor—was looking for a permanent priest to conduct the daily worship of his household deities. At Rokkhit Moshai's urging, Horihor went to meet the man. The moneylender liked him on sight. He was offered both the job and his own living quarters. There was no lack of reverence or care on the part of the man's family, either.

Durga Puja had been just around the corner when Horihor began his employment. When he sought leave from his employer to visit home, his employer gave him ten rupees as a mark of respect, in addition to a travel allowance for Contentment and back. When he went to Rokkhit Moshai's warehouse to say his goodbyes, he acquired another five rupees.

The sky above was a bright blue, glittering in the mellow autumn sun. The aroma of crisp sunshine rose from the land and air, filling his heart with unbound joy. The train sped through the fields, bending thickets of white kans flowers away from itself. Sitting on the train, all Horihor could think of was his family. A group of Shantipuri businessmen were on the same train, returning from Calcutta with their bundles of newly bought fabric. The wharf on the Churni river was bustling with life, people calling out to each other and loading things on boats. The joy of the season had spilled over everywhere.

Horihor went to the large marketplace at Ranaghat to buy new clothes for his wife and children. Durga loved saris with broad red borders; he sorted through piles to choose a good sari for her, then a few packets of good lacquer dye. Opu's *Poddopuran* couldn't be found anywhere, so he settled for buying him a copy of *The Illustrated Majesty of Goddess Chọndi, or the Story of Kalketu* for six annas. Shorbojoya had asked him to buy a few small things for the household, including a rolling board and pin. He bought those as well. Finally, loaded with presents, he took the train back to his homeland.

The walk from the station to the village took nearly all day—it was almost evening when he reached home. The roads had been fairly deserted, and even if there had been familiar faces, he had been walking far too fast to encourage conversation. He wanted to be home as quickly as he could.

Upon reaching his own courtyard, the first thing he noticed was the row of bamboo plants leaning unusually heavily on his boundary wall.

'Will you look at that!' he muttered to himself. 'Practically leaning over my wall, that one . . . no point telling Bhubon Uncle, he'd never bother trimming them. All the trouble's always on our plate . . .'

Then, as was his wont, he stepped on to the courtyard and raised his voice, happily calling for his children. 'Where are you, Ma Dugga? O Opu! Where are you two?'

No one answered his call. Only his wife came out of the house to meet him, but even she didn't say anything.

'Are you all right?' Horihor asked eagerly. 'Where are those two? Out as usual, I take it?'

Shorbojoya didn't answer. Instead, she relieved him of his bundle and quietly said, 'Come indoors.'

Horihor was too happy to notice his wife's unusual rectitude. His mind had already raced ahead to the moment of joyous reunion, when his children would rush into the room to greet their father. Durga, her face shining with anticipation and joy, would point to his bundles.

'What's in this, Baba?' she would ask, happiness bubbling in her voice.

That was when he would take out their new clothes, her packets of lacquer dye, Opu's illustrated book, and the toy railway carriage made of tin that was his special surprise. How his family would be amazed!

Following his wife indoors, he said, 'I got a good rolling pin and board for you . . . made of good strong jackfruit wood. You'll like it.' Then, still looking about the house in eager expectation, he said in tones of slight disappointment, 'So Opu and Dugga are really out, are they?'

Shorbojoya couldn't hold herself together any more. Letting all control dissolve in a loud sob, she exclaimed, 'My dear, she's no more, no more! Our ma has escaped us forever . . . oh, where *were* you all these days?'

~

The Ganguly household's puja was famous throughout the area. Even the poorest people of the village found respite from starvation these few days, for the Ganguly kitchen was open to all for every meal. The celebrations were steeped in aristocratic traditions. The household's potter would come several days ahead to start building the idol within the premises. The earthenware artists would arrive to begin the background decor. Florists and garland-makers would work on the daily supply of flowers for decor and worship. The lower-caste employees would go all the way to the bend in the river at Barashe-Modhukhali to bring back armfuls of lotuses. Deenu the flutist would arrive from Anshmali to play classical music throughout the day.

The festival began. The tune of the goddess's welcome song floated upwards from Deenu's flute into the clear blue sky. The mellow sunshine touched everything beneath with the affectionate touch of a tropical autumn: the ripening paddy in the fields, the first blossoms of the night jasmine, the flocks of brightly coloured shama birds flying south from the Himalayas, the dew-softened autumn evenings with their fresh-blossomed lotuses.

Horihor dressed his son in the new clothes that he'd bought, and took him along to fulfil their invitation at the Ganguly house meals. Along the way, he thought he could see a child's face peeking at him . . . her flyaway hair surrounding her thin little face, a bright-eyed request to be taken along written clearly on it. His attention slipped from the road and he faltered.

Then he collected himself and tried to make up for it by hurrying his son. 'Come along, Baba, don't dawdle . . . we're late as it is.'

The Ganguly house was a riot of sights and sounds. The courtyard was filled with beautifully dressed young people. Opu stared, looking for familiar faces. There was Shotu and his brother, dressed in the colour of ripe oranges. Ranudi over there . . . that green sari and new hairdo really suited her. Shunoyonee, one of the daughters of the household, had dressed up her bun in tuberoses. She was chatting and giggling with a group of girls in the veranda. Opu looked closely at the others, but couldn't identify any of them. Probably friends or family, visiting for the pujas. He had never seen such beauty, such wonderful clothes before. They were very likely from the city. Without quite realizing it, he stared at the laughing, beautifully dressed group, lost in thought.

In the background, the bustle of the pujas continued at full pace. Someone from the family was shouting at someone else.

'The large awning is still "on its way"? Excellent—just perfect! Now just wait and see what a mess this becomes . . . honestly, do you *want* the brahmon feast to begin at five?'

27

THE DAYS ROLLED by, one after another. Autumn passed, and now even winter was nearing its end.

Since Durga's death, Shorbojoya had been prodding her husband to leave this village for good. In fairness to her husband, Horihor had made several attempts to find a new place to settle in. But arranging a permanent livelihood was difficult business, and none of his efforts had borne fruit. Finally, after an autumn and winter of hoping and waiting, Shorbojoya had all but given up.

In the meantime, life in the village continued. The widowed wife of Neelmoni Roy—Horihor's former neighbour and late cousin—had arrived in Contentment at the beginning of winter. She had been staying at Bhubon Mukhujje's home, since her husband's family home had become derelict and overgrown in his years of absence. Horihor, of course, had offered his cousin's wife his own spare rooms, but she had declined.

Two of Neelmoni Roy's three children had accompanied their mother: Awtoshi, a girl of about fourteen, and Shuneel, a boy of eight. Her eldest, Shuresh, was enrolled in an English-medium school in Calcutta, and wouldn't be able to join the family till the beginning of his summer holidays. The general consensus about the two children was that neither was particularly attractive. Awtoshi was more pleasing to the eye than her brother, but even she wasn't exactly beautiful. However, they both had robust physiques. People attributed it to their childhood in Lahore, where—thanks to their father's job at the commissariat—they had lived till recently.

When the family first arrived at the village, Shorbojoya had attempted to establish a relationship with her rich sister-in-law. The information that Shuneel's mother was the outright owner of ten thousand rupees in cash and shares had commanded her immediate awe, and she made several determined attempts through the winter to get closer to the woman. Neelmoni Roy's widow, however, had absolutely no interest in her husband's poorer relations. She had made it clear, right from the beginning, that she considered herself and her children far above the rural branch of the family, and indeed above much of Contentment. Unlike these men who lived off inherited land, her husband had always held positions of influence within the government. The life of urban affluence she and her children were used to simply didn't compare with this dull village life. Even amongst the well-off families of the village, her children were set apart by their clothes, speech and manners. Neither of them left home at dawn for games or errands. They waited sedately till breakfast hour and their first cup of tea. Despite her youth, Awtoshi was never seen without a gold necklace, gold earrings and gold bangles. No matter what the hour, there was never a spot, stain or blemish on their faces or clothes, and their hair was always perfectly combed. Neelmoni Roy's widow had even brought along a servant from the west to do all her housework for her—such was the extent of their prosperity.

In short, the difference between the two branches of the Roy family was glaring. So when Shorbojoya began her overtures, her sister-in-law had no trouble implying, through both words and demeanour, that she didn't consider Shorbojoya in any way equal to her circle of acquaintances, even in this village. Shorbojoya was rather naive in these matters, so the first few rebuffs missed their mark, but eventually even she had to concede that she would never be considered fit company for her rich sister-in-law, familial ties or not.

In addition to curating her own social circle, Shuneel's mother had also explicitly forbidden her son from spending much time with the village boys, including Opu, for she feared their rural uncouthness rubbing off on him. If this made her unpopular in the village, she didn't particularly care. Contentment would never be her home, or even a place she planned to visit often. The only reason she had come this winter was to ensure that her property was protected during the survey. She was well aware that Bhubon Mukhujje hadn't offered her and her children a place in his house out of the goodness of his heart; he had plans to benefit from their local property. She had accepted his offer because it was convenient. Even then, to limit her degree of being beholden, she had ensured that her kitchen was separate from the family's. So though within the Mukhujje house, her two rooms, with her children and personal help, effectively functioned as a separate household.

Overall, though, she was prepared to treat Bhubon Mukhujje's family as her equals, for they, too, had money. Shorbojoya, on the other hand . . . well, she barely considered her a fellow human being.

Shuresh came to the village for ten days during his school break for Dol, the spring festival of colours. He was about

Opu's age, and currently enrolled in the fifth class at an English-medium school. Like his siblings (and unlike Opu), his skin was only medium-brown, but regular exercise had given him a strong, healthy physique. Although only a year older than Opu, his well-built frame made him look like a boy of fifteen or sixteen. One of the richer village boys—Ramnath Ganguly's son from the Ganguly household one neighbourhood over—was his classmate in Calcutta. The Ganguly household was famous for their elaborate celebration of Ramnobomi Dol, so Shuresh spent most of his time in that house. Like his mother, he made it clear that he didn't consider the other boys of the village to be fit company for himself.

Opu, on the other hand, felt an almost magnetic pull towards his new cousins. These were the people of that dilapidated old house and overgrown orchards—the places where he and his sister had had so many of their secret adventures! He felt an instant connection to all of them, but especially to Shuresh, for they were the same age. Ever since he'd come to know of Shuresh's existence, he had waited impatiently for summer so he could meet him. But now that Shuresh was here—unexpectedly early, at that—he realized that a friendship between them would be very unlikely. Shuresh's every word and action signalled that he thought the village boys beneath him. Opu had never seen such confidence and self-assurance. Despite being practically the same age, he was far too intimidated to approach Shuresh on his own.

On the day of Dol, when most of the local boys had gathered near the paved bathing steps at the Gangulys' garden, Shuresh had cornered and interrogated them about their academic prowess. His manner had been that of a victorious king lording over lesser vassals. Unlike Shuresh and his classmate, Opu had never been to a proper school after his stint at the village teacher's home. So when Shuresh had asked where he studied, he had simply said, 'My father teaches me at home.'

'Ah!' said Shuresh. 'Let's see, then . . . do you know where India's boundaries lie? Have you studied geography at all?'

Opu didn't even know the word 'geography', so he kept quiet.

'How far have you gone with algebra?' Shuresh asked again. 'Do you know your decimal fractions?'

Opu didn't. In fact, he hadn't known these words either. Despite the humiliation, though, a small part of him began to quietly rebel. All right, so he didn't know what 'geography' or a 'decimal fraction' was. But he *did* have several books in his old tin box! Just off the top of his head, he could name the *Instructions for Daily Rituals*, *Shubhonkori*, the book of counting and account-keeping, *The Ballad of Brave Women* (it had a few pages torn out, but still . . .), and his mother's copy of the Mahabharat. He had read *all* of those books. Several times! In fact, he still read them, for despite multiple rereadings, he never grew tired of the stories. On top of that, his father often brought him books that he had begged or borrowed from other people. It wasn't like he was completely ignorant!

Still, Shuresh's obvious academic superiority was a blow to his already weak confidence.

Horihor would have been upset to have heard of this encounter, for his one wish in life—a near-obsession, in fact—was to groom his son into an educated, learned young man. Unfortunately, his circumstances didn't allow him to send Opu to a good boarding school away from the village. And despite being better educated than most of his neighbours, he knew that he hadn't studied far enough himself to be his son's guide. In the brief periods when he was home, he would sit with his son and try to teach him this and that, and tell him stories. He had even procured a copy of *Shubhonkori* so he could refresh the lessons of his youth and introduce them to his son. If there was a piece of literature within his reach that he thought would enrich Opu, he gave it to Opu, or better yet, read it out to his son himself. He had also recently brought out his collection of old *Bongobashi* magazines. Back when Opu was still a child, Horihor had been able to subscribe to the famous weekly for a few years—a luxury he now sorely missed. Still, he had had the foresight to pack those old issues away, hopeful that his son would read them when he was old enough. This hope had been richly rewarded. Opu was obsessed with the yellowed issues. In fact, he adored *Bongobashi* so much that every Saturday morning he would abandon games and friends to go sit at the post box near Awnnoda Roy's temple courtyard, eagerly awaiting the delivery of that week's issue despite his family not being rich enough to be a subscriber.

It broke Horihor's heart that he couldn't even afford his son the simple pleasure of a magazine, but that was how things were.

Still, Opu had learnt a lot from the stories printed in the old issues of the magazine. He regularly narrated these to Potu, his new companion. The volcanic eruptions in St Lucia and the Raffaele Martinique islands, the fascinating story about magicians who could make gold out of other metals, and several others. But Shuresh was right: he had no school education. He could only do a few simple division sums, had no knowledge of history or grammar, hadn't even heard of geometry or trigonometry, and his knowledge of English only went as far as the first few pages of the *First Book*.

His mother had rather a different view of her son's future. Shorbojoya was a village girl through and through. She had no lofty expectations of scholarship. No one in her circle had ever seen the inside of a proper school, and they had been just fine. No, what she hoped for her son was a secure circle of rich disciples. When he was a little older, she wanted him to start making rounds of the homes of all her husband's scattered disciples—insert himself into inheriting them, and thus keep up the family tradition.

She did have another secret desire. The village priest, Dinu Bhotchaj, was getting on in years. His son Bhombol might have inherited his parish, but Bhombol was a known addict. In the absence of a clear successor, Shorbojoya thought Opu might be a good applicant for the post. Her boy was a simple-souled, beautiful child, loved by all the neighbours. They had told her so a hundred times! Indeed, Ranu's mother, Gokul's wife, and the eldest daughter-in-law of the Ganguly household had all informed her that they would like to have Opu officiating their domestic rituals as soon as possible. Quite apart from the honour of being wanted, it was a lucrative profession. The women's year was full of multiple deity venerations—from the worship of serpent goddess Mawnosha to the seasonal celebration of Lokkhi, the goddess of prosperity. If her son could secure the priestship of the local households in addition to inheriting his father's disciples, why, their lives would be perfect!

Shorbojoya's aspiration for her son might have been less exalted than her husband's, but as the daughter and wife of two impoverished families, she had never had the opportunity to develop an imagination that thought beyond the security of minimum daily comforts. Not having to worry about every meal and having a little respect in the village—these were the zenith of her ambitions.

The subject came up one day in Bhubon Mukhujje's house. Several of the brahmin women had gathered to play a hand of cards after the midday meal, as they often did. Shorbojoya decided to take the opportunity of having them together.

'All my elders and well-wishers are here,' she began in her best flattering tone. 'Our eldest aunt, grandmother, the second-eldest sister-in-law—everybody. If all of you take pity on my son, then we can have his thread ceremony in the month of Falgun and then let him start conducting the household rituals in this village. If that happens then I'll finally have no more worries left. We have eight to ten households of disciples, and if by the grace of Mother Shiddheshwori the Ganguly house pujo becomes a permanent job for him, then . . .'

Shuneel's mother was present in the women's circle of cards. She had smirked openly as Shorbojoya spoke. *Her* son was going to become a lawyer. Though he was only in the fifth class, plans were already in place to have him practise under her cousin, who was a lawyer in Patna. This cousin had often offered to take Shuresh into his family home and pay for his education, for he had no sons of his own to inherit his sprawling practice. But Shuneel's mother had always refused. Why should she surrender her son to another family? Even without her husband, she was more than capable of giving her children an excellent childhood and education. All of this information had been conveyed to the women of the village within a few weeks of her arrival, but not once did she have to descend to Shorbojoya's level of garrulous blabbering to do it.

Later, when they had left Bhubon Mukhujje's house that afternoon, Shorbojoya pulled her son aside.

'Listen. Why don't you go to your elder aunt and say, "Auntie, I don't have shoes. Will you buy me a pair?"'

'But why, Ma?'

'Arre, ask no! Your aunt is very rich. If you ask, she just might buy you a pair. Did you see the shoes that Shuresh wears? A red pair like that would look so good on you.'

'I can't ask, Ma. It'd be so embarrassing! They'd think I was a . . . no, Ma, I can't.'

Shorbojoya was surprised. 'Why would you be embarrassed? They are family, aren't they? Just ask . . . it'll be fine.'

'No-o-o-o . . . I can barely speak in front of elder aunt as it is . . .'

Shorbojoya's hopes turned to annoyance. 'Of course you can't! All your bravery is reserved for your mother, and within the four walls of the house! Roaming barefoot for two years now, but that's fine by you! Here we have some wealthy people close at hand, they're even family, you could get a nice pair of shoes out of them . . . but no. "I can't even speak in front of her!" Useless boy!'

On the next full moon, Opu went to Rani to bring offerings from their Shotyonarayon Puja. Rani smiled broadly when she saw him, but when she spoke to him, there was a note of complaint.

'You never come by any more, Opu. Why is that? You used to be over all the time!'

'Who said I don't? I come by all the time . . .'

'Kitchen ashes! As if I wouldn't know if you were in the house?' said Rani, clearly hurt. 'I worry about you so much . . . but do you even care about me? About us?'

'As if I wouldn't! What a question . . . ask Ma if you don't believe me!' Opu stuttered. Even to his own ears, this riposte sounded rather silly. But he couldn't think of a more satisfactory answer to Rani's accusations.

Rani went indoors to fetch him part of the offerings. When she came back, it was with a big plate of fruits, sweets and other food consecrated by the puja.

'Take it with the plate,' she said, smiling warmly at Opu. 'I'll come by tomorrow to take it back from Auntie.'

The smile warmed Opu's heart. Honestly, Ranudi had become positively beautiful with time. He had certainly never seen eyes as pretty as hers. Awtoshidi might be beautifully dressed and presentable at all times, but in terms of natural good looks, she couldn't hold a candle to Ranudi. But it wasn't just her beauty; Opu had known for a long time that Ranudi was, at heart, very different from the other girls in the village. If he'd ever loved any of his playmates apart from his sister, then it was Ranudi. And he knew Ranudi loved him back as well, as much as she loved her own brothers. Indeed, perhaps more than some of her own.

He was about to leave with the plate, but then he hesitated for a moment. This was the best chance he'd have to raise the matter.

'Ranudi . . . the books in the western room of your house? Shotuda never lets me read any of them. Could you get me one? I'll return it as soon as I'm done.'

Rani said, 'I don't know which book you mean . . . but wait, let me ask him and see.'

At first, Shotu absolutely refused. He wouldn't let Opu touch any of his family's books. Finally, however, he offered a deal.

'I'll let you read, but only if you do something. People have been stealing fish from our pond every day. Our eldest uncle has asked me to hide in the shrubbery and watch out for them. I don't like wasting my afternoons there alone. If you be the lookout in my place, I'll let you read the books.'

'That's not fair!' Rani protested immediately. 'He's only a child. An old lump like you can't go sit alone in those woods, but this child has to do it just to read books? You can keep your deal. I'll ask Baba for those books instead.'

Opu, however, agreed. Rani's father, Bhubon Mukhujje, lived abroad. That is to say, he lived outside Contentment. He visited only after long gaps, so who knew when he would come next? On the other hand, he really, really coveted those books. He had nervously made his way up to the western room a few times to stare longingly at the cupboards of books. Occasionally, he had managed to read a page or two too. But ever since Shotu found out, he had appointed himself guardian of the library. It wasn't that he wanted the books for himself; Shotu had no interest in reading. But he was determined not to let Opu read them. Just as the book Opu had sneaked out of a cupboard would reach its dramatic high point, Shotu would stomp into the room and snatch it away from him.

'That's my youngest uncle's books! Put it back, Opu—here, give it to me, you'll rip it.'

And now, in return for merely spending his afternoons in the woods, Opu was being offered unrestricted access to that treasure! It was like his fondest wish had come true.

From then on, he would choose a book from the cupboard every afternoon, and have Shotu hand it to him. Then he would head to the bamboo grove, make himself a mattress from young branches of the neighbouring sandpaper tree, and lie down to read the day's book. The cupboard had many, many books to choose from: *The Idol of Love*, *The Tale of Shawroj and Shawrojini*, *The Flower Girl*, *The Nun in Her Youth (Illustrated)*, *The Dacoit's Innocent Daughter*, *Consequences of Love (or, A Poisoned Ambrosia)*, *Gopeshwor's Secret* . . . he couldn't even finish listing the lot. And each as fascinating as the other! Once he started these books, he couldn't stop till he was done. As the shadows lengthened and merged with the mossy bank of the pond, his eyes would itch and redden, and his temple would throb with a long afternoon's reading. But he couldn't stop. These stories were magical, unputdownable. For instance . . .

Shawroj would be travelling with Shawrojini by boat to Murshidabad. But alas! The nawab's men would suddenly attack their boat, robbing them and taking them prisoner. On the nawab's orders, Shawroj would be killed and Shawrojini thrown into the dark dungeon. Then, in the dead of the night, the door of the dungeon would creak open and the inebriated nawab would enter.

'Beautiful Shawrojini!' he would proclaim. 'Your Shawroj has been put to death at my command. Then why keep denying me . . .?' and so on.

In response, Shawrojini would toss her head proudly. 'You fiend!' she would exclaim. 'You do not know the strength of a Rajput woman's virtue! As long as there is breath in this body . . .'

Suddenly, the dungeon window would be smashed open by a powerful foot! A bearded ascetic would leap inside, matted hair heaped on his head and power radiating from every pore of his magnificent body. Four or five men would jump in after him. To the nawab, they would look like the very guards of hell.

'Vile man!' the ascetic would roar. 'Preying on those you're bound to protect!'

Later, after the nawab had been subdued, he would turn to Shawrojini.

'Ma,' he would say gently. 'I am your husband's guru—Joganondo Swami. Your husband is not dead. The water from my prayer pot had restored his life! Come with me to my ashram. Your Shawroj awaits you there.'

Opu read these stories breathlessly till the end. He would finish a chapter in a rush, and find that there was a lump in his throat. Tears would threaten to spill out of his eyes at the travails of the characters. He would have to take a few deep breaths and look at the sky for a few minutes to process the richness of emotions, to really savour the buffet of feelings so enticingly laid out. Then he would plunge into the next chapter with bated breath. Never before had he read such magnificent prose. The way the author guided the reader's attention with every change of scene—for example, when he narrated the miracle of Shawroj's resurrection—held him absolutely captivated: 'Come now, dear reader. Let us peep behind the curtains of divine miracles to see how Shawroj was reawakened into life, after that most precious gift was snatched so cruelly from him.' His afternoons in the bamboo grove turned regularly into evenings. Above him, the birds of the grove would call out to each other as they sought shelter for the night. In this flurry of activity, Opu would think briefly about getting up, but his eyes stayed glued to the page. As the shadows lengthened, he would lean closer and closer to the page, till his nose was an inch away from the printed words.

Where had these books been all his life? Old favourites like *The Exile of Seeta* or *The Adventures of Duval* couldn't compare to the thrills of these books.

When he finally reached home in the evening, his mother would tell him off.

'Why are you such a stupid boy? Guarding other people's fish just so you can read a stupid book? A fine fool they've found in you!'

But then, his mother had no idea about the joys her foolish boy found in books. Right now, thanks to his lookout duty, he had been able to read two books at once: *Maharashtra: The Dawn of an Age,* and *The Dusk of the Rajputs.* In the backdrop of the termite mound and the circle of prickly-pear trees, scene after scene from the books play out in front of his eyes. Zulekha tending to the wounded Narendra in the shallows of a gurgling stream; the wrath of Shivaji, when in Aurangzeb's court he was labelled the leader of merely a five-thousand-strong army; his furious internal monologue, 'Shibaji a five-thousand's officer! Why doesn't the court come to Poona? I'll make them count how many officers in Shibaji's army *themselves* command five thousand people! Each!'

His mother might think he was spending his days in the woods, but really he spent them in the desert and hills of Rajabara, inside the theatres of Delhi and Agra, in mirror-panelled rooms in the company of gorgeous women dressed in full skirts and colourful dupattas. What a wonderful world, this! The golden light of the full moon shone upon every chapter, the friendship of beautiful faces and sword games was the norm, and on the occasion of the Aaheria hunt in spring, people went on long horse rides with their spears, racing through barren valleys and fields of golden maize.

A braveheart's duty, a Rajput's duty, the duty of a human being—Pratapsingh had fulfilled all of those to the best of his abilities! His story was etched into every stone on the mountainous roads of Haldighat. Ballads to his bravery were written upon the Deoar battlefield, in the life blood of twelve thousand brave Rajput soldiers. Decades after his own time, ancient soldiers would still gather their grandchildren around the fire on winter nights, and tell them about the unmatched bravery of Pratapsingh at Haldighat.

Though raised in the soothing shade of the woods of this fertile delta, in the embrace of plants and with the aroma of monsoon-dampened soil, Opu felt he knew every bit of the Bhil provinces of the Rajputana, the Mewar-Aravalli area, or the stunning beauty of the Nahara-Mogro forests. He could clearly see the majestic figure of Tejsingh descending the mountains, flashing weapons in his arms. What a magnificent view it was!

> In a Bhil village in the Chappan province, a woman's song could be heard in the second hour of the night, echoing in the solitary valleys and off mountain tops. Some travellers said that they had caught fleeting glimpses of a pale-faced woman in the solitary fields very early in the morning. Local folks said it was probably a perturbed woodland goddess, roaming over her domain.

While reading this, Opu was sure he could hear faint echoes of the song wafting out of the bamboo groves behind him.

Kamalmeer, the battle of Surajgarh, the battle commander Shahbaaz Khan, the beautiful Noorjahan, the singing lady of the forest, the forested Bhil province, the brave boy warrior Chandansingh—so far away, in time and place, and yet they felt so close to him, so real. He could clearly see the deserts of the Rajawada, the sycamores in full blossom on the blue-tinged peaks of the Aravalli, and the lacquer-red footsteps of the goddess Mewar-Lokkhi on the boulders by the banks of the Boonas and the Boree, on the pebbles by the springs, along the fields of millet and sorghum, and in the aromatic forests of mohua.

The chapters progressed to Chitor's final fall. Rana Amarsingh bent his knee to the emperor. How had his father Pratapsingh taken the news? He had spent twenty-five hard years fighting the emperor's forces with his army of Bhils. How did his ageing, broken heart contain this humiliation, this fury?

Warm tears blurred Opu's view of the forest. The termite mound, the plum bushes, the bamboo grove blurred into each other, as the pain of a dead hero suffused his heart.

One afternoon, his father came home with a packet for him. Handing it over with a big smile, he said, 'Something for you, Khoka. Can you guess what it is?'

Opu was lying down, but he shot up in excitement. 'It's the newspaper! Isn't it, Baba? Am I right?'

He was. Horihor had earned three rupees the other day by making an amulet for Behari Ghosh's mother-in-law. If his wife ever heard of the money, every bit of it would have disappeared down the hole of their never-ending needs. So he kept the three rupees a secret, and sent away two of them to the newspaper offices as soon as he could.

In the meantime, Opu had ripped open the package in excitement. Yes! There it was, in large familiar fonts: *Bongobashi*. That wonderful smell of fresh newsprint, the array of printed words containing many unread stories . . . finally, the thing that he waited for with such eagerness every Saturday at Bhubon Mukhujje's temple courtyard was his! He couldn't wait to start diving into the new stories within its pages. Who knew what new adventure was in store for him!

The look of unalloyed joy on his son's face made the rash expenditure of those two precious rupees worth it to Horihor. True, the last of Shorbojoya's valuables—a pair of earrings—was still at the pawnbrokers, and this money could have retrieved them. But no earring in the world could ever come close to the satisfaction he felt at his son's obvious happiness.

'Look, Baba!' Opu exclaimed, unaware of his father's thoughts. 'They've just started publishing "Letters from a Foreign Land". This has the first instalment! We got the newspaper at a great time, didn't we, Baba?'

Yet, beneath the joy, there was a bit of lingering regret in Opu. Back when they'd stopped taking the newspaper—a year back, now—he was in the middle of the story about the Japanese spider-demon. Now he would never get to know what happened to Raiko after she finally reached the king's court . . .

A few days later, Rani suddenly asked him, 'What's it that you write in your notebook?'

Opu was startled, 'What notebook? How did you . . .?'

Rani grinned. 'I went to your house the other afternoon, didn't I? You were out, so I chatted with Auntie for a long time. Didn't she mention it? Anyway, I saw you'd written a lot in that red notebook in your tin box—there was my name, then some man called Debi Shingho . . .'

Opu's fair skin had been turning progressively redder during Rani's speech. Hurriedly, he said, 'That was just some old story.'

'What was the story? Read it out to me sometime.'

The next day, Rani gave Opu a small bound notebook.

'Here, write a story for me in this notebook . . . a good story, mind! Awtoshi was saying the other day that she had heard you write well . . . write this for me and I'll show it to Awtoshi, too.'

Opu wrote the story in bits every night.

'Give me a small spoonful of oil no, Ma? I want to finish this part today,' he would say to his mother.

His mother would say, 'Don't do your studies at night. I only have two spoons worth of oil left . . . if I give it to you, there'll be no cooking tomorrow. Sit next to the fire when I'm making dinner—there'll be enough light for your writing then.'

Opu would protest strongly. How could he write in the light of the cooking fire? That wasn't enough!

'Then you should know better than to write only late in the night!' his mother would snap. 'No hide nor hair all day, and as soon as it's dark, "Ma, give me oil, give me oil!" There's no oil here, go! Shoo!'

Finally, Opu would give in and write by the kitchen fire. Shorbojoya would glance at her son as she cooked.

'Let him grow up a little more, then I'll arrange a good match for him,' she would think. 'We'll build a proper house, then once he gets his sacred thread this coming year and the pujo at the Ganguly household becomes permanent . . .'

Four or five days later, Opu gave the notebook back to Rani.

'Did you really write it?' Rani asked, taking it eagerly.

'Open it and see for yourself,' Opu said, smiling contentedly.

Rani saw the pages of writing. 'This is such a lot!' she said happily. 'Wait, let me call Awtoshi and show her.'

Awtoshi glanced at the pages and waved them away dismissively. 'As if that's his writing,' she said. 'He's copied it from somewhere.'

'As if!' Opu exclaimed, hurt. 'Why would I copy anything from a book? I make up all my stories myself—ask Potu if you don't believe me! Don't I tell him stories all afternoon when we sit on the banks of the river?'

'I'm sure this is Opu's own story, my sister,' said Rani. 'He does write lots and lots of stuff on his own. He had written such a wonderful play once in his red notebook—he read the whole thing out to me.'

Later, she told Opu, 'Oi, why didn't you sign your name, eh? Here, write your name at the end.'

Opu explained, with some embarrassment, that though he'd returned the notebook, the story wasn't finished yet. He would sign his name as soon as he finished the story. The truth was that he had begun his wholly original story in the fashion of *The Nun in Her Youth (Illustrated)*, but hadn't quite worked out how to bring all the dramatic threads together to a satisfactory end. But if he kept the notebook with himself for longer than four days, Ranudi—and especially Awtoshidi—might suspect that he was using something besides his native talent to write the story. That was why he had rushed to return the notebook to Ranudi, unfinished story and all.

A few mornings after this, Opu's father took him along to attend an end-of-mourning feast in a neighbouring village. The two of them walked the way with other men and boys from Contentment, including Shuneel. The crowd at the bereaved family's home was enormous. Brahmin men from every neighbouring village were in attendance, some having walked fifteen to twenty kilometres to attend the feast. Seating their guests became a nightmare for the bereaved hosts. Each adult had brought along five or six young boys, and the shoving for seating space almost devolved into a riot. The serving staff had been instructed to give everyone four luchis to begin with. But when the servers returned to serve the fried eggplants to go with the luchi, they saw that everyone's plate was empty—the guests had piled all their luchis on to their shawls or thin towels. Only one small boy, perhaps still unfamiliar with the ways of communal feasts, had been about to eat. But his father, Bishsheshwor Bhotchaj, had snatched his luchi away and stashed them into the child's towel.

'What's your hurry?' he had snapped at his son. 'They'll give you more right now, you can eat those. These are for taking home.'

The feast steadily progressed into a confusion of demands and outrage.

'Where's the basket of luchi? That was only the first serving!'

'The pumpkin seems to have skipped my plate entirely . . .'

'Watch it! That's hot!'

'Call this a luchi? It's a lump of raw flour!'

And so on. Some of the men began arguing with the bereaved family about how much food each brahmin was entitled to take away in his chhNada—a temporary sack made from his shawl or towel.

'Then you shouldn't have invited proper gentlemen like us, if you weren't prepared to shell out for the chhNada!' an enraged brahmin was screaming. 'At least twenty luchis per person—that's been the fixed rate for chhNada in these parts from the time of King Bollal Sen! Here . . . keep your measly parcel. Kondoppo Mojumdar doesn't accept charity in place of his just deserts!'

The men in charge of the brahmin feast had to beg and plead to placate Kondoppo Mojumdar, and to keep him from storming out. Along with the other men and boys, Opu too had managed to pack a large amount of food in his towel. Shorbojoya came bustling out at the sound of her son's return, and grinned enormously at the size of his takeaway bundle.

'Goodness, look at how much you've brought back! Open it, open it—let me see what they served. Oooh, luchi, pantua, goja—Opu, this is a lot! Keep it covered for the night, you can have it tomorrow for breakfast.'

'You must also have some, Ma,' Opu said. 'I especially asked for the pantua twice so I'd have enough for you.'

Shorbojoya was delighted by her son's consideration. 'Did you say, "Give me more, my mother will eat this"?' she asked, giggling. 'I wouldn't be surprised, given how silly you are . . .'

Opu shook his head vigorously. 'As if! I was very crafty! The way I said it, they thought it was all for me!'

Shorbojoya carried the bundle inside with a happy grin.

After a bit, Opu wandered over to Shuneel's place. He was about to step into their courtyard, when he heard Shuneel's mother shouting at him.

'Why would you bring this home? Who asked you to carry back food from a sit-down meal?'

Shuneel hadn't realized that not taking food home was an option. He had simply followed the lead of the other men and boys, and every one of them had made themselves large takeaway bundles. He tried to use that as a defence.

'It's what everyone else did! Even Opu brought back a big sack of food!'

His mother was livid. 'Of course he did! Why wouldn't he? Son of a worthless village brahmon! That's going to be his profession soon—going from house to house, performing pujos and bundling up food. That's all that family is good for. The mother's no better—a real greedy piece of work! These people are exactly why I didn't want to bring you to the village . . . already falling into bad company and picking up these disgusting habits! You were invited; you went, you ate, you came back. That's where the matter should have ended. Why wrap up a mound of food like a lowly beggar? Go give this sack to your Opu. Or throw it away—I don't care. But get rid of it!'

Opu decided he didn't have the courage to enter Shuneel's house. Instead, he quickly made his way back to the lane that would take him back home. As he walked down that familiar path, he couldn't work out why his elder aunt was so furious about something that made his own mother so happy. Was feast food like fistfuls of clay that Shuneel should just throw his bundle away? Calling his mother greedy and him the son of a bundle-making brahmin . . . like pantuas and gojas could be refused as easily as everyday food? Maybe his aunt had tasted things like that many times in her life, but his mother had seldom had the chance to even see them. In fact, how many times had *he* tasted them, despite being invited to brahmin feasts? Almost never. Perhaps packing food away from a feast was wrong for someone like Shuneel. But there was no way it could be wrong for someone like him.

It was true, however, that he didn't have much in the way of an education. Eating at ceremonies he had been invited to, bringing back bundles of food, going with his father to the houses of their various disciples, catching fish—these were the high points of his life. That once-small boy, Potu, who had been beaten up one afternoon in the fishermen's neighbourhood over cowries, was now his constant companion. He had grown quite a bit in the intervening year, and loyally followed his Opuda around all day. He came all the way from his own neighbourhood just to play with Opu; he didn't bother making other friends. He hadn't forgotten that it was Opuda who had tried to intervene to save him on that fateful afternoon, and had received a thrashing himself as a result.

Opu was a bit too fond of fishing. There was some excellent fishing to be had in the Kachikata canal, beneath the Shonadanga moors and along the banks of the Ichamoti. Opu would sit beneath the milkwood pine at the mouth of the canal and cast his line for fish. He cherished the seclusion of the place. The trees on either bank bent towards the water. There was a dense wood of breadfruit trees on the other bank, interspersed with burflower and silk-cotton. The shrubs were full of white morning-glory blossoms. In the distance, he could see the bamboo groves that marked the border of the neighbouring village, Madhobpur. It was the perfect hidden paradise. During late morning and afternoon, silence reigned in this part of the woods, broken only by stray notes of bird call. The sweet aroma of dates hung thickly in the air, and the gentle breeze from the river carried over the sudden calls of pied cuckoos and orioles. The cool green shade of the nook, the view of the forest, the sound of the river, and the musical warbling of the birds came together to weave him a place of near-enchanted bliss. In the evenings, when the sun god began to finally slip behind the big banyan tree on the Shonadanga moors, the glittering water of the river turned dark, and the air came alive with flocks of bank mynahs . . . an inexpressible joy would fill his heart. Looking around in wonder, he would tell himself that even if he never caught a single fish in these waters, he would still want to return here every day, just to sit under the shade of that milkwood pine tree.

Often, in fact, there was no fish. The bait sat still in the water, like the unwavering flame of a candle in the shade. Much as he loved fishing, Opu did not actually have the patience to sit in one place for long. So he left his fishing rod in place and explored the woods, looking for birds' nests in the undergrowth. Then he would catch a slight movement around his bait and run back, reeling in his rod eagerly. Almost always, it would be to sigh in disappointment: there would be nothing on the rod.

'Too many tiny shoals here,' he would tell himself. 'No point wasting my time here any longer.'

He would go a little further down the bank instead, and cast his line once more through the moss and water weeds. The deep, dark water promised large carps, glistening silver and fattened with age. But the fantasy dissolved when the bait steadfastly refused to twitch.

He brought a new book with him every day. There was plenty of time to read once the line was cast. He had managed to borrow one of Shuresh's old English readers from a previous year, and its companion guidebook in Bangla. The book had a lot of pictures. Though he couldn't really read English, he followed the stories by using the guidebook as his translator. They were exactly the sort of stories he loved best: tales of adventure, of bravery and valour, set in far-off lands. He read with relish about Christopher Columbus's discovery of America, about travails of people lost in the African wilderness, about the slow death of a traveller in a fierce snowstorm. There was a chapter about the English boy and girl who stumbled upon danger and intrigue while out picking eggs from seagull nests. There was the story of

Praskovia Lopulof, a girl who set out all alone across the trackless frozen waste of Siberia to find and bring back her banished father. These strange people, with strange foreign names, became so familiar to him in that wood by the canal that he felt he would be able to pick them out in a crowd.

The excerpt about Sir Philip Sidney filled his eyes with tears. He went back to Shuresh that evening with the reader opened to that page.

'Do you know what this is about, Shureshda? Can you tell me the whole story?'

'Oh, that,' said Shuresh dismissively. 'That's about the Battle of Zutphen.'

Opu was amazed, 'Zut . . . what? Zut-phen? Where's that, Shureshda?'

But Shuresh didn't know anything about Zutphen beyond the name.

Then, about a month later, Opu suddenly caught a big olive-barb fish. That was it; his love for the place now validated by this catch, he refused to move to any other fishing area. Instead, he piled soft broken branches to make a bed for himself so that he could almost start living under those familiar trees.

The beautiful spring days passed in lazy glory. Opu luxuriated in the silence of the river and woodlands, bathing in the dappled sunshine of the day, watching the white reed-flowers blossom along the banks, listening to the bird call as he read. Finally, when his old friend the red-gold dusk arrived, tinging the tops of trees with its last bright light, he wrapped up for the day and went home.

While borrowing a book from Shuresh, he had spotted the Mediterranean Sea on his large map of the world. He hadn't had time to locate France, but knew from that *Bongobashi* column, 'Letters from Foreign Shores', that it was close by. He had read about France in today's story. The story was set a long time ago, when France was struggling to survive under weak leadership, civil mayhem and the chokehold of foreign armies. So the heavens had called upon an unusual hero to deliver the land from its evils.

In a tiny village in Lorraine, a poor farmer's daughter used to take her father's sheep out to pasture every day. While they grazed, she lay back on the green grass, cast her blue eyes on the open sky, and thought about terror and humiliation plaguing her land. One day, she heard a voice whisper from deep within her pure, virgin soul: 'You are the guardian of France. You must take up weapons, assemble a national army, and protect the people. This country's fate depends on you.'

With the blessings of the goddess Mary lighting her way, and the heavens sending her message upon message to guide her, that simple village girl led a rejuvenated French army to battle, dispelled her nation's enemies, and personally crowned the rightful heir the king of the land. But alas, the blind people of France labelled her a witch and burnt her alive!

His afternoon had been coloured by the wide range of emotions he had felt while reading about the peasant-girl hero of France. Her final tragedy had filled his heart with sorrow, and he had shed copious tears at her fate. But when he lay back to think about this wonderful girl, he realized that he was not really thinking about battles and victories. He was thinking about a worried girl lying in the middle of an empty green field, surrounded by unconcerned cattle.

On the one hand: clashing swords, fierce foreign invaders, cruelty, rapaciousness, victory bathed in rivers of blood.

On the other: an innocent, blue-eyed country girl lost deep in thought; the earth beneath her, the sky above her.

It was the latter image that found permanent place in his heart.

The idea that staring into the vast blue sky would reveal secret routes to far-off lands was a favourite fantasy of his since his childhood. Thinking about the sky in Lorraine made him wonder if it looked the same over the other places he'd been reading about. What did it look like above the island of Martinique, surrounded by the deep blue sea? What sort of a place was the island? Fields of sugarcane all around, blue sky above the head as far as the eye could see, and an endless blueness of the sea all around, yet none of those blues were uniform. What would that feel like? He tried to imagine the scene, but it was indescribably alien. Instead, he rolled up his fishing rod and prepared to go home. The blood-red sun was just setting behind the big banyan tree on the Shonadanga moors . . . there was still some light left in the sky. He could clearly make out the bent-over gum trees up ahead, pouring their flowers into the dark water with every shake of the breeze.

Suddenly, someone pressed palms over his eyes from behind. As soon as he had forced the hands away, Potu came around to stand in front of him, laughing.

'I knew you'd be here, Opuda! Been looking for you all day. Let's see what you caught—nothing? Not even a single one? Aww, never mind. I'm going to untie one of the boats and go for a ride. You want to come?'

The Sahib's Wharf by the Burflowers received several boats throughout the year. Some of these were boats that had travelled from far-off shores, loaded with palm leaves, sacks of grain, heaps of seashells and other goods. The shell-picking boats were always here at this time of year—they began coming up from the south the moment the weather turned warm. Local fishermen used these boats to hang their larger nets across the breadth of the river. They would take several boats out to the middle of the black waters, then drop anchor and line them next to each other. While the nets were lined up and cast, the shell-pickers dove for their prize. Opu often spent his days watching them—a dark man bobbing up and down in the water as he sorted shells from the clumps of river-bed mud and sand, then throwing them on to the boat and diving again to the bottom for the next clump.

'Do you see how long he's holding his breath?' he would marvel to Potu. 'Can you hold your breath that long?'

The boats and boatmen fascinated him. He looked at the line of boats gently bobbing at the bottom of the grassy slope of the riverbank, and wondered how long they had travelled to reach his village. What were those lands like—the ones these boats must have crossed? Had they only rowed along big rivers, or gone through the smaller canals and tributaries through villages? Did they have to brave rapids and shallows? He wished he could just go up to the boatmen as they sat around in circles, and soak up all their stories. Ever since reading about famous sailors and their adventures in Shuresh's book, going sailing had become his fondest wish.

Potu, meanwhile, had gone up to the palm-leaf boat and struck up a conversation with the person inside.

'O boatman, how much for a bundle of your leaves? Where's your boat from? Jhalkathi? Where's that? How far is it from here?'

After a while, he returned to Opu and said, 'Opuda, let's go to the bathing steps by the tamarind tree. The dinghy boats will be tied there now—we'll untie one and go for a quick ride.'

So the two of them went to the tamarind tree, untied a dinghy, gave it a push to launch it into the water, then climbed aboard. The moist, cool smell of the rippling waters rose up to envelop them. Bronze-winged jacanas flitted between colonies of water-spinach as they went by. They could see farmers on either bank, weeding their fields of pointed gourd. Some were cutting the long grass into stacks. Flocks of bank-mynahs chirped in the dense bushes by the bend in the river. Multicoloured clouds decorated the sky against the light of the fading day.

'Sing a song, Opuda,' Poltu suddenly said. 'That one . . . the one that you sang the other day.'

'No, not that one. I learnt a new one from Baba—a very nice tune. Let's go a bit further out first. There are way too many people here. Just look at the banks.'

'Opuda! Why're you so shy? As if they can hear us! Look, they're too far inland. You're always embarrassed without reason. Come on, start!'

Opu waited till they'd moved a little further ahead. Then he began the song he had just learned. Once he began, Potu hauled the oars out of the water and sat quietly at his end of the boat, listening. Unguided, the boat began to drift gently with the current towards the big bend at La-Bhanga. When Opu finished singing, Potu picked up a song. Opu rowed slowly as he listened. The dinghy had come quite far from the tamarind tree steps already. The bend at La-Bhanga was now very close.

Suddenly, Potu stopped singing and pointed at the north-eastern sky. 'Opuda, look! The clouds! A storm's coming—you mark my words. Want to turn the dinghy around?'

'Nah. Let there be a storm. It's much more fun to row and sing in a storm. Let's go further.'

Even before they finished speaking, the black clouds that had been rising in a corner raced over the Madhobpur fields, and began to spread across the rest of the sky. The river darkened with their shadows. The birds in the riverside bushes broke into an alarmed twitter. Potu looked up at the sky in happy anticipation. From the middle of the river, they could hear the distant approach of the stormy winds. A cool breeze broke over the river, carrying with it the smell of freshly drenched earth. Dozens of winged seeds of the swallow-wort blew on to the water and into their boat from both banks.

And then the summer storm was upon them.

The milkwood pine and gum trees along the banks swayed and groaned, their branches breaking as the wind tore through them. A phalanx of white storks rose against the dark grey sky, braving the wind in perfect synchrony. Opu let go of the oars and raised his face to the storm, soaking in all its glorious majesty. At the other end of the boat, Potu had untucked the pleats of his dhuti and thrown it into the wind. Much to his delight, it had immediately arched like a mini-sail in high wind.

'Opuda . . . it's a big storm though,' he warned. 'The dinghy can't push forward any more, but what if it overturns?'

Opu wasn't listening. He sat at the prow of the boat, mesmerized by the wild wind. Everything around him—the dancing black water, the clouds above, the boatmen of the south with their shell heaps, the water hyacinths floating with the current—began to fade away as he imagined himself in the stories he'd recently been reading. He was the traveller who wrote about foreign lands in *Bongobashi*. His ship had just set sail from Calcutta. Now they were leaving Shagordweep behind . . . now they were at the mouth of the Bay of Bengal. Oh, so many tiny green islands left behind as the ship sailed past the coast and into the open sea. There! That was the Sinhala coast, dotted with the green of coconut trees. And now he was sailing past a land with blue mountains in the distance, basking in the red glow of the setting sun. New countries, new landscapes were beckoning him, but tonight was for sailing! Away, further away!

'Would the unseen sea be as dark as the waters of the Ichamoti?' he wondered. Would there be dots of green islands on the Arabian Sea, as there apparently were on the Bay of Bengal? He imagined being afloat on the Arabian Sea on a stormy evening. Or perhaps watching the sea from the safety of the Eden harbour, just like that writer of 'Letters from a Foreign Land'. He would ask a pretty Arab maiden for water, just as the writer had. If only he could take this dinghy further, just enough so he could look around the Elephant-apple's Bend, he was sure he would be able to see the flocks of seagulls that the writer had so vividly described in the paper.

One day. One day he would actually go to all of these places, see all these sights. He would go to England and Japan. He would first set sail on a commercial vessel, then eventually become a rich merchant himself. After that there would be no end to his adventures. He would travel across as many countries as he could, and sail across all the seas. He would face terrible dangers. His ship would almost sink in a sea storm in the middle of the Chinese sea, just like the sailors in 'My Fantastic Travels'. Just like them, he would scramble on to a jolly boat and survive by eating roasted snails scoured from the sides of underwater hills. Everything that was familiar and known ended right past that horizon—just beyond the cluster of blue clouds now rising above the bamboo groves of Madhobpur. If only he could find the way, he would be on an unknown sandy shore right now, lined with coconut groves. Or perhaps at the foot of a volcano, or walking across snow-covered fields. He would be meeting Zulekha, Shawroj, Grace Darling, Zutphen, that English boy and girl who went looking for seagull eggs, the scientist-magician Böttger, the blue-eyed girl Joan, lost in her own thoughts on the fields of Lorraine . . . and so many others. Everything he had ever read—from the old books in his tin box, his father's old *Bongobashi*, to the books in Ranudi's house and the reader he had borrowed from Shureshda—had convinced him that a group of people were waiting for him in those strange, far-off lands. They were just biding their time before they sent out a call for him. Once that call came, he would be off!

He didn't once stop to think how he would get to these places: Who would take him? How would he afford the journey? He was, after all, the barely educated son of a village brahmin. The pinnacle of his success was going to be making rounds of the village on puja days, conducting rituals for food and a pittance. He was still a boy who begged his mother for reading oil at night and got told off. He had no idea what decent clothes—or any of the finer things in life, really—even looked like. Why would anyone want to invite such an uneducated, unconnected, resourceless village boy to the great celebrations of life in the wonderful worlds beyond this village?

On the one hand, these questions had the power to bring his rich world of fantasies to a crashing halt. On the other, they could have spurred on the chariot of his youthful determination to overcome these very real barriers. But the truth is, these thoughts never even occurred to him. His fantasies functioned on the principle that everything would automatically start happening once he was 'older'. Opportunities for getting ahead would be strewn all around him; it was just a matter of time till he found them. Once he became a grown-up, invitations from all over would issue forth for him. And he would finally be able to set out on his quest—to know all of the world, and the people that lived in it.

The way back to the village passed in these vivid, delightful dreams. The rains had stopped after a brief spell, and left behind a pristine sky in their wake. The wind was no more than a cool river breeze. Opu finally relinquished his fantasies once the dinghy hit the shallows at the steps by the tamarind tree. The two boys tied up the boat, and for the rest of the way he walked jauntily ahead of Potu, whistling cheerfully.

Like his mother and sister, Opu too had learnt to weave happy, improbable dreams.

28

THE DAY HIS parents had The Conversation, Opu had not been asleep. He had been lying down with his eyes closed, listening to his parents talk. They would leave this land and go to Kashi—that was the plan. His father had been explaining the many advantages of Kashi to his mother. Horihor knew the land well, for he had spent a long time in Kashi as a young man. Everyone there either knew or respected him. Besides, things were cheap and plenty in Kashi, unlike in this village, and there were friends there who would be willing to help them.

His mother was so keen to leave that she would have packed up that very night if she could—she had no desire to spend a single day more in the village. From his father's words, Kashi seemed like a golden land of plenty . . . unlike this village of theirs, where sorrow was a constant companion from season to season. All they needed to do was muster enough courage to leave this place. And then the happiness of the golden land would be theirs! Finally, after much discussion, his parents decided that they would leave Contentment at the beginning of summer, in Boishakh, the first month of the local calendar.

This plan, however, presented a crucial problem. Sometime back, Shorbojoya had vowed an offering at the temple of Goddess Shiddheshwori in Gonganondopur. But the temple was almost ten kilometres away from their village, and this fact had kept her from fulfilling her promise. But now that they were leaving this land, she could no longer afford to put it off. Unfortunately, neither could she find a single volunteer to accompany her to the temple. In the end, Opu offered to go. He could travel alone, perform the puja on his mother's behalf, and finally visit the aunt on his father's side that he'd heard about but never met, given that she lived in faraway Gonganondopur.

At first, Shorbojoya dismissed him outright. 'Yes yes, *of course* you'll go alone . . . do you even know how far it is, you silly boy? Go alone indeed! It's almost thirteen kilometres one way . . . as if!'

But Opu was insistent. 'Why can't I go? Don't I have eyes and ears and legs? Or am I supposed to stay indoors for the rest of my life?'

'Oh yes, you have everything! Our big-man hero, you'll go alone to Gonganondopur! Go on, run along now. Don't bother me with this nonsense.'

In the end, however, she had to give in to his unrelenting pleading. And thus Opu set out alone, for the first time in his life.

The raised dirt road cut straight through the middle of the Shonadanga moors. The fields on either side were filled with crown-flower plants, their long white stems curved with the weight of the blossoms till they were almost one with the grass. Not a single other person was on the road. The morning was almost spent, and the shadows of trees were shortening rapidly as he travelled from the east to overhead. Opu's bare feet had become caked with a thin layer of warm, sandy soil. It made his feet toasty and comfortable. Bushes and woodlands bordered the road on both sides, and he lost count of the number of shrubs and plants that were in blossom. The fields were dotted with acacia trees, heavy with bright yellow blossoms. Certain bushes and plants had already begun to bear fruit. He passed one with clusters of small, bright, berry-like fruits, much like the inedible wild fig. An aroma of the sun-toasted, slightly wet earth permeated the entire stretch. From time to time, he bent down to rummage in the bushes for fallen ramontchi fruits, and stowed them in the two pockets of his home-sewn red satin shirt.

The journey filled his heart with joy. He could never find the words to make people understand how much he loved this fresh, sun-baked smell of the soil, these shadow-darkened clusters of scutch-grass, these sunlit fields, this never-ending road, the chirping birds, those flower-dotted bushes, the dangling clusters of fruit and berries on familiar plants: the velvet bean, the white morning glory, the bluebell vine. What was home, compared to this? If only his father would say to him, 'Son! You're free to roam all the roads and fields you like!' How marvellous would that be? He would walk through fields just like these, pass through the hanging flowers and shadowy bushes, going further and further . . . his eyes fixed on those far woodlands. Only the occasional cry of doves would keep him company, and the susurration of leaves in the bamboo grove. When the setting sun coloured the sky with its golden glow, he would watch as the brightly coloured birds sang on their way home.

Opu had been reared in the lap of rural nature. Here, the change of seasons always sent word ahead of itself—through trees, the winds, the sky and birdsong. The magnificent canvas of this riverine land had taught him to know instinctively what the first subtle changes in the surrounding trees, air and flowing water meant. This harmony was something he loved and cherished, and he couldn't imagine a life bereft of it. The shimmering heat of summer, the gradual gathering of deep blue, solemn, serious clouds across the horizon at the end of the hot months, the magical sunset colours above the Shonadanga moors, the uninterrupted stretch of white kans-grass flowers from here to Madhobpur as the month of Bhadro came to an end, the webs of moonlight that filtered through leaves on the golden full-moon nights, and wove patterns on the village roads . . . all of these had found an eternal home in Opu's young mind. From birth to boyhood, they had trained his senses in the grace and splendour of everyday life, had whispered chants of the infinite into his eager ears. Without him realizing it, freedom—in its aspect as untrammelled nature—had instilled in him an adoration of the pure and the beautiful. It was a devotion that would blossom within him for the rest of his life.

On his way past the blocked canal at Notidanga, he saw some people casting for fish. Unhurried by the demands of a companion, Opu stood and watched them for a while. Inside the village, a blind beggar was strumming his single-stringed instrument, singing for alms. Opu knew the song he was singing—he had sung it himself many times:

> If the moon rises in the afternoon,
> How then shall I spend my nights?

His grandfatherly friend, the Vaishnav Norottowm Daash, sang the song beautifully.

Once he entered the village of Horishpur, he saw a school in a small, tiled-roof house by the road. The boys were reciting their tables in a sing-song voice. He stood and listened to them for a while. The teacher was not very old; in fact, he was much younger than Proshonno Gurumoshai, the teacher in his village.

All through the journey, a thought kept pushing itself to the top of his mind: he must really have grown up. Why else would his mother have let him come on this journey alone? No one would let a child do that! So, since he was on the journey, it followed that he was indeed a grown-up. Which meant that he was already on his way to fulfilling his adventures! Today, Gonganondopur. Then, by this time next month, Kashi. It seemed like such a distant dream, the idea of Kashi, but in no time at all, he would actually be there. And from then on, the road only went further, beyond what he could see. All he knew was that he had to keep going forward.

He reached Gonganondopur towards the end of the afternoon. Once he reached his aunt's neighbourhood, however, a world of shyness suddenly overcame him. He managed to keep walking, eyes fixed on the road, but he was convinced that every single person he passed was scrutinizing and making assumptions about him. He felt certain that they all knew he was coming, and were now saying to each other, 'Ooh, take a good look! That's the one . . . there he goes now!' Maybe they even knew that he was carrying a handful of coconut-and-jaggery sweets in his bag. He was so overcome by acute self-consciousness that he couldn't bring himself to ask any of the people where his uncle Kunjo Chokroborti's house was. Only once he walked into a lonely lane and found an old, solitary woman could he gather enough courage to ask for directions. The woman was nice. She immediately showed him the way to the house.

The compound was surrounded by a fence. Opu entered the front courtyard through the main door in the boundary wall, but he couldn't see anyone. He coughed loudly a couple of times to announce his presence (his nerves hadn't calmed down enough for him to speak). There was no telling how long he would have had to stand outside in the harsh Choitro sun had a brown-skinned girl of around eighteen or nineteen not come out of the house shortly after on an errand. She was surprised to see a stranger's son standing by the door inside the fence. The boy was pleasing to the eye but clearly ill at ease, shyly clutching his small bag to himself.

'Who are you, Khoka?' she asked gently. 'Where are you coming from?'

Opu came forward a little and managed to say, 'From home . . . er, from Contentment. I, um . . . my name . . . I-I'm Opu.'

He was already regretting this visit. It would have been far better not to have come at all. Perhaps his aunt was going to be irritated by his sudden unannounced arrival. Maybe she would think him a nuisance. And frankly, even apart from all that, who could ever have guessed that speaking to strangers in a strange land would be so difficult? His forehead was beaded with worried drops of sweat.

But he needn't have worried. Upon hearing 'Contentment' and his name, the girl ran up to him with unfeigned joy and led him into the house by hand. She asked after his parents in detail, affectionately touching his chin as he spoke. Despite never having seen his sister—or indeed known of her existence—she shed genuine tears about her passing. She helped him take off his travelling shirt, poured out the water as he washed his face and hands, then wiped them dry with a soft cloth. A little later, she made him a sweet, replenishing summer drink. In short, she wasn't at all like the mental image that Opu had constructed of an aunt. Indeed, she was only a few years older than his neighbour Raji's elder sister.

His aunt seemed equally taken by him. She probably had no idea that her cousin's son was such a fair-skinned, handsome boy, or that he was so young. When a neighbour came by from the house next door, she proudly introduced him.

'This is my nephew from Contentment . . . my father's younger brother's grandson. It's a very close family relationship . . . just that the distance gets in the way.'

She finished by tilting her head towards Opu with evident pride, as if to say, 'Take a good look at this prince-like child! Now do you understand what superior stock I come from? It's not just any family, the Contentment Roys . . . yes!'

Kunjo Chokroborti came home later that evening. He was thin and wiry, and his gaunt face made it hard to tell his age. While meeting his aunt had made Opu shy and a little anxious, seeing his uncle filled him with fear. He reminded Opu of his former teacher Proshonno Gurumoshai. He expected his uncle to accost him at any moment and growl, 'Getting too big for our britches, eh, lad?'

The next morning, Opu went for a walk along the street that had led him to the house. This place was not a land of scutch-grass fields or fallow land. Dense woods surrounded the house, and lined the narrow roads. There was a stretch of woodland right after his aunt's house—a forest, almost—with only the road leading one through it. After a while, he came upon another house, but that was a little standalone place with the woods resuming right after. In many places, the winding village lane went right past people's courtyards. On the way, he did see a few boys of his age playing together, but they stared at him with such surprise and fascination that he felt like an alien object of curiosity. He could not even meet their eyes, let alone muster up the courage to go and speak to them.

The only thing left to do was to go back to his aunt's house, but that wasn't ideal, either. Ordinarily, at about this time at home, his mother would make him a meal of either flat-roasted or puffed rice, maybe a few coconut-jaggery sweets, or some leftover rice. But what would they serve him here? Last night, they had bought a dessert especially for him, so he could have it with a glass of milk before bed. If he went back now, right at the morning mealtime, mightn't they think that he was a greedy glutton, targetting mealtimes in the hopes of more delicacies? No, that wouldn't do. Anyway, it wasn't good to eat shop-bought food every day. He'd just spend the morning on the village roads, returning to his aunt's only when it was time for the midday rice. Yes, that's what he would do.

But really, how could he spend the hours between now and midday on these unknown roads? He had no idea where to go. And he could hardly just stand here, in the middle of the road, all day.

In the end, he slowly retraced his steps back to his aunt's house.

A little girl—no more than six or seven, at the most—ran just ahead of him into his aunt's courtyard, carrying a brass bowl in her hands.

'O Auntie, did you cook gourd?' she called from the bottom of the outer veranda. 'Gimme little?'

From inside the house, Opu's aunt replied, 'Who's it . . . Gulki? No, I'll cook the gourd this evening. Come along then and I'll give you some.'

The girl put her bowl down on the veranda and turned to look at the fence. She had curly, unkempt hair, cut short like a boy's. Her clothes were dirty, there was no oil in her flyaway hair, and her complexion was dark. When she caught sight of Opu just inside the fence gate, she suddenly grinned to herself, turned swiftly around to pick up her bowl, and ran out of the courtyard.

Curious, Opu asked, 'Who's the girl, Auntie?'

'Who? Oh, do you mean Gulki? She's not from this village. Only came here after her parents died. Nibaron Mukhujje's wife—you know, the woman next door? She's an aunt of sorts to her . . . don't know the exact relationship. Anyway, that's who she lives with now.'

The next day, a boy from the village came over to make friends with him and show him around the village. On his way back late in the morning, he saw the orphan girl Gulki once again. She was sitting alone by the narrow village lane, her legs stretched out in front of her, eating something out of the folds of her sari. When she saw him, she quickly tried to hide her food, but Opu had come close enough to see that the loose end of her sari was full of half-ripe medlar berries. Between last morning and now, Opu had found out much more about the poor girl from his aunt. Nibaron Mukhujje's wife did not treat her niece very well. They were, in general, not very good people.

'The way she acts, you'd never know she was the girl's aunt,' his aunt had said. 'Whenever she speaks to the child, she's furious. Half the days they don't even give her anything to eat—she has to go from house to house asking for food. True, she has several mouths of her own to feed, and this is an extra one on top of that, but still . . .'

Somehow, Opu didn't feel any of his natural shyness with Gulki. Instead, he felt an overwhelming sense of pity. Such a small girl, and already with no one to call her own! He wanted to make friends with her. So he walked up to where she was sitting and said, 'And what are you hiding in your sari, eh Khuki?'

By then, Gulki had swiftly wrapped the loose end of her sari into a makeshift knot of berries. She merely flashed him a mischievous smile and ran away. Her antics made Opu want to laugh out loud. While running, the inexpertly tied knot in her sari came apart, and the berries began to fall everywhere, marking her trail. Laughing, Opu began picking up after her.

'Everything is falling out! O Khuki, you're dropping all your berries! At least take your medlars with you . . . I promise I won't scold you! O Khuki!'

But Gulki had already disappeared down the unfamiliar roads.

Later, after he had had his bath at the local pond and returned to his aunt's house, he saw Gulki peeking through the side doorway. She would lean forward a bit, catch his eye, then quickly hide again. Every time she caught his eye, she gave him the same impish grin. After a while of this, Opu stood up.

'Just you wait!' he called out to the little girl. 'I'll catch you in one breath—you'll see!' Then he ran towards the back doorway.

Gulki immediately began sprinting down the lane to the pond. But she was no match for Opu. When she saw Opu was upon her, she gave up and stood, waiting for him to catch her. Opu playfully clasped the curly mass of her hair in his fist.

'A fast runner, eh, Khuki?' he said, mock sternly. 'But did you think you could escape me?'

Gulki froze on the spot. Life had taught her to expect a hail of fists at every turn. But when Opu let go of her hair and started laughing, she understood that this was a game. Then she relaxed and gave Opu another of her mischievous little grins.

A rush of sympathy overcame Opu. There was something about her expression that made Opu certain that she wanted to be friends with him, to play with him. But because she was a child, she hadn't yet learned the words to express this properly, and so had to rely on peeking, running away, and her sudden smiles. She reminded him very strongly of his didi. At her age, he was sure his didi had been exactly like this child: roaming the woods and bylanes by herself, carrying her little trove of black jujubes, wood apples and governor's plums in the loose end of her sari . . . no one to understand her, no one to look after her. This child was just as innocent, just as trusting, just as naive as his didi had been.

Opu decided right then that while he was here, he would play with Gulki. Poor child, without parents at such an early age, forced to roam the woods alone for food and entertainment . . . yes, he would give her his time.

'Do you want to play, Khuki?' he asked gently. 'Let's go towards the pond. No, wait, let's do something; we'll play catch-catch. I'll catch you, and you have to run away. That jackfruit tree will be our starting point. Come on!'

The moment he let go of her, however, Gulki started running. She had no patience with starting points.

'Oh, all right then!' Opu called after her. 'Let's see how far you can go before I catch you! Ooh, that's pretty far! But now watch me . . .'

And with that, he took a deep breath, held it inside, and began running at full speed. Gulki turned back to see how close he was, then tried to run faster. But her small legs were no match for Opu's. He caught up with her almost immediately.

'You're quite the runner, Khuki, but there's no way you can win against me! Want to test it? Okay, let's play thieves and police. You be the thief. Here, steal these jackfruit leaves and run . . . got it? I'll be the police, I'll try to catch you.'

Gulki's face lit up with joy. Perhaps she had been hoping to be friends with this handsome new boy, but had never dared imagine it would happen. She nodded her head to show she understood. Then, perhaps to contribute to the friendship, she said to Opu in a reassuring voice, 'Want some tamarind seeds?'

Her speech was not the gentleman's dialect. She spoke like the children of the cowherds and milkmen from his village. Opu told himself that she had picked it up from living in a farming village.

When his aunt called him in for his lunch, Gulki followed in as well. After Opu was done eating, his aunt looked at the little girl.

'Do you want some rice as well, Gulki? Yes? Then sit in Opu's place. There's curried banana flower . . . I'll give you some daal with that.'

Opu was once again overcome with pity. 'If I knew she was going to eat, I'd have kept a couple of pieces of fish for her,' he thought to himself.

Gulki, meanwhile, showed no hesitation in eating at a neighbour's house. She immediately sat down in front of Opu's plate, then asked several times for more rice and daal. In the end, though she sat in front of her plate and simply moved the food around. Her little body could not put away that amount of rice. Still, she showed no sign of getting up. She was happy to just sit with a surfeit of food.

Finally, Opu's aunt began to laugh. 'It's all right, Gulki . . . you can get up. Honestly, just look at the rice you've left on your plate. All your hunger is in the eyes . . . hardly anything ends up in your tummy!'

Later, she said to Opu, 'Did you see how irresponsible her aunt is? So late in the day, and her such a small girl—and *still* not a single call for her midday rice? Fine, so she's not one of her own . . . but she's still a young child!'

That Saturday, Opu went to the Shiddheshwori temple to fulfil his mother's vow. The priest was an old man, with a white beard that flowed almost to his chest. Opu thought he looked like a good man. His widowed daughter accompanied him in his duties at the temple.

'Why only four paise as offering, Khoka?' she asked him. 'This is not enough. For the ritual of promise fulfilment, you need at least two annas . . .'

'My mother has only given me these four paise,' Opu replied, a little worried. 'I don't have anything more.'

The girl didn't say anything, but collected a few pieces of fruit from the plates of offerings and wrapped it up in a big leaf.

'Here's some proshad from the goddess,' she said, handing it to Opu. 'I've also added some holy leaves and a smear of vermilion—give those to the women in your family, all right?'

Opu took the leaf packet silently, but inside, he was thinking how lovely these people were. If he had money of his own, he would definitely have added two more paise to the offering.

That evening, he and his aunt sat on the outer veranda by the light of the moon, chatting. Opu had just begun telling his aunt about his experience at the temple, when Gulki's screams from the house next door rent the skies.

'O Auntie! Please don't hit me, Auntie! Help! Help! Auntie, my back is bleeding again! Please don't hit me any more!'

Along with those pathetic cries came the enraged screams of a harsh older voice.

'You good-for-nothing rascal! You disgusting wretch! So greedy you went to the Choudhurys' house to eat? Just because they called you? See if I don't burn that tongue of yours with a hot ladle! Going around to people's houses to eat . . . and those worthless women, blind as a bat . . . how dare they say that I don't feed you? Don't we feed you in this house? Don't we? Say it—don't we feed you? What do they know? Just you wait and see what I do to you today . . .'

Opu's aunt said, 'See? That dig was meant for me. You can never speak the truth in society if you want to have friends. Speak the truth, and suddenly *you're* the bad person, stirring up trouble . . .'

Opu's mind was caught between pity, horror and second-hand agony. Unshed tears choked him so completely that he couldn't utter a single word in response to his aunt.

The next day, a little before evening, Opu ate his final meal at his aunt's place. Then he set off towards the local cowherds' neighbourhood, where he was supposed to meet a tobacco cart. The tobacco cart was supposed to leave this village today and go towards Nawbabgonj. His uncle had arranged for Opu to spend the night on the cart, and be dropped off near the road to Contentment early the next morning.

He met Gulki at one of the crossroads of the brahmin neighbourhood. She was on her way back to the Mukhujjes' house after her evening's games.

'Where were you all day, Khuki?' he asked. 'I was waiting to play with you. Now it's too late, I'm on my way back home . . .'

Gulki smiled disbelievingly. Seeing that, Opu said, 'It's true. I'm telling you the truth. See, here's my bag. I'm on my way to Kartik the milkman's house right now—the cart will take me from there. We don't have time to play, but would you like to walk with me a little towards his house?'

Gulki immediately began following him. She followed him for quite a while. After the brahmin neighbourhood, there was a wide expanse of open fields. The cowherds' neighbourhood began after that. Gulki came almost to the edge of the fields. Then she pointed at Opu's red satin shirt and asked, 'How much was this shirt?'

Opu smiled. 'Two rupees . . . do you want it?'

Gulki grinned her sudden impish grin, which probably meant, 'If you give it to me, su-u-u-u-re!'

Opu turned his eyes towards the road in front of him, and saw the dying daylight shining through the gaps in the surrounding trees. Suddenly, he thought of how far he would be from this entire area by next month. He turned back to Gulki and said, 'Don't come any further, Khuki. Go back home. You've already come very far . . . they might scold you at your house again. Go back. Maybe, if I come back again sometime, we'll meet again. Okay? But then again, I may never be back . . . this Boishakh we're leaving for Kashi, you see. That's where we'll be staying from now on, I don't know if we will ever come back . . .'

In response, Gulki merely flashed him her sudden grin.

There was a full moon that night. Or perhaps it was the night before full moon—Opu could never properly remember, later. He never did return to this land of his first solo journey, but for several years afterwards, a single picture from that evening shone brightly in his mind. It was the picture of a straight road cutting through the fields, with a full moon rising from between the trees at the horizon. And in front of it all was the image of a child he had known for only a few days. A naive, curly-haired little orphan who had followed him to the edge of an unknown field, as he left her village behind forever.

29

THAT SUMMER, AT the beginning of the local new year, Horihor decided to begin moving his family permanently out of Contentment. Things were sorted through swiftly, and anything they couldn't carry was sold off to meet numerous small debts. The unused rooms of their old house had been used as storage for a pile of ancient furniture—old jackfruit-wood divans, sitting stools, strongboxes. People came from two or three villages away when they heard such vintage furniture was being put up for sale. Horihor sold them at practically giveaway prices.

The elders of the brahmin neighbourhood had tried their best to make Horihor change his mind. They waxed at length about the abundance of fresh milk and fish in Contentment, and the unbelievable cheapness of prices. Instantaneous lists were composed orally, comparing the inexpensive cost of living in Contentment, vis-a-vis the terribly high expenses beyond its borders. Only Rajkrishno Bhottacharjo's wife, when she stopped by to invite Shorbojoya to the summer's Shabitribroto observance, was encouraging.

'What has this place to offer that I'll ask you to stay back?' she said. 'Besides, sinking one's paddles in the mud and vegetating at the same shores never did anyone any good. One becomes a frog in a well, small-minded. Travelling really does cure that—I've seen that in myself. I hate being stuck here for too long these days. If the divine father allows, perhaps we'll be able to visit his temple at the Chondronath hills this time . . .'

Ranu came over the moment she heard the news, full of hopeful disbelief.

'Opu! Is it true that you're going to leave the village?'

'Yes, Ranudi. Ask Ma, she'll tell you.'

Ranu refused to believe him till Shorbojoya did, in fact, confirm it.

Ranu stood blankly in the Roys' outer courtyard for a few seconds, trying to process the news.

'So . . . when are you leaving?' she finally asked.

'The Wednesday after the next.'

'And you're never coming back?'

Opu wisely kept quiet.

Tears filled Ranu's eyes. 'Then why did you always say "Our Contentment is the best village?" Why did you say "No other place has such a beautiful river, no other place has such vast fields?" If everything's so wonderful, why are you people going away?'

'It's not like I asked to go!' Opu finally protested. 'If Baba wants to move back to the west, what can I say? And anyway, we barely make a living here, so . . . I'll leave you my notebook, Ranudi, all right? Maybe, when we're both grown-ups, we'll meet again?'

'Notebook! You didn't even finish the story you were writing in mine. You said you'd finish it and then sign it with your name—what happened to that, eh? Some boy you've turned out to be, Opu!'

Then, before he could defend himself, she squeezed back her tears and all but ran out of the house.

Opu shrugged. What he said was true: *he* hadn't decided to leave Contentment. In fact, truth be told, he wasn't even leaving of his own free will. There really was no reason for Ranudi to be so upset with him.

Later in the day, he met Potu at the men's bathing steps. He thought it was as good a time as any to let him know as well. Unlike Ranu, village gossip had not yet reached Potu's ears. But when he heard, he became just as upset as Ranu—only he didn't cry.

'I went into the water myself to clean out the algae,' he said morosely. 'But you won't have time to fish even once before you go, will you?'

This year, the Chorok festival, the Goshthobihar fair, and the festival of colours celebrating the birth of Lord Ram on Ramnawbomi were scheduled to follow each other in quick succession. In any other year, this stretch of spring and summer would have marked a period of unbridled happiness for Opu. These festivals were the days when he and his didi were allowed to run free of most rules, spending all hours of the day either at the fairground or trailing behind the travelling companies of actors and performers. Of course, excitement wasn't in short supply from Opu's end this year, either. Despite circumstances, he was really looking forward to the joys of the season.

Then, on the day of Chorok, old Aturi Buri passed away suddenly. Her little hut was fairly close to the new fairgrounds, so Opu saw the crowd on his way to the fair. Curious, he joined them. The last time he had actually spoken to Aturi Buri was on that afternoon when he had run from her. Through the fields, through the bamboo groves—goodness, how scared he had been! It made him want to laugh now, that silliness. He was much younger then. A child, really. Now that he was older, he was certain Aturi wasn't a witch at all, much less an evil one. She was just a lonely woman living in a lonely little hut—poor, helpless, without a son or daughter to care for her. After all, if she really had been a powerful witch, would she have been lying in her hut, unnoticed and dead, for almost a day? Would finding enough people to take her to the crematorium been so difficult?

Meanwhile, Pachu the fisherman's younger son brought out an earthen pot from inside the hut. It was full of desiccated mango powder. The old woman would go slowly through the woods, picking up mangoes that no one wanted and grinding them into a powder when dry. She would then ferry this tangy spice from market to market. Opu knew this because he had seen her at it during the last rothjatra fair, setting up shop by simply putting her spice tray on the ground.

Despite his earlier excitement, Chorok this year seemed . . . empty. He vividly remembered how happy his sister had been just last year, when he had brought home a painted earthenware plate for her.

'Opu, see if you get a good painting of Sheeta's kidnapping,' she had called out when he had been about to leave home that evening. Apparently, she had forgotten that fight they had had that morning, but he hadn't. So to exact revenge, he had said, 'It's always those insipid paintings with you! I'm not going to buy that silly swoony stuff! Buy a Ram–Rabon fight scene, why can't you?'

'You and fight scenes!' Durga had hit back. 'What's wrong buying just plain paintings of gods and goddesses?'

Opu hadn't deigned to answer; he had never had a particularly flattering opinion of his sister's aesthetic sense. Yet now he could not stop thinking about her. When he spotted the first leadwort blossom of the season, his first thought was about how happy she would have been to see it. Every bird call from the forest, every new cluster of woodrose buds made him miss her more. She was his sole companion in sharing these delights, the person he ran to tell when he spotted these annual miracles. Now the land was blooming again, but she was gone. The land would blossom every year, just like it had in the past, but his sister would never return to marvel at its wildflowers or play with its inedible berries.

Someone was playing the flute in the fairground. The music wove through the cacophony, rising in the evening air. Enchanted, Opu followed it back to a small clearing, where Haran Mal from the wrestlers' neighbourhood was expertly advertising his bunch of bamboo-carved long flutes.

'How much for one?' Opu asked. He couldn't resist music.

Haran Mal knew him very well. He'd been down to the Roys' house several times over the years to thatch the kitchen roof.

'Is it true that you're leaving this village, Khoka?' he asked, lowering the flute. 'So where are you going, then?'

Opu paid a paisa and a half for a flute. Before bidding the man goodbye, he said, 'Show me once more, Uncle Haran. Which of these holes do I press while playing?'

He remembered, once, waking up deep into a moonlit night. At first, the only sounds he could hear were the monotonous splashing of the weights as the fishing nets went in and came out of the water. Then he heard the distant strains of singing. Someone was walking along the indigo-bungalow field, singing happily into the night air. It wasn't the first time Opu had woken up at night to people's singing; late-night travellers often sang to keep themselves company. But he seldom heard them from the direction of the indigo bungalow, particularly this late at night. What struck him most was the uniqueness of the song. Most often at night, he heard travellers singing folk versions of Vaishnav keerton—like the ones composed by Modhusudon Kinnor. 'Modhukaner gaan', they were called. The song that night, however . . . It was completely different from anything he had heard before. He tried to stay up, repeating the tune in his head so he wouldn't forget; but that night the goddess of music had merely been strolling through two halves of his sleep on a whim . . . he never chanced upon that song again, nor remembered enough to recall it later. But the memory of the ethereal beauty of the tune—that could never be taken from him.

Evening descended. Boys and girls from farming families—some wearing colourful shirts, some in new kora-cotton saris—began returning to their villages in a disjointed line along the narrow path. People had come from as far as twenty kilometres away to attend this Goshthobihar fair. On their way back, they carried toys and household items they had bought from the fairground market: cork birds, wooden dolls, colourful paper fans, painted earthenware, pieces of bath-scrub. Chinibash, the Vaishnav businessman, had set up a stall of batter-fried vegetables. Opu bought two paisa's worth of food from him and headed home. While walking back with the happy crowd, he wondered if the new place they were going to had Chorok and Goshthobihar fairs. What if it didn't? Had he just attended the last Chorok of his life?

No, wait. This was simple. If the new place didn't have Chorok fairs, then he would just ask his father to bring him back to Contentment every year during spring. There, solved! 'Let's go back for the Chorok fair, Baba—I can't miss it,' he would say. 'We'll just stay with Ranu Didi's family for two nights, no problem.'

The next day, Shorbojoya began wrapping up the household. They were due to leave the next afternoon after lunch. After the lamp-lighting hour, Opu sat down for his evening meal in the kitchen veranda. His mother served him from within, replenishing his plate one porota after another hot off the stove. Early moonlight glittered on the top of the coconut trees in his late Uncle Neelmoni's garden. Watching the silver-topped dark leaves shiver in the breeze, Opu was suddenly filled with a deep, regretful sorrow. When his father had first proposed moving, he had been very excited at the prospect of new lands and train rides. But now that departure was imminent, all he felt was an acute and abiding sense of loss. This house, that bamboo grove, the Sholtekhagee mango orchard, the quiet bank of the river, the secret place in the woods where he and sister had their picnic—he loved these places with his entire being. He and his sister had spent so many evenings on this very veranda, playing cowries as that very coconut tree glittered and shimmered above them. He had known that tree all his life. How often had he sat watching that tree in the moonlight and thought his Contentment the most wonderful, beautiful land? Would the new land have such a majestic coconut tree between the kitchen and the woods behind the house? Would he be able to go fishing there? Go mango-picking? Take boats out into the river? Play rail-rail? Would the new land have such large bathing steps as the ones at the Burflower's Wharf? They had been perfectly happy in Contentment for all these years . . . why leave now?

Then something happened the next afternoon. It was after lunch. His mother was out in the neighbourhood, honouring her various Shabitribroto invitations. Horihor was enjoying his afternoon nap in the next room. Left to his devices, Opu was rooting through the shelves of old things, sorting what he could and could not take with him to Kashi. While moving an old clay pot, something rattled and fell out of it, rolling away from him once it hit the floor. Surprised, Opu leaned down for a closer look. The thing was covered in cobwebs and dust, but there was no mistaking what it was; it was the small gold box that had been stolen from the third-eldest mistress's house the previous year.

Opu stood holding the box for several minutes. The breeze whistling through the bamboo grove echoed in his ears, like coded messages from a faraway land.

'Poor Didi,' he said to himself after a while. 'Stole and stuffed it here so no one would find it . . .'

Then he left the house by the back door and walked slowly to the edge of the bamboo grove. The grove stretched endlessly before him, still and silent, like a sunbathing behemoth. A seagull cawed from within, drawing each call out like its own echo. It's mourning the dying prince, thought Opu. The one from the poem, who lay defeated and forgotten by a secret pond deep within the grove . . . a pond that was really the Dwaipayon Lake in disguise. After a minute's quiet reflection, he raised his arm and hurled the gold box into the grove as hard as he could. It sailed over the dense bushes (the one that his sister's charity dog Bhulo used to jump out of, panting and desperate for food), over the pile of dead bamboo shoots and leaves, and finally landed beyond a governor's plum bush. Opu heard it hit the ground, then roll further into the dense undergrowth.

'Good!' he said to himself. 'It's out of harm's way now. Who's going to go into that forest and look for a gold box? No one.'

Once silence settled over the grove once more, he went back home. He didn't tell anyone about finding the box. Not on that day, and not for the rest of his life. He didn't even tell his mother.

Hiru the carter's cow-drawn cart arrived later that afternoon. There had been a slight cloud cover before ten that morning, but since then the summer sun had been raining down a fiery blaze. A forlorn Potu nonetheless followed the cart for a long while.

'They've booked a good company for this year's jatra, you know,' he said. 'But you won't hear them play, will you, Opuda . . .'

'Take an extra sheet of their advertisement and send it to me,' Opu called back from the cart.

The cart left their village lane. A little later, it trundled past the new fairground, empty of all signs of Chorok except a scattering of green-coconut shells. As the cart drew level with the field, a group of people came into sight, eating in a circle on the far side of the field. The ground beside them was scorched from a now-dead cooking fire. A soot-bottomed new clay pot lay on one side, further proof of cooking.

Horihor wasn't really taking in the view; he was thinking. Was leaving really the right thing to do? After all, the Roys had lived in Contentment for generations. True, their once-lavish lifestyles had long been history, but as long as he was here, there was still a flame that flickered in their name. His wife lit a lamp on the ancestral land at every lamp-lighting hour, keeping the memories of his ancestors alive. With his leaving, the evenings would only bring darkness. What would his late father, the scholar of logic, Ramchand, have to say about this selfish abandonment?

The cart finally left the last homes of the village behind. Opu stared at Aturi Buri's empty hut for as long as he could. Then the road turned at a date-palm orchard and blocked it from view. After the orchard, the cart finally left behind the village mud roads and ascended the paved road leading to Asharu.

With the last glimpse of the village fading behind them, Shorbojoya felt a weight lift from her shoulders. Life in Contentment had never been kind to her. In leaving the village behind, she felt she could finally leave behind her daily burden of poverty, shame and humiliation. The road forward was paved with hope—a new household, a new way of life, a new prosperity.

Daylight began to fade as the cart trundled through the Shonadanga moors. Horihor pointed to a large banyan tree, standing alone in the middle of the moors.

'Look! That's the Highwayman's Banyan, right next to the Pond of the Sisters-in-Law.'

Shorbojoya quickly leaned out from within the cart's awning. The tree was closer than she had imagined—on a low marshland only a short distance away from the road. Only fifty years earlier her ancestor-in-law would've been hiding in that darkness, waiting for his next prey. How many times had she been told the story of the old brahmin and his young son? Too many times, that's what. Poor, poor souls. Killed and buried in the middle of the moors—and not a word to anyone back home. Imagine being the mother, waiting for your little boy who could never, ever come back home. How many months . . . how many years had she waited, before she was forced to accept her loss? Goddess! Shorbojoya quickly pulled her head back within the awning, hiding the tears blurring her sight.

The Shonadanga moors were the largest moors in this region. They were dotted with cotton and gum indica trees surrounded by wildflower bushes. Every now and then a date palm made an appearance, hung low with clusters of date. Golden laburnum blossoms shimmered in the slight breeze. Cuckoos and golden orioles hid in the foliage, calling out to each other. Not even a little of the rich green land had been marred by farming or human habitation. The dusty orange road twisted and turned through the undulating greenness, like a wandering baul lost in the trance of his own music. Above this magnificence stretched the never-ending arch of the evening sky, its colour the blue of linseed flowers.

A little later, the cart went past the Barashe-Modhukhali lake. Some ancient river had once brought itself down to these moors to find its final resting place, and that resting place was the Modhukhali lake. The once-flowing water now stood still in the deep riverbed, contained within the vast greenness and replete with a wilderness of lotuses. Opu sat outside the awning, taking in the beautiful colours of the summer sunset. The beauty of the moors had brought back the fantasies of his childhood—the dreams of travelling to distant, unknown lands that opened into the realms of stories. Indeed, these very moors had been like a mythical land to him—heard of often, but never seen. And yet today he was trundling through them. If this is how the journey began, how wondrous would the rest of it be? Perhaps the life ahead would be a long, magnificent journey; perhaps he *would* reach the lands of his distant dreams!

Horihor pointed at a distant impression of huts against the horizon.

'That is Dhonche-Pawlashgachi. On the other side of the woods is Natabere. Every monsoon they have an enormous fair around the BonBibi darga—you'd never find cheaper pumpkins anywhere else.'

The moon rose as the marketplace of Asharu became visible on the opposite bank of the Betrabotee river. Their cart was loaded on to a large boat, luggage and all. The water around them shimmered and glittered in the moonlight. It was a market day at Asharu, so the other bank was still alive with people. Halfway across the river, a ferryboat from the Asharu pier crossed them, going in the opposite direction. The happy chatter of returning shoppers spilled on to the quiet waters.

Once on the other side, Opu slipped off the cart with his father's permission and went to explore the market. The shops were arranged in a dense line, all of them still open and doing a great deal of business. The goldsmith was hunched over his little anvil, hammering away rhythmically. There was a large crowd of carts in front of the date-palm jaggery storehouse. Majherpara station, where they were ultimately headed, was still almost thirteen kilometres away. The avenue leading to the station, though unpaved, was broad and well-maintained. Long-dead indigo planters had lined it with banyan, holy fig and mulberry trees. The once-young banyans were now old and majestic, each surrounded by a thick circle of aerial roots hanging from their lower branches. Moonlight filtered through the young summer leaves, transforming them into clusters of ghostly pale foliage. Brainfever birds hid within the thick foliage, piercing the hot summer nights with their wails.

Opu had never witnessed the beauty of springtime in Bengal on such a vast scale before. Through the blazing afternoon to the moonlit night, he had absorbed the majesty of the changing landscape: the lonely moors, the quiet, sunny woods, the shy fluttering of the fragrant rose-chestnut blossoms, the moonlit fields, the careless calls of the cuckoo. Each of these scenes had been permanently etched on to his soul that day, never to be forgotten. In his future life as an artist, it was the memory of this day that he turned to again and again for inspiration and sweet tranquillity.

It was almost ten when their cart finally reached Majherpara station. Opu had been waiting for this moment all day. The moment their cart rolled to a stop, he jumped off the back and ran on to the platform. But alas, the last train of the night had already left—at eight-thirty. He ran back to ask his father whether there was any hope of another train that night, but there wasn't. Opu almost stamped his feet in frustration. He had been so looking forward to seeing an actual train! It was all the fault of Hiru the carter's cows. Had they not been so horribly slow, he would definitely have been on time to see that last train! Now he had to wait till morning. Annoyed, he began looking around.

Moonbeams glanced off the railway tracks, making them shine. A part of the platform had been covered with a pile of tobacco bundles. Off to one side, two railwaymen were loading the bundles on to a machine that looked like a large, flat iron box, but had an enormous metal handle. On one end of the station, beyond the end of the platform, two tall red lights on a pole glowed in the darkness. There was an exact replica on the other end, also currently glowing red. Opu wandered over to peek inside the station office. A wooden table dominated the room. A large, four-legged oil-lamp shone on top of it. A bundle of official-looking papers was piled next to it. The stationmaster was working with a strange object that made a loud, wood-on-wood, 'tock, tock' noise. What was that thing? Opu ventured closer to the office door. It looked like the toe-grip of a wooden sandal, but he couldn't solve the mystery of its use.

Oh, the railway station! Such a magical place, full of mysteries. Just a few more hours amidst these fascinating new things . . . and then it'd be morning and he'd see a train! Not just see one, in fact, but ride in it! Unfortunately, his father came looking for him right then. He didn't want to leave the platform after such a short exploration, but his father insisted on taking him back. On their way out, Opu pointed out the strange 'tock, tock' instrument to his father. Apparently, that was the telegraph machine—the thing that actually sent messages through wires!

Horihor led Opu to the bank of the station's pond, where Shorbojoya was busy making arrangements for cooking dinner. A cart had already been tethered there when they had arrived at the station, its passengers a married woman of about eighteen or nineteen, and a young man. It came out in conversation that the woman was the daughter of the Biswas household in Hobibpur, and the man was her brother. He had come to escort her back to her parents' house for a visit. In the time that it had taken him to survey the platform, Opu's mother had already become fast friends with the woman. When Opu reached the cooking spot, she was washing the rice and lentils for the night's khichuri, while the other woman peeled potatoes. Dinner was going to be cooked together.

The train pulled into the station at seven-thirty in the morning. Opu had been waiting at the edge of the platform since much earlier in the morning, waiting for just this moment. But when the train actually became visible, his father began to worry and fuss.

'Come away, Khoka!' he called loudly, for all to hear. 'Don't stand that close to the edge—you'll fall!'

Almost immediately, a railway porter also appeared, driving people away from the platform's edge. Opu was forced to step back.

The train was hu-u-u-ge! And it made SUCH a racket! What was that strange thing at the front? Was that the 'engine'? Goodness—would you look at it! Even the married woman from Hobibpur lowered her decorous head-covering to stare at the oncoming metal beast.

As soon as the train entered, everyone rushed to load all their belongings on it. Inside the carriage, there were rows of wooden benches facing each other. The floor looked like it was made of cement. In short, it was exactly like a room in a house, with proper doors and windows. Even as he was pushed on to the train, Opu couldn't quite believe that this immense thing would move again. Perhaps someone would come and say, 'Listen, all of you! You have to get down now! Our train will not go anywhere today!' Through the windows, he caught sight of a man on the other side of the wire fence, a bale of hay on his head, waiting for the train to pass. Opu felt a surge of pity for him. Imagine being able to see a train, but not get up on it! How could a life of such deprivation be worth living! Through the windows, he caught sight of Hiru carter. He, too, was standing outside the station gates, staring at the train.

The train started to move. It was amazing! A magical side-to-side swaying while still moving forward! In no time at all, everything on the Majherpara station—the people, the tobacco bundles, the mouth-wide-open Hiru carter—fell away from the windows. The train began speeding through open fields of hay. The trees on either side went by with an impressive 'Whoosh!' Such speed! The bushes, trees, little thatched-roof huts, small farmhouses . . . all seemed to merge into a single smear of colour as the train sped through the landscape. From underneath the carriage, the noise of a hundred grindstones rose up. Up ahead, the engine made a din of its own. Behind them, the distant signal of the Majherpara station was slowly fading into the horizon.

Opu was suddenly reminded of a day from ages ago. That day, when he and his sister had set out to find their lost red calf, and ended up lost amongst the marshes in their search for the railroad. Making his way to the window, he quickly leaned out and looked back. The land of his birth was now behind him. There, marked by a row of trees in the middle of the open fields, was the Asharu–Durgapur road. On the other side of that road lay the winding village path that connected Contentment to the Shonadanga moors—a path they had failed to find on that fateful day. Looking back, Opu imagined his sister standing at the bend of that road, alone and forlorn, watching as the train carried her family further and further away from her.

Nobody had ever brought her to see the railroad. Nobody had thought to bring something of her with them. Everybody had abandoned her without a thought. True, technically, she was no more. But while he had been in Contentment, Opu had felt her presence everywhere: along the wooded paths, in the bamboo grove, underneath the many mango trees. The memory of her affection had surrounded him in every corner of their dilapidated home. He had never completely felt her loss while he was still there. But today . . . today he felt that he was truly abandoning his sister forever.

Watching the tree-lined Asharu–Durgapur road become smaller and smaller against the horizon, Opu suddenly felt that no one had truly loved his didi—not even his mother. No one had felt any sorrow at leaving her behind forever. In fact, they had barely seemed to remember her. His heart swelled with a sudden, overpowering emotion. It wasn't exactly sadness. Nor was it despair or desolation. He did not quite know what to call it, but he felt it intensely. It flooded his mind with countless memories of his beloved village: Aturi

Daini, the serene banks of the river, their old home, the lane to the elephant-apple tree, Ranudi, all those afternoons of roaming the orchards, years' worth of laughter and games, Potu . . . and above all, over and over, his didi's face. And his mind flooded with the memories of her many small but unfulfilled wishes.

He looked back again. At the bend of their village road, he could still see his didi standing, watching as the fast-disappearing train bore her brother away from her.

In the next instant, all the hurt that had remained unspoken in his heart came tumbling out in a hot flood of tears. 'I didn't want to go, Didi!' he wanted to shout back at the abandoned girl. 'I haven't forgotten you! I haven't left you behind! These people are taking me away, Didi. I didn't want to go!'

And he never did forget her.

Later in life, he had opportunities to become better acquainted with the blue skies, the infinite ocean, with the wonders of this earth. But whenever his body shivered with the thrill of speed, whenever he encountered the ever-changing beauty of the blue skies from the deck of an ocean-bound ship, or found himself in the forests at the foothills of towering blue mountains, he would remember those rain-filled nights, of huddling in one corner of a dark room in an old house, and the words of a poor village girl, beaten down by illness.

'. . . Opu, when I get better, will you show me the railroad one day?'

The distant signal of the Majherpara station grew fainter and fainter behind them, till it could finally be seen no more.

30

THEY HAD TO change trains at Ranaghat that afternoon. Opu had had powdered coal fly into his eyes twice already, but he couldn't bear to keep his head inside the large windows. There was so much to see! What were those things at every station? 'Signals'? Why were they going up and down? And look, wherever the train stopped, someone had built a raised platform at just the right height to help people get on and off—just like verandas in front of a house! Were these the 'platforms'? There were boards stuck on these verandas, with the name of the stations written in English and Bangla: Kurulgachi, Gobindopur, Baanpur. Just before the train left each station, someone would hit an iron disc four times with an iron mallet. Dhong-dhong-dhong-dhong! It was exactly four times, he had counted. And then the signal would go up and down. The signal was controlled by an iron disc with spokes sticking out in all directions. He saw a man in the Kurulgachi station turning it with some effort, and the hand of the signal moving.

Shorbojoya, too, was looking around. This was only the second time she had been on a train. The first time was . . . oh, years back, when *he* had first returned from Kashi. It was in summer, during the month of Joishtho. She had gone to Aranghata to see the Jugolkishor—a temple dedicated to a flute-playing Krishno, and his consort Radha. She was a new bride then, fresh from setting up her own home in Contentment. Ages . . . it had been ages back. She leaned out of the window like her son, and happily watched the crowds of people getting on and off the train. Look at those women, she thought to herself. Such nice clothes, such jewellery! At Jogonnathpur station, she saw a man peddling good moa—large balls of fluffed rice, jaggery and reduced milk.

'Opu,' she said eagerly, 'shall I take some moa for you? You love it . . . these are good.'

After a while, her son pointed at a bird on the telegraph wires accompanying the tracks in sudden excitement.

'Look, Ma! Someone's pet mynah has escaped its cage!'

The sun had begun to set when they changed trains again at Noihati, and thundered across the bridge over the Ganga. Shorbojoya stared mesmerized at the red-gold glow spreading from the horizon. The cool river breeze rushed past the train, bathing the travellers in its crisp freshness. Boats went languidly by on the river below. From her vantage point, Shorbojoya could see beautiful houses and gardens scattered on either side of the river. Never in her life had she seen such marvellous sights. When a steamship came around the distant bend, she clutched her son's arm in thrill.

'Opu, look! A real smoke-top ship!'

A few minutes later, she joined her palms and raised them to her forehead in silent prayer. 'Mother Gonga, forgive us for crossing you, Ma,' she begged earnestly of the waves below. 'I'll offer you a pujo with flowers and marmelos leaves once we see you again in Kashi. Keep my Opu well, and please, Ma, may our hopes for the new place come true. May we find true shelter there.'

Truth be told, this was the happiest she had been in years. The promise of a rewarding future mixed with the unfamiliar thrill of freedom as she leaned out of the train to drink in such sights and sounds as she had never before imagined seeing. While living her previous bamboo-grove-bound stagnant rural life, she had never even conceived of such speed or such rapid changes in scenery, or of goosebumps from joy, not fear. Now that she tasted the fresh air that whipped through the compartment, she felt that her previous life had been spent in building higher and higher walls to stay isolated and contained, cut off from the world outside for fear of change. But today those walls had been shattered! She had stepped over their debris to embrace a mysterious unknown. She felt every moment of that momentous flight—across rivers, through countless villages and towns, straight towards the molten gold of the setting sun. To think that only a year back, lying down in the silence of her Contentment house, she had told herself that travelling to Chakdah or Kaligonj for a dip in the holy river was an impossibly ambitious adventure. Yet look at her now!

As their train was pulling into the Bandel station, a much larger train thundered through the station at the speed of a gale. Opu stared after its speeding form in amazement. When they finally got off their train at Bandel, the noise and buzz of constant activity drowned out pretty much everything else. Engines kept going up and down on different tracks and freight trains thundered through every five minutes without stopping at the platforms. By now it was the lamp-lighting hour, but no one would have mistaken it for the quiet darkness of Contentment evenings. The engines whistled at a deafening pitch, people shouted instructions to each other, and a bright green signal glowed a short distance away to mark the departure of a passenger train. Even the darkness beyond the station was lightened by the glow of flocks of red and green signal-lights for the various tracks.

Later that night, their train to Kashi finally pulled into the station with a series of hideous clangs. Bandel was a much larger station than either Ranaghat or Noihati, and even at that late hour was absolutely swarming with people. When she saw the enormous crowd move as one towards the train, Shorbojoya lost all sense of bearing. Barely managing to follow her husband on numbed, shaking feet, she found herself propelled by the crowd towards the doorway of a compartment, but was unable to find a foothold of her own. Finally, Horihor had to propel his disoriented wife and son from behind till they were inside the compartment, and then fight to secure them seats on the bench. Then he had to battle the crowds once again to help the porter bring their boxes and bundles to their seat.

Shorbojoya woke up around dawn. The train was racing through the dissipating darkness at the speed of a storm. Her husband was close by, still sleeping. Horihor had not sent her and Opu to the women's coupe this time, because Bandel to Kashi was a night train. The compartment was emptier than it had been when they got on. People were stretched out on their benches, fast asleep. A trader from Kabul was snoring in one of the upper berths. Opu had clearly been awake for a while. He was next to the window, eyes glued to the scenery flashing by.

After a while, Horihor woke up. 'Come away from the window, Khoka,' he admonished his son. 'You'll have coal dust flying into your eyes any minute now.'

Hah, coal dust. Opu could not have turned away from the window if someone had threatened to scratch his eyes out. He had been sitting next to the window, staring out, for almost all of the night. His parents had been asleep, unaware of all the magnificent things that he had seen. Their train had whooshed past so many stations, full of light and people waiting to get on! He must have dozed off a little after passing several such stations, for when he woke up again the train was crossing a bridge over a small river. On the other side of the bridge he could make out a very large, very high dark mound rising out of the ground, covered in trees. The river water gleamed in the golden light of the full moon, and white clouds floated in the dark sky. When the train crossed the forested mound, he saw there was another one just like that behind it, and then another, and another—all of them covered in the same kind of trees. After crossing the high mounds, the train finally pulled into a large station. Suddenly, lights and crowds were everywhere again. A second passenger train stood on the next track. While their train waited at the station, a man had an enormous fight with a paan-seller on the station. There was a large wall-clock on the platform. Following the instructions learnt from his master moshai, Neeren Babu, Opu worked out that it was twenty-two minutes past three in the morning.

Then the train began moving again. The high mounds appeared soon after they left the station. Opu was dying to know what these things were, but to his exasperation, not a single other person in the entire compartment was awake. Why on earth did these people travel by the railway if they couldn't be bothered to stay up and see the scenery?! At one point, he stuck his head out of the window and tried to follow the ground to see how fast the train was really going. The wind blew his hair back from his face, and the ground slipped by too fast for him to work out the speed. All through the night he shuttled between the windows on either side of the compartment, determined not to miss anything on the way. Towards dawn, when the moon had begun to fade into the east, he suddenly looked at a moonlit field and wondered how far they'd come from home. What was this land of undulating fields and roads? He had fallen asleep briefly towards morning. But when the train pulled into an enormous station with a horrible metallic clang, he woke up again. A stone tablet on the platform proclaimed the station's name: Patna City.

Other stations followed after that, then an enormous, unending bridge. He saw signals change as their train went past. Factories and warehouses loomed in the distance. At one station he saw a railway official speaking into a pipe attached to an iron pillar: 'Private number? All right . . . sixty-nine . . . sixty-nine? One less than seventy, first six then nine . . . yes, that's right.'

'What is that machine, Baba?' he asked his father, bewildered. 'And why is he speaking like that?'

When the day was at the point of dissolving into evening, Horihor said, 'We're about to reach Kashi. Look to your left. There's a bridge over the Gonga up ahead. You'll see Kashi the moment the train's on the bridge.'

Opu, meanwhile, was thinking of something else. All through the night and day, he had had the chance to really observe the structure of telegraph poles and wires. That one time with his father, he'd barely formed an impression of the whole thing.

If he ever played train-train again, he would make sure to set up the poles correctly. The last set-up had been such a mess! This Kashi place that they were going to . . . would its woods have moonseed vine?

~

Fifteen days had passed since the great railroad adventure. Horihor had found rooms for his family on the ground floor of a three-storey house in Banshfatka Alley. He hadn't been able to track down any of his old acquaintances. New people had taken over their old haunts, and claimed to know nothing about their predecessors. Only the old confectioner, Ramgopal Sahu, still lived at his old address at the Vishweshwar lane.

The top floor of the house was occupied by a Punjabi family, and the middle floor by a Bengali businessman. The road-facing rooms were his shop and storeroom; the other two or three rooms served as his kitchen and sleeping quarters. In the last five or six days, Shorbojoya had visited several parts of the city with her husband. Never in her wildest dreams had she imagined a place with so many people, such imposing statues of deities, such magnificent temples. All her life she had held up the Jugolkishor temple at Aranghata as the epitome of architectural wonder. But now that she had seen the Vishwanath temple, the Annapurna temple, the redstone temples above Dasaswamedh Ghat, she could barely contain her awe. They were wonders on a different scale entirely.

One evening she had gone with the Punjabi gentleman's wife to see the arati at the Vishwanath temple. Words defied her experience there. Once the lamps and incense were lit, the temple filled with the perfumed smoke and seven or eight priests began chanting the mantras in perfect harmony. The crowds, the splendour, the richly dressed women from well-known families . . . it was a spectacle beyond anything she had ever dreamt of. There was an actual queen in attendance that evening, accompanied by four or five of her own maids. In Shorbojoya's eyes, she was the embodiment of every fairy-tale queen she had grown up with: stunning large eyes, perfectly shaped brows, and a face whose beauty declared its superior lineage even from a distance. A true queen indeed! When the priests each lifted their arrangement of five lamps in the air for the fire salutation, the golden-threaded kalka patterns on the loose end of her Banarasi silk sari glittered in the semi-darkness. Once the arati was over, Shorbojoya honestly couldn't be sure whether she had spent more time watching the ceremony, or staring at the queen.

And then there were the houses. Back home in Contentment, she remembered how envious she had been of the Ganguly household, with their double-storey home, a separate temple portico, and their own cemented bathing steps. Once, when invited for the Gangulys' Durga Puja, she remembered telling her daughter, 'See the splendour of rich people's houses, Dugga? It's like Lakshmi herself designed it.'

Now she marvelled at her past naiveté. The Ganguly house, once the epitome of wealth to her yearning soul, couldn't hold a *candle* to the mansions she saw casually lining the streets of Kashi.

The traffic was a spectacle of its own. She had never seen anything except cow and bullock carts in the villages. There had been a few horse-drawn carriages in Noihati—she had seen them from the station—but nothing close to the sheer variety of vehicles she saw in just a few minutes on the road. There were so many vehicles with no animals attached! Every time she went out, she wished that she could just stand by the side of the road for a few minutes and watch this wonderful parade. But then the Punjabi gentleman's wife always accompanied her on these trips, and it would be too embarrassing to confess her little desire to a neighbour.

Kashi had sent Opu into a state of permanent astonishment as well. For all his daydreaming, he had never, ever thought that a place like this could exist. Their house was fairly close to Dasaswamedh Ghat—just a short walk away. It was like having a Chorok fair at the doorstep every single day! Music on one end, ballad recitals on the other, someone reading out verses from the Ramayan in the middle, hundreds of people milling about, laughter . . . it was like living inside a permanent festival. Ever since he had learnt the route, he went to the ghat every evening, then came home full of stories and vivid descriptions.

There was a little boy who was brought to the ghat for his evening walk. Opu had made friends with the child. He was called Poltu, and he was too young to speak clearly. Because of his size and extreme restlessness, his family only allowed him out like a jailer allows his charges—with a rope tied around his waist. The other end of the rope stayed in the hands of a servant who accompanied him. Opu found this arrangement hilarious. He tried to convince the servant to set Poltu free, but the servant had clear instructions, and was afraid to go against them. And poor Poltu, of course, was too young to rouse to rebellion.

When he returned home each evening, his anxious mother scolded him for staying out on his own.

'Why do you have to go out at all?' she would complain. 'These are city streets, not like home. What if you get lost?'

Opu would then have to launch into passionate self-defence, and explain why it was absolutely impossible for him to lose his way, even though they were now in Kashi.

Horihor's income had gone up since settling into the city. After a few daily visits to plead his case, he was finally given the job of reciting sections of the Puranas at a few temples. Then one day Shorbojoya said, 'Why don't you sit with your books at Doshashwomedh Ghat in the evenings? People find so many ways to go out and make money—you just want to sit at home and make plans!'

So Horihor began taking his volume of the *Kashi Khanda* to the Dasaswamedh in the evenings. Reciting the Puranas was not new to him—he had done it often enough in his disciples' homes during rituals and ceremonial festivities. He would open the volume, and in his musical voice begin singing the introductory salutation:

A beautiful piece of peacock-plume, musk smeared on his
forehead,
His earrings touching his cheek.
. . . a smile on his charming face, a flute resting on his
lower lip
. . . Brahma, in the skin of Gopal, I praise.

The crowd that gathered was not bad for a newcomer.

After coming home, he would sit down to write his ideas on rough, inexpensive paper.

'No one wants to hear dry shlokas,' he would tell his wife. 'That Bangladeshi balladeer draws a far bigger crowd than I do. I'm thinking of composing a few acts myself . . . put in a few songs, some ballad-like storytelling. No one wants to listen otherwise. I actually spoke to that Bangladeshi gink day before. He doesn't even know the Devanagari alphabet, can you believe that? Just recites rhyming stuff to fool women, and it works! I barely clean up six annas at the end of the evening—his bowl never has less than a rupee! Anyway, do you want to listen to a bit of what I've written so far?'

Then he would recite some of the verses he had composed.

'I'm thinking of lifting the description of the woods from that balladeer,' he confided in his wife. 'But do you think he'll allow it?'

'Where exactly do you sit?' asked Shorbojoya. 'I want to go listen to you one of these days.'

'Yes, of course—I sit right beneath the Shoshti temple. Come tomorrow. I'll launch the new act tomorrow evening. It's the eleventh day of the lunar cycle, a good day to start new things . . .'

'On your way back, bring four paise worth of water-chestnut jilipi from the Bishsheshwor alley. That Hindi-speaking woman from upstairs invited me the other day—some pujo of theirs at her home. She said you can get jilipi made of water-chestnut flour at Bishsheshwor's alley. I kept thinking of how much Opu loved jilipi, but then she'd served them as refreshments—how could I ask to bring some downstairs with me? Bring four paise worth tomorrow, don't forget.'

Over the next few days, Horihor noticed an increase in the number of people stopping to listen to him. A few days after that, a maid from the Naradaghat Kali temple delivered a large basket of food to his house. Shorbojoya was overjoyed.

'Is this from the weekly pujo?' she asked eagerly. 'And do you know if my husband is on his way home yet?'

After the maid left, she called her son into the veranda, where the basket of food had been deposited.

'Look, Opu—puffy coconut. Don't you like these? You know you do! Raisins, bananas . . . such large mangoes! Come eat, find a place to sit on the floor. Let me serve you.'

His wife's prompting had lit the old spark in Horihor. The other day Shorbojoya had said to him, 'People's ears are ringing with your repeated recitation of "Dhrubochoritro". Why don't you start something new?'

So Horihor had taken his old writings out for inspiration, and for the last few days he had been concentrating on recasting the Jarabharat story from the Mahabharat as a solo ballad-style play. Bent over his papers, he remembered the days from twenty-two years ago, when he had sat in this very city and translated the *Geet Gobindo* in verse. Back then, Kashi didn't really have a culture of musical storytelling. He discovered that particular culture when he went back to Bengal, to a rural society steeped in local music and folk-rhyme. Surrounded by such icons as Dashu Roy's *Book of Ballads*, Dewanjee's songs, Gobindo Odhikari's 'The Parrot and the Myna', and Moti the singer's choir in Loka Dhopa's travelling company, he gradually realized his true purpose in life. One night he finally told his wife about his plans.

'Saw a stand-up singing show going on at the marketplace, you know?' he said. 'Stopped to listen for a bit. Just simple rhyming verses—nothing to it. I'm just waiting to settle us down well. Then I'm going to introduce a completely new kind of act. As I pointed out to Raju yesterday, the problem here is that these people don't innovate. All these years, and still singing the same ancient verses . . .'

Some nights he would leave the rooms to sit in the open veranda after his family had fallen asleep. Looking up at the night sky, he would feel as light and carefree as a feather. Finally, after decades of hardship, Horihor Roy was going to have that elusive bright future that he had always dreamt of. In the darkness of the alleys at night, he could almost see the golden glow of chandeliers lighting up prestigious concerts. His poems, songs, acts and devotional verses would spread from state to state, village to village. Travelling companies would be playing his pieces night after night. People would come from across fields and rivers with little bundles of food, just so they could stay up all night and listen to his stories and songs. The manager of those travelling companies would travel all the way to his house, begging him to give them his next musical.

'What a fantastic verse! Whose is it?'

'Every poet's guru, the Thakur Horu.'

No, that didn't quite catch the spirit. Horu Thakur was too . . . common. Perhaps . . . 'The Master of Poetry'. Yes, that was better. 'The Master of Poetry, Horihor Roy Esquire; from the Abode of Contentment'.

Smiling at the thoughts of future success, he would then think of the dreams he had once had on this very Dasaswamedh Ghat, all those years back. The naive ambitions of youth had dissipated like so much wispy morning mist under the brutal sun of middle-age needs. His bundle of writings had been stashed away in the corner of a box, hidden for years from the light of day.

Couldn't he reset the clock just once? Get those youthful years back—relive them?

Opu, meanwhile, had made several friends from amongst the boys who came to the riverside for their evening stroll. The only problem was that all of these boys were in school. Back in Contentment, he had been perfectly happy spending his days fishing and trawling the river in boats, but here he was embarrassed to confess his lack of enrolment to these boys.

The other difference was that all of these boys came from well-off homes. Poltu's elder brother had once casually mentioned that his father had to travel a great deal for work.

'Is that because your family has a lot of disciples?' Opu had asked, for he had known no other reason for fathers to travel.

'Disciples? How do you mean?' Poltu's elder brother had responded, puzzled. Then, without waiting for an explanation, he had clarified, 'My father is a contractor. He has to travel to visit all his sites. Besides, we have a small landholding in Kanthi—he has to look after that, too. But then again, these days, what's really left over after taxes?'

Some evenings Opu wandered up to the crowd around his father at the top of the bathing steps. Sitting on the portico of the Shoshti temple, he listened to his father narrate the emotional devastation that wracked the king Bhorot after wounding a deer cub. As his father's musical voice took the audience through Bhorot's helplessness, pain, and the cub's eventual death, his eyes filled with involuntary tears. Then, as the story progressed to Rohugon, the king of Sindhu Shoubeer, appointing the now sage-king Bhorot as a palanquin-bearer without knowing his true identity, his tears give way to a rapid beating of the heart.

'Something's going to happen now,' he would tell himself. 'Someone's going to snap!'

But his favourite part of the narration was the blessing that his father recited at the end of the evening's session:

May the clouds and rain be timely
May the earth blossom with plenty
May the land be free of discontent
May the good people live without fear.

As Horihor's voice recited the benediction, the late-evening conch-calls from surrounding temples would melt into the floating strain of Purvi in the air, smearing the red-gold sunset with the quiet despair of a deer cub's passing.

One night, when his father returned home from the ghat, he brought him a pen and a piece of paper.

'Write that verse for me, Baba,' he said. '"May the clouds and rain be timely"—that one.'

'So you come to my readings, Khoka?' his father asked, delighted.

'Yes, I'm there every day. Yesterday, when you were telling the story of Bhorot's mother's death, I was sitting behind you, on the steps of the Shoshti temple.'

'So how do you like it? I mean . . . do you like it?'

'I re-e-e-e-ally like it, Baba! I go every day to hear you speak!'

This, however, was not exactly true. Opu went to his father's sessions often enough, but never when he was with his new friends. One day, when his group happened to walk by his father, his father had caught sight of him. 'Khoka! O Khoka!' Horihor had called out, happy to see his son. But Opu had walked on without responding, pretending obliviousness. One of his friends had asked him about it.

'Does that gentleman know you?'

Opu had only nodded. The rest of that evening, he had avoided coming anywhere near those bathing steps. He couldn't bring himself to confess to his new friends that his father was a bathing-steps storyteller. With the exception of Poltu's brother, he had told all his friends that his family had an enormous house back in their homeland—that they were only in Kashi for a holiday. His father was a busy man, he had explained, what with all the site visits he had to do on account of being an important contractor. Plus, he also had to travel to look after their landholdings in the village. He usually concluded this description by saying:

'But then again, these days, what's really left over after taxes?'

His mates were too young to see the discrepancy between his worn clothes and tall tales. Then again, the allure of his handsome face and musical voice fitted well with a history of invented nobility, so perhaps there was an inherent believability to his story.

On the next full moon, the crowd around the Bangladeshi balladeer seemed to really swell. After the evening's session was over, the man went down to the river to wash his hands, feet and face. Horihor was resting in his usual place when the man returned to the top.

'There you are, sir!' said the balladeer. 'Did you see the disaster today? It's an auspicious, full-moon day, so I thought: let me set up an extra brahmon-charity bowl. A single day of brahmon charity would've brought in anything from five to forty kilos of rice in Kashi once! But now? Even a special charity for brahmons can't lure the people . . . no one cares about the virtue of giving, sir, no one. Barely five quarters in my bowl, all told, and two of those pennies are bad! But enough about me. Where has sir done his schooling?'

'I studied here in Kashi,' Horihor responded. 'But I've only been back recently. I was living at home all these years.'

'So is sir's new home close by? If it is, could sir get me a cup of tea? All this recitation really hurts the voice . . . been thinking a little salt tea might help. I've actually been walking around the last few days with tea-leaves tied at the end of this shawl, thinking perhaps if nothing else works I'll get hot water off a confectioner . . .'

'No no, please, it'll be my pleasure,' said Horihor, getting up. 'This way . . . my house is very close.'

The Roys had never had the custom of drinking tea at home, so the water had to be boiled in a wok. Opu served it to the balladeer in a brass glass, along with a plate of refreshments. The balladeer was overcome; after strong-arming an invitation to tea, he had not expected Horihor's spouse to serve him food. His delight bubbled over into generous praise of Horihor's family.

'Is this your son? Such a handsome boy! Ah, no no . . . bless you, my boy, bless you. It's salt tea, right? Here, let me try a sip . . .'

'Are your children in Kashi?' asked Horihor.

'Children? Hah! A man needs a wife first, sir, to have children! Forty acres of land I lost for it, and still no family to show. Do you think I'd be here if that land was still mine? Hah! No one lives in Kashi unless they have to. It's all very well to have Baba Bishsheshwor watching over me, but not a drop of date juice in winter . . . not a single bit of date-palm jaggery! Back in my village, sir, I myself owned forty trees of date palms, but in this foreign land . . .'

'So where is sir's village?' Horihor interposed.

'Near Shaatkheera . . . do you know Badure-Sheetolkati? The Sheetolkati Chokrobortis are very well-known in that area, maybe you've heard of them?'

A little later, Horihor prepared a hookah indoors and brought it out to the guest. The balladeer accepted with alacrity.

'Thinking of going home at the end of winter,' he confided. 'There's still an orchard left—let me go sell it off. We're shrotriyo brahmons, you know? Bride price, that's our custom. So back in the day I put forty acres of land as collateral to meet the bride price. Her and me, we lived together for ten years. Then, wouldn't you just believe my luck . . . she was bitten by a snake. While cutting down a pumpkin from our own roof! On top of that, I was away from home that day . . . so who knows if someone even called for a doctor or a kobiraj. The next day—I had reached the quay at Patuli by then—I see Mohesh Shadhukhan from our village hurrying towards me. "Go home, you're in grave danger," he said—but didn't say what the danger was. By the time I reached . . . well, sir, she had died the previous night. So that was that. No land, no wife, nothing left to sell for another wedding. So then I thought, what's the point? Might as well head out to seek shelter at Baba Bishwonath's feet. At least I'll get my daily rice. That was eight years ago. These days my cousin has taken over my remaining land . . . tells me, "None of this was yours anyway." "Fine," I say. "If you want to rob me, then rob me. I'm never going to fight for mere property—never!" So that's my story . . . anyway, thank you for the tea, sir. It's time I headed home. Where did your boy get to? He's a good lad, that one.'

The balladeer shook out the dust from his worn canvas shoes, patched with old leather, and slipped them on.

'I'll put out the brahmon-charity bowl again tomorrow,' he called out as he left. 'Let's see if that succeeds.'

31

HORIHOR'S ACCOMMODATION WASN'T particularly good. He had managed to secure two rooms in the damp, dark ground floor of a three-storeyed house. Even during the day, anyone coming suddenly out of the rooms was dazzled by daylight for a few seconds. Shorbojoya had never lived in such a joyless place. Their home in Contentment might have been old, but they had large doors and windows to let in unending amounts of air and light, and the walls remained dry throughout the year. This dampness and lack of daylight began giving her regular headaches.

Opu spent as little time as possible at the house. Much like a sapling, his body and mind turned towards sunlight and open spaces. He was raised in such spaces, amidst the sun, rain and wind. The rejuvenating greenness of Contentment's fields, woodlands and sunbathed rivers had surrounded him all his life. He felt strangled in the damp darkness of the rooms. In general, Kashi had disappointed him. Yes, there were imposing houses and temples everywhere, and the roads and carriages had been impressive at first, but where were the woods? How could such a famous place be so bereft of trees? How was he going to gather things to play with?

In the middle of all this, the ballad singer visited Horihor's place again one evening. After some polite catching-up, he asked, 'Where's your son? Doesn't seem to be around . . .?'

'Probably gone outside to play,' supplied Horihor. 'Somewhere around Doshashwomedh Ghat, most likely . . .'

The balladeer began untying something from a knot at the edge of his shawl.

'I've become good friends with your boy,' he told Horihor. 'Had a long chat with him the other day. Said he loved cowries. So when I got this in my bowl the other day, I thought . . . Here, you keep them with you for now. Give them to him when he comes home.'

He held out two large sea cowries to Horihor.

Towards the end of the dry season, Opu pleaded with his father to go to school.

'Everyone here goes to school, Baba! I want to go too. There's a good school just around the corner, at the end of that lane . . .'

Horihor agreed. Though the school was a charitable institution, they did teach English. In all his years, this was only Opu's second experience of classroom learning, the first being his stint at Proshonno Gurumoshai's two-in-one shop and school.

Towards the end of that winter, the ballad singer visited Horihor at home again, this time with a piece of paper.

'Take a look at this,' he said, offering Horihor the document. 'Do you think this will hold up?'

Horihor read the text. It was a document drawn at the behest of one Ramgopal Chokroborti, bestowing ten bighas of his own land—located in the village of Shwogram—to the ballad singer. It was witnessed by so and so, at Dasaswamedh Ghat at Kashi, on such and such date.

'It's like this,' explained the balladeer, when Horihor finished reading. 'Ramgopal Chokkoti was a learned man from Kumure, a village near my ancestral home. Much respected. Now, a few years before he passed away, he said to me, "Ramdhon, my boy, you have nothing. If I donate, say, ten bighas of land to you, will you accept it?" I thought, if such a learned brahmon wants to give me something of his own volition, who am I to refuse? So we made a verbal agreement. But back then, I had planned to live out my days in Kashi. What use did I have for a few acres in a far-off village? So I forgot about it. Now, though, I've been thinking. What's the point of living if there are no sons to carry on the family line? I don't mind telling you, I've actually managed to save some three hundred rupees. If I can manage about two hundred more, I can afford to marry a girl from a shrotriyo brahmon family. But then I'll need the land to make a living. But remember, Chokkoti Moshai's promise had been verbal. What if his sons refuse to believe me? That's why I thought I'd make this document. All of this writing is my own, heh heh. Even the signatures. Those witnesses are just made-up names. Perhaps a written document will convince them. I'm going to try, anyway: go to the sons and say, "Look, boys, your father had willed me this land, so now that I'm back . . ."'

A little later, at the point of taking his leave, he said, 'Oh, by the way, this coming Tuesday is the full moon of the holy bath—Maaghi purnima. The Kashi household of the maharaja of Teota always feeds brahmons on that day. It's close, right next to the Maanmondir.' He stopped for breath, then added proudly, 'They personally invite me every year—send a letter and everything. Good food, too. I was thinking of taking your son along this year. How about it? I can come by on Tuesday evening and pick him up. Tell him it'll be a royal feast!'

On the day of the holy bath, Shorbojoya was amazed to see queues snaking from the direction of the bathing steps at the crack of dawn. She was told that the crowds had been lining up since the middle of the night, making sure that they had the chance of a dip while the auspicious hours lasted. The bathing steps were teeming with both men and women, determined to brave the bitterly cold winter waters. Chants of 'Jai Vishwanath ji ki jai' and 'Bolo Bom!' reverberated through the air.

A little later in the day, Shorbojoya went with the Punjabi woman for her own holy dip. The bathing steps, the shallows at their bottom, the temple area . . . every bit of space was overflowing with men and women, resplendent in their festive finery. Wading through them to reach the water seemed like an impossible task. Above them, the red flag fluttered in the breeze from the spire of the Shoshti temple.

Just before evening, the balladeer arrived to take Opu to dinner at the maharaja's household. Shorbojoya had happily consented to this adventure.

'Aww, poor man, let him take Opu,' she had said to her husband. 'Fellow has no one of his own. Besides he's taken a liking to Opu. Opu says they sit and chat at Doshashwomedh Ghat . . . apparently one day he even bought a papaya for Opu to eat. Let the poor man take him, he seems like a good fellow . . .'

After picking him up from home, the balladeer first took Opu to his own house. It was a mud hut, roofed with earthenware tiles. On one of the inside walls, there was a list of scribblings:

Queen of Siyarsol's house: Reading the Bhagvad . . . 4/-
Musammat Kunta's temple courtyard: Same as above . . . 2/-
Daily allowance: Laalji Dobe . . . 4/-

There wasn't much furniture in the room. One narrow bed, a small tin trunk, an indoor clothesline, a pair of slippers. On the wall, a big garland of lotus blooms hung from a nail.

'Do you want an orange?' the balladeer asked.

Opu nodded easily. For some reason, he felt none of his usual shyness or hesitation with this man. 'Do you have one here?' he asked.

A little later, while peeling the orange, he asked the balladeer, 'Do you know that verse? "May the clouds and rains be timely"?'

'The "Kaale varshatu parjanya"? Of course I know it! I recite it every day. You should come and listen to me some day.'

'How about now? Can you recite it for me now?'

The balladeer launched into the tune. Opu listened, but he felt immediately that his father's rendition of the blessing was far superior. Horihor's voice was naturally musical. The balladeer's voice, on the other hand, was too rough to be good for musical invocations.

The balladeer then showed Opu his collection of things to take home with him: an assortment of clay and stone knick-knacks—dolls, toys, garlands made of small replicas of the holy phallus, pretty stones from the ghat and fields. He showed them to Opu.

'You know how everyone always says, "So what did you bring back from such-and-such place?" Well, I'm taking these to show them what I brought back from Kashi . . .'

A little later, the two of them left the hut for the royal household. After walking down several narrow lanes, the balladeer finally stopped in front of a dark house. The main gate was locked, but a low, narrow door had been left open for people to use. Opu followed the balladeer through the door. The courtyard inside was dark and quiet. Opu felt certain that the building beyond it was deserted—that they had come to the wrong place. The balladeer didn't seem deterred, however. He cleared his throat noisily a few times in the empty courtyard. In response, a figure rose sleepily from a small bed on one of the verandas. Once he located the two figures by the door, he barked something at the balladeer in Hindi. Opu understood nothing of it, but it sounded to him like the man was demanding to know who they were. Even after the balladeer introduced himself, it seemed to Opu the man didn't recognize him; nor, it appeared, was he expecting anyone to turn up that evening. After a while, clearly irritated, he went inside to talk to someone else. He was indoors for such a long time that Opu was certain he would come back to tell them that there had been a mistake, that no one had invited them. 'You can leave right now!' he imagined that irritated voice snapping.

A good fifteen minutes passed before the man finally reappeared. He led them sullenly to a passageway, then gestured for them to sit at a dark corner. A few minutes later, he came back with a couple of shal-leaf plates and a brass tumbler of water. Perhaps the lack of warmth from his host was finally beginning to bother the balladeer, for he took his seat in front of a plate a little hesitantly. Opu, on the other hand, was finally looking forward to the meal. This was a royal household, after all! Who knew what delicacies they'd be served?

The man disappeared once again. A further twenty minutes passed. Just as Opu's anticipation was once again beginning to give way to doubt, he finally reappeared with their dinner. Thick pooris of whole wheat, a tasteless brinjal curry, and enormous laddoos—that was the extent of the royal feast. The laddoos were so hard that Opu couldn't even pierce the surface with his teeth. His spirit was absolutely crushed.

The balladeer, on the other hand, seemed delighted with the meal. He eagerly ate about ten of those thick pooris, then asked for more when the first mound had been decimated. Mistaking Opu's reluctance for shyness, he jovially urged him to keep up.

'Eat up, eat up—don't be shy! They serve such good food here, don't they? These laddoos are great! Thank goodness for my teeth, heh heh! I can still eat these with ease!'

Sensibility is a strange thing. Sometimes we become so inured to even the most blatant disrespect that we fail to notice that it's happening. On the other hand, the slightest thing can tip off even a trusting heart. Opu was only a small boy, but even he could see the clear disdain, the utter lack of respect, that lay behind the 'feast'. The balladeer's innocent joy at the inedible food filled his heart with pity.

'Poor man,' he thought to himself. 'He has no one to feed him . . . that's why he likes these awful laddoos. I'll ask Ma to invite him to lunch one of these days . . . he can have a real meal with us.'

Compassion is one of the central foundations of affection. Without him realizing it, Opu's compassion for the balladeer—a near-stranger—had secured the man a permanent place in his heart, right beside his sister and the child Gulki. All by virtue of the man's pathetic relish at a dreadful meal, dismissively served.

A few days after that evening, the balladeer left Kashi to move back to his village. Horihor took Opu with him to see the man off at Rajghat railway station. As the train pulled out of the station, taking the balladeer towards his new life, Horihor thought about a similar journey he had undertaken almost twenty-two years ago. He had still been a young man then. The balladeer was eight years older than Horihor was now, with the same dream of finally starting his own family. So why did he, Horihor, think of himself as old and burnt out? Clearly, no age was too much if he really wanted to do something.

Standing beside his pensive father, Opu's eyes filled with tears as the train left the station. In the short while that he had known the balladeer, Opu had come to both pity and care for the man. Children's souls are sensitive, and they do sometimes imprint a permanent affection for an older person. Such affection may be rare, but it was that very rarity that made it all the more valuable.

Towards the end of the month of Maagh, Horihor came home one day from his day's work and abruptly collapsed in the courtyard. Shorbojoya was working indoors. When she heard the sound of his fall, she came out running.

'What happened? Why did you . . . ?' she began, but one look at her husband's face stilled the words in her mouth.

Horihor's eyes were bloodshot. His right hand was shaking. As Shorbojoya bent to help him up by his arms, she heard him whispering the same thing over and over, clearly in delirium: 'Where's my boy? Where's my khoka? Where is he?' When she put her palm on his forehead, it burned under her touch.

'Opu is on his way,' she said in a soothing voice. 'Nondo Babu from upstairs had called him . . . probably taken

Opu with him to his shop at the Godhulia crossroads. Don't worry.'

She was mistaken, however. Opu was not in the shop, though he was in the building. He was reading a book outside Nondo Babu's room on the roof. For about a month now, he had built a great rapport with Nondo Babu. It was hard to tell the man's age, but Opu guessed he was a few years younger than his father. His chief attraction, as far as Opu was concerned, was a small library of books in his rooftop room. Opu had slipped into the habit of taking a book from his shelves and reading it on the roof. Though he only did it when Nondo Babu was home, there was a tendril of fear at the back of his mind that the tacit permission to read might suddenly be withdrawn. Something had happened a few days back to put the fear in his head. He had been sitting in a corner of the roof, reading a book, when Nondo Babu had come upstairs, looking for something. When his eyes fell on Opu, he had snapped. 'Hey! Keep my book back!' he had shouted. 'All you people coming in and taking my stuff—and I never find anything when I need it!'

Opu had never touched anything apart from books in that room—certainly nothing Nondo Babu might have been looking for. But ever since then, he had been wary of another scolding. The fear spiked whenever he took a book from the man's shelves.

Nondo Babu went out most evenings: sharply dressed, every hair in place, a fragrance from a bottle sprayed all over his clothes. Once, he'd spritzed a little of it on Opu—it had a wonderful, mesmerizing, lingering smell. On the few evenings that he stayed at home, Opu sometimes went up to his rooftop room to read a little more. But Nondo Babu had a habit of drinking a reddish medicine in the evenings when he stayed at home. It came in a bottle and stayed locked in his cupboard all day. One evening after he had had his medicine, Nondo Babu shouted at Opu for no reason at all. Another evening, Opu had gone upstairs to get a book, only to come face-to-face with another person in Nondo Babu's rooms—a well-dressed woman. That room had a separate set of stairs leading to the road from the other side of the roof, so he had no idea that Nondo Babu had a guest.

When Nondo Babu saw him, he had said, rather sharply, 'You should go downstairs, Awpurbo. I'm now speaking to my elder sister-in-law. She's just stopped by to meet me, and will be leaving soon.'

He had turned back and was about to come down the stairs, when he heard Nondo Babu say, 'That's the renter's son from downstairs. Don't worry, he's a simple child—doesn't really understand anything.'

The one thing Nondo Babu consistently asked Opu about was his mother. He would say things like, 'Why don't you ask your mother to prepare this bunch of betel leaves for me, Awpurbo? My servant has no idea how to properly make paan.'

So Opu would take the betel leaves and beg his mother to prepare them for Nondo Babu. When he took the set back, Nondo Babu would invariably ask, 'So, does your mother ever ask about me? No?'

Opu would climb downstairs and say, 'Nondo Babu is such a nice man, Ma. He always asks about you. He says, "Tell your mother I was asking about her." Such a good man, no?'

Oddly, his mother was never pleased about this.

'Let him ask!' she would snap. 'Unruly child . . . why do you need to go upstairs so often? What do you do up there all afternoon?'

Over the next few days, Horihor's fever came down a bit. When he heard Opu come back from school and put down his books, he would call out, 'Come sit by me for a while, Khoka . . .'

Opu usually sat down and started to chat about school.

'You know, Baba . . .' he confided one day, in a low, shyly pleased voice. 'It's only been two months since I started school, but everyone already likes me a lot. I sit on the first bench every day. Baba, they've taken me on the team to publish the class magazine. I'll show it to you once it's printed.'

Horihor's chest clenched with fierce affection for his son.

One day after school, Opu showed his father a sheet of paper. 'I've written a story, Baba. The school said they'll print it in the class magazine with my name! But Baba, only those that pay two rupees for a subscription will have their writings published. Can I have two rupees, Baba?'

Horihor eagerly took the sheet of paper from his son's hands and began reading the story. He had no idea that his son dabbled in writing. The story was about a prince on a hunt. Horihor thought it was beautiful. He was so overjoyed by his son's hidden talent that he pushed his weak body up on the pillows in an attempt to sit up.

'*You* wrote this, Khoka?'

'Yes, Baba! I've written so many other things! Ghost stories, stories about princesses . . . when we were at home I used to write so many stories and plays in Ranudi's notebook . . .'

But Shorbojoya refused. Her husband's illness had already drained their meagre savings. She was not prepared to waste any money on printing things on paper. Horihor had to invest a great deal of effort to convince her.

'Give the money to him,' he said. 'He really wants to have his story printed—let him have it. As soon as I get well, I'll start the Bhagvad reading at the Thakurs' again. They'll give me ten rupees for it, they said . . .'

A couple of days later, however, Opu came to his father after school, pouting.

'It won't happen, Baba. They said at school that the printing people have been asking for more money. So now they'll only print things by those who pay a four-rupee subscription.'

The dismay on his son's face pierced Horihor's heart. He tried to distract his son with talk of other things for a while. Then, in a low voice, he asked, 'Is your mother around, Khoka?' When Opu confirmed that she wasn't, he took a set of keys from under the pillow.

'See that wooden box? The one that has all my writing things? Open it quietly. How much money is hidden in that corner?'

As Opu clumsily did his best impression of trying to stealthily open a safe, Horihor watched his son with a blossoming warmth. Innocent, innocent—such a wonderfully innocent child! The moon-like paleness of that beautiful forehead, those beautiful eyes . . . all of it inherited from his lovely mother. When he had first brought Shorbojoya home to Contentment, years after their actual wedding, her face had lit up with exactly the kind of relief and joy that now brightened his son's face.

A sudden tide of affection for his son brought tears to Horihor's eyes. Opu was, to him, the rejuvenation of spring. The joy on his face was like the rays of the sun on a clear dawn. In the slight blue of his wide, hopeful eyes, Horihor saw the dreams of his own long-forgotten past—the joyous exultation of young forests on the blue mountains, the echoes of the songs from a forgotten ocean.

Opu turned around from the wooden box.

'Baba,' he quietly whispered. 'There's four rupees there.'

This was Horihor's emergency fund—something his wife didn't know existed. Given the fortuitous absence of his wife, he was now able to tell his son, 'You take that money, Khoka. Go pay your subscription. Just . . . don't tell your mother, all right?'

'I'll show you the magazine when it comes out, Baba,' Opu said happily. 'They said it'll have my full name. Monday after next Monday, then I'll bring it home.'

The next morning, Horihor's fever came back. Alarmed, Shorbojoya called her son. 'Go ask that Nondo Babu if he can come take a look . . .'

Nondo Babu came immediately and took a look.

'Tell your mother he needs a doctor immediately, Awpurbo,' was his pronouncement.

Later that evening, he himself brought a doctor to Horihor's rooms.

'Broncho-pneumonia,' the doctor pronounced after his examination. 'It's from this cold we're having. What he needs is good nursing . . . god, how does one live in this dampness? Awful! Listen, Khoka, you need to bring a bottle to my chamber immediately—I need to send home your father's medicine.'

For the next few days, Opu went regularly to the doctor's dispensary at Dasaswamedh Ghat to bring the medicine. But there wasn't much improvement in his father's health. Horihor grew weaker by the day. What little money the family had managed to save was completely drained by his medical costs and the healthy diet that the doctor insisted he be on. At least a litre of milk and several fruits—that was his injunction to keep Horihor from becoming weaker. He had also prescribed a few foreign medicines—those alone had cost three-and-a-half rupees. Shorbojoya was completely lost. In this strange land, with no familiar faces to help her, she had no idea how to pay for any of these things, or indeed for the daily necessities of her household.

And on top of everything else, she had to endure a new unpleasantness. The inside of her kitchen was visible to anyone who stood by the inner wall of the roof and peered downstairs. It wasn't that she hadn't noticed Nondo Babu peeking at her from the vantage point of his rooftop room, but things had really begun to get out of hand after Horihor's relapse. He now used the flimsiest of pretexts to come into their ground-floor rooms several times a day. In the beginning, at least, he used to conform to the civility of speaking to her through Opu. But lately he had started addressing her directly, and with a familiarity that he hadn't remotely earned. At first, Shorbojoya had been so consumed with her husband's illness that she hadn't thought much of the man's frequent visits. Indeed, she had been grateful that this near-stranger had taken an interest in her family in their hour of such terrible need. But increasingly, she felt that he was pushing things too far, taking liberties that didn't sit at all well with her. A few days after Horihor's relapse, for example, Nondo Babu had bypassed calling out to her from the common courtyard or from Horihor's room, and had come straight into her kitchen, carrying a bunch of betel leaves.

'The servants cannot make paan at all, sister-in-law!' he had complained jovially, as if he and Shorbojoya shared the kind of relationship that allowed such proximity. 'What's left in life if a man cannot get a good paan in his own home?

Here, make these for me—let me have some good paan for a change.'

Shorbojoya had been fine with even this, at least in the beginning. Truth be told, she'd felt a little pity for this lonely man, living alone so far away from his homeland. But then his behaviour began to very obviously cross the boundaries of acceptability. Lately, he had begun bringing bunches of betel leaf into the kitchen, and instead of putting it down, holding it out at her. Clearly, he wanted her to walk up to him and take it out of his hands. When she didn't comply, he admonished her, as if the awkwardness was somehow her fault. 'Arre! What's wrong now? Come take these, sister-in-law!'

If only Opu stayed home, Shorbojoya would have felt safer. But that crazy boy of hers could barely be kept indoors. And Nondo Babu seemed to know exactly when Opu was out and Horihor was unconscious in the other room. He would come at precisely those times to 'see the patient', then find excuses to stay for at least another hour. He'd hover about Shorbojoya, dishing out such platitudes as, 'Don't be scared, sister-in-law. I'm always here for you. If you need anything—even if Awpurbo is not at home—just come upstairs to let me know. What is politeness in times of trouble? Eh, this paan doesn't have enough lime . . . oh, don't bother with the leaf stalk, just smear some lime on your finger and give it to me.'

Whenever he came to, Horihor would search desperately for his son. He would try to lift his weak body off the bed to look for his always-missing child. 'Opu! Where's Opu? Where's my son?' he would call hoarsely, voice shaking with panic.

Shorbojoya would come running to pacify him. 'He'll be home soon. That crazy boy is always out of the house! Can't get him to sit in one place for a second. Probably playing at the ghat once again.'

Later, when Opu came home, she would roundly tell him off. 'Why can't you stay home and sit by your father? What royal mission do you have at the bathing steps? Poor man—goes mad searching for his son whenever he's awake. But does the son care? No! Playing is more important! Go—go sit by your father right now. Run your hand down his chest and head. Give the poor man some comfort in his illness . . . or is that too much to ask of you?'

Embarrassed, Opu would drag his feet to sit next to his father. But after only a little while, he would begin to feel bored and restless.

'This is so unfair!' he would complain to himself. 'Like I have no games to attend to, or friends to play with? It's Baba who is ill, not me . . . why am *I* not allowed to go out?'

The biting cold of the damp room would soon numb his legs. Images of good times that could be had outside in the bright sun would fill his mind, making the dark dampness of the room all the more unbearable. The rippling water, the crisp fresh breeze, the crowds of well-dressed men and women . . . Poltu, Gulu, Shubeer, Potol, Poltu's older brother . . . he would recreate the entire Dasaswamedh Ghat in his mind. There was going to be a boat race this evening, he would suddenly remember; beginning from the peacock-headed boat of the king of Ramnogor, at four in the afternoon. Embarrassment and guilt forced him to stay at home, but he was bitter about every moment of it.

One morning, Shorbojoya suddenly asked her son, 'Do you know the alms house next to the white building?'

'No?'

'What? You've been in Kashi all these months and haven't eaten at an alms house even once? Silly boy—don't you know it's a blessing to eat at an alms house? You must try it!'

'But why, Ma?'

'Didn't I just say? It's a blessing! Go straight to that alms house today after you finish your bath at Doshashwomedh Ghat, do you hear me? Have your meal there.'

Later that afternoon, when Opu came back after having his lunch at the alms house, he saw his mother sitting in the kitchen, eating something out of a single bowl. Shorbojoya's first instinct was to hide the bowl, but Opu had already come too close. If she tried hiding, he might suspect something. So she said in a casual voice, 'So did you eat? What did they feed you?'

Opu saw that his mother was eating raw soaked lentils.

'Ew, horrible!' he said. 'Some inedible gourd curry . . . and I got so tired of just sitting and waiting. And the people eating there had such dirty clothes! I'm never going back to an alms house. I don't need divine blessings . . . why're you eating raw lentils, Ma? Do you have a ritual or something today?'

'Arre, don't you remember? It's the Koluichondi ritual today. That's why . . . anyway, I really like these soaked lentils. Do you want some for dinner?'

There was no cooking that night, either.

'Why don't you try some of these soaked lentils?' his mother asked. 'Go on, give it a try. You'll like it. I didn't feel like cooking tonight. And anyway, given how much you eat—just a few grains of rice!—I didn't think you'd eat anything after a few mouthfuls of soaked daal.'

The next afternoon, Nondo Babu gave a bunch of betel leaves to Opu. 'Tell your mother to prepare them for me,' he said.

Shorbojoya was sitting in the room next to Horihor's, preparing the paan, when Nondo Babu's footsteps could be heard entering her husband's room. After only a few seconds, he left that room and came into the adjoining room. After a full night of staying up with Horihor, Shorbojoya had been drowsy that afternoon. She jerked up when she heard someone come in, and then tried to hurriedly adjust the loose end of the sari over her head.

Standing in front of her, Nondo Babu asked, 'Is the paan ready, sister-in-law?' Shorbojoya wordlessly held up the plate of prepared betel leaves to him. Instead of taking the plate, Nondo Babu simply picked one up and put it into his mouth, as if Shorbojoya had been offering the plate to him as a hostess.

'You put too little lime in the paan, sister-in-law,' he said. 'Here, move a little, let me take some myself.'

The container of lime was near Shorbojoya's lap. There was no one else at home in that quiet afternoon—Opu was out somewhere, as usual, and Horihor was unconscious under the influence of his medicines. Despite her drowsiness, Shorbojoya suddenly felt that Nondo Babu, under the pretext of taking some lime, was coming far too close to her. Letting out an involuntary cry, she quickly stood up and stumbled out of the room. She felt like a flash of lightning had just gone through her body. Shaking, she looked at Nondo Babu and pointed at the stairs.

'Go upstairs—now!' she said in an unsteady, intense voice. 'Never come to our rooms again! If I see you again, I swear I'll kill myself. Why do you keep coming here? Never, ever come to us again!'

After Nondo Babu left, Shorbojoya almost collapsed from exhaustion and helplessness. Here she was: a woman on her own in a foreign land, with a sick man in the next room unable to get up. There wasn't a single familiar face around, not even one person they could turn to. The last penny in the house had long been spent. Her son was only eleven years old—and an immature, innocent eleven at that. And now this new trouble. What was she to do?

After much thinking, Shorbojoya decided to go upstairs. The Punjabi woman who lived in the rooms above seldom came down, and though she had invited Shorbojoya once or twice to her rooms, Shorbojoya's total lack of Hindi—despite almost six months in Kashi—meant that the friendship hadn't really developed. But now, with no one else to turn to, Shorbojoya went up to her rooms and broke down in tears, while narrating the afternoon's incident. It turned out that the woman was called Surajkunwari. Both she and her husband were from the Rewalsar district of Punjab. The husband was employed by the railways as an overseer. Surajkunwari was not a young woman, but with her fair complexion, large eyes and robust frame, she looked considerably younger than her actual years.

'Don't be afraid, sister,' she reassured Shorbojoya. 'You don't need to live in fear of that man. If he ever tries anything again, you just let me know. I'll get my husband to cut that lecher's nose off!'

A few days passed. Shorbojoya had fallen asleep on the floor in the afternoon, after several nights of staying awake to keep an eye on Horihor. A ray of sunshine from the northern window had lit up the courtyard. Opu had optimistically planted marigolds in a few earthen pots, and some flowers had finally begun to sprout, almost in exasperation at his hopes. A kitten lay curled up next to one of the pots, basking in the sun. Opu was home that afternoon. He was sitting next to his father's bed. Horihor had been feeling better that morning, and the doctor had come by and given them hope that this might be a sign he was about to shake off the persistent illness. He was still very weak, though. At the moment, he was in one of his phases of near-unconscious sleep. Suddenly, he opened his eyes, looked straight at Opu for a while, and mumbled something. Opu thought his father was asking him to come closer. Once he came closer, Horihor enveloped his son in his weakened arms, then lay silently staring at his young face for a long while. Opu was a little surprised, for he had never seen such a look in his father's eyes before.

Around ten at night, after everyone had long gone to bed, a sudden noise woke him up. The room was lit by a single flickering lamp. His mother was deep asleep on the floor . . . and a strange noise was coming from his father's mouth. Suddenly, Opu was very scared. The cobweb-covered rafters, the damp floor, the biting cold, the fumes from the doused charcoal fire—everything came together to make the inside of the room seem like a scene from a nightmare. When would his father get better? He couldn't wait for things to return to normal.

Towards the end of the night, he woke up again to his mother's frantic shaking. 'Opu! Opu! Wake up! Quick, call the Hindustani woman from upstairs—your father's not well!'

The strange noise from his father's mouth had grown louder. Opu ran out of the room, still half asleep, to get Surajkunwari from upstairs.

At four o'clock that morning, only a little while after Surajkunwari came down, Horihor closed his eyes for the last time.

In those wet, monsoon-ridden, fog-encrusted days, sunlight sometimes seemed like a figment of one's imagination—something out of an impossible dream. Clouds and darkness surrounded the land, the only company for an infinite future of cold misery. Spring seemed like a forgotten dream on the distant horizon. Summer was barely a memory. It felt impossible that a bright happiness would ever return.

Shorbojoya lived within an envelope of impenetrable darkness. She could see no road through it, find no friends in that hopeless mist. She was certain it would never be lifted again—not even when the real sun shone through the skies. She now always saw the darkness of a vast, horizon-spanning cloud of an untimely monsoon behind it.

The Punjabi overseer, Zalim Singh, and his wife turned out to be really good neighbours. Zalim Singh missed work for the day so he could walk around the local Bengali neighbourhoods and round up enough people to fulfil the cremation rituals. A few monks from the local branch of the Ramkrishna Mission also arrived to help once they heard about the death.

The cremation took place just above the river, beside the steps of Manikarnika Ghat. After he lit the pyre, a freshly bathed Opu stood shivering in cold westerly winds. Nondo Babu and one of the Ramkrishna Mission volunteers had draped a shawl over him, but he barely felt the warmth. It was late in the day. The red rays of the sun shone off the tops of surrounding stone temples. Bewildered and exhausted, Opu felt oddly unmoored from his surroundings. All he could think of was his father as he had grown used to seeing him at this time of the day: sitting in front of an eager audience near the bathing steps, concluding the day's reading with a musical benediction in that eternally familiar, comforting voice:

May the clouds and rain be timely
May the earth blossom with plenty
May the land be free of discontent
May the good people live without fear . . .

The father that they had brought earlier today to Manikarnika Ghat to cremate, the father defeated by illness and the many ravages of life . . . Opu did not know that man. That man was a stranger to him—almost part of a dream. The man that he knew as his father—the man he had relied upon all his life without question, the man with the familiar, reassuring, smiling face . . . that man was not on that pyre. No, *that* man—his father—was sitting somewhere else, above the rushing river water, singing a benediction to the land in the forlorn strains of the Purbi.

May the clouds and rains be timely
May the earth blossom with plenty
May the good people live without fear . . .

32

A MONTH PASSED. Shorbojoya lived in a constant state of hopelessness, fear and hardship. She thought constantly about different ways to stay afloat with her son, but nothing remotely useful came to her. Throughout it all, the temptation of returning to the soothing familiarity of Contentment kept popping into her mind, but each time she squashed it mercilessly. Going back wasn't an option. First, they had nothing left in Contentment except the dilapidated old house, for all their land and possessions had been sold to either meet debts, or to finance their move to Kashi. Second, for a month before she left, Shorbojoya had taken great pleasure in painting the picture of her family's imminent success to all the women and girls of the village. The stagnant little pond of Contentment didn't have the wherewithal to understand her husband's true worth, she had explained loftily, but the world outside was simply dying to bestow him with wealth and honour. It wouldn't even take a full year, she had predicted, for their poverty to turn into a life of plenty.

That had been last Choitro—less than a year ago. How could she go back to that neighbourhood now, newly widowed and completely penniless? The very idea made her want to melt into the ground in shame and embarrassment at herself. She couldn't bear to look into familiar eyes. No, she was not going to go back to Contentment. Whatever happened, she was going to stay here. Even if she had to beg on the streets with her son by her side, at least there would be no one to see her, no one to know who she was.

But then, at the end of the month, a new avenue opened up. A gentleman from Kedar Ghat came to the Ramkrishna Mission, asking after brahmin women in need of work. A rich Bengali family was looking for a woman from their own caste to move into their house and help with domestic chores. After some back and forth, the Mission decided to recommend Opu and his mother to the gentleman. When Shorbojoya heard the news, she felt like she had finally sighted land after months of being cast away. Two days after this, the gentleman sent word that mother and son should prepare to leave Kashi permanently, for the employing family had only been in the city for a visit. They would be leaving for their hometown soon, and needed their new employee to travel with them.

The hometown house turned out to be an enormous yellow mansion. Opu had seen several enormous multi-wing mansions in Kashi, with several verandas and courtyards. This house was exactly like those. Shorbojoya entered the house behind the long line of travelling family and staff, trying to make herself small and unnoticeable. When the group finally made its way to the inner wings, a roll of cheer went up. Not for her and her son, but for the people ahead—family members and relatives who had just returned from Kashi after a long stay.

Once the first peal of exclamations abated and the crowd dispersed a little, the mistress of the household came to meet Shorbojoya. A rather plump, pleasant-faced woman, it was obvious she had been quite a beauty in her youth. When Shorbojoya bent down to touch her feet, she said, 'Bless you, child, bless you . . . poor girl, to be widowed at this age—is this your son? Lovely boy. What's his name?'

Another woman of the household said, 'So are you originally from Kashi? No? Oh, then did you . . .?'

All the scrutiny began to close in around Shorbojoya. She mumbled her answers half-heartedly, barely able to look up at the group gathered around her. When one of the upstairs' maids finally delivered her to the tiny ground-floor room assigned to her and her son, she breathed her first sigh of relief in the house.

The next day, she formally joined the household as a cook. There were four or five cooks already employed by the family, to handle the daily duties of the many different kitchens: the fish kitchen, the vegetarian kitchen, the milk room, the sickroom kitchen, the kitchen for staff and visitors . . . and a few more. Shorbojoya gave up on trying to count the number of maids and servants employed to keep just the kitchen complex functioning smoothly. Although part of the inner wings, the kitchens were housed together in a separate building, and ruled by the brahmin maids and cooks. The women of the household stopped by once, in the morning, to lay out and explain the tasks for the day. Beyond that, they were seldom seen in the kitchen complex.

Shorbojoya had always believed herself to be an excellent cook. So when the cooks and maids began discussing which duties she could be assigned, she said, with some confidence, that she could look after the vegetarian cooking for the family. This led to barely hidden smirks.

'You want to cook for the masters?' the senior cook Mokkhoda asked, grinning derisively. 'That'll be the day!'

Then she called out to the kitchen maid Panchi to explain Shorbojoya's ridiculous ambition in detail. 'O Panchi, have you heard what this lady from Kashi's been saying? She wants to start here by being in charge of the masters' curries! What was your name again, my dear? I keep forgetting these little details . . .'

Their overt contempt and mockery nearly crushed Shorbojoya to the core, but in a few days, she realized that her public shaming had, in fact, done her a favour. With skills developed to suit a rural, poverty-plagued kitchen, she would have been utterly lost in this household's expectations of vegetarian cooking. Never in all her life had she seen anyone mix such piles of sugar into thin gravies, or known that there was such a thing as cabbage 'fritters'.

The mistress of the household had taken good care of Shorbojoya for the first two months. She asked after her often, and assigned only light kitchen work to her. But once Shorbojoya had settled into the household, her duties increased to match the rest of the kitchen staff. It was harder than she'd ever have imagined. To meet the needs of the household, the kitchen fires remained stoked from early morning till two in the afternoon. Shorbojoya had never had to work such long hours, and that in such constant high heat. By the time her duties were done, she was too drained to even eat her lunch. The other cooks hid bowls of fish and curries from the main kitchen for themselves; Shorbojoya could barely eat the simple food that was put in front of her.

The scale of things in the kitchens continued to astonish her, even after she had been part of the household for a while. Using three litres of oil *per day* seemed like the stuff of fables to her—too unreal for real life, at least as she had known it so far. Working in the kitchens amidst this unbelievable excess felt like living permanently in the middle of a festival. Yet there was very little in the festival that was joyous. One day, unable to take an enormous pot of boiling rice off the flames by herself, she called out to Mokkhoda for help. Mokkhoda promptly turned away, pretending not to have heard. Shorbojoya waited a few minutes, but when the pot of rice—fine-grained, for the family's lunch—came close to charring, she tried to take it off the flames by herself . . . and immediately splashed her foot with boiling starch water. The mistress of the house reassigned her to the bread room that very evening, and gave her leave to only do light work till her foot healed.

The room she'd been assigned to live in with Opu was on the ground floor, in the western corner of the house. It was right off the veranda, just like the rooms upstairs. But unlike the upstairs' rooms, the ground-floor rooms were so low, so dark, so damp, and so permanently smelly that even their room in Kashi would have been a significant improvement on them. The owners of the house did not consider them fit for human habitation, and had therefore distributed them amongst their cooks, maids and servants.

While his mother worked, Opu spent his first few days walking along the upstairs veranda, looking into the family's rooms. They were dazzlingly beautiful, all of them. The chairs were all fitted with thick cushions. The tables gleamed with regular cleaning and polishing. Had he dared to go inside, he was fairly certain he could have seen his reflection on all of them. The floors were covered with thick carpet. They used to have woven carpet-mats in Contentment, but these were far superior to those, thicker and softer even from a distance. And then there were the mirrors. Enormous pieces of framed glass, so large that even from the doorway Opu could see his whole body reflected in them. How on earth did these people find glasses that big? The question puzzled him for days. Did they take several normal mirrors and glue them together?

There was one room along the upstairs veranda that was almost always locked. Opu wanted to desperately know what it contained. The maids and servants occasionally opened its door and windows to air it out, and after several futile visits, Opu finally found himself in front of it on an airing-out day. The room was amazing! The walls were covered with lots and lots of paintings. Large doll-like things, made of stone, were scattered across the room. And, of course, there were enormous mirrors that reflected the room back to itself. Large chairs fitted with deep cushions were neatly arranged in groups throughout the room. Opu had lost himself in the wonder of the mystery room, when the upstairs' steward Chotu Khansama stormed in, furious at the intrusion. 'Who the hell are you?' he demanded. 'How dare you come in?'

Opu would certainly have been given a sound beating that day had it not been for a maid who was passing by. 'Hey Chotu, let him go—his mother works here,' she called out to the steward. 'Let him look, it isn't harming anything.'

Once the various groups of residents were done with their lunches, Shorbojoya finally had leave to go to her room. She had a lie-down during this break, before the evening shift began in the kitchen. This was also the only time during the whole day when mother and son could talk to each other in peace. Since joining this household, Shorbojoya had felt a distance grow between her and her darling boy. Work, work, work all day—that was her new life. She never even had time to look up, much less seek out her child. And by the time she was able to return to the room at night, Opu was usually fast asleep. Which is why the afternoons were so precious to her; her heart thirsted for this little slice of the day, when she could see her son and talk to him.

So when she heard footsteps at the door one afternoon, Shorbojoya sat up eagerly. 'Opu, is that you? Come in!'

It wasn't. Bamni Mashi, a senior member of the kitchen staff, came through the door. Shorbojoya immediately stood up and greeted her with respectful warmth. Though employed in the kitchen, Bamni Mashi was distantly related to the family, so it was probably best to be on good terms with her. Bamni Mashi accepted her invitation and sat down, but didn't return her smile. She had come to the new cook to vent safely about the many wrongs done to her by the ungrateful family, not to socialize.

'What an awful scene our eldest daughter-in-law made today!' she began, referring to the mistress of the household. 'How was I even at fault? I mean, you were in the bread room all along, you saw me putting down the fish and ghee, right? I thought perhaps a curry with the leftover cabbage . . . I mean, if she wanted the cooked fish to be eaten with polau instead of rice she could just have sent word—I would have made it differently then. Such an insult—and in front of everybody! I'm telling you, it's all that maid Shodu's fault. Beloved mole of the upstairs ladies, that one—has the mistress's ear! Takes the littlest details of the kitchen upstairs, and makes it sound like seven times a catastrophe!'

Opu had come into the room shortly after Bamni Mashi, but Bamni Mashi's presence meant he couldn't have a private moment with his mother. The conversation carried on in this vein till almost four o'clock, when Bamni Mashi finally felt that she had vented enough to match the injustice she had suffered.

'Well, I'll leave you two to talk,' she said, rising. 'Let me go start the dough for the early evening's meal.'

After Mashi left, Opu came and sat flush against his mother. Shorbojoya touched his chin and grinned.

'What do you do in the afternoons?' she asked gently. 'I barely see you.'

Opu grinned back. 'They're playing the music machine today, so I was in the upstairs veranda, listening.'

This seemed to please Shorbojoya. 'So the masters' children speak to you, then? Do they ask you to sit in the actual rooms?'

'Oh, of course!' Opu said immediately. 'All the time!'

This was a complete lie. None of the masters' children took any notice of him whatsoever. When they put records on the gramophone in the afternoon, he went hesitantly up the stairs, never quite sure whether what he was doing was allowed in this household. Once upstairs, he would stand outside the gramophone room's door and warily listen to the songs. Once the people in the room were done with the music, he would quickly come downstairs again, relieved that no one scolded him.

'And why would they scold me?' he reassured himself. 'It's not like I go inside the masters' rooms. I just stand outside and listen to the songs. I'm sure nobody here minds that. How could they? They're good people.'

The boys of the household routinely ignored him. He had tried to hang about the periphery of their activities, perhaps with some faint hope of being included, but they never even acknowledged his presence. The other day, he was watching four of the boys—Romen, Tebu, Shomeer and Shontu—play a game on a large, flat board. Carrom, they called it. You had to play it by sliding flat black tablets on the board. In his opinion, the hopscotch they played back in Contentment had been a far better game.

At the beginning of Boishakh, the house came alive for the wedding of the eldest master's eldest daughter. Relatives began arriving, with family from Gaya, Munger, Allahabad, Calcutta, Kashi and other places. All of these families brought their own personal maids and servants along, and the empty rooms on the ground floor filled up fast. All night long, there would be someone or another chatting and laughing, both upstairs and downstairs.

The mistress of the household cancelled Shorbojoya's bread-room duties for the next few days. She, along with the upstairs maid Mokkhoda, was put in charge of edible gifts brought by the relatives, or sent by friends and associates of the family.

'Separate the food by type, Awpurbo's mother,' the mistress instructed. 'If it's sweets, keep them in the bread-room shelves. But if it's fruits or anything delicate, send it straight upstairs with my maid Shodu. Or keep it aside for Bamni Mashi to bring in after the early evening meal is served.'

Shorbojoya lost count of the number of gift trays that had come from the groom's family alone. The shelves of the bread room were filled to breaking with sweets. Even rarer presents, such as little silver bowls of sandalwood paste, accumulated in a pile of fifteen or sixteen. It wasn't hot enough for mangoes, yet she had to keep aside one of the large cane baskets for mangoes alone. While piling the day's presents into Bamni Mashi's waiting hands, Shorbojoya thought of her son.

'Poor boy—having to eat his two fistfuls of rice in one corner of the bookkeepers' workroom,' she thought with sorrow and some bitterness. 'Can't give him two pieces of fish, or a bowl of the fancy curries, or even a ladleful of milk.

That bitch Shodu will immediately fly upstairs to complain! But of course, *her* son gets all the best bits from the masters' kitchen . . .'

The crowds really swelled on the day of the actual wedding. The groom and his wedding party had arrived by the morning train, and had been put up at a house a short distance away to rest for the day. In the evening, they arrived at the house in an enormous formal procession, with great pomp and fanfare. By then, the outer courtyard was teeming with guests. Carpets had been rolled out so shoes didn't touch the ground, and a canopy of gold-laced blue satin stood shielding the guests from the evening sky. Thick, three-strand garlands of Arabian jasmine connected the bamboo poles holding up the canopy. The smell of the flowers mingled with the aroma of rose water and foreign perfume, which was being spritzed into the air and on guests. A throne-like chair covered in gold-edged red velvet stood at one end of the courtyard; this was where the groom was meant to sit till he was called for the actual wedding ceremony. Several thickly cushioned couches surrounded the groom's chair, reserved for members of his wedding party.

Opu missed most of the evening's festivities, for he had fallen asleep in his room. He had only gone inside the house once, and that to look for his mother. At that point, the inner wing had been in the middle of celebrating pre-wedding rituals with the bride, and it had been impossible to locate his mother amongst the laughter, music and crowds of unfamiliar women moving around in brightly coloured Banarasi saris. On his way out, he had seen Oruna, the youngest master's daughter, instructing servants to bring the large living-room organ to the inner wing. That was the last he saw of the wedding festivities.

Two days after the wedding, the house hosted an amateur theatre performance. A raised stage was constructed in one corner of the outer courtyard, richly appointed with roses and orchids. The five-hundred-branch chandelier had been unhooked from indoors and set up above the stage. The whole household thrummed with eager anticipation for the evening.

Opu didn't know what a theatre was, but it was clear to him that whatever it was, it was going to be a spectacle. So he went into the outer courtyard as soon as evening began to turn to night, and secured himself a seat at the front. Slowly, the seats behind him began to fill up. The musicians began warming up, and as the evening deepened, they began playing their opening set. It was almost time for the drop scene to go up. Just before the family and their guests made their entrance, the bookkeeper Girish Ghosh came by for a final inspection. He didn't know Opu by name, but his position in the household was apparent at a glance.

'What are you doing in the front rows?' snapped Girish, bearing down on him. 'Get out, get out quickly! The masters are probably on their way even now, we barely have time . . .'

Opu was immediately terrified, but didn't understand why he had to give up the seat he'd been saving all evening.

'But I've been sitting here for hours . . .' he tried to plead, in a terrified, anxious monotone. 'I came here early so I'd have a good seat . . . Everything's full now, where will I go?'

Girish Ghosh lost his temper. He leaned forward and began yanking Opu by his wrist.

'You mouthy little servant's son! Sitting in the front rows like family, bold as brass! We have to find him another good seat or he won't move—the nerve of you! I don't care where you park yourself, get out of that seat now! Go sit behind that pillar for all I care. Useless kitchen sprog!'

The household manager was passing by. Hearing raised voices, he came in and said, 'What's the trouble, Girish?'

'Look at this troublemaker here, Manager Babu,' Girish Ghosh said instantly. 'He's sitting in the family's seats and refusing to move. And here I am, waiting to show the Chondonnogor branch into these seats . . .'

'Give him a couple of whacks and toss him out,' the manager advised casually. 'That'll sort him out.'

Opu staggered blindly out of the audience. He wanted the earth to open up and swallow him whole. Everyone in the makeshift theatre arena was looking at him, waiting to see how the little kerfuffle would end. At first, he thought he'd start running flat out till he was out of the range of those mercilessly curious eyes. But in the end he could only drag himself to the shaded area behind a pillar before collapsing. His legs, his arms—his entire body was shaking. It was as if someone had turned up his sense of shame, anxiety and fear to their maximum capacity, and his body couldn't stand the strain. Suddenly, it occurred to him that the upper verandas of the inner wing had a clear view of the theatre courtyard. Bamboo screens had been placed around areas to make sure that the women could watch the theatre without joining the men in the audience. The area was currently swarming with beautifully dressed people, laughing and talking to each other. Was his mother hidden in their midst? Did she see him being publicly humiliated? The thought made him want to curl into himself even further.

After a few minutes of agony, the shaking finally subsided. Opu calmed himself down enough to peek out from behind the pillar. The courtyard was even fuller than it was earlier. Manservants were everywhere. The women and their guests were crowded behind the bamboo screens.

Most of the household's maids and cooks had gathered in the ground-floor veranda that went around the courtyard, eagerly watching the goings-on. They must have all witnessed his humiliation—every last one of them. Goodness knew what they thought of him now! Honestly, how was he to know those seats were reserved for the masters? He hid behind the pillar again, trying to convince himself that no one had actually recognized him. The house was swarming with relatives, daily guests, their servants and lots and lots of tradespeople. Surely no one would have recognized him in the melee!

The performance began. For all his earlier enthusiasm, Opu barely heard a word of it. The scenes, the cheering of the crowd, the floating chatter of gatekeepers and servants from beyond the courtyard, the stuffy heat of the arena—nothing registered with him. When Chotu, the upstairs steward, began distributing paan from a silver swan-shaped tray to the first rows, he immediately thought of his mother, and his stomach dropped once again. He craned his neck from behind the pillar and forced himself to look around, scanning the courtyard and verandas once more for his mother. What if one of the other servants had seen his public shaming, and rushed indoors to spread the mortifying gossip? How would he face his mother then?

He need not have worried. His mother was in a completely different part of the house at the time, and too exhausted from the day's long hours to have the time to listen to gossip.

33

THOUGH SHE NOW had a certain degree of security, living in someone else's house as a servant was a bitter pill for Shorbojoya to swallow. For all her poverty and hardships, she had always been independent—the sole mistress of her own household. Their house in Contentment might have been dilapidated, and the rooms in Kashi damp and dark, but she was no less a queen of those realms than the rich women upstairs were of this household. Her authority in both places had been absolute.

But here? Here she was the lowest of the low—the smallest cog in an enormous wheel. She had to watch her every step, mind her every word, constantly worry about leaving the slightest possible room for complaint . . . and not just with the masters. As the newest drone, she had to make sure she was on the good side of the senior servants and maids.

Never in her life had she had to work so much, for so little. The hours were unrelenting and the work back-breaking, but was there ever a word of appreciation? Of acknowledgement, even? No. On the rare occasion that a token of appreciation arrived from upstairs, it was casually tossed down as charity. One had to kneel to pick it up, or risk offending.

It was intolerable, this life. But what could she do? Where else could she go? Who could she seek shelter from? How else, apart from domestic work, would she be able to stay on her feet? Perhaps she was doomed to end up like Bamni Mashi, every hour of the rest of her life consumed by someone else's kitchen.

What a dreadful thought. But she simply didn't have anywhere else to go.

The wedding celebrations were still going on. Tonight was the night of the women's dinner. Cars bearing female friends and relatives had been pulling up at the back gate all evening. The broad marble staircase just inside the main entrance at the back—the one that led directly to the inner wings—had been lined with a thick blue floral carpet. The staircase and verandas of the women's wing were lit like day with gas lamps. Two glittering gas chandeliers warmed the stair landing and the middle of the veranda. The family's younger daughters waited just inside the main back gate to welcome guests and direct them to the stairs. Two of the family's daughters-in-law were also in attendance, greeting guests at the foot of the stairs and making small talk. Bourani, they were called in this household: the bride queens of the household. Once directed to the women's wings, guests floated up the stairs in their glittering finery. Some carried themselves with slow, stately dignity, bestowing gracious smiles upon the crowd. Others flitted up in groups, surrounded by peals of tinkling laughter. But every single one of them looked like they had stepped out of a dream: beautiful, graceful, wonderfully elegant.

Opu had been watching from the ground-floor veranda. This was the first time he had witnessed such a spectacle. The wedding festivities had been extravagant, but he'd fallen asleep that night—the auspicious wedding hour had been too late for him to stay up. One of the family's daughters, Shujata, caught his eye the most. She descended the stairs at regular intervals, greeting guests and tossing affectionate complaints at new arrivals.

'At eight in the evening, Monidi! We've been waiting all evening . . . isn't our sister-in-law from Medlar Gardens with you?'

The beautiful woman thus greeted smiled back. 'I had the car ready to go at six. But leaving the house and its responsibilities isn't easy . . . you know how it is, my dear.'

Shujata was wearing a sleeveless, China-crepe blouse the colour of a purple orchid. It contrasted beautifully with her fair skin. As the guest began going up the stairs, Shujata matched pace with her, putting her fair, perfectly rounded arm around the woman's shoulder, and tilting her head to rest lightly on the woman's right shoulder.

'Ma said that our Medlar Gardens sister-in-law is going to go to Calcutta this coming month,' she said, as the two went up the stairs. 'She heard it last Wednesday. Has anything more been planned since?'

The second-eldest daughter-in-law of the household appeared at the top of the staircase. She was richer in years than the other women greeting the guests—probably above thirty. Her beauty was breathtaking. Unlike most of the crowd, she was dressed simply; a silk sari the colour of lilies, bordered in red, and a thin gold chain around her neck. The loose end of the sari was draped decorously over her head, and secured on one side with a diamond clip. The gold of her chain glittered under the light of the chandelier. Despite her years, her skin was flawless, her fairness the pink glow of milk tinged with vermilion. There was a natural reserve about her, deepened by the recent loss of her brother. The tinge of sadness, coupled with her sombre beauty, lent her an aura of quiet gravitas, even amidst the cheerful crowds.

Shujata's Monidi stopped when she caught sight of the second-eldest bourani, then eagerly approached her. Once in front of her, however, she seemed somewhat flustered.

'Second-eldest sister-in-law! How are you? I meant to come much earlier this evening . . . all day I've been saying to myself, "Oh, I want to go right now", but . . . Actually we had guests come in really late last night from Ettwa . . . we went to bed really, really late, so . . .'

Opu paid no attention to the conversation. He had been mesmerized by the second-eldest bourani from the moment she had appeared at the top of the stairs. How could a human be this beautiful? None of today seemed real to him. The swarm of beautiful women, the light perfume of fresh-cut flowers, the tinkles of musical laughter . . . it was intoxicating. Why couldn't things like this happen all day, every day?

Despite the crowds, the second-eldest bourani had noticed the boy almost hiding behind a pillar. He was a bit of a mystery. First, he appeared to be alone. And second, he didn't look like he was part of the invited guests. But if he was a part of the household, then why didn't she know him? Perhaps he had arrived while she had been away? Her own family was phenomenally rich, and unlike most other daughters-in-law of the family, she spent a good part of the year in her father's household.

She decided to solve the mystery of the hiding, beautiful child herself. Once at the base of the staircase, she called to Opu.

'Khoka, why are you loitering at the bottom of the stairs? Come upstairs. Where are you coming from?'

Opu had turned, just then, to watch a new set of guests arrive. When he realized the second-eldest bourani was addressing him, his wits completely deserted him. How . . . how was this happening? The most exalted member of the masters' household was speaking to *him*?

Receiving no answer, the second-eldest bourani came closer to the boy. 'Where are you coming from, Khoka?' she asked again, gently.

Opu couldn't decide if he should run away from the veranda, full tilt, or if he should fly up the stairs at her invitation before anyone changed their minds. Willing himself—with considerable difficulty—to stay put, he managed to stumble out a few words.

'I . . . I . . . my mother—we live here.'

The moment the words were out of his mouth, he almost recoiled in fear. Now that she knew he was one of the employee's sons, would the second-eldest bourani demand that the steward throw him out of the area? Would she be furious with him for daring to intrude upon the family's festivities?

But the second-eldest bourani didn't seem the least offended by his status. Instead, she peered at him, trying to puzzle exactly who he was.

'Your mother lives here? Where does she . . . what does she do, do you know? When did you start living with us?'

Only a little reassured, Opu managed to relay the story of his mother's arrival in the household.

The second-eldest bourani must have heard about the new cook once or twice, for she connected the dots after a few seconds. 'Ah, so you're the family that came from Kashi. What's your name?'

Then, taking pity on the fear in his innocent, beautiful young eyes, she said, 'Why don't you come upstairs, Khoka? No need to stand here. Here, come with me.'

Opu followed her up the stairs, feeling acutely self-conscious. He felt like a thief who had been caught, and then invited to take a tour of the house. Once upstairs, he found the least obtrusive corner in the veranda, and quickly pushed himself into it. The entirety of the long, broad veranda had been taken over by the women's festivities. Enormous vulcanite pots of rose bushes and areca palms marked the length of the space, ending in the large organ that had been brought out from the sitting room. After much begging and pleading, the assembled women managed to get a girl out of her seat and on to the small cushioned stool in front of the organ. The girl stalled for a few seconds, lightly pressing a few keys. Then she smiled to herself and started playing the opening bars of a song. She wasn't as good to look at as most of the other women, for her complexion was middling, not fair; but she had a marvellous singing voice. After her, a second girl took the stool to play and sing. She wasn't too pretty, either. Then the second-eldest bourani's daughter, Leela, took centre stage to recite a funny poem. She was a beautiful girl, truly her mother's daughter. And she had a wonderfully sweet smile.

'I wish Ma could've seen this,' Opu thought, watching the women dissolve in laughter at Leela's exaggerated expressions. 'She never gets to see anything of what goes on, stuck in that kitchen of hers. Poor thing—she'll never even know things like this can happen in real life.'

Just then, a loud commotion floated up from the outer courtyard—from the area near the kitchens. Girish Ghosh's voice dominated a confusion of threats and shouting. A few minutes later, Shodu, the upstairs maid, came upstairs, laughing.

'Oh my rotten head! Of all places! Hee hee hee! Inside the belly of his hookah, they said . . . hee hee!'

Some of the invited women leaned forward eagerly, 'What's going on, girl? What?'

'That daily-wage cook . . . who knows where he's from, was hired for the wedding. He was sitting in the veranda of the accountants' dining room, frying luchi—oh, this is too funny! Says, "I need to take a quick break", fills hookah with half a kilo ghee . . . hee hee hee . . . and the steward catches him! Now Ramnihor Singh is working on him . . . dragged him by the hair to the courtyard, hee hee!'

Shorbojoya had been assigned to the fish kitchen that day. Nearly eighty kilos of fish had been delivered to her in the morning, ready to be cleaned, cut and made into perfect, meal-ready fries. She had been sweating over the enormous wok when the trouble first broke, wholly unaware of things outside the hot little room. She only ran out when the shouting began. A thin, dark-skinned brahmin man of about twenty-five or thirty—clad in worn, unwashed clothes—was being dragged into the middle of the outer courtyard. Three or four of the male domestic staff immediately swooped down on him. Within seconds, punches and slaps began landing with brutal precision. From the other kitchen staff, Shorbojoya discovered that this man had been hired for the day to help with the wedding festivities, but had since been caught trying to sneak the cooking-ghee outside using his hookah. From the beating he was being given, it was clear that his crime considered severe . . . but no one seemed to actually care about the stolen ghee. The hookah was lying in one corner of the courtyard, the precious ghee inside spilt on the ground.

Meanwhile, the man's clothes were coming undone in the shower of blows. In a shaking voice, he was trying to convince everyone that carrying ghee inside one's hookah was perfectly normal. That in fact, he always carried ghee in his hookah, and he was merely taking out of the house what was already his. This ridiculous claim seemed to enrage the already-furious bystanders, and the doorman Shambhu Singh inserted himself inside the circle to give the man an almighty shove. The man screamed in terror and went whirling out of the circle, straight towards a corner of the courtyard. His head hit a pillar with a resounding thud. Then, next second, he had collapsed in an untidy heap. A small amount of blood appeared on the ground near his head.

Shorbojoya sidled up to the senior kitchen maid, Khemi. 'Why are they being so harsh, Khemi Mashi? To beat a brahmon this badly . . . poor man . . .'

'You think this is bad?' snarled Khemi. 'Just you wait till they break his bones. Grind them to a powder, they will! He'll rot in jail for this, you mark my words. Trying to rob a tiger's cave . . . he doesn't know what he's . . .'

Shorbojoya looked up as Khemi abruptly swallowed the rest of her words and stood rigidly to attention. An elderly woman was coming down the main staircase at the front of the house, accompanied by the mistress of the household. Two of the household's bouranis followed respectfully behind, in turn followed by two of the family's daughters, Oruna and Shujata.

At almost lightning speed, an awed hush spread over the group of servants and maids. Everyone quickly rearranged themselves such that they were lined, perfectly at attention, all the way along the ground-floor veranda right up to the outer courtyard.

'Who's the lady, Khemi Mashi?' Shorbojoya whispered, confused.

'A real queen of somewhere . . . don't know where,' Khemi the maid whispered back. But Shorbojoya was only half listening. Now that they were closer, she realized that the elderly woman looked familiar. Very familiar, in fact. But where could she have seen her?

After they reached the bottom of the stairs, the mistress of the household indicated that the visiting lady's palanquin should be brought around to the main doorway. It was only then that Shorbojoya noticed that the three or four women bringing up the rear of the little procession were not members of this household. From their attire, they were probably the woman's personal maids, brought along to make sure she was adequately taken care of in someone else's house. In the meantime, the mistress of the household had begun the polite ritual of leave-taking. Broad smiles were generously exchanged, as the women of the household thanked their royal guest humbly for gracing their residence, and their guest, in turn, bestowed gracious thanks and compliments on them.

When the enormous, sixteen-bearer palanquin drew up in front of the front gateway, all the assembled servants and maids dropped to their knees and bent forward to touch their foreheads to the ground. Shorbojoya was astonished at this extreme show of subservience. She wasn't used to seeing humility in this household, not even amongst the domestic staff.

'If these incredibly rich people are bowing and scraping in front of her, she must be some queen!' she thought, as the woman slowly made her way towards her palanquin.

The maids and servants stayed put in their worshipful position till the women settled inside the palanquin, the guards took up position at the front and back of the vehicle, and the bearers finally lifted it off the ground. Only once the palanquin started moving forward did the women of the household turn back towards the stairs, and things began to go back to normal.

'Did you see the whole circus?' Bamni Mashi whispered a few minutes later, in the privacy of the bread room. 'She has her own huge estate, you know . . . donated two lakhs to some college somewhere in the eastern districts of Bengal. Money—it's all about the money. Do you think they care about her? Oh no, it's her money they adore. Otherwise I'm here too—her age, give or take a few years, and their own relative on top of that! Do they care about me? No. It's into the kitchens with me, day in and day out . . .'

Once again, Shorbojoya was only half listening. She had suddenly realized why the elderly queen had looked so familiar. Take away the fine clothes, the jewellery, the regal bearing and the personal maids, and the woman was a striking replica of her elderly sister-in-law, Indir Thakrun. That Indir Thakrun, who had to tie knots over tears in her ancient saris because they had become too fragile for patching. That Indir Thakrun, who used to eat raw hog plums and rice because she had nothing else to put on her plate, whom she had once so brutally insulted over a mere custard apple. What a life that old woman must have led in those last few years—no one to respect her, no one to ask after her . . . thrown out of her own home on that fateful afternoon, that awful, helpless death beside the public road.

At this point, Shorbojoya realized tears were running down her cheeks.

She had no idea whether heartfelt repentance could breach the barrier between the living and the dead. But today, in the wake of this spectacle of wealth, she silently begged her long-departed impoverished sister-in-law's forgiveness for the atrocities she had made the woman endure in her own immature youth.

34

A FEW DAYS later, Opu was passing through the broad ground-floor veranda just as the second-eldest bourani's daughter, Leela, was coming down the stairs.

When she saw him, she called out, 'Hey! Wait a minute. What's your name? Opu, right?'

Opu was rather taken aback. The children of this household never stooped to talk with him—certainly not in such a social way.

'Opu is what I'm called,' he said hesitantly. 'Properly it's Shree Awpurbo Kumar Roy . . .'

Leela ran down the remaining stairs, then ran up to him. Opu realized, up close, that she had a stunningly beautiful face. He had seen beautiful women before; for example, his Contentment neighbours—Ranudi, Awtoshidi, Awmoladi—had all been good-looking. But his idea of beauty had been turned on its head ever since he had arrived at this household. The women here were from a different world altogether! Especially Leela's mother, the second-eldest bourani. Opu had never seen anyone as stunningly beautiful as her. And Leela had inherited those looks. The other day, when she had been reciting funny poems at the women's gathering, he had been so mesmerized by her face that he'd barely heard her actual words.

'When did you come to our house? I didn't see you the last time we returned—I would have remembered.'

'We came in the Falgun . . . this last Falgun.'

'Where from?'

'From Kashi. That was where my father passed away, so we had to . . .'

Opu still couldn't believe his luck. Not only was someone from the actual household finally talking to him—out of their own volition!—but it was the only daughter of its brightest star, the second-eldest bourani. Delight coursed through him.

'Come to my study,' Leela invited. 'My master moshai is supposed to come any minute now. Let's go wait for him in the study.'

Once again, Opu was taken aback. 'Me? You want me to go to your study?'

Leela grinned. 'Didn't I just invite you? Goodness, you really *are* shy! Haven't you seen my study before? It's the room at the other end of the western veranda.'

Leela's study wasn't large, but it was beautifully appointed. Her table was small, round and stone-topped. The two chairs bracketing it were fitted with leather-covered cushions. A large calendar full of pictures hung from one wall, while the others were scattered with framed photographs. There was a small bookcase, and on top of it, a timepiece clock in a green vulcanite shell. Leela opened an attaché case and took out a sheet of transferable pictures—little designs that could be transferred to paper or skin with just a few drops of water and a good scrub.

'Master moshai bought me these,' she said. 'He's going to get me more when I learn division. Do you know how to transfer these pictures?'

'You don't know division?'

'Do you? Have you done division sums before?'

Opu curled his lips in disdain. 'Oh, *ages* ago.' The expression sat beautifully on his handsome face.

Leela laughed. 'Aww, the way you speak! It's funny!' Then she reached forward and put her finger on a little freckle under his lower lip. 'Oh look, you have a freckle. It looks good on you. How old are you? Thirteen? I'm eleven—that's two years younger than you . . .'

Opu said, 'I really like the poem you were reciting from memory the other day. It was funny.'

'Do *you* know any poems?'

'I do. My father had a book . . . I learned a few from that.'

'Let's hear one, then!'

Her voice was so sweet! He had never heard such a lovely voice on a girl before. Without needing to be prompted, he began reciting, nodding his head in time with the rhythm:

If raised to sleep on mats of leaves, or on bundles of hay
By fate
Can a man rest on mattresses and beds
Or in a mosquito net?

Then he looked at Leela and bobbed his head in inquiry. She was laughing so hard that she nearly rolled out of her chair.

'You're so funny! How do you know these things?'

Opu was beyond delighted with this praise. 'It's from Dashu Roy's *Book of Ballads*. Do you want to hear another one?'

Then he looked at the support beams above, riffling through his memory. 'All right, listen to this,' he said after a few seconds, then began nodding in time to the rhythm again:

An ascetic desires only his god; he has no other wish
The lazy thinks of rolls of dice, or a deck of cards' swish.
The rich thinks of his wealth, and of numbers to fudge
The Vaishnav thinks of Jagannath, the fakir thinks of Hajj
The householder thinks only of making his roof stronger
A child thinks of his mother; an animal, its hunger.

Leela didn't understand this poem too well, but she dissolved into laughter again anyway.

'Wait, I'm going to write this down!' she exclaimed.

After she took out a pen from the attaché case, Opu began reciting the poem again. After a few lines, he stopped in confusion.

'How is that pen still writing?' he asked. 'Where's your ink?'

'Oh, this is a fountain pen,' Leela said. 'Haven't you seen one before? You don't need ink—it's all inside.'

Opu took the pen from Leela and examined it. 'This is wonderful,' he said, impressed. 'A pen without ink—who would've thought?'

'Not without ink . . . the ink stays inside. When it runs out, you have to fill it again. Here, let me show you how to do it . . .'

'This is great!' Opu exclaimed. 'Can I see it again?'

Leela put the pen in his palm, then grinned. 'You don't have to give it back,' she said. 'It's a gift.'

Opu was caught so completely off guard that he simply stared at her. Then he tried to give it back, embarrassed. 'I . . . I can't take this,' he said, not looking at Leela.

'Why not?'

'No-o-o . . .'

'But why?'

'Nah.'

Leela looked genuinely hurt by his refusal.

'Why won't you take it?' she said. 'I'll just ask Baba for another one—it's not a problem. Here, show me your hand . . . there, that's your pen now. You can't give it back.'

The whole thing struck Opu as wildly improbable. 'What if someone scolds us?'

'Scold us? Why? For the pen? No one will say anything. I'll tell Ma, "I gave that pen to Awpurbo." Then I'll ask Baba to give me another one. Have you seen Baba? That's his photograph next to the calendar—wait, let me bring it down.'

Leela also took down several other photographs. Then she took out a few books from the bookcase.

'Master Moshai bought me these books,' she said. 'So which school do you go to?'

Opu had gone to a school for a few days in Kashi, but that had been the extent of his formal education.

'I used to go to school in Kashi,' he said. 'Never seen the inside of a schoolroom since then.'

Because he was acutely embarrassed to admit this fact, he said it with a great deal of dismissive bravado, like it was a matter of pride not to have gone to school. Then he pointed to a book that had a lot of pictures. 'Will you let me read this? Just once?'

'Of course! Take it,' Leela said. 'I have many more books with pictures, too. Ma has three years' worth of *Mukul* magazines in her almirah. I'll get those for you, too.'

'I have some books too . . .' Opu ventured. 'Should I bring them here?'

'No,' Leela said, getting up. 'I have a better idea. Let's go to your room!'

Abruptly, Opu wished that he had kept quiet. The room they had been given was bare and damp, their pillow covers were torn, and their old quilt the only thing hanging from the clothes' horse. But Leela insisted.

Once in the room, Opu took out a thin volume from his tin box of books. 'I wrote for this,' he said, grinning with obvious pride. 'Look, here's my name in print.'

Leela leaned forward eagerly. 'Show, show! Let me see!'

It was the school magazine from his school in Kashi. Horihor had not been able to see his son's story in print—the magazine had come out three days after his death. Now, as Leela sat down next to him to read, Opu began following her eyes and reading his own writing, re-savouring the elation at being a published author.

After she finished reading, Leela stared at Opu for a few seconds in open admiration. Then she took the magazine. 'This is really good,' she said. 'I'm taking this with me—I'll show Ma.'

Immediately, Opu's old shyness overcame him. 'No, no . . .' he protested.

Leela took the magazine anyway. 'It says "Abode of Contentment" here,' she said. 'What is this Abode of Contentment?'

'Contentment is our old village,' Opu explained. 'It's where our home is. Kashi was just a place we were in for a year or so . . .'

Just then, the younger Mokkhoda thrust her head inside the room. 'Didimoni, you're here! Oh my rotten head—I've been looking for you all over the house. Your master moshai has been waiting and waiting for you in your study . . . who knew you'd be in this damp, dark room? Come on, come on, let's go back up!'

Leela didn't move. 'You go,' she said, waving dismissively at the maid. 'I'll be coming in a bit.'

'This is not the place for someone like you!' Mokkhoda protested. 'Even we get headaches in these dank holes—how can you even sit here? No no, you come upstairs with me right now. Those north Indian grooms . . . they neither sweep the stables nor wash them. Ugh! You can smell the horses and dung from here. You have to get out of here. Now come on!'

At this steady stream of scolding, Leela lost her temper.

'I'm not going anywhere!' she said vehemently. 'If you don't like it here, then get out. Who asked you to stand here and blab? I'm not going to study today . . . now go tattle to my mother. Out!'

The younger Mokkhoda left in a temper, stomping down the corridor.

'Why did you have to speak to her like that?' Opu asked nervously. 'What if your mother scolds you?'

The next afternoon, Opu was woken from his afternoon nap by someone shaking him. Startled, he snapped out of sleep. He had been sleeping on a long woven mat on the floor. When he opened his eyes, Leela was kneeling next to it, her face alight with amusement.

Grinning broadly at his confusion, she said, 'Is this how deeply you sleep in the afternoons? I called you so many times from outside the door—no movement, no nothing . . .'

Opu sat up hurriedly and began rubbing the sleep out of his eyes with the end of his dhoti.

'Didn't you come down to study this morning?' he said. 'I'd gone there to look for you. I waited, but when you didn't show up . . .'

Leela handed back the magazine she'd taken the previous day. 'I read your story out to Ma last night,' she said. 'Then she read it once more, on her own.'

A shiver of pleasure shot through Opu. The second-eldest bourani had read his story! And then came the wave of bashfulness and embarrassment. Goodness—the *second-eldest bourani* had read his story!

'Come to my study,' Leela said. 'I've brought down bound volumes of *Shokha-Shaathi* for you.'

Opu glanced at the clothes horse in the corner of the room. His only good dhoti was still wet from the wash. The one he was currently wearing was not good enough to be worn outside their little room. So, despite the pull of the magazines, he said, 'I'm not going to go right now.'

'Why not?' Leela demanded, surprised.

Opu didn't say anything, merely pressed his lips together and hid a secretive little smile. He had no idea how beautiful this mischievous expression looked on his handsome face.

'Come on, don't say no!' Leela begged.

Opu didn't say anything this time. He merely smiled again.

'Why're you so stubborn?' Leela exclaimed, exasperated. 'At least tell me why you won't go . . . no, a smile's not going to cut it, you tell me why you won't go!'

Opu still didn't say anything, but he inclined his head towards the clothes horse and grinned.

Leela finally caught on. She went up to the clothes horse and felt the dhoti. 'It's only a little dry,' she said, dejectedly. 'All right . . . you wait here, I'll run and get the book. Have you been using the fountain pen? Doesn't it write really well?'

A little later, the two of them were on their knees on the mat in the little room, flipping through the various volumes in the bound digest. Leela's silk-soft hair brushed Opu's arms, sending a slight shiver down his body. After some time, Leela suddenly looked up and said, 'Do you know how to sing?'

Opu nodded.

'Then sing a song.'

'How about you? Do you know any songs?'

'A few . . . didn't you hear me during the wedding?'

Just then, the younger Mokkhoda peeked into the room.

'There you are. I knew straight off, if Didimoni is not upstairs or in the study, she must be in that . . . well, if you must sit here, at least come and drink your milk. Been roaming the whole house with it, looking for you . . . it's probably gone cold by now, too . . .'

Once again, Leela showed no sign of moving. 'Put the glass down and go. You can come back for it later,' she commanded.

The younger Mokkhoda put the small silver glass of milk down in the room and went away. Opu and Leela returned to the books.

After some time, Leela picked up the glass. 'Here, you drink half of this first,' she said to Opu.

Opu blushed in embarrassment. 'No . . .' he said.

'Why does one have to beg and plead with you to get you to do the smallest thing? That's not good behaviour! This milk is from our multani cow—as sweet as wok-thickened milk. Drink up, there's a good boy.'

Opu jerked his eyebrows together. '"Good boy", eh? Like you're some sort of a . . . as if!'

Leela held the glass up to his lips. 'Enough of this silly shyness. Here, I'm closing my eyes—take the glass and drink half the milk.'

Opu lowered his mouth to the glass and swiftly downed some of the milk in a short gulp. Then he straightened, cleaned the milk from around his mouth with the end of his dhoti and grinned broadly. Leela brought the glass to her own lips and finished the rest of the milk. Then she, too, began laughing.

'Wasn't the milk sweet?' she asked.

'Why did you eat my seconds?' Opu countered. 'Don't you know one shouldn't eat others' leftovers—especially from utensils that someone has already eaten from?'

'I ate your seconds because I wanted to!' Leela riposted. Then, after a brief pause, she said, 'You said the other day you know how to transfer pictures. All lies! Transfer a few for me if you can—then I'll believe you!'

35

TOWARDS THE MIDDLE of that summer, Shorbojoya finally managed to beg and borrow enough to hold Opu's holy thread ceremony. It wasn't anything like she had imagined her son's initiation into potential priesthood would be. To begin with, it had to be done quietly, in one little corner of the bigger courtyard, for fear of offending or intruding upon the convenience of the people whose house they lived in. Bamni Mashi helped Shorbojoya wok-roast the coconut-jaggery mix for celebratory sweets. A couple of brahmin cooks from the kitchen building were invited to fulfil the requirement of a brahmin feast. Among other notable guests were Beeru, the rent collector for the family's lands, and the household manager, Deenu.

A few days after the ceremony, Opu was sitting in his room reading the bound issues of *Mukul* that Leela had given him, when he heard someone come into the room. Looking up, he couldn't believe his eyes. After gaping at the entrant for a few seconds, he finally found his voice.

'You?! But . . . when?'

Leela simply stood there, grinning at him with her laughter-filled eyes.

'You're some girl!' Opu said. 'When you left you said you'd be back from Calcutta by Monday. Monday after Monday passed . . . but no sign of you!'

Leela sat down on the damp floor, laughing.

'And how was I supposed to come? Baba has put me in school in Calcutta—no more coming and going at will! Besides . . . he has not been well. So from now on, we'll stay at the Calcutta house instead of here. I could only come with my mother because I have a few days' holiday at school. We'll have to go back on Wednesday . . .'

The smile vanished from Opu's face. 'You won't be living here any more?' he asked.

'I don't know . . . we might come back once Baba gets better.'

Then she grinned. 'Now close your eyes for a bit!'

'Why?'

'Arre, close na?'

Opu closed his eyes, and immediately felt something heavy descend on his hand. He opened his eyes to the sounds of Leela's laughter. A cardboard box sat on his lap. Leela opened the box to show him his presents: a dhuti with a matching shawl, and a raw silk panjabi kurta. 'Ma bought these for you when she heard you had your thread ceremony,' Leela explained.

The dhuti and chador—and especially the panjabi—were of excellent quality. It was clearly a very expensive gift. Opu had never even seen anything of its kind before, much less held it in his hands. While he admired his present, Leela scrutinized his face.

'Your face has changed a lot in this past month,' she observed after a while. 'You look grown-up now. Where's the new brahmon's sacred thread—show me? And didn't you need to pierce your ears? One of my younger cousins also had his investiture ceremony recently, he started sobbing during the piercing . . .'

In the middle of her words, Opu flipped to an earlier page of *Mukul.*

'Have you read this story?' he asked her, interrupting her.

'No . . . which one?' said Leela. 'Show me?'

So Opu read it out to her. Almost two, three hundred years ago, a treasure-laden Spanish ship had been wrecked at sea. Many, many people have searched for it since, but no one has found the exact location of the wreck. Opu had been inordinately thrilled by this fact when he'd read the story.

'Do you know how much treasure there was?' he said excitedly. 'First there's ten, then hundred, then thousand, ten thousand, *then* lakhs . . . this ship had *fifty lakh* pounds' worth of gold and silver! One pound is thirteen rupees—just multiply and see!'

Then he pulled a piece of paper to himself and eagerly worked out the sum.

'See? That's the total!'

He had already done the sum by himself when he'd first read the story.

'I'll go find the ship when I'm older,' he informed Leela, his face bright with hope. 'I'll definitely find it, you'll see. Nobody had been able to find it yet, which means it'll stay where it is . . .'

Leela didn't seem entirely convinced. 'You'll go all that way? But how will you know where to look?'

'Look, it's right here—"On the shores of the ocean, near Porto Plata". I'll go there and look till I find it!'

When he'd read the story, his first thought was that it was good no one had found the wreck so far. If everyone went ahead and found all the lost treasure, then what would he do when he grew up? Now he just hoped that this wreck remained undiscovered till he was sufficiently grown up . . .

Despite her youth, Leela was quite an intelligent child. She thought over Opu's plans for a while, then said, 'But where will you find a ship like these people's? You'll need a ship of your own if you go looking for treasure, just like these others . . .'

Opu dismissed these petty details. 'Don't worry about that. I'll be very rich when I grow up. I'd easily buy whatever ship I wanted.'

This seemed to finally convince Leela a little. At least, she didn't press him further on the subject. Instead, she asked him if he had ever been to Calcutta. Opu had to admit that he hadn't.

'Is it very big?' he asked. 'Even bigger than here?'

Leela laughed. 'Oh, much bigger than this!'

'Even bigger than Kashi?'

'I haven't seen Kashi, so . . .'

Then she took Opu up to her old study. She began showing him her new books and notebooks. 'Look, I've drawn a flowering plant,' she said, opening her drawing book. 'How is it?'

After a while of this, Opu said, 'I'll have to go lie down for a bit. I have a headache . . .'

Leela said, 'Wait, I know a little magic for headaches. Here, let me see . . .' Then she started vigorously massaging his temples with the fingers of both hands. It was such a sudden attack that Opu started laughing.

'Stop!' he cried. 'It tickles!'

Leela laughed as well. 'My cousin learns wrestling from a champion—I learnt this from him. Isn't it good? Do you feel better now?'

After a few days, Leela and her mother went back to Calcutta.

After much pleading, Opu had convinced his mother to let him start attending a nearby school. The building was just down the main road from the masters' house, in a narrow alley to the left. It was a small single-storeyed building, housing five masters, a few chairs with broken armrests, an old, scratched blackboard, and a few maps. An open drain ran right along the front of the school. The only view from the sole window in Opu's classroom was the exposed brick wall of the house next door. On his way in, he would see manual scavengers cleaning the drain, stacking solid waste in small piles as they went along. The whole building had an air of cloistered suffocation about it. Around midday, a Hindustani savoury maker would fire up his coal oven right next to the school, and the sickly-sweet smell of raw, charring coals would pervade every room of the school. It would suffuse Opu's senses and leave his head throbbing and heavy. The unpleasant sensations would stay on long after he had left the school building.

He did not like this life—did not like it at all. The brick, cement and mortar life of the city trapped him in a choking embrace, killing his breath in his throat. His soul withered from the loss of something vital to its existence, but he couldn't put a finger on what it was. There was no grass along the roads he now treaded, and barely any trees. The main road was made of red cement, lined with cemented drains. Yet it was not a clean place. There were piles of refuse dumped between houses, ditches of dirty water on the cemented roads, pieces of discarded cloth and paper everywhere. One day he had been invited by a classmate to their house. It had been a single-storeyed house of slate, with several rooms around the cramped courtyard. Each room had been rented by different families. Old sack-cloth served as curtains to the rooms, and the floor—being only slightly higher than the ground outside—was damp throughout. There was no breeze—no air at all—through any of the rooms. The courtyard was crowded and dirty to begin with, but then the families began lighting up their coal stoves at the same time, and Opu was assailed by the familiar smell of sickly-sweetness. A sense of inescapable hopelessness hit him so hard that he thought he could feel his heart shrinking inside his chest. His friend's family asked him to stay longer, but he simply couldn't stay in that place for a moment more. The road, at least, would give him a little more air to breathe.

A similar air of suffocation pervaded their room in the masters' house. In fact, it felt worse because it was now his only home. Everything in the house, including the courtyard, was paved with either marble or brick and cement. All his life, Opu had constantly felt the earth as he walked—he couldn't live without the feel of soil beneath his feet. Here, not only was soil hard to find, but the little bits that he did manage to seek out felt alien and wrong . . . nothing like the rich earth he'd grown up with. And on top of it all, his freedom had been severely curtailed. He could no longer come and go wherever and whenever he liked. Every waking moment was spent in treading cautiously, like a thief, lest someone take offence. He couldn't even speak normally, for fear that someone would think him loud and disruptive.

Some days, he would go into the records room just to see the old bookkeeper. The man sat inside a small, metal-caged room-within-a-room, with a pile of ledgers on one side and a wooden box in front. He would sit like that all day, propped up by a greasy little pillow. The room was so dark that even during the day he had a small lamp of rapeseed oil on his box. The family's rent collector, Girish, would sit in the collections room close by. This room was not as dark as the records room—it even had a few large windows. But the light that filtered in only served to highlight the mess and filth of the room. Girish both lived and worked in this room. An unwashed bedspread lay over his low bed, upon which he both slept and worked. The sides of the bed were piled high with ledgers tied up in once-white cloth bundles. The collection room's daily refuse was piled under the bed: charred remains of tobacco cakes, bits of paper, and a miscellany of other things. Cobwebs and dust covered the rafters, greasy with lamp soot. When the clerk, Beeru, sitting amidst all that, would casually call out, 'Hey Ramdoyal! Check how much was spent on the musicians last quarter!' Opu's soul would fill with sudden revulsion.

One morning, Opu came to one corner of the outer courtyard to see the boys of the house playing with the family's sedan chair. The sedan was new and shining, with thick iron handles, plush leather seats and big wheels. He came a little closer to the group and stood there, watching them, when suddenly one of the older boys, Romen, called out to him.

'Hey, you! Come here. Push us while we ride the chair.'

Opu had been coveting a ride on the sedan ever since it had arrived. So to be included in the game delighted him.

'I'll push you, but then can I have a ride at the end?'

'Yes, yes, we'll see about that,' said Romen. 'Now come here and push us, boy. Push hard!'

Opu gave everyone rides for quite some time. Then, suddenly, Romen declared, 'All right, that's enough for today. Let's all go inside.'

Seeing everyone immediately begin to leave with the chair, Opu said, 'But . . . what about my ride?'

Romen waved him away with impatience. 'No no, no more rides. You'll break the chair with more rides. You can have your ride later.'

The betrayal and insult made Opu's eyes water. He had been pushing around the chair for these boys with all his might, all in the hopes of just one ride at the end of it.

'But . . . that's not fair! You promised. I pushed for so long, and now . . . you did exactly this the other day . . . I push all of you and then . . .'

'If you don't like it then why come back again? You could have refused, but no. Go on, shoo! Nobody promised you anything. Let you ride our chair indeed! Do you think we got it for free?'

'But you said! You said, Shontu said . . . my arms are aching after all that pushing, and now . . . I just wanted one ride, but you . . . you . . .'

Romen's impatience morphed into anger. 'I didn't say a thing. You joined us on your own. Now get lost!'

Shontu said, 'Hey stupid, look at this: furrr, furr. Go on, fly away like a crane!'

And then, out of nowhere, the eldest master's son, Tebu, came over and began to shove Opu out of the courtyard by pushing him at the throat, screaming, 'Get out! We won't let you ride our chair . . . what'll you do about it? Go hide in your servant's room! How dare you come to play with us?!'

Maybe it was because Tebu was several years younger than him, and so his insults stung more, or maybe it was because everyone stood around laughing at his humiliation, but something in Opu snapped. He angrily shrugged off Tebu's hand at his throat, and shoved him away from himself. At this unexpected retaliation, Tebu staggered away and hit the wall, his forehead banging against it and beginning to bleed. The boy immediately let out a blood-curdling shriek, and started wailing.

In the next few seconds, the place became a circus. The servants came running, the guards and valets rushed out, and even the eldest master—who was holding court in the upstairs lounge—came running downstairs with his associates. Water bowls and washcloths appeared from several directions. People crowded around Tebu and began demanding that everyone else move back to give him some air. Someone started shouting for a cold compress.

Once everything calmed down a little, the elder master said, 'Who hit him? Bring him to me.'

The guard Ramnihor Singh immediately began shoving Opu forward from the back of the crowd, till he was deposited in front of the eldest master.

'Who's this?' the master demanded. 'It's the son of that brahmon cook from Kashi, isn't it?'

Girish the rent collector pushed forward through the crowd. 'A complete no-gooder, master. If only you knew of his impertinence . . . way beyond his years! On the day of the theatre, found him sitting in the front row. Wanted to sit with the family! When I asked him to move back, he started arguing with me! Just the other day I saw him near the Seth's house, wearing an expensive red panjabi and smoking a cigarette! Totally debauched, master! And at such an early age, too!'

The eldest master turned sternly to Romen. 'Hasn't your tutor come today? Don't you have lessons to attend to? And who asked you to mix with boys like these? Hey, you over there! Go inside and bring me my cane whip!'

Romen was clearly terrified at this turn of events. 'We . . . we don't mix with him,' he quivered. '*He* comes to us, tries to get in our games. Why should we seek him out? Ask Shontu . . . the other day he asked to see those English magazines of yours—the ones with the pictures. He also comes into the big drawing room and touches everything inside . . .'

'Such impertinence!' breathed Girish, right on cue.

The eldest master finally turned to Opu. 'You! Come here, in front of me. Why did you hit Tebu?'

Opu was already half dead from terror. It was undeniable that he had shoved Tebu, but he had done so in the heat of the moment. He hadn't remotely been prepared for the whole thing to spiral into a huge public hearing.

'Te . . . Tebu hi . . . hit me first,' he managed to stutter. 'I only . . . I . . . I . . .'

'Do you know exactly how many years older you are to that child?' the master growled, incensed at this attempted defence.

Had Opu had the nerve, he might have pointed out that while Tebu was indeed young in years, in worldliness he was riper than Opu's worldly-wise uncle, the late Neelmoni Roy. He might also have wanted to point out that Tebu—along with all the other boys of the household—constantly taunted him for his speech, calling him 'Bangladeshi' because of it, hit him on the back of the head for sport, and teased him incessantly. But in front of a courtyard full of hostile people glaring at him, his tongue tied itself into knots. All he could manage was, 'Tebu . . . me . . . for no reason . . . they only . . .'

The eldest master lost control of his temper.

'Stupid boy!' he screamed. 'Why were you even here? Who gave you permission to try to play with the boys of the family? Someone hand me my whip! You—come here right now!'

Then, before he quite knew what was happening, the master's whip rose in the air, and lashed down hard on Opu's back.

Opu was absolutely stunned. Never before had anybody ever raised a hand to him . . . not even his own father. He simply stared at the eldest master, his eyes disbelievingly following the whip as it arced up again, and came whistling down on his back. For the first few lashes, his mind simply couldn't accept what was happening. That he was being beaten, actually beaten, and that too in public! Once the reality of his situation sunk in, his hands rose almost inadvertently to meet the whip, as if to shield himself from the blows that were now raining freely down on his back. The rhythmic whistling of the whip had silenced even Tebu's wails; he stared transfixed at the rising and falling piece of supple cane, pain forgotten.

The eldest master was forced to stop the whipping far sooner than he would have liked because of exhaustion and shortness of breath. However, he had the satisfaction of knowing that he had taught Opu—and everyone else—an excellent lesson in knowing one's place. No son of a mere cook would ever make the same mistake again, not in this household. A lesser whip might have broken under the strain of such a vehement lesson, but this was clearly an expensive whip of superior stock.

'This is your final warning, you stupid, dissolute scoundrel!' he growled at Opu after he had recovered his breath. 'If I ever catch you trying to pal around with the boys of this household again, I'll drag you out of this house by your ear!'

Then he turned to an associate of his, and began lamenting the bitter fruits of his kindness.

'Just look at this boy, Dheeren Babu. Our manager Shoteesh Babu brought his widowed mother from Kashi. I thought . . . well, she's a poor, helpless woman of our caste, let her stay. But the son! This is how he pays us back! The mother spends her days cooking rice, and this lout roams about wearing silk panjabis and smoking cigarettes!'

'There's nothing one can do. It's how these people are,' commiserated Dheeren Babu. 'Today it's cigarettes, tomorrow it'll be cocaine. Next he'll break his mother's savings' box and abscond. It's the fault of his class. On top of that he was raised in Kashi. So . . .'

Not much of the outdoor news made its way indoors in this household, but people made sure that Shorbojoya heard about Opu's beating. Indeed, they made sure she heard about it in great detail. The eldest mistress personally called her in for a talk, and said, 'If you're going to bring such a lumpen son into our household, my dear, then I'm afraid . . .', and then proceeded to make other veiled threats.

Shorbojoya heard it all, and then spent her morning dutifully rolling out and toasting flatbreads for breakfast. When she finally had a moment to stop by her room, she saw that Opu had already left for school. Even after such a catastrophe, he hadn't sought her out, hadn't tried to tell her anything. In fact, Shorbojoya now realized, he had never told her about any of his humiliations or fights. In the privacy of her dark little room, Shorbojoya's body finally began to shake with the morning's pent-up anger, sorrow and bitterness. Waves of heated fury began to radiate from her.

After a while, she couldn't bear to remain inside the damp little room, and ran out on to the narrow veranda outside.

Someone—these people—had laid hands on her Opu. Her son, who still came to her and said, 'Just you wait, Ma! One day I'm going to give you such a scare when you come back from the kitchens late at night. Hee hee!' Her darling, innocent, childlike son, who didn't yet have the practical sense of a child! How could they hurt him like that? Was there even a single person in the audience who had cared about his cries? Had anyone tried to soothe his pain?

In the narrow veranda, Shorbojoya's tears turned into anguished, heartbroken sobs.

That night, when a solitary star twinkled to life over the dark courtyard and the leaves of the gooseberry tree near the stables undulated gently in the breeze, Shorbojoya went out to the courtyard alone and sat next to the reservoir of water in the corner. Under the cloak of darkness, her body shook with fresh sobs as she thought about her son.

'God, almighty god . . . you know he's my sole treasure . . . my dearly beloved treasure,' she prayed silently. 'I can't rest if he's out of my sight for even a moment. If there's punishment in his destiny, then please, almighty, give it to me. Don't let him suffer. My heart breaks when he's hurt—I can't stand it! Please, god, I beg you. Please!'

Opu's school let out early that day. Thrilled, his classmates decided to meet in a nearby field for football, and asked Opu if he'd be the referee. Opu had only recently learned about the game—hadn't known anything like it existed till he came to the city. Nor could he play it well. But he was always delighted to be the referee. His classmates often chose him for the job, because despite his newness to the game, he was very well liked by nearly everyone.

'Let me go home and get my big whistle,' he told them happily. 'I'll see you at the field at four!'

But on the way back, the morning's incident kept coming back to him. He had thought about it all day, off and on. Such terrible lies they had said about him! Well . . . it was technically true that Girish the rent collector had spotted him with a cigarette, but that didn't mean he smoked every day! The day Girish had spotted him, he had been returning from school wearing the red panjabi that the second-eldest mistress had given him. It had occurred to him that the men of the house smoked cigarettes while wearing just such panjabis. With that thought, he had had the sudden urge to smoke a cigarette himself. So he had taken this saved-up lunch money and bought a cigarette, just like he had that one time back in Contentment. Just like that day, however, he hadn't enjoyed smoking at all, and immediately regretted spending his savings on it.

'I should have bought a paisa's worth of fried peas instead,' he had thought wistfully. 'Can't imagine why people keep wasting money on this horrible cigarette thing.'

And that was what had happened. Why did the rent collector have to talk about things he knew nothing about?

At least Leela wasn't here. That was the only good thing about the morning. Had he been humiliated like this in front of her, he would never have been able to face her again. As it was, he hoped that his mother hadn't been told of the incident. He had left the house earlier than usual today, lest he meet her and discover that she had heard all about it. He couldn't bear his mother knowing about his public shaming.

Speaking of Leela . . . she hadn't been back for a long time now, had she? She had come once last year, but hadn't been back since.

Anyway, even if she did come back, would these people ever let her talk to him again?

As he approached the gateway of the house, he heard a song being played in the upstairs sitting room. He stopped walking and turned his face upwards, towards the open window of that room. It was hard to make out the words from this distance, but the tune was beautiful. Haunting, almost. As he stood there, listening, everything else—school, football, refereeing, the beating he had suffered that morning—slowly vanished from his mind. He was transported back to happier times, back when he used to roam freely on the riverbanks of Contentment. When he would regularly see the green fields and the bright red flowers of the silk-cotton tree in the backdrop of a vast, bright blue sky; when he had run through fields of hay, walked by wildflowers, and heard birdsong every dawn and dusk.

He could see that beautiful land now, like a scenery painted on canvas. But the days of his being amongst it seemed like a lost, faraway country . . . one that he had left behind forever. The landscape seemed almost foreign to him now, like a land he had never visited. Yet they invariably came back to him in moments of happiness. And from within the fields and orchards, he could almost hear a beloved, familiar voice calling out to him: 'Opu-u-u-u-u!'

And his mind would instantly answer, 'I'm coming-g-g! I'm coming ba-a-ack!'

Though he knew he couldn't actually return to that place across time, the voice always made his heart hum with happiness for several minutes after.

When he finally got back to their tiny room, he found his mother waiting for him.

'They let you out early today?' she asked.

'The older boys won a match, so they gave us a half-day,' he responded.

'Come sit with me for a bit,' she invited, gently patting his shoulders. After he sat, she hesitated for a few seconds and asked, 'I heard the masters called you inside today? Did they scold you?'

Opu rushed to reassure his mother. 'Oh, no no, not at all. Tebu had been hurt a little while playing. So the eldest master was calling everyone to ask what had happened, that's all.'

'So they didn't scold you?'

'Not in the least!'

His mother sat quietly for a while. Then she said, 'I've been thinking, Opu . . . do you ever want to go away from here?'

Opu turned to look at his mother's face, surprised. How did his mother know his dearest wish?

'Where shall we go, Ma?' he asked eagerly, his voice filled with joy. 'Can we go back to Contentment? That would be wonderful. Let's go! I can be the local priest . . . now I even have my holy thread. We'll be on our own land, in our own house . . . it'll be great. No more of this place!'

'I've been thinking about it these past two years,' Shorbojoya said slowly. 'You say we should go back . . . but really, what do we have left? All your father had was the house, and that has been unoccupied for almost three years now. I doubt if the walls are even standing . . . it was an ancient house even when we lived in it. What little land we once had is no more, either. We would be stranded without a roof if we went back there . . . all our enemies would point and laugh . . .'

Mother and son stayed silent for a few seconds.

'We could go to Kashi,' Shorbojoya mused. 'Maybe that's something we could do . . .'

In the end, nothing concrete could be decided upon. Shorbojoya had missed lunch to talk to her son, so after a while of sitting together in silence, she left to take her bath and return to the kitchens. Opu sat alone in the little room, thinking. His sister used to say that he had a good singing voice. Even his friend from the travelling band of performers had said so. If he went to a troupe, would they take him on? Then he could come back and take his mother away from here. These people made her work way too hard.

The heat in the small room grew intense. Smoke began coiling out of the kitchen pipes, and the afternoon sun blazed heat on the brick-and-cement veranda. The inside of the room was already dark. He could hear the groom Matabiya muttering to himself in Hindi, and the horses stomping their hooves on the stable's cobbled floor. The smell from the drains seemed to slowly fill the room. Opu's head began to pound so hard that he thought it might fall off his shoulders.

'I'll just lie down for a few minutes before going to the field,' he told himself. 'It's only three o'clock. The sun is anyway too harsh to go out right now.'

A thought came to him as he lay down. Though he hadn't realized this earlier, in his heart he had always been convinced that no matter what, Contentment would always wait for them at the end of the day. It was the one place they could always return to. But after the eldest master's threat of throwing him out, and his talk with his mother about their old house in the village, he had begun to realize how truly homeless they actually were. This wasn't something he had had to consider before. Did it mean they would never be able to return to Contentment? Would they have to stay on in these hostile foreign lands forever, with people like that rent collector Girish, skulking about like thieves? Say they left this house . . . what then? With going back to Contentment being out of the question, would mother and son be forced to roam the streets like vagabonds?

In the stable, two grooms had begun quarrelling. Flocks of crows had gathered on the roof of the kitchens, hoping for leftover rice. After a while, Opu realized that he had been thinking the same thought over and over again. With the constant thunder of hoofbeats coming in from the stables, he felt like he was sinking into the ground . . . deep, deep, inside the ground . . . like someone below was pulling him in. Oddly, it felt good, very good. There was no more pounding in his head. It was blissful.

The midday sun was beating down on the Contentment woods. His sister was crazy! Who organized picnics in this heat? He kept trying to dissuade her, saying, 'Have a lie-down instead, Didi . . . a picnic in this heat, really?'

Ranudi sat at his head, prattling about this and that. He saw that her large eyes were full of hurt and brimming with tears. But what could he do? They couldn't survive in Contentment—they had to go. Wait, was that really Ranudi? Or was it Leela?

Haran Kaka was playing one of the wooden flutes from his bundle. He was such a talented flutist! Opu ran up to his father.

'Can I have a paisa, Baba? I want a flute, they're a paisa each.'

His father affectionately tucked his long hair behind his ears.

'Your story was lovely, Khoka,' he said, warmly. 'Will you show it to me when your magazine is printed?'

'What is cocaine, Baba?' Opu asked. 'Girish Shorkar said I'll have cocaine next . . . what is it?'

Then he saw that his father was wearing a garland of lotus seeds, just like the balladeer in Kashi used to.

At long last, their train finally pulled into Majherpara station. He could see the big wooden board that proudly proclaimed the name: 'MA . . . JHE . . . R PA . . . RA'. He left the train ahead of his mother, wearing the red silk panjabi, carrying their big bundle on his shoulders. The canopy above made the road from the station wonderfully inviting and cool. The evening stars were beginning to rise in the vast sky above. The aroma of ripe banyan flowers filled the air.

The road to Contentment seemed never-ending. He and his mother walked on, and on, and on. He had never navigated this road on his own before, and was unsure of the way. While passing a field, he called out to a man working in it.

'Hello, uncle-with-the-scythe! Can you help me? Can you tell me which road leads to Contentment? Yes, Joshora-Contentment—the one across the Betroboti river.'

The next thing he knew, his mother was back in the room, waking him up.

'Opu! Get up! Daylight's almost over, my darling. You've slept for hours . . . and at such an odd time! Didn't you say you had to go out to play? Get up, it's evening already.'

Startled into being fully awake, Opu looked around. It was indeed very late. The sun had disappeared entirely while he had been asleep.

'Didn't you say you were going to go to the field?' his mother asked again. 'Do you want me to take out your big whistle?'

Without waiting for his response, she took out the whistle from the box and kept it on the bed, before leaving for the kitchens again. But Opu did not show any interest in the whistle. He was no longer keen on going out of the house, not even to referee a match. The inside of their room was already very dark. He left the bed and went to stand at the window. For a few minutes, he stared outside without really seeing anything. The daylight hours were over, but the heat was still suffocating. The stench from the drains seemed to have increased even further. He could hear the enormous clock at the entrance of the house sounding its gong. It was six in the evening.

The darkening sky stretched above the stables. On its other end of it lay his village, his beloved Contentment. It has been so long since he had laid eyes on that land . . . three years, almost. It felt like forever. These days, he could feel the place calling out to him constantly, at all hours of day and night. The Shellcutter's Pond called out to him, the bamboo grove called out to him, the Shonadanga moors called out to him, the Burflower's Wharf called out to him. Even the goddess Bishalakkhi entreated him to return.

He thought of their old, dilapidated house, scented with the sweet aroma of lemon flowers and shaded by drumstick trees. When would he return to that place? When again would he hear the familiar birdsong from the neighbouring lebbeck and golden laburnum trees? At this time of the year, the Ichamoti would have already been flooded by the monsoons. Indeed, the water must have drowned the riverside roads and reached the silk-cotton trees. The leadwort and yellow-nickers in the woods would be in full bloom, as would the wild bluebell vines. Most branches and treetops would be covered in their bright blue flowers. It was late enough in that day for Raju Kaka to be at the bathing steps, by the crab's-eye bushes. Bathing at odd hours was his little quirk. Okrur the boatman must have already laid his nets at the

Chaltepota bend, next to the new cluster of reeds. Today would be market day on the banks off that bend. As the sun set in a blaze of colours behind the solitary banyan at the Pond of the Sisters-in-Law, the neighbourhood boys—Potu, Neelu, Teenu, Bhola—would be returning home from the market through the fields under its red-gold light.

Surrounded by woodland and the bamboo grove, their own courtyard would already be veiled in shadowy darkness. Birdsong would have filled the air. Oh, how he yearned for those sweet, peaceful evenings! The yellow bird would have flown in to sit on the split-bamboo boundary wall, as it always did. The lemon plant that his mother had planted was probably already heavy with fruit.

In a little while, true darkness would settle on their compound. But there wouldn't be anyone to dispel it with the light of the evening lamp. There would be no evening prayers, no fairy tales for the children. The only sound would be from the crickets, who now lived amongst the wild kalmegh bushes of their empty, overgrown courtyard. Much later at night, the snow owl would hoot from the wild-fig tree behind their house.

Very soon, the lemon tree his mother had planted would be lost to human eyes, hidden behind the encroaching woods. The flowers of the white morning glory in their compound would blossom and wilt unseen. The berries and custard apples would ripen and fall for no one, and the yellow-winged bird would sing into the empty air. At the edge of those woods, the magical evenings would descend and die without a single soul knowing about them . . .

Earlier today, when he had been whipped for no fault of his own, in front of a courtyard full of people, not a single tear had escaped him. But now, standing alone in the dark little room, staring blindly out of the window, hot tears flooded his cheeks. Sobbing desperately, he raised his palms to stem the tide and prayed with all his heart:

'Please, god, let us return to Contentment. That's all I ask . . . just let us go back to our village. I won't live if we don't return to Contentment, god. Please take us back, I beg you!'

In response, the God of the Travelled Road smiled down at him.

'Silly boy,' he said, affectionately. 'Do you think my road ends at the edge of your village? Or at the solitary banyan tree where Biru Roy's highwaymen marked their boundary? No, my child. It stretches past your Shonadanga moors, across the Ichamoti, past the Modhukhali pond teeming with lotuses, across the Betroboti ferryway. My road goes on, further and further, never ending. The only way on it is forward. Past this country and into foreign lands, past sunrise and towards the sunset, past the known and into the unknown. The road goes past days and nights, births and deaths, months and years, famines and sufferings . . . past the time when the pristine marble of your dreams acquires the weight of life's moss and mould. On, and on and on . . . it goes ever forward. Its unceasing music plays across the infinity of time, spreading across all skies.

When I first made you homeless, I also anointed you with the invisible mark of this strange, joyous, never-ending road. There is no going back on this road, only forward.

So come, my child. Let us go forth.